F
LYN

Lynn, Jack, 1927-
Hallelujah flight

$15.95

DATE			

The Hallelujah
Flight

Also by Jack Lynn

The Professor
The Turncoat
The Factory

The Hallelujah Flight

JACK LYNN

St. Martin's Press
New York

Library of Congress Cataloging-in-Publication Data

Lynn, Jack
      Hallelujah flight / Jack Lynn.
          p.   cm.
      ISBN 0-312-04324-4
      I. Title.
    PS3562.Y444H35   1990
    813'.54—dc20   89-78051
                                                CIP

First published in Great Britain by Robson Books Ltd.

First U.S. Edition
10 9 8 7 6 5 4 3 2 1

For my wife Linzi
and my son Alexandre

Prologue

IT WAS WHILE I was researching the subject of another book that I came across, and became fascinated by, an old newspaper clipping. Its two brief paragraphs alluded to a couple of remarkable black men and their extraordinary accomplishment – in the depths of the Depression, in a country of dust-swallowing migrants, restless street bums and belligerent bigots.

Determined to gather more facts, I ransacked libraries, newspaper morgues, and other worldwide research sources, but found very little information of value, because the achievement of Thomas C. Allen and James Herman Banning in 1932 had not received proper recognition and widespread publicity.

Finally, after months of investigative work, I managed to locate Allen in Oklahoma City, Oklahoma. Lengthy conversations, personal diaries, and a file of revealing documents, gave me the exclusive material I needed to write this story, based on true experiences.

The reader will find certain errors of fact. Times, places, names, and situations have sometimes been distorted purposely to suit this fictionalized account of a little known historical event.

Tom Allen was born in Quitman, Wood County, Texas on 2 April 1907. His parents were school teachers. His father, who died three months after the boy's birth, was the President of a Negro Methodist College. Later, his mother taught at a small country school, and ran a farm.

In 1918, planes were flying from Fort Worth, Texas to Roanoke, Arkansas. Allen would watch until they flew out of sight. One afternoon, a plane circled the pasture of his farm, hit a tree stump, and broke a propeller. Standing with his brother Hardy, Tom Allen decided then and there that he would become a pilot, or a mechanic.

His mother eventually remarried, and the family moved to Oklahoma City in 1919. An airfield was located nearby. Allen would hang around, observe, pester, and tolerate white racial attitudes with a smile. A young man of average height and

7

weight, with pleasant looks, a mischievous expression, and a warm, cheerful nature, he was well-liked.

After becoming a familiar figure on the airfield, he was finally allowed by the owner, Bob Tarbutton, to work with the flight mechanics and learn his trade. He was also given some flying lessons by Tarbutton in his spare time. But Allen handled aircraft tools with a lot more skill than he did the controls in a cockpit. Right from the start, he was an instinctively capable mechanic, and a lousy pilot.

After Tarbutton's training, Allen moved around the country, fighting hard times and prejudice, working on engines when and where he could, always with the same even-tempered attitude, regardless of the circumstances.

But even though Charles Lindbergh's flight in 1927 sparked more general interest in aviation, Tom Allen's search for decent wages and challenging opportunities ended unsuccessfully. He returned to Oklahoma City.

By this time, with two planes – a Stinston Detroit and a Ryan Brougham – Paul Braniff had started Tulsa–Oklahoma Airline, later renamed Braniff. Allen was given a job: that of cleaning, fumigating and servicing the planes; and the boss was very pleased with the results. Friends envied him, because times were bad, and respectable work had become almost impossible to find, especially for Negroes. But Allen had a problem. Paul Braniff was unable to pay anyone a salary. The Tulsa–Oklahoma City Airline employees received free lunch and a few dollars whenever the proprietor had some cash.

It was 1929.

Allen heard that the Bessie Coleman Aero Club in Los Angeles – named after the pioneer black woman aviator who had learned to fly in France, after World War One – was organizing a national air tour featuring Negro pilots and parachutists. The club needed an experienced mechanic. Braniff urged Allen to go for the job, promising that he could always return, if there were any problems.

After some thought, Allen left for California and joined the Coleman team, where he met James Herman Banning, the chief pilot. They began to prepare for the air tour.

Banning was born in Canton, Oklahoma on 17 February 1900. The family moved to Ames, Iowa at the start of 1919, where James Herman entered Iowa State College to study electrical engineering. However, he left after a year and a half to pursue a childhood obsession with learning to fly.

A tall, slim, very good-looking young man, Banning's intelligence and sense of humour made him very popular. He had a sharp, confident attitude, and his smooth dialogue, especially with females, usually produced a variety of positive results. In addition, he was a determined and ambitious character, keen to make his way in his chosen field regardless of the obstacles.

However, there was another side to him, quickly detected and carefully handled by close friends – a churning resentment of discrimination by whites, a chip, not only on his shoulder, but lodged deep in his guts. He insisted on standing up for his rights at a time when other blacks preferred to keep a very low profile and avoid trouble. Above all, he was determined to go for his wings; not dream-stuff, with cheap balsa wood and glue, but the real thing.

Sadly, he soon discovered that the real thing was ugly and prejudiced, and his great expectations were quickly smothered by flying school admission clerks in Chicago, Minneapolis, St Louis, and Kansas City. He was bitter and disillusioned.

He returned to Ames, Iowa, where he heard about an airfield and an instructor in Des Moines, thirty miles from his home. The information was to change his life, although it seemed unpromising at the time, since the school's owner and teacher was a white man, an Army officer named Lieutenant Craig Meredith.

Banning cycled to the field one day, found an isolated spot, and watched the flight activities with great interest, envy, and a firm conviction that he was just as capable as the white students.

He began to spend more and more time at the airfield, believing himself an unobserved spectator. However, the Lieutenant had spotted Banning on his first visit, and noticed him every other time he appeared. Intrigued, he talked to the young man, and was impressed enough to take him on as a student, despite opposition from his wife and colleagues.

Ignoring racial slurs and indignation, Banning and Craig Meredith concentrated on the job at hand, steadily building up a mutual respect, becoming friends.

Soon Banning had absorbed everything the instructor could teach him, and they both agreed that it was time for him to leave the Des Moines flying school and find his own way in the aviation world as a qualified pilot.

On 2 May 1926, after many episodes of discrimination, almost constant frustration, and a very complicated and, at times, needlessly extended series of tests, James Herman Banning, at twenty-six, became the first black aviator to obtain a licence from the United States Department of Commerce.

Still based in Ames, Iowa, he started to earn money flying as a stunt pilot and racer, performing in numerous air shows around the country. And he flew passengers for a fee. But black flyers had a difficult time getting financial backing, and their planes were old, or rebuilt, and in constant need of repair.

Consequently, Banning left Ames on 8 September 1929 and settled in Los Angeles, where he became chief pilot for the Bessie Coleman Aero Club.

As the newly-wed Tom Allen helped Banning and his colleagues organize the Club's national tour, a financial hurricane was brewing in the United States, and it hit with full force on the last Tuesday of October, 1929, when Wall Street crashed.

All of Bessie Coleman's planes and equipment were impounded by the banks, and the Negro flight club was grounded. All her employees found themselves out of work and had to go their separate ways in search of similar employment; an extremely difficult task even for the most highly qualified among them.

James Herman Banning carried passengers from Los Angeles to Tijuana, and organized stunt flying exhibitions in Arizona and California. He made a living – just – but it was quite a feat, considering his colour, the tightly-circled flying game, and America's problems during the Depression.

Thomas Allen picked up jobs as a mechanic whenever possible, mainly at Butler and Lockheed. For extra cash, he worked in the glass division of a factory, helping to make the new milk bottle which held the cream separate at the top of the neck. Every moment of his spare time was spent hanging out at a local flying club, goofing around with the white pilots while he conned them out of free and precious air time. He practised forced landings and rough take-offs in wheatfields and pastures – without a licence. And he continued to be considered a fine mechanic, and an utterly hopeless pilot.

His wife, Celene, urged him to forget about aircraft and take up fixing automobiles and bicycles instead. Flying was for white men.

But Thomas C. Allen and James Herman Banning refused to be swayed by anyone, as they pursued their own goals, on different courses, until finally in 1932 a challenging proposition brought them together again for the adventure of a lifetime.

JACK LYNN
November 1988

1

The Cotton Club
Harlem
New York
18 August 1932

'This is the most exciting goddamn thing I have ever seen!' the fat man shouted in a thick Southern accent, as he sat at a table with four boozy-eyed companions watching a chorus line of beautiful, half-naked black dancers. 'All niggers have rhythm, but these gals shake their asses wilder than epileptic tomcats. And listen to that music! Really special!' He glanced at the others. 'Was it worth the bus ride from Norfolk, gentlemen?!'

His friends agreed that it was, nodding their heads, gulping their drinks, and staring lustfully at the female members of the elaborate floor show.

The fat man was right. This was a special night at the famous Club on Lenox Avenue at 142nd Street. Harold Arlen and Dorothy Fields had written and produced a magnificent revue with a cast of show-stoppers that included Ethel Waters, Fats Waller, Adelaide Hall, Carolynne Snowden, Peg Leg Bates, Aida Ward, Louis Armstrong, Lena Horne, and the music of Duke Ellington's orchestra.

This particular night had been geared up for Mr Bill Robinson. The dancing star's film, *Harlem Is Heaven*, was being premiered at the Renaissance cinema, and after the glittering ceremony some of America's leading show business personalities were scheduled to arrive at the Club with the great Bojangles in order to take bows, drinks, and possibly a few cues for impromptu performances.

The fat man was Mr John Cunningham, a fairly successful cut-rate department store owner from Norfolk, Virginia. His companions also had small businesses doing moderately well in the same town, when so many others were struggling for existence or going under.

11

'How about that!' Cunningham shouted, applauding the chorus girls loudly as they made a spirited exit past a realistic plantation cabin and rows of cotton bushes. 'Every goddamn one a beauty! Special! Really special!'

The fat man turned back to his friends when the lights dimmed and the music softened, and Ethel Waters moved downstage for a ballad.

'They shake their asses real good,' one of the businessmen commented drily, feeling his drinks. 'Pity they can't use the more important parts of their bodies for useful purposes.'

'Now just what the hell does that mean, Kingston?' The fat man lit up a cigar before continuing. 'You always have been an outright nigger hater.'

'A lie, Cunningham.' Kingston had a small face and, in profile, it had the lines of a falcon with a sharp beak. 'I am stating a published medical fact.'

'Andrew is right.' William Pringle inclined his bald head to lower a high pitched voice. 'They can't get their arms and legs to function properly because of underdeveloped brains. That's why they have slow reactions and poor co-ordination. It's not their fault. I read a –'

'Bullshit.' The fat man blew cigar smoke until Pringle moved back in his chair. 'Poor co-ordination?' He pointed backwards to the stage where Ethel Waters, in a soft spot, was concertizing a Eubie Blake number. 'Did you ever watch Bojangles – or Fats Waller – or Louis Armstrong? Poor co-ordination?'

'That's rhythm,' said Kingston. 'Like you said, all niggers have rhythm. They can tap their feet and shake their asses and blow their horns. But I'm talking about complicated things. Brainwork. Technology. And stuff like that. And you know damn well what I mean, Cunningham.'

'Your cigar is upsetting my stomach, John,' the other member of the group complained. 'At least blow the smoke up instead of at us.'

'Sorry, Wilfred.' The fat man co-operated at once and then asked, 'How do you stand in this nigger debate? You've got four or five on your payroll. Are they reliable? Co-ordinated?'

'Lazy,' Wilfred Treadwell replied without hesitation. 'And just plain ignorant. And Bill Pringle is right. You can't blame these people. They have to operate with what God gave them. And it sure wasn't enough.'

Treadwell, a sombre, rather scholarly-looking man, wearing steel-rimmed glasses, poured himself another large gin, and the

12

others did the same, while Ethel Waters was being enthusiastically applauded. Her encore was 'Am I Blue?'

The four Norfolk businessmen drank, and listened, and watched, and appreciated the great talents of the black entertainers.

'Did you hear that Lindbergh is flying transcontinental for Hoover's re-election campaign?' the fat man asked his friends, while smartly groomed men and women danced to Ellington's music. 'A waste of the Eagle's time,' Cunningham added, beginning to slur his words as the alcohol took hold.

'Absolutely correct,' Kingston agreed, displaying identical symptoms. 'Roosevelt by a landslide.'

'Now that's a damned good example,' William Pringle mumbled, drunker than all of them. 'Lindbergh.'

'What about him?' Kingston asked.

'Co-ordination,' Pringle replied, swaying a little in his chair. 'Sending proper signals from his brain – to all parts of his body – and getting immediate results. Co-ordination. How the hell do you think he made it to France alone?'

Treadwell stared with the others for a moment before speaking. 'I don't get your point, William.'

'Niggers,' said Pringle. 'Can you picture a nigger flying an airplane across this country like Charles Lindbergh?' His laugh was thin and it resembled a childish giggle. 'You can't get out and tap dance at ten thousand feet in a storm cloud.'

'And navigation?' Kingston stretched his arms out wide, like wings, and see-sawed them, to simulate a plane in trouble. 'Straight as the black crow flies,' he mocked, appreciating Pringle's grin.

'There are nigger pilots around now, Andrew,' said Cunningham, not amused. 'And I understand they do pretty damn well.'

'As clowns in travelling circus shows,' Kingston retorted, lowering his arms. 'We're talking about navigating an airplane across the United States like Charles Lindbergh. It has never been done by a nigger. And I claim that it will never be done by a nigger. Because they are just not equipped mentally or physically.'

'I agree,' Treadwell joined in. 'My delivery boy is a high school graduate and he gets lost three blocks from the store. Sometimes with the wrong order. And then he panics and comes back telling lies or blaming others.'

'An isolated case, Wilfred,' said Cunningham. 'You hired a dumb ass. And that happens – white or black.'

'Wrong,' Treadwell insisted. 'This boy is typical. No sense of direction. Unreliable. And no damn good in a crisis.' He removed the steel-rimmed spectacles, blinked, and rubbed his eyes. 'Andrew is right. A coast-to-coast flight will never be completed by a Negro.'

'Want to bet?' Cunningham asked, draining his glass. 'There are niggers out there who can fly an airplane across this country.'

'I hear a lot of talk,' Kingston chided, winking at the others. 'Put your money where your mouth is, John.'

'That is exactly what I'll do, gentlemen,' said Cunningham, trying to focus on the Norfolk businessmen. 'Well, now – accept this as an official proposal – from Mr John Radcliff Cunningham.' He took a long draw on the cigar and remembered to blow the smoke upwards instead of across the table. 'One thousand – I repeat – one thousand American dollars to the first Negroes to make a successful transcontinental flight.'

'That's better,' said Pringle, laughing with Kingston. 'But you should put it in writing. Make a formal pledge. This could be historic, Mr Cunningham.'

'Are you serious about the proposition, John?' Wilfred Treadwell inquired. 'Or are you drunk?'

'Both,' Cunningham admitted. 'Even so, I never go back on my word. One thousand dollars to the first niggers who fly a plane transcontinental.'

'A safe gamble,' Treadwell commented, as the group began to take the conversation seriously. 'You can't possibly lose the money. But go all the way. Announce your intentions to our Negro population.'

'Want me to scream it from the Harlem rooftops, Wilfred?' Cunningham asked sarcastically, realizing that he was now truly on the hook. 'Or should I visit all the nigger churches on our way home?'

'Put an advertisement in a black newspaper,' Treadwell pushed on. 'The *New York Defender* has a big circulation. And the word will spread to all of your coloured Lindberghs.'

'You have a deal, Wilfred.' Cunningham poured a bit more gin, raised his glass, and the others did likewise. 'To the first nigger transcontinental pilots,' he toasted dramatically. 'The J.R. Cunningham prize is waiting.'

'Hallelujah!' shouted William Pringle, as the four clinked, swallowed, and switched their attention back to the Cotton Club stage. The patrons were applauding and cheering wildly for an animated Negro performer. Cab Calloway, a special guest introduced by Bojangles Robinson, began to wail his classic, 'Minnie The Moocher'.

Los Angeles
California
4 September 1932

In a bright and cloudless sky, an old fashioned light plane dipped
and rolled crazily on what appeared to be a suicide course, flying
low, clipping tree tops, until it finally crash-landed on a small plot
of ground, just missing a house.

The antiquated 0XX6 Eagle Rock, a war surplus model, broke
into sections on impact. After the loud bang – slam – rip –
crunching noises of the accident, dust and debris settled, and
there was an eerie silence for several moments.

Eventually, miraculously, a short and pudgy white man climbed
from a piece of wreckage and stood dazed for an instant, before
collapsing on his back, fully conscious, his eyes wide open, as if he
could not believe that he was still alive and breathing, or possibly
wondering if the crash had indeed been fatal, and this was the way
it was in the dead zone.

Actually, Phil Nash, a very lucky fellow, was only suffering
from temporary shock, bruises, and a few superficial cuts on his
face and arms.

Seconds later, a black man, even shorter, though of slighter
build, crawled out from under a chunk of twisted fuselage, moved
slowly to Nash on all fours, and then flopped down beside him,
head to head.

Douglas Boyd, known on Central Avenue as Little Dandy, had
a gash dripping blood over his left brow, several broken teeth,
multiple sprains, and worse bruising than Nash. But no shock.
Little Dandy knew exactly where he was and he didn't like it at all.

'Your damn fault,' he sputtered, breathing heavily, through a
busted mouth. 'Why did you cut the switches?'

Phil Nash groaned, closed his eyes tightly, and turned away
from Little Dandy without answering.

'The motor was hot and losing revs.' The Negro wiped away
blood with the back of his hand. 'Did you forget the throttle?'

'Leave me alone,' Phil Nash pleaded hoarsely. 'I feel like I'm
dying. Call for some help.'

'You're not dying – yet,' Little Dandy declared, attempting to
raise himself up on one elbow. 'But you might be – when I get
my strength back.'

After a painful struggle, and a lot of back alley cursing, he
managed to wriggle into a contorted sitting position. Still stunned,

15

bleeding, and spitting teeth, he surveyed the damage around him and shook his head in despair.

'Four hundred and twelve dollars shot to hell,' he moaned. 'A fortune gone. All because of you.' He watched some people rushing towards the wreck. 'Our partnership is over, Phil Nash. And I really do mean it this time.'

'Not my fault,' the white man said in a choked voice. 'We bought an old plane. You can't fly the damn thing any better than me.'

'I didn't smash her.'

'You've had more lessons.'

'Just a couple.'

'Well, it's all over now,' Phil Nash announced, finally opening his eyes. 'I don't want to fly any more.'

'You won't,' Little Dandy assured him. 'Not with me.' He took another slow look around. 'And not in this heap of rubbish.'

Phil Nash groaned and closed his eyes again. 'We'd better get help,' he repeated, trying to move one leg, and then the other. 'I need a doctor.'

'You need a banker and a big hit.' Little Dandy pressed a handkerchief hard against his wounded forehead, in a futile attempt to stop the flow of blood. 'We're out four hundred and twelve dollars, and I expect proper compensation, Phil Nash.'

'If I survive.'

'You will,' Little Dandy replied at once. 'A rescue party is almost here. And don't forget. *You* nearly tore the roof off that goddamn house. Not me. Looks like a white lynch mob is on the way.'

Douglas Boyd, a perky little thirty-year-old dude, was always capable of putting together some cash by pimping high class whores, or banking the numbers racket, or setting up a wide variety of Central Avenue business ventures, most of them sleazy and illegal, but none of them outright vicious or physically harmful. Little Dandy was a popular member of the Negro sporting class, and his silk shirts, bright ties, and stylish clothes helped to prove the point. On Sunday afternoons, he would usually strut down Central Avenue with a tall beauty on each arm, and a friendly greeting for just about everyone who passed by.

He had taken up flying mainly for the image it conferred, and was learning the basics, slowly, and not very well. Splitting the cost, he had purchased the old Eagle Rock with his sometime business partner, Phil Nash, another novice aviator.

16

Nash, at thirty-two, had been living in the coloured sections of Los Angeles for over fifteen years. He was a carpenter by trade, with neither a decent education nor a particularly sharp mind. After his parents divorced, his mother was given possession of the modest family house, and she refused to leave, even when the blacks started taking over the neighbourhood. Phil grew up with them, became friends with them, made love to them, and was accepted by them, with only a few exceptions over the years.

Using his carpentry skills, he picked up odd jobs, mainly in the nearby white sections of town. He also used the house, after his mother's death, as a rental for boarders. And he did business with Little Dandy, sometimes using his whiteness to help organize or clinch particularly sensitive inter-racial deals.

Thus, even with his unprepossessing appearance and rather dim wit, Phil Nash was able to put his hands on some cash. And, for the record, learning to fly, and buying the plane, had been Little Dandy's idea, and not really Phil Nash's type of action, as the last flight had demonstrated quite clearly.

'That's all we need,' Little Dandy sighed, as vehicles with screaming sirens joined the oncoming rescue team. 'Cops and a meat wagon.'

'We should be grateful.' Phil Nash had forced himself to lift his head and squint at the ambulance speeding in front. 'It could have been a hearse.'

'Exactly,' Little Dandy snapped angrily, kicking a bent motor part. 'And don't you ever forget it, man.'

17

2

Two days later, a battered moving van with faded paint and a flat tyre, was parked in a large yard adjoining the Mosby brothers' automobile garage. Located about six miles from the site of the Eagle Rock crash, in a black neighbourhood of Los Angeles, the crudely built wooden shack, a barn-like structure, was a popular haunt for car owners, motor enthusiasts, and anybody else who had time to kill.

This afternoon in September 1932 was different. An important meeting had been scheduled, and the owners, Booker T. and Floyd Mosby, had bolted the doors and put up a sign formally declaring that the garage was temporarily closed for business.

Little Dandy and Phil Nash, heavily bandaged, had been given the most comfortable seats: two soft leather chairs, normally reserved for cash-paying clients.

The Mosby brothers, two fat-lipped, pop-eyed, very black bean-poles garbed in overalls, were seated behind a work bench piled with an assortment of tools. They had a reputation for doing sloppy mechanical work, but at a reasonable price, and credit was usually extended, along with plenty of hospitality, so no one complained.

James Herman Banning, the pilot, and one of the most popular and respected characters in the neighbourhood, sat before the group, straight faced, all business, determined to run the show.

'Let's unload the truck and lay out every scrap neatly in the yard,' he said authoritatively. 'And then we'll build ourselves an airplane.'

'Impossible,' Phil Nash challenged. 'That's a total wreck.'

'A fucked up jig-saw puzzle, Banning,' Little Dandy added. 'With a lot of missing pieces. You will never get the damn thing put back together again. A waste of time. Salvage a few parts and dump the rest in Mosby's garbage patch.'

'Douglas is right, James Herman,' said Floyd Mosby, in his usual monotone. 'We can hang on to a couple of bits and pieces. But the rest ain't useful. You won't build no airplane with that junk. Not one that flies anywhere. Why are you so mule-headed about this?'

Banning stared thoughtfully at the automobile mechanic. He had borrowed the old van from a friend in order to gather up everything on the ground where the Eagle Rock had crash landed – damaged remnants of wings, fuselage, motor, and other parts, right down to nuts, bolts, and wire. Nothing was missed during the salvage operation.

'I need an airplane as soon as possible,' he announced, switching his gaze to Little Dandy and Phil Nash. 'Can you gentlemen raise the money for a new one?'

'Not a chance,' Nash replied adamantly. 'Even if I could – which I can't – I wouldn't put another dime in this aviation business. Make a deal with Douglas Boyd.'

'What?' Little Dandy looked at Phil Nash, scowled, and then turned back to Banning. 'My former partner must be suffering from brain damage,' he said. 'There is no way for me to find airplane cash, James Herman. I have business problems just like everybody else these days. Even my girls are home with their legs crossed. And besides, this four hundred and twelve dollar humiliation will lose me a lot of credibility on the Avenue. Thanks to Phil Nash. Now if you –'

'Floyd?' Banning interrupted and looked over at the Mosby brothers behind the work bench. 'How about you and Booker T. lending me the cash for a plane – a used one – but reliable enough for a long flight?'

'Ain't discussable, James Herman,' Booker T. Mosby snapped back, gruff-voiced, but friendly in manner, his usual way. 'We've got kids to feed. And things are real bad. This here garage is like a Hooverville soup kitchen now. And you know that's a true fact.'

'I know it is, Booker T.,' Banning agreed. 'And that's the reason we'll unload the truck and put the Eagle Rock back together again. Piece by piece. Little by little. And to hell with beauty and standard design.' The pilot, dressed in a slightly worn, but smartly fitted leather jacket and khaki trousers, stood, and paced the room, unable to keep his excitement down. 'Just help me build an airplane,' he said quietly, almost to himself. 'One that I can fly.'

'That junk outside ain't goin' anywhere,' Floyd Mosby stated, watching the pilot move to a small window and peer up at the sky. 'How far are you reckoning to travel, James Herman?'

'From here to New York City,' Banning replied without turning around. 'And into the history books. The first successful

Negro transcontinental flight. That's how far I reckon to travel, Floyd.'

The group remained silent for several moments, allowing the astonishing information to sink in, and register properly.

'Now we've got two brothers suffering from brain damage,' Little Dandy finally commented. 'From here to New York City in a pile of glued-up rubbish?'

Banning turned, walked back to his chair, and sat facing four curious expressions.

'Listen carefully,' he told them. 'There is a very interesting East Coast newspaper report circulating.' He glanced slowly from one man to another before continuing. 'A rich white guy by the name of Cunningham has pledged one thousand dollars to the first successful Negro transcontinental pilots.' Another pause stimulated even more curiosity. 'I intend to pick up the money and make history.'

'Dear Lord Jesus,' Little Dandy murmured, folding his arms and smirking at Banning. 'You do believe in miracles.'

'I believe in smart heads, strong backs, and determination,' Banning corrected. 'And we have all of these requirements. Along with a truck-load of basic airplane parts and the knowledge to piece them together. And that's just what we're going to do.' He focused his attention on Phil Nash. 'Unless you and Douglas want to dump the mess in Mosby's garbage patch. After all – it is your property. Well, Phil?'

Nash stared at the pilot for a long moment and then shrugged his shoulders. 'Go ahead and try,' he said. 'Sounds crazy and impossible. But – go ahead and try – as far as I'm concerned.'

'Will you help?'

'I'll stick around – and give you a hand – but I don't know too much about building airplanes.'

'Good enough.' Banning smiled warmly. 'Douglas?'

'You don't stand a chance of getting off the ground,' Little Dandy replied. 'But suppose a miracle does happen?'

'What do you mean?'

'The one thousand dollars.'

'A split,' Banning fired back, ready for the question. 'All of us share. We'll agree percentages this afternoon. Along with other business. This is a joint venture.'

'A fairy-tale for nut cases.' Little Dandy copied Phil Nash's shrug. 'But I guess anything is better than Mosby's garbage patch.'

'Well?'

'Use the damn junk,' he answered. 'Just don't ask me to climb into the cockpit of this lunatic contraption – if it ever gets pasted together.'

'Will you help?'

'That depends entirely on my schedule, James Herman.' Little Dandy checked his watch with an exaggerated gesture. 'At the moment I have some free time – so I can help you make history – or a goddamn fool out of yourself.'

'Thank you, Douglas.' Banning grinned. 'And what about the Mosby brothers? Floyd? Booker T.?'

'You're a real fine pilot, James Herman,' Floyd Mosby recited, without an inflexion. 'Even so, there ain't no way you're gonna fly a wrecked airplane to New York City. Patch it all up like new? We don't believe in miracles.'

'You'll go through all this bother – and risk your life – for some white money?' Booker T. asked quietly. 'And to get your name put in a book?'

Banning thought for a while before speaking. 'The money is sure as hell important these days,' he admitted, getting up and walking to the work bench. 'And the same goes for setting a record – the first Negroes to fly across the United States – proving that Lindbergh and other white men are not the only Eagles who have wings.' His mind elsewhere, he tapped a screwdriver lightly against an old-fashioned grindstone, while the others watched and waited patiently for him to continue. 'A successful transcontinental flight will get young black kids interested in aviation. And they won't feel so damn limited – and inferior – and defensive all the time. Like a white guy once told me – they have a right to the sky – just like everybody else.'

There was silence in the garage again, until Little Dandy applauded, one loud clap at a time, not in a disparaging way, but the unexpected action broke the serious mood, and drew a smile out of Phil Nash, and Banning, too.

'Call the meeting to order, General,' Little Dandy instructed jokingly, 'before you have us all in tears.' He fingered the bandage on his forehead and glanced at the sling supporting Phil Nash's arm. 'The walking wounded are now ready for orders, sir – at your service.'

Plans were discussed. Because he had worked on every type of automobile motor for years, and had a smattering of aircraft knowledge, owing to his association with Banning, Floyd Mosby was selected to accompany the pilot as mechanic on the pioneering flight. Floyd had not volunteered for the assignment, and it was clear that he had mixed feelings about the awesome responsibilities involved, and the prospects of becoming a hero, a celebrity, a black legend – or a very dead man. Booker T. had refused at once. He did, however, agree to participate as a neighbourhood promoter, publicist, and fund-raiser during the flight, along with Little Dandy and Phil Nash.

After a heated debate, it was agreed that if miracles did happen, and the Eagle Rock became a plane again, flew across America, and touched down in New York City, Banning would receive forty-five per cent of Mr Cunningham's prize money; Floyd Mosby, the mechanic, twenty-five; and the three promoters, Little Dandy, Phil Nash, and Booker T. Mosby, ten per cent each.

Then Floyd and Booker T. Mosby, sombre types by appearance and attitude, but always good hosts, decided to celebrate the new joint venture by hauling out some beer, cheese, and crackers.

'Imagine the shindig we'll have after the final landing,' said Banning, enjoying the beer, with an eye on his new flight mechanic. 'Ever been to New York City, Floyd – Harlem?'

'Never.'

'I haven't either,' Banning told him, the exhilaration showing in his face. 'But we're going, man. First stop? The Cotton Club. Music – and beauties – and glamour – and hooch – and food – and –'

'You can't get in,' Little Dandy interrupted. 'Only whites at the tables. Are you a singer and dancer, James Herman? They do allow black boys to perform.'

'I'll get in, Douglas.'

'Because you fly?'

'No,' Banning answered, running a hand playfully over his cheek. 'Just light enough,' he remarked, grinning. 'I'll pass.'

'That's doubtful,' Phil Nash contradicted, belching after a long swallow of beer. 'And Floyd doesn't stand a chance.'

'We'll both get in,' Banning persisted. 'I'll pass. And Floyd will begin using Fair-Plex Ointment and Cocotone Skin Whitener as part of our flight preparations. And we'll straighten his hair with Wonder Uncurl and Kink-No-More – Conk for short.'

The pilot looked over at Floyd Mosby and smiled as the others laughed, guzzled beer, and crunched cheese crackers. 'How about that, Floyd?' Banning asked jovially. 'Worth the trouble for a visit to the Cotton Club?'

'No,' Mosby replied, taking him very seriously. 'I'll stay black – out of trouble – and where I'm wanted.'

Instead of ignoring the remark, Banning glared, his smile fading completely. He turned away from Floyd and faced the others. 'Let's unload the van,' he said, all business again.

Work on reconstructing the Eagle Rock proceeded slowly and painstakingly by day, and with flash-lights, by night, to the accompaniment of arguments, confusion, impatience, elation, frustration, laughs, feasts, drunkenness, brawls, and many threats to abandon the project by every member of the group, including Banning, who lost his temper on numerous occasions.

However, they persevered, and made progress.

Because the project needed constant attention, and since the Depression had fouled up most of his dubious ventures anyway, Little Dandy's business meetings on the Avenue were reduced to a bare minimum. Phil Nash accepted only quick, simple carpentry assignments, and ignored his boarders completely, in order to make his contribution in Mosby's backyard. Floyd and Booker T. had turned away two 'pay later' automobile repairs for the sake of the cause. And James Herman Banning was the tireless, driving spirit behind the enterprise, determined to follow through with all plans.

Early on the morning of Monday, 12 September 1932, five days and six nights after the unloading operation, the weary task force stood back and stared in reverent admiration at something resembling an airplane, sitting on the plot of ground next to Mosby's garage. The fuselage, wings, tail, and wheels had been ingeniously patched up and pieced together in the shape of something that might possibly fly. An engine, a broken propeller, and numerous other parts were set out neatly beside the remodelled Eagle Rock – or whatever the unorthodox new design might be called.

'Looks like a big floppy bird,' Little Dandy commented, gazing at the contraption. 'Some kind of bastard species.'

'It is, Douglas,' Banning agreed proudly. 'And I love the damn thing because we actually gave birth. We did, man. And I can't wait to test our baby's wings.'

'Not with that fourteen year-old smashed-up engine,' Floyd Mosby advised, glancing at his brother. 'Ain't no sense in puttin' a decent tool on it.'

'No sense at all,' Booker T. confirmed. 'And how ya gonna use that busted pro-peller?'

'The Mosby boys are right, James Herman,' Phil Nash joined in. 'That crazy heap will sit there forever.'

'It won't.' Banning walked over to the parts on the ground beside the plane, and his team followed, one after the other. 'But we do have some problems,' he said, kneeling to get a closer look at the engine and propeller. 'We need two Scintilla magnetos – and a steel prop – for additional revs – to help us clear the high ranges.' He stared up at Floyd and Booker T. 'And – just as important – this motor needs a complete overhauling – a professional job.'

'Costing what?' Little Dandy asked. 'And where in the hell do you intend to find the money? Another miracle, James Herman?'

'We can buy two magnetos for a hundred and twenty dollars – sixty for each,' Banning replied, getting up. 'I don't know the exact price of a steel propeller. And the overhaul?' He glared at the Mosby brothers. 'That depends on the mechanic's ability and experience. Shame you gentlemen can't put a decent tool on that motor.'

'You need a new one, James Herman,' Floyd insisted. 'No kind of mechanic can get that mess workin' properly. And fly across this country with it? Nobody.'

'I'll check around,' said Banning, turning to Little Dandy and Phil Nash. 'Any place to find the money on the Avenue, Douglas?'

'No chance right now.'

'How about a white neighbourhood, Phil?'

'Things are bad and –'

'Listen to me,' Banning interrupted, pacing slowly back and forth. 'While I'm scrounging for a motor overhaul – and a few other favours – maybe you two hot shot promoters can hit the Avenue and – well – spread the word about our transcontinental attempt – history – a Negro flight record.'

'Holy shit, man.' Little Dandy shook his head in mock disbelief. 'Want to give us a couple of jingle bells and tin cups?'

'I'm serious, Douglas,' said Banning. 'Go to everybody you know on the Avenue – and people you don't know – brief them – Reverend Johnson, too, at the Second Baptist Church – he'll beg the congregation. Try, God damn it – raise some funds – we're flying to New York City in the plane that's sitting right over there – and nothing can stop us – absolutely nothing!'

Once again, the eyes of every member of the group were on Banning, and all were silent.

'I'm starting to believe you, James Herman,' Little Dandy finally stated. He took a hard look at Phil Nash. 'Want to conduct a little business on the Avenue?'

24

'Maybe,' Phil Nash replied in a friendly tone of voice. 'But why the hell should I want to make black history?'

'Because you fucked up our airplane, that's why,' Little Dandy explained, just as friendly. 'Now help us raise some repair money to get it flying again. Well?'

'Well,' Phil Nash hesitated, glanced around the group and then back at Little Dandy. 'I'll do my best,' he said. 'Just don't push me too hard.'

'Come on, partner,' Little Dandy ordered genially. 'Let's get dressed up real snazzy – and do the Avenue – and bring home a couple of magnetos and a steel prop for America's first black transcontinental fly boys – Amen – Amen – and I do mean Amen!'

Another meeting was held in the garage after the fund-raising operation had been completed. Little Dandy and Phil Nash plonked thirty-two dollars and fifty cents on the work bench in front of the Mosby brothers and considered it to be a major achievement, considering the rough times, the outlandish excuse for panhandling, and Reverend Johnson's reluctance to risk his collection plate donations by dipping into skimpy pockets before the Sunday service – especially for any cause connected with Douglas Boyd.

Phil Nash claimed to have guilt feelings about taking eight dollars and twenty cents from widow Letty Walker, an old cripple who lived alone, but he had promised to repair her back door free of charge, time permitting. However, most of the cash had been extracted from Little Dandy's friends and business associates on the Avenue, some of whom were unable to decline his request, for a variety of mysterious reasons.

Even though the Mosby brothers slapped down an additional fifteen dollars, and Banning contributed ten, the Eagle Rock organization was still in serious financial trouble, holding a grand total of fifty-five dollars.

Banning summed up the situation. They were still five dollars short of the sixty required for one magneto, and they needed two, and a steel propeller, new or used. They also needed a compass, and several other important bits and pieces, technical items, essentials for a coast-to-coast flight in a homemade aircraft. He figured they would have to find at least another two hundred dollars and a free motor overhaul even before getting off the ground. And then there was the question of gasoline, hangar rent, living expenses, an emergency fund, and other necessities en route.

25

'We'll just concentrate on our prime objective right now,' Banning continued. 'Getting the airplane ready for take-off and a reasonably safe flight. All the other – obstacles – will be dealt with one at a time – as things progress.'

'How you gettin' two hundred bucks and free engine work, James Herman?' Booker T. asked, speaking for everyone, to judge from their expressions. 'Nobody here can squeeze another dime. And Floyd ain't good enough to fix that kind of crazy machine.'

'I know that,' said Banning, in a pensive mood. 'But we might be able to lay two gals in the same bed. In other words, Booker T., pick up the money and the overhaul from the same source. Maybe. A big maybe. But – maybe.'

He proceeded to tell his task force about an excellent aircraft mechanic, an experienced professional, a former colleague who had worked with him at the Bessie Coleman Aero Club.

'Thomas C. Allen is our man,' Banning stated emphatically. 'I know him well. He is sure to be fascinated to hear that we're attempting the first Negro transcontinental flight. I'm sure we can count on his full co-operation.'

26

3

The Allens lived at number 18 Buchanan Drive, Alhambra, a very small, modestly furnished, but comfortable house, attached to an identical one, in a long row of very small, modestly furnished, but comfortable houses, on a narrow street without trees or hedges or anything green, just off busy West Pico Boulevard. Despite the traffic noise, occasional gang fights, and the slow deterioration of both residents and property due to the Depression, this was a fairly respectable, better than average Negro neighbourhood.

Celene Allen, a short, bouncy, rather plump young woman, with a quick wit and attractive features, had prepared and served her speciality dinner, crispy fried chicken and sweet-potato pie. Allen and Banning were drinking their coffee in a living-room crowded with models and photographs of aircraft and diagrams of engines. There were books on aviation, too, and magazines. The main attraction, deeply resented by Celene, because it was a symbol of her husband's obsession with flight, was a real wooden propeller, dangling on a short chain from the ceiling – a bizarre ornament which could be spun with a sharp flick of the wrist, something Allen did frequently.

After the men had brought each other up to date with personal happenings, gossip, and recent flight news, the pilot leaned forward and broached the subject of his visit.

'Did you hear about the one thousand dollar prize?' he asked. 'Put up by the white guy from Virginia?'

'I heard,' Allen replied, sipping his coffee. 'To the first coloured transcontinental flyers.'

'Right.'

'So?'

'We're going.'

'Going?' Allen put the cup down and stared. 'Who is we?' he asked. 'And going in what?'

'Floyd Mosby and myself,' Banning answered, meeting his gaze. 'In an 0XX6 Eagle Rock that belongs to some friends of mine.'

Tom Allen grinned. 'Are you referring to that old crate which was smashed up by Douglas Boyd and Phil Nash the other day? Floyd Mosby must have become an overnight mechanical genius. Did he get the wreck put together for you? Using the well-known talents of Booker T.? Or are you jesting with me, Banning? An excuse to gobble up a free Celene Allen chicken delight?'

'The Eagle Rock is now in one piece and solid enough to fly,' Banning responded seriously, ignoring the light remarks. 'But we need a professional motor overhaul – a steel prop – and some other parts.'

Tom Allen finished his coffee, pushed the cup aside, and settled back against a sofa cushion. 'You act like a man who is about to make me a proposition,' he said. 'Go right ahead, Mr Banning.'

'Will you do the motor overhaul?'

'Floyd Mosby is –'

'Come on, Tom,' Banning interrupted sharply. 'You know damn well that Floyd can't repair an airplane engine. He has trouble with automobiles.'

Allen rubbed a finger under his chin, thoughtfully. 'I'll take a look and give you an estimate,' he said. 'How much do you people have to spend?'

'Nothing.'

'*Nothing?*' Allen laughed. 'You sure have a high-class operation going. Better haul one of Little Dandy's whores instead of Floyd Mosby. Then you'll probably make it to New York.'

'All right, that's enough, smart ass!' Banning was through playing games, and his expression showed it. 'I'll put my entire proposal on the table and you give me a positive or negative response without the comedy routine.'

Allen took a long and careful look at his friend, then smiled, and nodded good-humouredly. 'You've got the floor, James Herman,' he said. 'This business appears to be more serious than I thought. What's going on?'

Banning outlined his plans for a transcontinental attempt, and explained that it was not just the prize money that was at stake: a Negro success in the field of aviation would be a terrific boost to the morale of the black population, particularly the young. It would show them – and the whites – that they were just as capable of doing what highly trained white men could do.

'But we need free mechanical labour and about two hundred dollars just to get off the ground and start flying,' Banning concluded, ignoring Allen's look of exaggerated incredulity. 'Requirements en route will have to be begged, borrowed, stolen, or done without. But – for the first time – an airplane is going to leave this coast and land on the other one – with a couple of nigger flyers.'

'That ugly word is never used in my home, Mr Banning.' Celene Allen had entered the room, in a happy mood, obviously ready to join the discussion. She sat next to her husband on the sofa and tapped her hand playfully on his leg. 'What exactly does this hot shot operator want from you, Thomas?' she asked, throwing a sidelong glance at Banning. 'I caught snippets of the conversation in between plate rattling.'

'Slave labour and no wages, Celene dear,' Allen replied, putting his hand on hers. 'For the sake of Negro history. Am I right, James Herman?'

'That's only part of it,' Banning corrected, seriously. 'I want you to overhaul the motor and come up with about two hundred dollars' worth of take-off money.' He waited for the statement to be digested before proceeding. 'You'll get it back – plus a little extra – from Mr Cunningham's cash prize. And – you become a part of aviation history, Tom Allen – a black hero.'

Celene's smile developed into a chuckle, and very quickly it became a laugh, and grew louder and nearly uncontrollable, as her husband joined in with his head back and eyes closed. Banning studied them both, deadpan, until Allen had recovered enough to cough and splutter a response.

'You – want me – to overhaul your cracked up motor – and pay two hundred dollars – for the privilege of getting my name in the history books – as a black hero? *A black hero*? Man, what the hell are you talking about?'

'You know damn well what I'm talking about,' Banning lashed back, raising his voice. 'A transcontinental flight record for Negroes.'

'Floyd Mosby as a black hero defies the imagination, James Herman,' said Allen, with an unfamiliar touch of jealousy. 'That thick bumpkin wouldn't be able to drain oil or change a plug. It's all a joke. And you talk about *my* comedy routines?'

'Nobody has a contract with Floyd Mosby, Thomas,' Banning explained, keeping a sharp eye on Allen's reactions. 'Want to discuss an arrangement?'

'Just hold it right there, brothers,' Celene interrupted. 'Get whatever you have in mind out right now, James Herman, and I'll tell you why in a few blunt words.'

'Celene, nobody asked you to –'

'Close your big flapping mouth, Thomas Allen,' Celene instructed. 'I am a pregnant lady. We have exactly two hundred

29

and fifteen dollars saved. And things are real bad in this country. Do you believe that I'll give up one penny of this precious money for some crackpot ego trip to make black points? And have my husband work his ass off on a motor for nothing? And risk that same ass barnstorming across the United States in a toy plane?' She got up and stood over Banning, glaring down at him. 'No, James Herman. Tom has been floating around on his own long enough. Now I want him home, at least until the baby arrives, taking local jobs. And getting paid for them. So hunt your money and repair work elsewhere, and forget about Thomas C. Allen. Right? Did you receive the message?'

'Faster than Western Union, Celene,' Banning replied, smiling. 'I do understand your wifely feelings.'

'Good.' Celene's smile was as warm and friendly as his. 'I'm going over to my parents for a coffee while you boys talk.' She looked at her husband and faked a frown. 'You had better concentrate on things other than transcontinental shenanigans. I'll be home in an hour.'

'Celene.' Tom's voice stopped her at the door. 'You have jumped the gun once again,' he said, stretched full length on the sofa. 'Nobody made any proposals and consequently nobody has accepted.'

'Just anticipating, Thomas,' said Celene, preparing to leave, 'based on past experience and a certain sneaky glint in your eyes tonight. I know all the signs. Bye.' She waved and was gone.

After a few moments of silence, Banning poured two more coffees, and watched Allen slowly sit up.

'You are definitely a married man, Thomas,' Banning teased, observing his friend closely. 'But that gal sure puts out great chicken and pie – and I'll bet a lot of other enjoyable things too. Am I right? Lucky devil.'

Allen appeared to be offended for an instant, but he quickly composed himself, and changed the subject.

'Are you really serious about this damn flight?'

'Dead serious.'

'That's how you'll probably end up – trying for a coast-to-coast in a wrecked 0XX6 – with a pooped-out engine – no money – and a dumb-bell like Floyd Mosby.'

Banning knew his man well, and could tell that the excitement of the project was beginning to appeal to his sense of adventure.

'Nobody is forcing you to join this expedition, Thomas,' he said toying with his victim. 'I heard you were back. And I know how much you love the business – and challenges – and maybe even some good times. Hell, man, that's all. So I came over to brief you.' He looked Allen straight in the eyes. 'Now wouldn't I have been a proper bastard if we had gone for a black flight record and one thousand dollars without informing you – a good friend – and the best damn mechanic in the game?'

Allen yawned on purpose, stood up, walked casually to the centre of the room, spun the wooden propeller, and watched it revolve a few times, before speaking.

'The honey just oozes past those sparkling white teeth of yours, James Herman,' he said, gazing at the ceiling prop as it slowed down. 'Where do you keep this magnificent flying machine?'

'In the yard,' Banning replied, certain now that he had made some progress, 'next to the Mosby garage.'

'A perfect resting place.'

'Want to come over and take a look at her?'

'I might,' Allen replied, turning to his friend. 'But only out of curiosity. That 0XX6 Eagle Rock was a wreck before the accident. I just have to see how you and the Wright Brothers pieced it together for a transcontinental attempt.'

'But the motor and some other –'

'Forget that,' Allen interrupted. 'The body alone is worth a visit. You don't get a chance to inspect aviation magic every day. This is a great opportunity.'

'Don't start messing around again, Thomas,' Banning warned quietly. 'Are you coming over to the garage?'

'Yes.'

'When?'

'Name it.'

'Tomorrow afternoon.'

'I'll be there.'

'Fine.' Banning smiled, let it fade, and hesitated a moment before asking his question, a touchy one. 'What about Celene?'

'What about her?'

'The lady's speech,' Banning reminded him. 'She doesn't want you anywhere near this project. I did get the message, brother.'

'I'll tell you something, James Herman.' Allen walked back to the sofa and flopped down heavily. 'You worry too much about women. And that's bad. Especially when they belong to other men.' He leaned his head back on the cushion again and used the coffee table for his feet. 'Besides,' he said, with eyes closed. 'Who said I was joining your ding-a-ling circus anyway? All you can expect is a snoopy visitor. Nothing more. Is that understood?'

'Yep.'

Both men were silent until Allen opened one eye slightly and asked, 'How many horses in that beat-up old motor?'

'A hundred,' Banning replied, watching the eye close again. 'But two Scintilla mags and a steel prop would give us some extra revs. That is, if the old beat-up motor had a real overhaul – by an expert. Don't you think so, Thomas?'

'Always a slight possibility,' Allen answered, pretending to be half asleep and hardly paying attention. 'I do hope you recruit a good man for the job. Otherwise – with Floyd Mosby – you won't get *off* the ground – you'll be buried *under* it.'

Tom Allen arrived at the Mosby garage, as promised, after assuring Celene that he was only going to take a look out of curiosity, and to placate his old friend Banning, who wanted a professional opinion about the flight, nothing more. Celene was furious and worried and utterly unconvinced by her husband's casual attitude. However, to avoid a major quarrel prematurely, she had accepted a kiss on the forehead and a light smack on the behind before the mechanic's early afternoon departure.

Deciding to keep Allen's grand inspection for later, without even allowing him a curious peek out of the one window facing the yard, the project team enjoyed lunch, and heard a short lecture from Banning about the plane, the flight, the problems, and the rewards. Obviously prepared for the ceremony, Allen listened in a friendly and polite manner, although he failed to ask a single question, or make any comment whatsoever.

Finally the time had come. Banning led Allen and his task force out of the rear door to the large plot of ground where the born-again 0XX6 Eagle Rock was displayed.

'OH! OH! OH! OH! OH!' screamed Allen, doubling over and falling to his knees. 'OH! OH! OH! OH! OH! OH!' he continued, shaking violently, his head down and face hidden, apparently out of control.

At first all the men, except Banning, who knew Allen too well, were shocked and frightened by the mechanic's hysterical behaviour.

'I'll call and get us an ambulance,' Floyd Mosby spluttered, his eye-balls bulging even more than usual. 'That man has been struck down with somethin' really awful.'

'Forget it, Floyd,' Banning advised calmly. 'Mr Allen is just reacting to our aircraft. He's laughing, that's all. Like a mental case. We must have built a very funny airplane. Right, Thomas?'

Slowly, while the others inspected him with bewildered interest, Allen stifled his hilarity, lifted his head and pointed at the Eagle Rock.

'What the hell is that thing?' he yelled, making an awkward move to get up. 'Are you people having a joke on me?'

'No, Thomas,' said Banning, watching the mechanic brush dirt off his trousers. 'We're flying to New York City in that thing.'

'Have a nice trip,' Allen countered, glancing over at the plane. 'Anyway – you don't need a steel propeller. Just buy a large pencil and a strong rubber band. Save your money.'

'Why dontcha go on over and take a closer look, Tom?' Booker T. suggested. 'Everybody worked mighty hard on this job. You got no right to poke fun at a distance.'

'Booker T. is right,' Banning said, leading Allen by the arm towards the Eagle Rock. 'Do a proper inspection before you sound off and ridicule people.'

'I can tell you now,' Allen persisted. 'That crate won't get off the ground. And if it did, you might fly about two inches above it – for a couple of minutes, and then – wham.'

They stopped in front of the plane. Allen gave the body a quick once-over, a cursory examination, without pausing. 'One thing is sure,' he commented mockingly. 'If you do manage to lift off in this strange object – it will scare every bird out of the sky – and cause panic on the ground below.'

Little Dandy and Phil Nash were about to challenge the mechanic, but a gesture from Banning shut them up abruptly, because Allen, with an apparent change of attitude, suddenly began touching the fuselage, poking at the tail section, yanking on the wing fittings and, for the first time, treating the reassembled Eagle Rock seriously. No one spoke as he moved around the plane, giving it a very deliberate and thorough inspection. And then, ignoring his audience, he went to the motor, and the other accessories, which had been set out neatly on the ground. With a screwdriver, a wrench, a few other tools, and some rags, Allen spent some time huddled over these important parts, loosening and tightening, fiddling and tapping, staring and thinking. Finally he stood up, wiped the oil and grease off his hands, dumped the rag, and faced Banning and the task force.

'A pathetic junk heap,' he said quietly. 'But a little more usable than I thought at first.' He glanced at the eldest Mosby brother and spoke in a sincere tone of voice. 'You boys probably did work mighty hard on this job, Booker T. Frankly, I can't believe the damn thing. Who could?'

'Me.' Banning took a step forward and stood eye to eye with the mechanic. 'Can this plane be rigged up to fly across the United States?'

'Very doubtful indeed.'

'With an engine overhaul, two Scintilla magnetos, a steel propeller, a few extra bucks for a compass and some other equipment – and two guys with ability – and plenty of luck?'

'That depends on many –'

'Yes or no, Thomas?'

The two men stood without moving, and there was silence, while the rest of the Eagle Rock team gathered around them, straining to hear the response.

'We'd better have a long talk this evening, James Herman,' Allen finally replied. 'A very private one.'

The two friends met at Banning's place, where they drank bootleg hooch, and talked and joked and predicted and criticized and argued and cursed and eventually, just after midnight, Allen slurred a proposition, and Banning agreed instantly. Allen would overhaul the engine, and put up the funds for the Scintilla magnetos, steel propeller, compass, and other essential items needed to get the aircraft up and on its way: approximately two hundred dollars. He would accompany Banning as mechanic, instead of Floyd Mosby, and also be given an opportunity to fly the aircraft on at least two hops, before reaching New York City. In addition, Allen demanded that, if a miracle did happen, and the flight was successful, the one thousand dollar prize money should be distributed differently, according to the real contributions made by the members of the Eagle Rock team. Banning, the organizer, and chief pilot should receive three hundred and fifty dollars; Allen, the mechanic, co-pilot and financial backer, four hundred dollars (in reality a two hundred dollar split after deducting his two hundred dollar outlay); Little Dandy and Phil Nash, owners of the wreck, promoters and possible fund-raisers, eighty-five dollars each; Floyd and Booker T. Mosby, promoters, possible fund-raisers, and suppliers of backyard facilities, forty dollars each.

After shaking hands on the agreement, Allen and Banning swallowed a little more illegal booze, set a time for a planning meeting, and then whispered a quiet prayer for the mechanic, before he went home to face a young lady called Celene, who had a sharp tongue, a good right hook, and parents nearby with a spare room.

34

4

On the following day, the pilot, mechanic, and the support group, including an uncomplaining Floyd Mosby, had their conference, accepted the new percentage arrangements, and went to work on the flight preparations at the garage.

The plan was to leave from Dycer Airport, Los Angeles. Allen laboured over the engine while Banning was out negotiating the best possible prices for the engine parts they needed. In the meantime, Little Dandy, Phil Nash and the Mosby brothers were trying to organize free – or very cheap – transportation for the Eagle Rock's move from the yard to Dycer Field. At the appropriate time, the idea was to dismantle the wings, strap them carefully to the fuselage, and load the plane on a large truck of some kind. During the journey to Dycer, the priceless cargo would be held securely in place and kept under constant surveillance by task force members. Reassembly, and the finishing touches, were scheduled to be done at the airport by Allen and Banning, it was hoped with the assistance of field staff, if any could be recruited – men willing to donate their services for a place in aviation history.

Finally Allen finished his work, as far as the Mosby yard was concerned. Banning had made excellent deals for the parts, and Little Dandy, Phil Nash and the brothers had arranged for the conveyance of the aircraft, courtesy of a friend of Booker T. They were proud of their efforts: the deal would cost the organizers absolutely nothing. But, free or not, Allen and Banning exchanged irritated glances when Phil Nash explained that a large commercial hay wagon had been reserved, a perfect size for the Eagle Rock. And, also thanks to Booker T.'s friend, four work horses would be available to pull the load, although the friend, a farmer, was certain that two were sufficient for the job.

The thought of arriving at Dycer Airport in this primitive fashion, on the first leg of their history-making flight, did not appeal to the pilot or the mechanic. Nevertheless, rather than hurt their feelings, both men congratulated the support group members and decided to make the best of the arrangement.

Floyd and Brooker T. Mosby, as established businessmen, were also acting as bookkeepers for the operation. After making all purchases, and setting aside money for facilities at Dycer, the brothers reported a balance of fifty-three dollars and thirty cents – enough for gasoline, oil, and other basics needed for take-off.

The journey to Dycer Airport was uneventful, apart from the bewildered stares, head-scratching, and finger-pointing of people on the streets. Crowds collected, and at times automobile traffic became congested, as the wagon moved slowly along, with Allen and Banning sitting up front beside the huge, black, whip-snapping driver. The others, standing at the back next to the plane, took to waving at the perplexed onlookers, like performers on a float during a circus parade. A policeman at a busy intersection chased away a group of kids who were running behind the strange vehicle.

To crown their discomfiture, just after making an inelegant but spectacular entrance at the airport, the two old work-horses simultaneously let go and plopped a trail of manure along one of the runways.

A belligerent white ground crew, led by a burly, loud-mouthed supervisor, made it very plain at once that co-operation would be limited, and given reluctantly, on a cash basis only – a favour, as far as the airport was concerned.

Tom Allen instantly abandoned any thoughts of asking for assistance, and nothing was said about the purpose of the flight. Before arranging for hangar space and repair facilities, the Eagle Rock task force accepted shovels, pails, sweep brooms, and a large dose of humiliation. Urged on by Allen, they ignored abusive remarks, and cleaned the runway without back-talk or complaints, in order to avoid a useless and time-consuming confrontation. It was especially difficult for James Herman Banning to follow through so placidly. But, this time, he kept his head down and his mouth shut, as he grimly shovelled shit, and dreamed of landing in New York City.

On Sunday morning, a day before the scheduled take-off, Allen discovered that the overhead valve action was gone off the engine. Someone had obviously removed it Saturday night. And that someone had to be a member of the Dycer Airport staff. Again Banning and, on this occasion, Phil Nash too, had to be controlled, at times physically, by Allen and the Mosby brothers.

Leaving the other members of the team brooding and cursing in the hangar, Allen went to the field office and purchased a Miller valve action for fifty-two dollars and fifty cents, and the white Dycer employee smirked and said, 'Thank you kindly, sir,' as he took the money.

The 0XX6 Eagle Rock was ready for take-off at noon on Monday, 19 September 1932. But according to the Mosby books, and Tom Allen's pocket count, the flight organizers now had a balance of eighty cents, and they needed gasoline.

Banning was at the limits of his patience and tolerance. They had all worked too long and too hard to be grounded at the last minute because of some Dycer propeller cranker with bad intentions. Ignoring Allen's warnings, he informed the group that he would go to one of the airport supervisors and explain about the transcontinental flight – the history books – the prize money – and the problems, including the suspected valve theft, and the desperate need for gasoline on credit.

Floyd Mosby stood with the others watching Banning stride confidently across the field towards the main office.

'That man is gonna end up in real trouble over there,' he mused, shaking his head concernedly. 'We should be ready to fetch him in a couple of minutes.'

'Don't leave the hangar, Floyd,' Allen ordered, keeping his eyes on Banning, as the pilot entered the building without a hesitation. 'Nobody else either,' he added, glancing around. 'I have a peaceful alternative in case of trouble.'

'Like what?' Little Dandy asked, mockingly. 'Offer a full-time shit-cleaning service in exchange for airplane fuel?'

'Not a bad idea, Douglas,' Allen replied, used to him by now. 'But mine smells better and I can do it alone.'

He left the hangar before anyone could say another word. 'Stick around and wait!' he yelled over his shoulder. 'I'll be in the hall outside the supervisor's room!'

The Dycer Airport's assistant facilities chief was a dark-haired, beefy character in his early fifties, with a large round face, a flat nose, and the kind of eyes which always made Banning feel uncomfortable: cold and grey and piercing, they never changed, never matched his mood or expression. Thick layers of flab were jammed into a military-type khaki jacket and trousers.

'Did you say transcontinental?' Mr Peter Osborne was hunched over a very small wooden desk. Banning sat ramrod straight in a chair facing him. 'You intend to fly that – aircraft – from here to New York City tomorrow?'

'That's right.'

'I don't want to be a party to suicide, Mr Banning,' said Osborne, forcing his mouth into something resembling a smile. 'This is a reputable airport with an excellent safety record. We're concerned about every plane taking off from here. Forget about this coast-to-coast nonsense for the moment. Let's just think about our log books. Have you had formal flight instruction?'

'You must be new around here.'

'I beg your pardon?'

'Mr Dycer knows who I am.' Banning tried not to let his voice and expression reflect the antagonism he felt. 'Where are you from, Mr Osborne?'

'Allegheny Municipal in Pittsburgh.'

'Good airport,' Banning remarked. 'How long have you been here with Dycer?'

'Six weeks,' the assistant facilities chief replied, obviously smothering the same emotions as Banning. 'And that ends your interrogation, mister.'

'Fair enough.' Banning removed some papers from his leather jacket pocket and flashed them at Osborne. 'For your information, sir,' he continued, with just a touch of sarcasm coming through. 'I've been licensed by the United States Department of Commerce since 1926. And I have almost 800 hours of flying time to my credit. Stunt work, too. And training others. No, Mr Osborne. You don't have to worry about the Dycer log books. I know how to fly an airplane.'

Osborne kept his steely gaze fixed on the pilot and it was difficult to read the man's true feelings. 'Sorry, I wasn't aware of your flight experience, Banning,' he said, and it might have been genuine. 'But,' he went on, evidently choosing his words with care, 'you have to admit, we don't have too many – professional – skilled – licensed –'

'Nigger pilots?'

'I didn't say that,' Osborne snapped back. 'You did.' This time, he displayed his irritation by sitting up abruptly, and pressing the palms of his chubby hands on the desk. 'What are you doing here, Banning?'

'We need some help.' Banning explained the purpose of his flight, and the problem that had arisen owing to the missing valve.

'Are you insinuating that a member of the Dycer staff took your goddamn valve?' Osborne's face seemed to puff up and folds of overlapping skin nearly hid his eyes. His anger had finally surfaced. 'Watch your step, boy,' he warned threateningly. 'I don't care how many flying hours you have doing circus tricks. How dare you accuse our employees of theft?'

'I didn't accuse anyone, Mr Osborne,' Banning said calmly, keeping his mind on the gasoline. 'But the valve disappeared Saturday night on these premises. And we had to buy a new one.'

'That's your problem.'

'Accepted.' Banning put up his hand to ward off another outburst. 'The main thing is – we had to spend the last of our money – and we need gasoline.' He stood up and walked closer to the desk. 'Hell, man. I'm not here to cause trouble about missing valves or anything else. Just let us put some gas in our plane so we can take off tomorrow. You'll get the money back as soon as we return from New York. That's a solemn promise.'

'We don't give credit,' Osborne told him bluntly. 'Company policy.'

'Make an exception.'

'For you?'

'Right.'

'Why?'

'Because we're going to make aviation history, Mr Osborne,' Banning replied, raising his voice a little. 'The first Negroes to fly transcontinental.' He leaned forward. 'Lend us some gasoline. What the hell is the big deal? You and Dycer will take part in a very special event.'

Instead of answering, the assistant facilities chief suddenly burst out laughing, folded his arms on the desk, and rested his forehead on them, making snorting, pig-like sounds.

Banning watched until his fury erupted. He leaned close, just a breathing space away from Osborne's ear. 'Go ahead and laugh, you honky bastard,' he snarled. 'And stick the gas hose up your fat ass and pump – *pump* – until your big belly explodes.'

Osborne lifted his head instantly, no longer laughing. He rose up, fast.

'Get out!' he screamed, pointing to the door. 'You'd better run like a son-of-a-bitch, black boy!'

Banning was standing, fists clenched, ready to swing, when Tom Allen knocked loudly and entered the room.

'Sorry to interrupt your chat, Mr Osborne,' the mechanic apologized, with a broad, idiotic grin on his face. 'May I speak to my partner in private?'

39

'You had better pull him away from here fast!' Osborne yelled. 'He's looking for serious trouble!'

'Come on, James Herman.' Allen walked to him, gripped his arm, and started urging him towards the door. 'We have to discuss a practical idea of mine.'

Banning finally loosened up, but took one last shot at Osborne before moving away.

'Pay close attention when you log our take-off tomorrow, Osborne,' he asserted coldly. 'Two black boys will make your fucking airport famous.'

'Come on, James Herman.'

'Banning!' Osborne called out, as they left the office. 'Keep your noses clean around this place, or that horse shit-wagon might have to return for your crate – and you won't make history after all.'

'Come on, James Herman.'

Tom Allen's plan for raising the money for the gasoline was quite simple. One of Celene's uncles in Alhambra had some burial cash put away. A popular member of the local Elks Lodge, Wallace Hawkins loved to show off, brag about celebrities he had never met, and places he had never seen, and exciting things he had never done.

Allen proposed to leave the airport immediately, pay Uncle Wallace a surprise visit, brief him about the transcontinental attempt, make him feel a part of it, and then do everything possible to relieve him of some coffin money – hoping that he would not drop dead before they had a chance to claim the Cunningham prize, and make repayment.

Allen's mission succeeded, but there were bothersome strings attached to the loan, and Banning was not particularly pleased. Even so, they had no alternative but to accept.

Wallace Hawkins had been greatly impressed by Allen's account of the transcontinental flight attempt. It was juicy material for an Elks Lodge gathering. Consequently, he had agreed to extract twenty-five dollars from his burial fund, on certain conditions. The first was understandable and easy to accommodate. Hawkins wanted his money returned, plus two dollars' interest, after the prize money had been collected. Condition two was that the Eagle Rock should fly to Alhambra after leaving Dycer, and land, so that he and his family and a small group of friends – mainly Elks Lodge members – could

40

wave and cheer as the plane took off again for New York City and its place in the history books. As Banning said, it was a niggling, time-wasting, completely absurd and degrading pain in the rectum, but they had gasoline money, and a little to spare.

Floyd Mosby went to pick up Celene Allen while the other members of the task force held a final pre-flight meeting behind the hangar. Maps were studied very carefully. Allen and Banning would be leaving Los Angeles, bound for New York City, with less than twenty-five dollars in their pockets. A smart route had to be laid out, with stops in 'friendly' towns, preferably where they had acquaintances or relatives, former work colleagues, or contacts, people who might have heard about them, or possibly recognize them – Banning as an air chauffeur, stunt flyer, and touring member of the Bessie Coleman Aero Club – Allen as a well-travelled company and freelance mechanic.

They would have to beg for gas, oil, lodgings, food, and other expenses, including hangar rent. Emergencies might also cost money. Every possible source of quick funding had to be considered: unknown brothers and sisters, preachers, civic and social groups, whites both sympathetic and hostile; everyone and everything en route had to be fair game, and to hell with pride, dignity, and the prospects of a punch in the mouth, or worse.

Certain important rules were set out, and both men pledged to follow them, regardless of the circumstances: no passengers, no commercial stunts, and each time the plane left the ground it would be heading for New York City, a Negro flight record, and a one thousand dollar prize.

After handshakes, embraces, tears, jokes, and thumbs-up gestures, Celene, Little Dandy, Phil Nash and the Mosby brothers stood in a cluster off the runway watching Tom Allen and James Herman Banning climb into the cockpits of the reconstructed 0XX6 Eagle Rock.

Peter Osborne, the assistant facilities chief, observed coldly from the office building door. Sneering members of the Dycer ground crew were grouped closer to the action.

Four dollars and seventy-five cents' worth of gasoline had been added to about six gallons already in the tank. Allen's clothing was wrapped in a tight bundle to cut down weight. Banning's small, dilapidated bag stood upright on the seat, next to Allen, away from the controls. Both men were wearing flying gear, including goggles, and helmets.

Ignoring Osborne and his other employees, Mr Dycer, the airport owner, a man who knew Banning and had a quiet respect for him, walked to the plane with the log book, and signed, making the flight official. Little Dandy, doing an unusually efficient job as a promoter, took several photographs of the historic proceedings. The Mosby brothers finally smiled, Phil Nash shook a clenched fist over his head like a victorious athlete, and Celene cried.

At exactly 4:45 on Monday 19 September 1932, with Banning at the controls, and Allen blowing kisses from the rear cockpit, the salvaged wreck began a slow and wobbly move down the runway. There were cheers and waves as the plane picked up speed. Mr Dycer held his arm up high in the form of a salute. Osborne stared blankly without moving from his position, while some of the ground crew members faked wild support with exaggerated applause and whistles, and one or two yelled racial obscenities.

But Allen and Banning didn't hear a thing except the wind, and the motor, and the creak of makeshift fittings, as the aircraft finally left the ground, and strained to gain altitude. There were no yells or whoops of delight from the pilot and mechanic on this occasion; this was a test flight, in a very strange piece of equipment, without proper instruments, or parachutes, or flares, or navigation and landing lights.

They headed west for a while to get high enough for a safe turn. And then, a long sweep, and eastward, making a large circle around the outskirts of Los Angeles, always staying over clear country, in case of a forced landing. A sharp swing left and they were over the Los Angeles stockyard and in a few minutes, down below on the right, Sprott's Airport, and soon, the Midwick Country Club, and then, straight ahead, the Alhambra Air Drome, their destination, about seventeen miles from Dycer – and nothing had blown up or fallen off yet.

Banning flew over the field, turned back, landed bump-de-bump, and taxied unsteadily to a hangar where Mr and Mrs Wallace Hawkins, their two young daughters, and the Elks Lodge representatives were waiting in an embarrassing formation with hand-printed good luck posters and miniature American flags.

'Here they are!' Allen shouted, as the plane came to a halt, and the small group of well-wishers ran forward, led by Hawkins. 'We are twenty-five dollar whores, James Herman!'

'To hell with them!' Banning clambered out of the cockpit and pointed to the ground under the motor. 'What's that? Gasoline?'

42

Allen also jumped out, crouched, took a look, and sniffed. 'Water,' he finally replied, dejectedly. 'The goddamn pump is leaking.'

'How badly?'

'Just a little now, but –'

'GOD BLESS YOU, THOMAS ALLEN!' Wallace Hawkins shouted, as he approached. 'And God bless you, too, James Herman Banning,' he added, as the others gathered around the two aviators, holding up their posters, and waving their flags.

'Oh, shit,' Banning mumbled, exchanging a hasty glance with Allen. Then, both men smiled awkwardly as the welcoming committee hip-hip-hoo-rayed in a badly rehearsed fashion.

'Thank you very much,' said Allen, after a few hand gestures had produced some quiet. 'Nice of you to come and give us support. We do appreciate it.'

'We do indeed,' Banning interjected, doing everything possible not to show his annoyance. 'But we have a slight problem with our aircraft – a minor one – and we have to check things out before take-off. So – may I ask you wonderful folks to stand over there?' He indicated a spot a short distance from the plane and runway. 'Just for a couple of minutes,' he added, with a friendly smile. 'We'll give you a complete report – and a departure time – as soon as our inspection is over.'

Hawkins nodded, looking a little deflated, like the rest of his entourage, but they turned and moved away slowly, quietly, with their posters and flags lowered temporarily.

'Uncle Wallace is sure playing on this one,' Allen commented, turning back to the plane with Banning. 'I should have nailed him for more than twenty-five.'

'What about the pump?'

'It has to be fixed.'

'How long?'

'An overnight job.'

'You said it was a small leak,'

'Small leaks become big leaks, James Herman.'

'We've still got about an hour of daylight,' Banning said firmly. 'Let's take off for Riverside and repair it there.'

'That's sixty miles!'

'Is this plane heading for New York or not?' Banning smacked the fuselage like a baby's bottom. 'Besides,' he continued, 'the compass has to be checked. It's a few degrees off and we'd better know exactly how many. Riverside will give us a chance to mark the deviation.'

'I vote to stay and fix –'

'We don't vote on this ride, Thomas,' Banning stated with easy-going authority. 'I am the pilot and senior partner.' He started to move. 'Come on. Let's give your Uncle Wallace something to bullshit about at his next Lodge meeting.'

They did. While the Hawkins contingent watched proudly, ready with posters, flags, and vocal cords, the Eagle Rock taxied jerkily down the runway, and suddenly ground looped. It had no brakes.

'CRAZY BEAT UP SON-OF-A-BITCH!' Allen screamed at the plane, just before he jumped out, nearly breaking his neck, got up, and held a wing until the aircraft was straight on course again. After running alongside, and eventually clawing his way back in again, he bellowed at the pilot, who had been roaring with laughter, enjoying his acrobatics, 'GET US UP, YOU SADISTIC BASTARD!'

Banning raised his arm, pointed to the sky, and they took off, over the good luck posters, American flags, the waving, cheering money-lender, his family and friends from the Elks Lodge.

Turning due east, flying over the San José hills and the Los Angeles County Fair Grounds, the rattling Eagle Rock swung to the right a little, and headed for the Arlington Airport, at Riverside, California.

5

Apart from some body-shaking vibrations, unscheduled climbs and sudden falls, and a strange thumping noise under the fuselage, the flight from Alhambra was uneventful. As Allen had predicted, the small leak in the water pump became a large one, but it held up; and Banning used the flight to measure the compass deviation accurately.

However, he had trouble controlling the unsteady junk heap on descent, and the 6:00 pm landing at Arlington was nearly as humiliating an experience as the horse shit-wagon arrival at Dycer. The Eagle Rock slammed down hard, spun, and missed ramming the corner of a hangar by inches, while members of the airport staff watched in open-mouthed amazement.

Nevertheless, the reception was much warmer and friendlier here, because several airport attendants remembered Banning's expert stunt flying when the Bessie Coleman Aero Club performed at Arlington Field. In addition, a black former parachutist with the Club who had worked with the pilot on numerous occasions, now had a ground crew job at Arlington.

Allen and Banning felt able to speak openly about their transcontinental attempt, and no one laughed out loud, or heaped verbal abuse and ridicule on them, although there were a few snickering references to the crudely reconstructed aircraft, and most of the Arlington employees, including the former parachutist, obviously doubted that there would be a successful landing in New York City. However, they were polite, and even made an important contribution – the Eagle Rock was staked down for the night free of charge, a gesture very much appreciated by Allen and Banning.

A big man called The Greaser who had a friend who owned a restaurant in Riverside, a chilli joint, promised to call him and arrange for a late dinner, on the house. This unexpected gesture was also appreciated by the aviators.

Eventually, the Arlington Airport staff members dispersed to go about their various duties. The ex-parachutist, a tall, broad-shouldered man named Claude Wilkins, offered to give the aviators a lift into town, if they could wait for him to finish his shift at seven-thirty. The invitation was accepted gratefully.

Out of curiosity, and thinking about restrictions, Banning asked Wilkins about The Greaser, and the restaurant in Riverside.

'Well,' said Wilkins. 'The Greaser has never caused me any trouble. He's a good-natured man. I never did meet his friend, but I've been to the Hot Spot – that's the restaurant he probably means. It's in a Chinese neighbourhood. They get a few Negroes, but most of the customers are Chinese. The room is always full of people and busy. Great chilli. You'll like it. And The Greaser said on the house. How can it be bad?' Because of a previous engagement, and a lack of hard cash, Wilkins turned down Allen's invitation to join them.

Banning got up and started to move towards the hangar door as soon as Wilkins had disappeared.

'Where are you going, James Herman?' Allen remained seated on the ground with his back propped against a large wooden packing case. 'It's only 6.45,' he said. 'We have plenty of time.'

'Did you say plenty of time?' Banning asked, inspecting Allen closely. 'Man, you are still in your flying suit, complete with helmet and goggles.'

'That's the idea.'

Banning stared for a moment, perplexed. 'What the hell are you talking about?' he demanded. 'Let's get our clothes out of the plane. They have a wash-room and toilet in the Administration building. We can change and be ready for dinner when Claude Wilkins finishes here. And we don't have plenty of time.'

'Now just cool down for a minute, James Herman,' said Allen. 'I have a plan. And we had better discuss it right now.'

Banning hesitated for a moment, mumbled something under his breath, and then walked back to Allen. 'Go ahead,' he ordered, checking his watch. 'But don't waste time with foolishness. We have free chilli on the agenda tonight. And I am hungry.'

Allen reminded Banning that they had a balance of twenty-one dollars and five cents, and New York City was a long way off. They would have to solicit money and other contributions at every stop en route and, as they had agreed, everyone and everything was fair game.

'Fine,' Banning agreed. 'I'm with you. We'll scrounge around town after dinner. Claude Wilkins is broke but he must know of a few likely targets. And we'll hit them together. Or split up and do solo jobs. OK?' He prepared to leave. 'Now let's wash and get dressed before Wilkins gets here. It's almost seven o'clock.'

'You didn't hear my plan, goddamn it!' Allen's insistent tone of voice stopped Banning as he was about to turn away. 'It'll be too late to go begging after chilli and beer, even if Wilkins does have a suggestion.'

'So what do you have in mind?'

'The Hot Spot.'

'What about it?'

'Our target.'

'It's already been hit.'

'Only the boss,' Allen explained, warming up to his idea. 'We're after the customers.'

Banning stared at him for a long moment. 'I should have taken Floyd Mosby,' he said finally. 'Or one of Little Dandy's whores.'

'Don't interrupt,' Allen warned, continuing in the same enthusiastic vein. 'We'll use the airport facilities to wash, and then we'll dress up – like this.' He pointed to his attire. 'Flying suits – helmets – and goggles, firmly in place over our eyes. That's how we enter the Hot Spot tonight.'

'You are definitely out of your mind.'

'We stun the customers,' Allen went on excitedly, ignoring the remark. 'Get their attention. And then move from table to table – or stand in the centre of the room – explain the purpose of our flight – and ask for donations, so they can help make aviation history.'

Banning watched incredulously as Allen straightened up, smoothed his flight jacket, adjusted his helmet, and placed the goggles over his eyes.

'One thing is sure,' he continued, standing proudly. 'None of them will ever have seen real aviators – in full dress – up close – and black ones, too – men going for a world record.'

'The customers are mostly Chinese, you meat-head.'

'All the better,' said Allen, without a pause. 'These people are known to be courteous – hospitable – and very wise.'

'I've just lost my appetite.'

'Listen to me, James Herman.' Allen gripped Banning's arm. 'I've been thinking about something else. We'll have a Gold Book on this flight. The lower left wing tip. Every person who helps us en route – regardless of the size or type of donation – gets to sign his or her name on the wing tip – our Gold Book.'

'You won't be on it.'

'I mean this, James Herman,' said Allen determinedly. 'Like The Greaser for his meal. Wilkins for his ride. The hangar guys for free rent. And we'll add Wallace Hawkins for his loan. Anybody who donates anything gets to sign our Gold Book. If they can't sign at the airport, we'll sign for them.'

Banning studied Allen with a spark of interest.

'Any customer at the Hot Spot who puts up a dollar – or a penny – or a slice of bread – whatever – ends up in our Gold Book. And we follow the same policy, at every stop, all the way to New York City.'

'That's one hell of an incentive to make a contribution.' Banning was now unsure of his own reaction to the idea. 'Help the cause and get your name scribbled on a busted wing tip. Can you pitch that proposition and get away with it, Thomas? Especially to some Chinese chilli-eaters?'

Allen slowly removed his goggles and helmet, and stepped forward, until he was eye to eye with the pilot. 'The 0XX6 Eagle Rock is destined to rest forever in Washington in the Smithsonian Institute – as a part of aviation history,' he declared. 'All Gold Book names will be on display for future generations to examine and admire. Yes, James Herman. I can pitch that proposition and get away with it. Even to some Chinese chilli-eaters.'

Banning's good-looking features, stern and jaw-muscle-tight during most of the discussion, finally relaxed, and he smiled broadly.

'I like it,' he said, motioning for Allen to follow him. 'Let's go.'

An elderly Chinese man, stooped and trembling from some kind of physical disorder, was slowly making his way down the Hot Spot stairs, gripping the wooden banister, taking one very careful step at a time. Nearing the bottom, he heard noises at the front door, looked up, and suddenly froze in his tracks. With eyes and mouth wide open, he emitted a chesty gasp, almost a scream, without any power or volume behind it.

Two strange black creatures dressed unlike anything the Oriental had ever seen before, were preparing to mount the stairs. He caught a fuzzy, head-spinning glimpse of dark leather helmets, and goggles where their eyes should have been. And then, taking a firmer hold on the banister, the old man turned away in horror and faced the wall, shaking violently.

'This was a bad mistake, Thomas!' Banning yelled, as he bounded up the stairs to aid the victim. 'We'll scare hell out of these people – instead of money!'

A few minutes later, in the large, crowded, plainly furnished restaurant, the sounds of munching, jabbering, and laughter began to die gradually away, until the room was eerily silent. Waiters eased down their trays of steaming dishes and stood motionless. All movement stopped. All eyes were riveted on the two extraordinary-looking figures who were posing like museum pieces in the entrance.

'Good evening, ladies and gentlemen,' said Allen cordially, bowing from the waist, with helmet and goggles still in place. 'I am Thomas C. Allen.'

'And my name is James Herman Banning.' The pilot removed his helmet and goggles. 'We are aviators on a very special mission,' he announced with confidence. 'A transcontinental flight.'

'That's right,' Allen chimed in, beginning a slow and measured walk down a narrow aisle, between the tables. 'Now don't let us ruin your meal,' he advised, realizing that the customers and waiters were still staring, dumbfounded. 'We'll explain later, while you digest this wonderful Hot Spot food.'

Banning followed close behind, smiling now, amused by the bewildered Chinese expressions, and Allen's comical handling of the situation.

A small man dressed in a business suit emerged from a door somewhere, and gestured nervously to the flyers. 'Over here, over here!' he called, pointing to a table in the corner of the room, a table nearly hidden by a pillar and a jutting wall, an undesirable table, evidently reserved for undesirable clients, the only empty table to be found. 'Quickly, quickly!' the small man shouted, waving arms and fingers to emphasize the urgency of his order. 'Don't upset my customers!'

Allen and Banning obediently took seats at the table, which was close to the kitchen's swinging doors, an isolated spot, from which they could just about view half the room.

'Please remove those stupid airplane glasses,' the fidgety owner pleaded, leaning close to Allen. 'Coburn should have warned me.'

'Coburn?' The mechanic obliged by taking off his goggles and helmet and placing them on the table. 'Is he The Greaser?'

'Yes, yes. The Greaser, The Greaser. My friend, my friend,' the Hot Spot owner answered, in his clipped, repetitive style. 'He phoned about you. But I didn't expect costumes and a floor show.'

'We do apologize, Mr—' Banning hesitated.

'Pipkin, Pipkin,' the owner replied instantly. 'I'll serve you chilli and rice. And two beers in the kitchen. On the house because of Coburn. But don't get my customers sick. They are very simple people.'

'Understood, Mr Pipkin,' said Allen, in his most courteous manner. 'And we certainly appreciate the food. But can I ask one more favour?'

'Be quick,' said Pipkin, gesturing to one of his waiters who was evidently not moving fast enough for him. 'I have business to conduct.'

'We can see that, Mr Pipkin,' said Allen, noticing that a few of the diners, the few who could be observed from the mechanic's table, were going back to their food, but the loud munching, jabbering, and laughter had been replaced by whispers and low mutterings about the alien visitors. 'After things quiet down in the restaurant – later – will you let us tell your customers about our flight – the first transcontinental attempt by Negroes?'

'Nobody will know what you're talking about, nobody,' said Pipkin. 'These people are mostly Chinese. Some don't understand English. Transcontinental Negro flights? You must be kidding. What do you want from these people?'

'Money,' Banning answered, without blinking an eye. 'We have to raise funds for gasoline, oil, and other necessities. Your customers might want to donate a few cents.'

'Ever heard of the Depression?' Pipkin asked, glancing around to see how the room was doing. 'A few cents buys food. What do they care about your gasoline and oil? Most of them have never seen an airplane.'

'We're flying all the way to New York City,' Banning persisted, 'Your Hot Spot customers will help make aviation history.'

'History, history, history.' Pipkin stared curiously at Banning. 'I saw you do some great tricks at the airport two years ago. Coburn took me. It's a wonder you don't break your neck.'

'Give him time,' said Allen, taking advantage of an opportunity. 'Can we speak to your customers later, Mr Pipkin?'

'Speak, speak, speak,' Pipkin repeated, as a waiter brought bowls of chilli and rice to the table. 'But you won't get anything but dumb looks, believe me. Unless you explain in Chinese.' He started to walk away. 'Enjoy your food. Good luck. And don't scare my customers with those crazy airplane glasses. They'll get indigestion.'

'Mr Pipkin!' Allen stopped him. 'Thank you for everything. We're putting your name in our Gold Book.'

'In your what?'

'Everybody who helps us on the way to New York gets their names written on the lower left wing tip,' Allen explained patiently. 'A place of honour. Because our plane – the Eagle Rock –

will end up in the Smithsonian Institute in Washington – a part of aviation history.'

'Good, good, good,' said the owner, on the move again, directing waiters, inspecting tables, and nodding to customers.

'Mr Pipkin!' Allen interrupted once more as the man was about to enter the kitchen doors. 'What's your first name?'

'Why?'

'For the Gold Book.'

'Oh, yes, yes, yes,' the owner mumbled, thinking for a moment. 'The Gold Book.' A waiter, holding a full tray, suddenly booted a kitchen door open with his shoe to make an exit. 'Idiot!' yelled Pipkin. 'Elbow and shoulders – easily – and carefully!'

'Yes, sir.' The waiter smiled, evidently used to his boss, and fond of him. 'Elbow and shoulders – easily – and carefully,' he repeated, before rushing away.

'The Gold Book,' Pipkin said again, now anxious to enter the kitchen. 'Just write Pipkin's Hot Spot, Riverside, California.'

'You've got a deal.' Allen nudged Banning who had already dug into his chilli and rice. 'A little free publicity, right, Mr Pipkin?'

'Of course,' Pipkin agreed, pushing the kitchen door, while nodding approvingly at one of his waiters who had made a perfect elbow and shoulders exit. 'So don't smash my advertising on the way to New York,' he shouted at the aviators, before disappearing.

Late, after devouring chilli and rice, and gulping two beers each in the kitchen, Allen and Banning decided that Pipkin's Hot Spot was quiet enough and ready for their unorthodox flight briefing and charitable appeal. The room would be split in half for the operation, Allen working all the tables on the left, while Banning handled those on the right. Two round metal pans had been supplied by Mr Pipkin to receive the anticipated donations, along with more predictions from the owner that they were about to waste their time, come over as lunatics, and succeed only in confusing, embarrassing or irritating his very special customers.

'How many of you nice people have ever seen a real airplane?' Allen stood in front of his tables, addressing an audience which, except for a small group of Negroes near the back, was wholly Chinese. 'Raise your hands if you've seen a real airplane. Not a picture. A real one. Please raise your hands.'

51

Many of the customers stared blankly, some were amused, several appeared to be intrigued, a few shifted restlessly in their seats, and three raised their hands timidly.

'Good,' said Allen, pacing back and forth, warming up, getting to the point carefully, theatrically. 'Now, my partner and I are flying an airplane all the way across the United States, from here in California to New York City. Do you understand?'

'Charlie Lindbergh,' a young Chinese at a front table blurted, while his pretty girlfriend stifled a giggle with her hand. 'You do just like Charlie Lindbergh,' he repeated, gaining some confidence. 'Fly coast-to-coast.'

'Exactly, my friend,' said Allen, moving closer to the young man's table. 'But – we are Negroes, like our brothers and sisters at the back there, and Charles Lindbergh is white.' He studied their faces, saw a little more interest in a few, and continued, ignoring the many vacant expressions, assuming these were the customers who did not speak or understand English. 'We are trying to be the first Negroes to fly across the country. If we land in New York, we will make aviation history – it will be a world event.'

'God bless you, brother!' one of the Negroes at the back shouted. 'Count on our prayers and blessings all the way!'

'Thank you kindly, brother,' said Allen, as he stepped back to the aisle, and lifted the pan supplied by Mr Pipkin. 'But you see, we need more than your prayers and blessings in order to succeed.' Carrying the pan reverently, like a religious object, he started a slow pilgrimage, pausing first at the table where the young Chinese and his giggling lady friend sat.

'We used our money to build the plane,' Allen explained, his voice breaking slightly. 'Now we need gasoline – and oil – and hangar rent – and –'

'Charlie Lindbergh is rich,' the young Chinese man interrupted, enjoying the attention, and not caring about the brief hint of annoyance on Allen's face. 'He flies across the ocean. And Charlie Lindbergh don't have to beg in Pipkin's chilli joint holding kitchen pot. Not fair. You should fly with Charlie Lindbergh.'

Allen stood, holding the kitchen pot, and feeling like a damn fool, as Pipkin had predicted. 'I would love to fly with Lindbergh – and not only because of his money,' he said finally, attempting to head off a ludicrous and time-consuming exchange. 'But, he is very famous – and busy – and prefers to fly alone. Mainly – Charles Lindbergh is a white man – and we want to be the first – coloured people to fly across the country. And that's why I'm holding a kitchen pot and begging in Pipkin's chilli joint.'

Disregarding the owner's strong warning about giving his customers indigestion, he put on his helmet and goggles and explained about the Gold Book.

'Anything you donate will be greatly appreciated,' he said, pretending not to see or hear some of the animated reactions to his appearance. 'In this case – a penny becomes a dollar – a dollar is a million – and if you have no coins to spare – which is certainly understandable – we'll accept a smile and a word of encouragement with just as much gratitude.'

'You look like a big black bug!' The comment came from a Chinese matron sitting with her family, one of the many who had appeared to be indifferent to the entire proceedings, whether because of a language problem, or shyness, boredom, or total shock. 'Bring pot here!' she ordered, laughing and pointing to Allen's helmet and goggles. 'I give fifty cents to big black bug – so he can fly away.'

The Chinese woman's family also laughed, and began to gather and count coins, and others in the room followed their example, including the young Chinese couple on the front table, the Negroes at the back, and even a few of the waiters. Mr Pipkin, observing from a position near the kitchen doors, did not seem to be annoyed by the disruption. In fact, he looked unusually relaxed and good humoured.

'The big black bug is flying your way!' Allen exclaimed happily, moving from table to table with his pan. 'Don't forget, write your names down for our Gold Book, so the world can remember Pipkin's Hot Spot customers!' Coins clinked into the collecting pot. 'Thank you, lady! Thank you, sir! Thank you, my brothers and sisters! God bless you all!'

When Allen's fund-raising spectacular was over, he removed the helmet and goggles, gave an appreciative wave to Mr Pipkin, now busy again, and returned to his isolated table in order to calculate the haul. One dollar and eighty-two cents. An excellent result from a predominately Oriental gathering. Riverside, California had been a worthwhile stop indeed, considering free hangar rent, the Hot Spot donations, chilli, rice, and beer.

At that precise moment, Allen thought of James Herman Banning, and realized for the first time since beginning to address his assigned targets, that the sounds drifting intermittently from the right side of the large room, Banning's territory, had been the sounds of munching, jabbering, and laughter, normal restaurant noises, nothing more. What the hell had Banning been doing? Had he left the joint? Deserted? Was he in some kind of serious trouble?

Hastily and clumsily jamming coins and scraps of paper covered with mostly Chinese names into both flight jacket pockets, Allen grabbed his helmet and goggles, and made a fast move towards the right side of the room, smiling politely, albeit a shade uneasily, as some of the familiar customers caught sight of him and started pointing, grinning, and commenting again.

'A great job, Thomas!' Banning called out, as Allen angrily approached an unusually neat and carefully set corner table, one of the best-situated in the entire restaurant. 'We loved every minute of it!' he added. 'Didn't we, folks?'

Banning, at ease and in good spirits, was sitting with three well-dressed and obviously well-off Negroes; a middle-aged man and woman, and a beautiful and very shapely young girl.

'Waiter!' Banning snapped his fingers authoritatively, while his new friends watched him with undisguised respect and admiration. 'Another chair, please, for my distinguished mechanic, co-pilot, and fund-raiser. And, would you check his flying gear, the helmet and goggles, please?'

The waiter obliged in record time.

'Now for the introductions,' said Banning, after a sullen-looking Tom Allen had taken a seat. 'This is Mrs Hazel Du Bois and Dr Adam Weldon Du Bois. Dr Du Bois is one of Riverside's best known and most experienced dentists.' Allen nodded courteously and the Du Bois couple reciprocated. 'And this vision at my side,' Banning gushed on, is Miss Lucille Du Bois, their charming daughter, who has brains as well as beauty, Thomas.'

Allen nodded politely again, and the girl smiled, tilted her head to one side in a practised way, and murmured, 'Pleased to meet you, Mr Allen.'

'Care for something to eat or drink, Mr Allen?' the dentist asked. 'You must be hungry and thirsty after working so hard over there.'

'No thank you, sir.' Allen was both hungry and thirsty, and mad as hell, too. 'I've had my dinner.'

'Go ahead, Thomas,' Banning urged, winking at Lucille. 'Don't be bashful. The spare ribs are much better than Pipkin's chilli.'

'You had spare ribs?' Allen asked harshly, unable to hide his resentment. 'I was on the left working my – my head off – and you had spare ribs?'

'I did, indeed,' Banning replied, 'and now it's your turn, Thomas, thanks to the generous Du Bois family. You impressed them. And me, too, as a matter of fact.'

'How kind of you to say so, James Herman,' said Allen, glaring at his partner. 'I was praying for your approval,' he added sarcastically. 'And wondering how you were doing over here.'

'He was doing extremely well,' Lucille Du Bois purred, glancing at the handsome pilot, 'Mr Banning explained all the technical details while you were performing for the customers. We are very proud to meet both of you.'

'That's quite true,' Mrs Du Bois remarked, before Allen had a chance to dig at the pilot. 'I'm especially taken by the Gold Book. A marvellous idea.'

'And this flight *will* be a great incentive for Negro youth,' Dr Du Bois added. 'We hope and pray that everything goes well.'

'I have no doubts, Papa,' said the vision, with her large, expressive eyes on Banning. 'History is going to be made by our guests at this table. They will land in New York City and thrill the world. I have no doubts at all.'

'My dear Lucille,' said Banning, patting her gently on the arm, 'no man could fail with a supporter like you cheering him on.' He caught Allen's slightly disgusted look. 'And now the big question. How did we score over there, Thomas?'

'*We?*' Allen shook his head slowly from side to side and forced a sardonic laugh. '*We* collected exactly one dollar and eighty-two cents. And that's pretty good – considering *we* only pleaded with half the room – and they were mostly Chinese.'

'And these are difficult times for everyone,' Dr Du Bois interjected. 'I think the folks did their best for you.'

'Some can't even speak or understand English,' Mrs Du Bois added. 'I think you did very well, Mr Allen.'

'Thank you, ma'am.' He looked directly at the pilot. 'This side of the room is your territory, James Herman, remember?'

Banning answered, glancing at his watch, 'The Du Bois family have to leave in about five minutes.'

'Sorry to hear that,' Allen said, honestly. 'But you can do the job afterwards. There are still plenty of customers in the joint.'

'Don't be impetuous, Thomas,' Banning advised pleasantly. 'The Hot Spot fund-raising exercise is over.' He exchanged glances with Lucille. 'We are leaving with the Du Bois family.'

'Leaving?' Allen was confused. 'To go where?'

'Home,' said Dr Du Bois, motioning for the waiter. 'You and Mr Banning will be our guests tonight. There's plenty of room.'

'And we'll drive you to the airport in the morning after a nice breakfast,' Mrs Du Bois promised. 'It will be a pleasure and an honour.'

Allen sat for a moment, allowing the unexpected and very welcome proposition to sink in, and then, taking his time, he smiled at each face around the table, even the gloating one belonging to James Herman Banning.

'We'll have some personal Gold Book signing at Arlington Field, Thomas,' said the pilot. 'Did you get the names from your territory?'

'On paper,' Allen replied, still smiling stupidly. 'Mostly Chinese. And we have Pipkin, The Greaser, and the hangar boys, too.' From his position, unlike the parents, he could see Lucille take Banning's hand under the table. 'Yes, indeed,' Allen commented, as the helmets and goggles arrived. 'Riverside has been quite a first stop. May all the rest be just as pleasurable.'

'Amen,' Mrs Du Bois murmured, and her husband did the same, followed by Lucille, Banning, and then Allen.

After the dentist had settled the bill, and they were all preparing to leave, Banning studied his mechanic and co-pilot, paying special attention to the helmet and goggles in his hand.

'I have just discovered something about you, Thomas Allen,' he said. 'You really do look like a big black bug – about to fly away.'

Everyone laughed, including Allen, as they left Pipkin's Hot Spot, in Riverside, California.

6

Allen, Banning, and the Du Bois family were up at six o'clock the following morning, ready for breakfast, although there were a few shaky hands cutting up the bacon and eggs, and for very good reasons.

After a brief conversation and coffee the night before, everyone had retired to their rooms, in anticipation of their early rise. The dentist owned a small detached house, on the outskirts of town, with an old wood-shed in the backyard, where hay had been stacked as a bed for the family dog. At 5:15 am, Tom Allen had woken up and squinted at the cot next to his own. It was empty. Everything had connected instantly. He had crept down the stairs, out the back door, and across the yard to the wood-shed. And there in the hay, instead of a dog, he had seen the dim but unmistakable shapes of James Herman Banning and Lucille Du Bois, half naked, locked together, and fast asleep.

He had knelt beside Banning and whispered in his ear, 'James Herman – James Herman! Get up! Come on – Get up, fast!'

Instead of waking, Banning had only smiled, and pulled the girl closer.

Angry, and anxious, Allen had taken hold of Banning's ear lobe and squeezed hard, until the pilot had opened his eyes wide, lifted his head about an inch off the hay, and become temporarily paralysed.

Still applying pressure, Allen had whispered again, louder this time, 'Grab your naked vision and run like a son-of-a-bitch! It's almost five-thirty in the morning! That dentist will put a drill up your ass if he finds you out here with his daughter!'

He had then dashed back to the house and into his bed. Seconds later, hearing a noise, he had turned to see Banning in the cot beside him, with the blanket pulled up to his chin.

'I owe you one, partner,' Banning had promised, grinning, with his eyes shut tightly. 'My balls are still trembling.'

*

At Arlington Airport, the Du Bois family inspected the Eagle Rock with great interest while listening to a running commentary by the pilot. Next, they watched Tom Allen open his tool kit, remove the leaking water pump and make the necessary repairs. Later, the group participated in a brief Gold Book ceremony. Allen, writing neatly, signed for The Greaser, the hangar boys, Pipkin's Hot Spot, and the customers who had donated. Then, proudly, Dr Adam Weldon Du Bois entered his name for posterity, followed by Mrs Hazel Du Bois, and finally Lucille. While the girl signed, Banning glanced at Allen.

'What a contribution *she* made to the flight,' his look said.

At eleven o'clock, with Banning at the controls, the Eagle Rock started her lumbering, rumbling, wobbling move down the runway, until she got up unsteadily, with a slight tail wind, flying east. Soon March Field appeared. And there were orange groves below. A short time later, they vibrated through the Sangorgonian Pass, flying at 3,800 feet. To the left, at a distance, the San Bernadino mountains. And, to the right, not so far, the San Jacinto range.

Swinging south-east, towards Palm Springs, they noticed that the truck farms were disappearing, as this was semi-desert country. Checking the course at Indio, where the White Water River meets the Southern Pacific Railway, Banning decided to continue on the same route. Minutes later, the Eagle Rock was crossing the desert proper, and they began to feel the heat.

In time, the temperature had risen to an unbearable degree, and both men were perspiring, and breathing heavily. After a struggle in the cockpit, and a few jerky plane movements, Banning managed to get out of his overalls, and unbutton his shirt. Eventually, he found his pad, scribbled a note, and held it up for Allen to read.

STRIP!

Allen read the message, found his own pad, and positioned his answer in Banning's line of vision.

WHAT DO YOU HAVE IN MIND?!

The pilot ignored the response and removed his shirt. Feeling the blistering desert heat, Allen began to follow Banning's advice. Deciding to go all the way, and to hell with it, he took off everything, including his underwear, and sat in the cockpit stark naked, imagining how eye-witnesses would react if, for some reason, the Eagle Rock were forced down, or smashed up.

Because his quarters were already cramped, with his other belongings in a bundle, and Banning's bag on the seat beside him, he tied his clothing into a ball, attracted the pilot's attention, and handed it over for safe keeping, until the approach at Yuma, Arizona.

The plane rattled on above the hot sand, and Allen, flying nude, felt a wondrous sense of freedom, of complete abandon, up so high, with no risk of being observed, or reprimanded, or put away for indecent exposure.

By the time they saw the Chocolate Mountains, on the left, and the Sand Hills, on the right, the water was boiling in the radiator, and the slip-stream from the propeller had started blowing it through a hole in the cowling. But in a short while things began to cool down a little, when the Colorado River appeared.

As the Eagle Rock crossed the river, and awkwardly banked left, Allen decided that the time had come to begin dressing, before Banning made his approach at Yuma, a few minutes away. The air was light and the plane would be coming in with plenty of speed. He wrote a note, banged for attention, and held it up for the pilot.

MY CLOTHES!

Banning took his time, completed the turn, and prepared for the descent to Yuma.

MY CLOTHES!

The pilot finally grabbed his pad, made a hasty notation, and flashed it for the benefit of the naked mechanic.

SORRY – BUSY LANDING!

Allen was furious; he slammed and pounded the fuselage, writhed, cursed and screamed into the wind. Urgently, he scribbled a final note, furious now, because Banning's shoulders were shaking – a sign that he was laughing, enjoying the mechanic's embarrassing predicament.

BASTARD – WANT MY CLOTHES NOW!!!

It was too late. Banning brought the plane down, wham-bang style again, while Allen shook his fists and shouted obscenities.

After they had taxied to the gas pump, Banning, still highly amused, grabbed Allen's ball of clothing, jumped out and ran to the small administration building, deaf to the threats ringing in his ears. The mechanic was trapped, naked. To make matters worse, he could see a woman employee carrying some documents into the office. He cursed Banning again, slumped in the cockpit, and debated whether or not to unfasten his bundle of spare clothes.

Banning entered the administration building and hurried to a counter where the woman had just deposited her papers in a wire in-tray. No one else was there. 'Excuse me, ma'am,' he said excitedly. 'Is there a doctor available?'

'A doctor? The woman looked at him with a mixture of concern, suspicion, and curiosity. 'We don't have a doctor here,' she replied finally. 'Are you sick?'

'No, ma'am,' Banning replied. 'But my mechanic and co-pilot is suffering from the desert heat. We just came in from Riverside. And he can't seem to get out of the cockpit. Nothing serious, I'm sure. But, I thought somebody should check him, before we continue on to Tucson.'

'Are you flying that old crate?'

'Yes, ma'am.'

'Next to the gas pump?'

'Yes, ma'am,' Banning answered. 'I'll be fuelling up now for the next hop.'

'Like I said,' the woman drawled, 'we don't carry any medical help. But I can phone the local ambulance service. You'll have to taxi away from – '

'That won't be necessary, ma'am,' said Banning, reversing gears at once. 'He'll probably be feeling better in a few minutes.'

'Well, all I can do is bring him a glass of cold water, and see how he is,' the woman suggested, trying to be helpful. 'You go ahead and deal with Pancho about your gasoline. Over there, next to the hangar. And move things along. We've got that new 525 hp Douglas Army plane landing here this afternoon. My husband wants the area cleared as soon as possible.'

'Yes, ma'am,' said Banning, 'I'll move things along. And thank you very much for being so kind and helpful.'

Back in the cockpit, Tom Allen had decided to remain naked, rather than disturb the neat package of clothing which had been arranged with such loving care by Celene. Banning, the sadistic bastard, would have to hand over his underwear and flying gear without delay, certainly before the motor check-out, and refuelling. Thus he waited patiently, expecting his belongings to be returned in a matter of minutes, knowing that Banning could not possibly continue horsing around, because the Tucson hop was serious business, and they were on a tight and steady course.

With head back and eyes partially closed, Allen took his mind off his immediate problem by conjuring up an image of Celene, her stomach, and the brilliant, handsome, rough-and-tumble baby boy kicking around inside.

Allen smiled, chuckled, and then nearly choked when, through narrow slits, he recognized the hazy figure of a woman moving towards the plane with what appeared to be a glass in her hand. In a flash he was bolt upright, wide awake, fumbling desperately for the bundle of spare clothing – but it was too late.

The woman, a large, masculine type, in her late thirties, with huge, bra-less breasts flopping under her shirt, had walked right up to the rear cockpit, at eye level. Shocked, and on automatic, Allen grabbed Banning's bag and covered his lap. The woman stared at him, and he stared back, until he finally grinned, sheepishly.

'Sure was hot up there,' he remarked feebly, leaning on the bag for extra protection. 'I almost fainted.'

'Your partner told me,' the woman drawled, still holding the glass of water, and looking him over without a trace of embarrassment. 'He said you were ill,' she added, inspecting his neck, shoulders, and arms, in a rather provocative way. 'But, I can't see anything wrong with you, mister.'

'No, indeed, I'm just fine,' said Allen nervously. 'Now – if you'll kindly give me a bit of privacy – I would like to put on my clothes and – '

'Move the bag away for a minute,' the woman ordered huskily, peering down into the cockpit. 'Only for a minute,' she repeated, becoming impatient. 'Before they come over to gas up.'

'Lady, if I move this bag – '

'Never seen a black one in all my days,' the woman admitted, still gazing down at the appropriate spot. 'Give me a fast peek. Is it true what they all say?'

Allen sat, without turning her way, obviously contemplating his next move. 'Yes, indeed,' he replied finally, drumming his fingers on Banning's bag. 'All true. It's longer than an elephant's trunk – and harder than rock candy.' He reached under the bag. 'I'll whip it out now and give you a quick look. It'll reach from here, you know.'

'Nigger!' the woman suddenly shouted contemptuously, pouring the glass of water over his head. 'Don't ever mention this!' she warned. 'Or we'll set the hounds on your ass – for indecent exposure – and attempted rape! I've got a very touchy husband!'

The woman twisted around abruptly at the sound of approaching voices. 'Remember what I said, black boy,' she cautioned again, before plodding away.

Banning and a short, swarthy, bow-legged man were walking towards the plane, deep in conversation. Allen sat in the cockpit, expressionless, looking straight ahead, with the water dripping from his hair. He did not turn or react when Banning spoke to him.

'This is Pancho – what the hell is that?' he asked, pointing to Allen's face, a study in wet granite. 'You were supposed to drink it – not bathe in it.'

'Give me my clothes, James Herman,' Allen growled, with eyes front, and mouth barely open. 'Now! Before I climb out of here naked and break your damn neck!'

'What a disgusting thought.' Banning grinned, and tossed the bundle of clothing into the cockpit. 'By the way, Thomas,' said Banning, 'Pancho tells me that gasoline jumps to twenty-nine cents a gallon in Tucson. And it won't go back to twenty-five until after El Paso. It's still twenty-five here. Should we fill up? Or will that be too much weight?'

Allen, still putting on his clothes, refused to answer.

'We've got a long ride to Tucson,' Banning continued, watching the pouting mechanic with a touch of sympathy, and guilt. 'But maybe we should get just enough for the hop. Right? Pay the price in Tucson and keep the weight down from here. What do you say?'

'I say – get the hell out of my way.' Allen, fully dressed now, climbed out of the cockpit, and Banning and Pancho stepped aside. Allen picked up a rag and wiped some grease off the cowl. And then he tested the oil, without saying a word.

'Snap out of it,' Banning suggested soberly, walking over to the mechanic and standing beside him. 'Hell – it was only a gag. A little fun. Don't be so damn sensitive.' He threw a playful punch at Allen's arm, and said, 'Come on, Thomas. This is not your style, man.'

Allen took his time, finished the motor check-out, and then turned, and faced Banning. 'Listen to me carefully, James Herman,' he said, in a firm tone of voice, wiping oil and grease off his hands with the rag. 'I pulled you and your Du Bois vision out of a haystack in Riverside, just in time. Am I right?'

'Right.'

'Saved your tail and her reputation.'

'True.'

'And you owed me one.'

'I confirm that.'

'And you left me here – in this airplane – naked – and exposed to a big white nympho.'

'A *what*?'

62

'A sex maniac.'

'A *what?*'

'You heard me, James Herman.'

'That enormous, butchy-looking hunk of flesh?' Banning stared at the mechanic incredulously. 'How do you know?'

'She wanted to inspect my jewels.'

'Your *what?*'

'My prick, goddamn it!' Allen shouted, tossing the rag to the ground angrily. 'She has never seen a black one before. And she sure as hell didn't see mine. The bitch!'

Banning tried hard, but it was impossible to prevent a sudden outburst of laughter, which forced him to lean against the plane for support.

'Get it out of your system, James Herman,' said Allen, waiting patiently for Banning's spontaneous reaction to subside. 'I haven't finished my speech yet.'

While Banning simmered down, and Allen watched and wait-ed, the airport attendant called Pancho was busy putting water and the requested amount of gasoline into the Eagle Rock – enough for the hop to Tucson, and no more, in order to stabilize the weight.

'Sorry to laugh, Thomas,' said Banning, now almost under control. 'But, the picture of you naked, and trapped in the cockpit, with this flabby – '

'Forget it,' Allen snapped. 'I want to finish my speech right now.'

'Go ahead.'

'Considering the haystack and the – cockpit incident – I figure you owe me two favours,' said Allen. 'Agreed?'

'I'll buy that.'

'Fine,' said Allen, losing all of his previous irritability. 'Com-bine them and pay me off with one big one.'

'Like what?'

'I'll pilot to Tucson and you ride in the back,' Allen replied, with confidence. 'We did agree that I would get some flying time on this run. Mechanic *and* co-pilot. Remember?'

'No deal,' said Banning, shaking his head. 'A tough hop,' he explained. 'Mountains and desert and very light air. Wait for an easier – '

'It's open country,' Allen interrupted sternly. 'A perfect stretch. Want me to fly us over buildings and people?'

'God, no,' Banning answered, cornered. 'I honestly don't want you to fly us anywhere. You are an unreliable pilot, Thomas.'

'Hog manure.'

'A great mechanic but a – '

'You owe me,' Allen announced with conviction and finality. 'Now pay up like a gentleman. I am flying this aircraft to Tucson, Arizona.'

'God help us.'

Allen did not hear the remark, because he had started on his way to Pancho, who was waiting, after completing the refuelling operation on the Eagle Rock.

'Hey, Thomas!' Banning called, following a short distance behind. 'Be honest. Did you or did you not show that big lady your precious jewels?'

'Go to hell, James Herman,' Allen replied, without looking back. 'Let's get this plane in the air. I am the pilot from here to Tucson.'

'What a pity if you did,' Banning persisted. 'The poor soul will be thinking that every black man in the world is hung with a little pecker like yours. And that would be unfair to me and all the others.' He caught up with Allen and Pancho. 'I'd better set her straight personally – if we stop here on the way back.'

Using all of the field, and missing a wooden fence at the end by inches, Tom Allen's take-off was enough to wipe the smile off Banning's face, and produce the symptoms of a fatal heart attack. But, they were finally up, first heading east, and then slightly north from Yuma towards Gila Bend, over Antelope Hill, which stands between the Castle Dome Mountains on the left and the Mohawk range on the right.

Allen felt a joyous sense of excitement and pride, as he guided the shivering, ungainly, handcrafted flying machine across a stretch of desert, barren except for an occasional ranch house. Banning sat upright in the rear cockpit, nerves on edge, body rigid, cursing himself for giving up the controls, regardless of the deal made back in Los Angeles. It would be much wiser and a lot more practical to break your word than your neck.

Emergency landing fields, with facilities for radio communications, weather reports, and gas and oil, were situated about thirty to fifty miles apart on this hop. But few pilots ever stopped at these locations, because it was much too difficult to gain altitude in the very light air, on take-off. However, the fields were well marked, and a flyer who happened to be lost could always circle, pick up the marker, check it on his map, and set a proper course, without landing.

Tom Allen's altimeter read 6,000 feet. At intervals along the way, beacon lights had been installed, but obviously they were not operating in the daytime. Allen felt comfortable and satisfied with his performance so far. The Eagle Rock had struggled along, in one piece, as hoped and prayed for. But Banning's anxiety was growing as Painted Rock Mountain rose to the left, and they approached Gila Bend. He lashed out at himself for allowing his mind to wander at times away from the difficult task at hand, an inexcusable blunder, which had placed most of the navigational responsibilities on the shoulders of the man in the front cockpit.

Swinging towards Tucson, Allen flew unsteadily over the southern part of Maricopa Divide, another mountain. Casagrande Mountain was sighted on the left, and then Allen coaxed the plane, just clearing the summit of Picacho Peak, on to Red Rock, Arizona.

At this point, Banning knew that there was a very good reason for the queasy feeling in the pit of his stomach. He checked the course, searching in vain for a spur track which, according to the map, was supposed to run into the main line of the Southern Pacific. After waiting the appropriate amount of time, Banning searched apprehensively for Naviska, a small town located ten miles from Red Rock, where the Santa Cruz river flows almost parallel to the railroad all the way to Tucson. The river and the railroad, about two or three miles apart, formed a lane which most flyers used to follow. But Banning was unable to locate any of these landmarks, and realized that, somehow, they had strayed off course, and were now in serious trouble somewhere between Yuma and Tucson.

He found his pad, wrote a terse note, attracted Allen's attention, and held the paper in a position for reading.

OFF COURSE!

After a brief wait, the response came back:

NO – ALL OK!

Banning's next communication started an exchange, while Allen flew on nonchalantly, as though everything was in perfect order – a late Sunday afternoon pleasure ride.

WE ARE LOST!

NO – APPROACHING TUCSON!

WRONG – TURN BACK – FIND EMERGENCY FIELD NEAR GILA BEND – NOW!

CALM DOWN – ON COURSE!

MANIAC – YOU ARE LOST – MUST LOCATE FIELD BEFORE DARK!

Allen, beginning to doubt himself now, because of Banning's superior flight knowledge and experience, finally produced a conciliatory message.

OK – BUT A MISTAKE!

The Eagle Rock was flying aimlessly over the desert, somewhere between Yuma and Tucson, and Tom Allen had lost all traces of bravado, as the quivering wreck pulled up, and banked, and circled, and dived, and jangled the nerves of the helpless aviator in the rear cockpit. Twice Allen nearly ripped the plane's belly on Picacho Peak. And once, with seconds to spare, he gained just enough altitude to avoid crashing into what might have been an unfamiliar section of the Casagrande, or the Maricopa, or even Painted Rock. Allen, completely off the charts, and disoriented, was rattling towards everything from strange and perilous angles. Low flying, to pick out recognizable markers, had produced nothing but more trauma, and a series of near pile-ups. And Banning, after ranting and raving like a wild man, had become a petrified figure behind Allen, a zombie, ready to accept his fate.

Later, the nightmare both men had been dreading since the Los Angeles take-off slowly became a waking reality. Darkness was falling, and they were airborne, off course, without flares, navigation or landing lights – and with a head strong, unlicensed mechanic at the controls.

At last the revolving beacons were operating, and Allen headed straight for the first one in his sights. After a sweat-flowing, lip-trembling approach, he reached it, and attempted to fly a blind but steady course from this illuminated marker on to the next signal in line, and then to the next, and the next – possibly a heaven-sent flight path to Tucson. Banning, back to shouting, cursing, and waving his arms madly, had managed to point out the direction he felt Allen should take, and the mechanic had complied without delay or question.

At the controls, Allen was doing everything possible to steady his nerves, as the Eagle Rock lumbered along from beacon to beacon. He looked down for several moments, and found himself mesmerized by the rays of light travelling back and forth on the highway below, a fascinating pattern of busy, silent movement. The sudden and chilling thought of a forced landing made him turn away, and check the gauges. Although the gasoline supply was low, he figured that the plane had enough to reach Tucson, if they were hugging the right beacons, and flying in the proper direction.

Allen glanced at the flames spitting from both exhaust pipes and decided that the colours were fine – meaning the carburettor was adequately adjusted. And he felt certain that the two new Scintilla magnetos would hold up well for quite a few hops to come. And the air was getting cooler. And Banning had finally shut his mouth and lowered his arms. So Allen relaxed just a bit, until he remembered that they were up in a dark sky, without any lights, flying on a blacked-out, guesswork route, with a crate that should have been dumped a piece at a time on the Mosby brothers' garbage pile. An uncomfortable tingling sensation inched up both arms and legs, as he swallowed hard, cleared his throat, and waited anxiously for the next revolving beacon.

Eight suspenseful minutes ticked away. Something was definitely wrong, Banning thought. By now, they should have been able to recognize another rotating signal, somewhere in the distance. There were no beacon flashes to be seen. Had he given Allen instructions to go west instead of east, or north, or south, or left, or right, or up, or down? Because of the desert and unremarkable terrain, and Allen's abrupt and erratic flight manoeuvres, and the darkness, the aircraft, and his own negligence – they were lost – and in serious trouble – and the map and compass were useless – and –

Suddenly, a giant blanket was thrown over the plane, and they had no vision whatsoever. Fog! The thickest patch he had ever flown into. A huge, claustrophobic, suffocating wad of cotton. You could actually feel it, taste it, gag on it – and he did. He knew that Allen, at the controls, must be doing the same. And he was right.

Allen had panicked the moment the dense fog enveloped them. His nervous fingers and sweaty palms were unable to control the aircraft properly. After a dangerously steep, unnecessary climb, the engine sputtered, and then cut out completely. The Eagle Rock seemed to be suspended in the air, motionless for a few seconds, as though it was debating whether or not to make the next move – an obvious one – and the aviators braced themselves for the worst. As expected, it came, without further notice.

Every part of the wreck that Banning and his task force had pasted together at Mosby's garage was shuddering, and clattering, and threatening to break away, as the aircraft plunged nose-first, faster and faster, deeper and deeper, into the seemingly endless wad of floating cotton. A loud cracking sound, coming from somewhere near the left wing, could be heard above the whistling rush of air, as the Eagle Rock continued to dive uncontrollably.

Soon it was joined by more creaks and bangs and knocks, and a staccato pounding under the fuselage, while Banning screamed unheard orders, and Allen struggled to pull out and take over. Possibly thoughts about Celene, or his unborn child – a son for sure – or God, or pride, or just the fact that he did not particularly fancy the idea of being splattered on the barren Arizona landscape, gave Thomas C. Allen what Banning later referred to as a sudden gush of superhuman strength, and an unexpected and very temporary touch of flight savvy: miracles usually reserved for more saintly souls who make stupid mistakes while flying airplanes. Because, for no logical reason, and at the last safe moment, the Eagle Rock's engine fired up, and the plane began to defy all the odds, by straining, and quivering, and convulsing itself into a fairly level position, like a badly injured elephant being hoisted upright with the aid of a giant sky hook. And, seconds later, to complete the amazing phenomenon, the unlit rattletrap was out of the fog, under bright stars, with the city lights of Tucson gleaming below.

The men in the cockpits whooped, and hollered, and punched the air with their fists, as Allen urged the Eagle Rock onward, over the city, to the airport, five miles out. They circled, and the attendants obviously saw that the noisy, unusual-looking silhouette had no navigation or landing lights. Almost instantly, the floods came on, and the field was as bright as day, ready for the arrival.

Allen, relieved and elated to the point of recklessness, dropped the aircraft full force against the runway, bounced up again, and repeated this outlandish rubber ball action until the Eagle Rock finally normalized, and taxied close to a hangar.

For a couple of minutes, the plane and crew just sat there in the glaring spotlights, cooling off, coping with an assortment of delayed technical and emotional reactions.

'We made it!' Allen eventually yelled, grinning broadly at a group of silent, astounded, cold-faced airport employees, who had gathered around the strange machine and the Negro aviators. 'Many thanks for snapping on the floods,' Allen added, subduing his voice and high spirits, because of the somewhat hostile expressions facing him. 'We do appreciate the service.'

'Mr Dunlop wants to see you people in his office right away,' a stern-voiced, overall-clad worker ordered, ignoring Allen's remarks. 'Better jump out of that fucked-up contraption and move fast – nobody keeps Mr Dunlop waiting.'

Still in the cockpit, Allen glanced back at Banning before

climbing out and waiting next to the plane for his partner to follow. Banning, without looking at the curious, belligerent airport staff, took his time, and when he did step down, he took even more time, stretching his arms, massaging his neck, and doing a few deep knee-bends. Then he walked directly to the man who had relayed Dunlop's message, and stood facing him, with controlled anger in his eyes. The tall, stockily-built worker stood his ground.

'Got something on your mind – stranger?' he asked, itching for trouble. 'Sound off and maybe I can oblige.'

Banning stood rigidly, arms at his sides, ready for action. Then, he seemed to relax, after making a sudden decision.

'I do have something on my mind – sir,' he admitted, sighing heavily. 'But I just can't pump up the energy to mess around with you – at the present time.'

'Come on, James Herman!' Allen shouted, beginning to walk towards the office. 'You heard what the man said! Nobody keeps Mr Dunlop waiting!'

7

'You can't put that monstrosity in our hangars tonight,' said Mr Dunlop, a sandy-haired, pompous little man with a starchy shirt and a meticulously knotted tie. 'And that's my final word on the subject.'

'There's a storm brewing,' Allen persisted, standing beside Banning in front of Dunlop's highly polished and well-organized desk. 'We've got to keep the plane under cover.'

'You call that thing a plane?' Dunlop's smirk appeared to be a permanent part of his expression. 'It's a menace. It should not be flown by anyone, for any reason. Especially without lights and proper training. And you have the audacity to fantasize about a transcontinental flight?'

'You've already been shown my credentials, Mr Dunlop,' said Banning, maintaining his composure. 'And I'll be doing most of the flying. But that's really our business, isn't it? We're just asking for overnight hangar access. I'll be taking off early in the morning.'

'No available space.'

'I saw plenty of room in Hangar Two,' Allen interjected politely. 'Are you worried about money?' He smiled and tapped his pocket. 'We're paying customers, Mr Dunlop. Cash on the barrel head.'

'That's not what we're talking about.'

'What *are* we talking about, Mr Dunlop?' Banning was tightening up again.

'Not what you're thinking.'

'What am I thinking, Mr Dunlop?'

The door of the office opened and a lanky young man in a Stetson hat and smartly tailored, cowboy-type accessories, entered without knocking or excusing himself. The visitor, clean-cut, freckled, and pleasant-looking, slumped down in a chair, and inspected the Negro aviators thoughtfully.

'This is a business of skilled professionals, Banning,' Dunlop suddenly began to lecture them, ignoring the youth. 'We need technical excellence, orderly flight operations, astute management, and well-educated, dedicated, forward-thinking, and courageous recruits, in order to progress as an industry. And this is an industry, Banning. And in time, it will be a major industry. Beyond our wildest dreams.'

'I'll buy all that, Mr Dunlop,' said Banning, eyeing him suspiciously. 'But what does your eloquent speech have to do with refusing us hangar access tonight?'

'We have no room or time for sloppy, barnstorming circus stunts, and publicity schemes to promote – a few cheap dollars – inflated egos – and well – causes.'

'Oh, yes,' Banning responded, nodding his head knowingly. 'Now I do understand exactly what you're talking about.'

'Have you looked around this airport, Banning?' Dunlop asked, gesturing with a wide sweep of his arm. 'The grounds? The runway? The hangars? The cleanliness? The upkeep? The efficiency? How long did it take for our floods to become operational once your – airplane – was spotted?'

'The lights were smack on the button, Mr Dunlop,' Allen agreed cordially. 'But there wasn't enough time to get a close look at the field.' He shot a quick glance at Banning before returning his attention to the airport manager. 'However, we did see a few of your reliable ground crew men, with their friendly and charming faces.'

The young cowboy's unexpected laugh was cut short immediately by Dunlop, who turned to him, glared, and then faced the aviators again.

'Members of a civic group will be visiting later this evening.' His tone indicated that the meeting was about to adjourn. 'I don't want that flying eyesore of yours to be on display. Mr Gilbert will have it rolled behind Hangar Three, on the edge of the field. These are emergency accommodations. And consider yourselves lucky.'

'Our beat-up heap might cause you some civic embarrassment,' said Allen, following Dunlop's thinking, on purpose. 'And I assume we should get lost as soon as possible, too.'

'It would be helpful.'

'Like we moved into your neighbourhood, right, Mr Dunlop?' Banning asked icily. 'Downgraded your standards and property value?'

'This is not a racial issue,' said Dunlop, ready to finish the exchange. 'All I want is a – '

'Do you have wash-room facilities here?' Banning interrupted rudely. 'We'd like to clean up and get dressed before heading into town.'

71

'Sorry,' Dunlop retorted, standing up, giving a clear exit cue to the aviators. 'The wash-room and changing lockers are reserved for employees and regular users of the airport facilities. You can do your business a short distance from here. Out the front gate and turn right. Mohawk Service Station.'

Allen, sensing that Banning was losing control, jumped in quickly and asked, in a very courteous manner, 'Any scheduled or unscheduled transportation to town tonight, Mr Dunlop?'

'Not at this hour,' he replied, feeling the knot of his tie. 'We have some crew members going home later. Ask Mr Gilbert. He might be able to arrange a lift.'

'I'm sure he will,' Banning said sarcastically. 'All the boys seemed to be extremely helpful and full of brotherly love.'

'You flew over this airfield in a weird cardboard box without lights or a sane approach,' Dunlop chided. 'We lit the floods at once and you slammed down in a fashion which can only be described as stupefying. Whether you were white, black, yellow, green, or blue, would have had absolutely nothing whatsoever to do with a professional ground crew staring in amazement, and perhaps acting in a – hesitant – unsociable – or even unfriendly manner.'

Dunlop glared, until Banning muttered something under his breath, turned away, and walked briskly towards the door, with Allen following.

The two aviators, dressed in their flying gear, and without a suitcase or clothes bundle, trudged along a gravelly, dimly-lit side road on the way to the Mohawk Service Station. Allen had made a few comical remarks and personal observations about Dunlop and the airport staff, but after a while Banning's detached attitude had shut him up. The pilot was silent, brooding, deep in thought.

Bad weather was developing fast. The pitch-black sky was ominous, and a strong wind had kicked up, swirling dust and grit. Anticipating another cool reception and a swift brush-off at the Service Station, they had decided to leave their clothes in the plane, return as soon as they had finished using the Mohawk's wash-room, and spruce up for town at the airport, behind Hangar Three. The next scheduled move was by far the one they dreaded most – begging Mr Gilbert to arrange a lift from one of Dunlop's well-educated, dedicated, forward-thinking, and courageous professionals.

'Hey, you guys!'

A gleaming pick-up van pulled to the side of the road, and stopped beside Allen and Banning. The young man in the cowboy outfit poked his Stetson-topped head out of the front window and asked cheerfully, 'Want a ride?'

Surprised and cautious, the aviators thanked the young man, but explained that they were only going to the Mohawk Service Station.

'No problem,' the young man told them. 'I'll wait outside and then drive you into town. Not all the way to the main drag, but close enough.' He hesitated for a moment before inquiring, 'Would a coloured neighbourhood be helpful?'

Allen explained that it certainly would, although their street clothes were still at the airport, and they had planned to return there and change.

'I don't want to go back there now,' the young man said, with a hint of impatience. 'Dunlop might find an assignment for me. Besides, you guys look sharp in those flight outfits. I'd like one myself. Why change?'

Allen and Banning felt ridiculous and out of place in their flying gear, but the chance of a wash-up and an immediate lift into town, especially to a coloured section, outweighed the prospect of crawling on hands and knees to a sneering Mr Gilbert later in the evening.

They accepted the young man's offer, thanked him again, warily, and climbed into the roomy front compartment of the pick-up van.

'Dunlop isn't really a bad character,' the cowboy was explaining as they headed for town, after stopping briefly at the Mohawk Service Station. 'He's a flight nut who gets his pleasure on the ground – the business end. Know what I mean? Like running an airport. And he does it very well.'

While the young man rambled on about Dunlop, Allen and Banning nodded their heads frequently, forced polite smiles, and said very little. Mainly, they watched with growing concern as the wind howled and twisted and began to develop into a full-blown whopper, a near cyclonic Arizona dust storm, blinding and destructive. The young man, apparently used to these weather conditions, and unaware of his passengers' preoccupation, continued assessing the character of Mr Jonathan Dunlop, airport manager.

'The guy is not a racist,' he went on, squinting at the road, which was rapidly becoming a blur because of the storm. 'It's just that everything in his life has to be – orderly. You should see his house, and his garden, and his wife. And take me, for example. I can wear this Stetson at the airport. But not tilted forward, or pushed back, or cocked on a slant. It has to rest straight on my head. Nothing can be out of place around Jonathan Dunlop.' The young man shrugged his shoulders. 'That's the way the guy is. Take him or leave him.'

'Hopefully we'll leave him in the morning, if this storm eases up,' said Allen, glancing anxiously at the revolving dust clouds and flying gravel all around them. 'Then your Mr Dunlop can be – orderly – again.'

'But he's not a racist,' the young man insisted, shoving the cowboy hat forward to eyebrow level, evidently the way he preferred to wear it. 'Your funny-looking airplane landed on his field and it was different – out of order. It disturbed him. The same goes for your colour. Black is different on this airfield. All of his guys are white. You are both out of order. And that disturbs Jonathan Dunlop.'

'An unusually sensitive man,' said Allen, chuckling, and discreetly nudging his quietly amused co-pilot. 'But glad to hear that he's not a racist.'

'He's not,' the young man repeated, leaning forward to peer at the murky, wind-swept, nearly obliterated side road into Tucson. 'If all the people on the field were black – and Dunlop was in charge – and P.T. Gilbert reported for work – a white guy – *he'd* be different – out of order – and that would disturb Jonathan Dunlop. See what I mean?'

'Not completely,' Banning answered, taking his eyes off the storm for a moment. 'If all the people on the field were black, and Dunlop was in charge – a white guy – *he'd* be different – out of order.' The pilot finally smiled. 'Wouldn't that disturb his orderly nature?'

'I guess so.' The young man appeared to think again about the situation, before adding, 'He'd probably end up firing himself.' And then he laughed, in a friendly, sociable sort of way, and the aviators joined him.

By the time they reached a coloured neighbourhood on the slummy edge of Tucson, the wind had peaked to a ferocious velocity, hurling dirt and trash and garbage lids in all directions. Trees swayed, and branches snapped, and the dark streets were deserted, except for an occasional Negro tramp or a terrified stray cat.

74

On the way, and upon request, Allen and Banning had told the young man all about their transcontinental flight attempt, and he had been genuinely impressed and supportive. In fact, when the pick-up van stopped to unload the flyers at a dismal and blustery intersection, he gave them a much-needed one dollar bill, a good luck prairie wolf's tooth on a cowhide key-ring, and his sincere best wishes for a safe landing in New York City.

'Hey!' Allen, remembering something, stopped the young man just before he slammed the van door. 'What's your name – for the Gold Book?'

'Dunlop!' the young man shouted, with a big grin on his freckled face. 'Randolph Scott Dunlop!'

'Did I hear you right?!' Allen stepped a little closer to the truck. 'Randolph Scott – *Dunlop?*'

'That's it!'

'Any relation?!'

'He's my father!'

The young man laughed, slammed the van door, tipped the brim of his Stetson, and drove away fast.

Allen and Banning stood on the lonely Tucson corner, watching the vehicle disappear into the night, while the wind howled and twisted and whipped up dust and bits of tenement debris.

'Holy Christ!' Banning wailed, as though he had suddenly been jolted out of a deep sleep. 'We'd better get to a telephone on the double!'

'What's up?'

'The plane!' He turned, faced the wind, and tried unsuccessfully to survey the area, as pellets of sand and filth tore into his flesh. 'It's in the open – behind the hangar!!'

'Don't worry!' Allen consoled him, gasping for breath. 'Somebody must have stashed it away in a storm like this!'

'Bullshit!' Banning yelled. 'Let's find a phone! I don't trust any of them! We'll have another wrecked Eagle Rock!'

'Wait a minute!' Allen put on his helmet and goggles and smiled a wise-guy smile. 'Perfect for this weather!' he exclaimed, adjusting the flight equipment. 'Do the same, James Herman. And we'll go frighten some of the Tucson black folks.'

The goggles and helmet were helpful, as Allen and Banning struggled along a very narrow business street, bent forward against the wind, dodging an assortment of flying objects. They passed a cramped row of small, dilapidated shops, including a laundry, an Orthodox Religious and Department Store, a basement grocer, and a rickety dining place, with a sign in the front window advertising 'All You Can Eat For 40 Cents'. The restaurant, like the other neighbourhood establishments, was closed, bolted, and dark.

On the corner, Allen tripped, recovered himself, and cursed a peppermint-striped barber-pole, which had somehow broken away from its foundation, evidently due to the storm. The shop, another run-down basement location, with a squalid residential structure above, had a light on behind a cracked plate-glass front, and someone could be seen moving around inside.

The aviators fought their way to a rusty iron railing, as the wind lashed at them, practically heaving them down three cement steps and up against a splintered wooden door.

Without a hesitation, Banning pounded hard and, at the same time, both men began to remove their goggles and helmets in an attempt to minimize the shock that their outlandish appearance might cause. Another light snapped on. There came the sound of someone, a trusting soul indeed, unfastening a heavy bolt.

When the door finally opened, Allen and Banning stood like a couple of swaying drunks, politely battling the wind and swallowing dirt, while squinting at a sombre, very slender man, with a dark skin and a fragile body. He stared back, vacantly, without a word.

'Hate to disturb you, sir!' Banning managed to yell, over the clang of a tin can, which bounced crazily past the shop. 'This is an emergency! Do you have a telephone?!'

Instead of answering, the man began to cough uncontrollably, a rasping, phlegmy, tubercular sound.

'Sorry about this!' Allen apologized, not knowing exactly how to handle the situation. 'You'd better get away from the air!'

As the violent hacking subsided a little, the man beckoned with a bony finger. The aviators entered the barber-shop hallway, and the ailing, speechless proprietor closed the door and led them to the main section.

It was a standard hair-cutting establishment, but smaller, older, and poorer than any the flyers had ever seen, even in the worst Negro tenements in Los Angeles. Jessup's, as the shop was called, according to a cheaply printed sign taped on the window, had two old-fashioned barber chairs, and a counter full of lotions, powders, creams and other grooming accessories. There were also three unsteady wooden chairs, and a low table strewn with tattered magazines and newspapers, for waiting clients. Allen and Banning watched the frail man lower himself very carefully into one of these customer chairs. And then he spoke for the first time, in a harsh whisper which seemed to come from somewhere deep in his stomach or groin.

'My name is Walter Jessup,' he croaked, apparently straining every part of his body to get the words out. 'I saw you boys walking on the street from my apartment window upstairs. A terrible storm. You need some hot coffee – or a shot of hard liquor. Which?'

'That's extremely hospitable of you, Mr Jessup,' Banning answered. 'A drink would be very welcome. But first we need a telephone. It's an emergency. Do you have one?'

'Local or long distance?'

'The Tucson airport. Our plane is sitting there without any cover. We'll gladly pay for –'

'I knew you were air pilots,' Jessup interrupted, after taking a quick breath. 'My big dream,' he revealed, blinking his sad eyes. 'Flying must be a heavenly thing.' He attempted to smile. 'Will you tell me how it feels up there?'

'Absolutely, Mr Jessup,' said Tom Allen, sitting in the chair next to him. 'We'll have a drink and paint you a complete and Gospel-truth picture.' He saw Banning fidgeting. 'But we'd better make our call first.'

'Over there.' Jessup pointed to an outmoded apparatus propped on the end of the counter, near a cracked wall mirror. 'I'll go upstairs and bring down a few things.'

The emaciated barber-shop proprietor fell into another chest-rattling fit of coughing and wheezing, as he left the shop, doubled over, and in obvious pain.

With Allen watching and listening intently from his sprawled position in the chair, Banning telephoned the airport. A woman answered. He made inquiries. Mr Dunlop was busy with visitors from a local civic organization. Mr Gilbert had been called to an emergency on the field. A Mr Lester Sanders was available and in the office building at the moment. Banning asked to be connected.

'Yeah?'

'Mr Sanders?'

'Speaking.'

'My name is Banning.'

'Who?'

'James Herman Banning,' the pilot replied, anticipating a problem. 'I think we have a plane sitting behind Hangar Three – on the edge of the field. Do you know the one I mean?'

'Oh, yes,' said Sanders, after a pause. 'P.T. Gilbert had your plane rolled out there by order of Mr Dunlop.'

'Is it still exposed?'

'Don't know.'

'Will you please find out?' Banning toughened his attitude. 'This storm is a crusher and getting worse. We need a hangar for the night. Can I talk to Gilbert?'

'He's busy on the field.'

'What do you suggest, Mr Sanders?'

'Give me a minute.'

'Filthy trash,' Banning remarked quietly to Allen, his hand over the mouthpiece. 'I knew they would jerk us around tonight. Efficiency – professionalism – an orderly airport – *hypocritical bastards!*'

'Banning?'

'Here.'

'I spoke to P.T. Gilbert about the situation.'

'Good,' said Banning. 'Is our plane under cover?'

'Not yet,' Sanders replied. 'The civic group members are still on the field. I understand that Mr Dunlop has already explained the – '

'Sanders!' The pilot was unable to control his temper any longer. 'I don't give a damn about Dunlop's civic group! We have an airplane on your field! And you people have an obligation to take care of it properly! Get us in a hangar, right now, or I'll come to that fucking airport and handle things in my own way! Will you pass the message on to P.T. Gilbert for me? I'll wait!'

Banning expected a violent outburst, profanity, racial abuse, or an immediate disconnection. Instead, Sanders responded in the same level tone of voice, 'Hold on for a moment, P.T. Gilbert just walked into the office. I'll give him your message now.'

Allen was now sitting upright, dividing his attention between Banning's phone call and the increasing fury of the wind. The plate glass window of the shop was being peppered like buckshot by a variety of unknown flying objects.

'Mr Banning?'

'Yes.'

'This is P.T. Gilbert. Mr Sanders has given me your message – word for word.' Gilbert's tone was deceptively pleasant. 'I can understand your concern. You must have worked hard on that old Eagle Rock.'

'Many people did.'

'And your destination is New York City?'

'Right.' Banning was unable to gauge the man's sincerity. 'Has our airplane been damaged by the storm, Mr Gilbert?'

'No reports yet,' he answered, sounding genuine and friendly. 'But I've been occupied. We've had an emergency landing. Understandable in a blow like this – as you can appreciate – being a licensed and experienced pilot.'

'Mr Gilbert – will you please put our airplane in a hangar right away? We have a morning take-off scheduled after a check-out and some minor repairs.'

This time Gilbert took a moment before replying. 'I'll do my very best for you,' he said, apparently meaning it, although Banning thought he heard the sound of muffled laughter. 'Good luck for tomorrow. Hope the weather clears.'

'Thank you.' Banning replaced the receiver slowly, while Allen kept his eyes on him, waiting for a report.

'Mr P.T. Gilbert will do the very best he can,' the pilot announced. 'And he wishes us good luck and clear weather.'

'There you are, James Herman,' said Allen, gesturing with both hands appropriately. 'Like I told you – these people are running an airport. Somebody will stash the plane away on a night like this.'

'I hope so,' Banning commented, as worried as ever. He leaned his back against the grooming counter and stared pensively at the rattling plate glass window. 'But I just don't trust these damn characters.'

'You don't like or trust anything white, partner – except maybe a clean sheet – with two big tits under it.'

Banning finally smiled, and Allen did the same, just as Walter Jessup staggered into the shop, wheezing louder than the storm, and dragging something resembling a large, fully-packed potato sack behind him.

The aviators moved quickly. Banning grabbed the load and hauled it close to the magazine table, and Allen helped the skeletal little barber into one of the creaky wooden chairs.

After some minutes spent gasping for air, he bent forward, and started coughing loudly into a napkin-sized handkerchief.

Allen and Banning watched him helplessly. Eventually, he pointed to the sack near the table, and gave a brief, strained, painful-sounding description of the contents. From his upstairs apartment, Jessup had collected half a salami, four tomatoes, some cheese, bread, two apples, an almost full bottle of whisky, two pillows, and two blankets. There was a pot of coffee, sugar and cups on the counter, next to a small electric cooker, in case the aviators wanted a milder drink.

'I can't guzzle liquor or invite guests upstairs,' Jessup explained, matter-of-factly. 'My wife is bedridden, very righteous, and dying of cancer. I'm not exactly a healthy specimen myself – as you can surmise. It's just like a hospital up there. Or a morgue.'

'This is all very kind of you, Mr Jessup,' said Allen, sitting next to him again. 'But we don't want to inconvenience you and your –'

'No trouble at all,' Jessup interrupted, with a wave of his hand. 'You boys can sleep in the barber chairs. Very comfortable. And there's a toilet in the hallway. Everything you need.'

'We certainly appreciate your help, Mr Jessup,' said Banning sincerely. 'I don't know what we would have done in this storm tonight.'

'Get drunk,' the barber suggested, doing his best to smile. 'Have some food, drink some liquor, and sleep well.' He thought for a moment and took a deep breath at the same time. 'Are you due back at the airport in the morning?'

'Yes, sir,' Allen replied. 'We've got to prepare our plane for an early take-off. If the wind stops.'

'It should,' said Jessup, speaking like an authority on Tucson weather. 'She'll blow herself out before sunrise. Where are you boys heading?'

'New York City, Mr Jessup,' Banning answered proudly. 'We're making a transcontinental flight. The first attempt by Negroes.'

'Good Lord Almighty,' said Jessup, his eyes glistening. 'That really is something. I can imagine all sorts of problems.'

'You happen to be right,' Allen told him. 'And that's why we appreciate all you've done for us.'

'Wish I could do more,' the barber sighed, having a difficult time breathing again. 'I'm mighty low on cash – and paying customers too,' he explained. 'It's the same with everybody on the block. No business. The Palm Grove restaurant is closed, you know. Most folks don't eat out anymore. But Alvin Simpkins, the grocer, trades me produce for haircuts sometimes. That's how we push along now.'

'You've been generous enough, Mr Jessup,' said Banning, indicating the sack near the table. 'We keep a record of all the people who help us during this flight.'

'Our Gold Book,' Allen chimed in. 'On the lower left wing tip. We'll sign your name there along with the others. And people will see it years and years from now – in the Smithsonian Institute – in Washington, DC.'

'That's quite an honour,' Jessup remarked, shaking his head in wonder. 'I always did love reading about planes and flying.' He stared at the aviators for a long moment, oblivious to the frightening slam of a storm-blown cardboard box against the plate glass window. 'Being what you are – you boys must have worked real hard – to become so privileged. I envy you. And I'm very proud that God led you to my front door on this blustery night.'

'You wanted to know what it's like up in the sky, Mr Jessup,' said Allen, unable to think of anything more appropriate to say. 'We can tell you how it feels to us, if that would be of interest.'

'It certainly would,' said Jessup, looking extremely pale and unsteady. 'But it's late now and I have to join my wife. And besides, I'd better keep my fantasies unspoiled. You boys know too much about the real thing.'

With Tom Allen's help, the barber rose slowly to his feet and stood for a moment, fighting for breath and steadying himself in preparation for his journey upstairs.

'Eat, drink, and sleep well,' he said. 'I'll phone Alvin Simpkins, the grocer, and arrange a ride to the airport for you in the morning.' He hesitated and managed a full smile with his parting remark. 'I do wish my miserable body was able to accept one large shot of that bootlegged hooch. What a pity. I'm scheduled to choke to death anyway – even without it.'

Allen and Banning devoured Jessup's provisions together with enough whisky to make them forget about coffee, the storm, and just about everything else. They laughed and clowned and swung in the barber chairs, and doused and smeared themselves with Walter Jessup's powder, cream, and lotions. And finally, drunk and exhausted, they adjusted the chairs straight back, and fell asleep.

8

Feeling as though they had spears in their heads, and eels in their stomachs, Allen and Banning arrived at Tucson airport courtesy of Mr Alvin Simpkins, who must have been intimidated by the flying gear, because he did not utter one word during the journey – and the aviators were grateful.

Jessup's forecast had been accurate. The savage wind had become a pleasant breeze and the Arizona skies were clear.

As the two aviators walked anxiously towards Hangar Three, Dunlop's employees were busy clearing the field of debris, and brushing away storm dirt in the administration area. A few looked up, recognized the Negroes, and turned back quickly to their work. Most ignored them completely. There were no greetings of any kind, not even taunts or insults. Allen and Banning realized very quickly that this was a performance, an indication of serious trouble ahead. They walked faster and faster, and finally broke into a run.

A rapid inspection of Hangar Three confirmed their worst fears, and a heart-pumping mixture of anger and apprehension gripped them as they dashed outside to the back of the hangar.

The Eagle Rock was still on the edge of the field, exactly where his crew had rolled it on Dunlop's orders the night before.

Allen and Banning stared grim-faced at a buckled wing, a damaged tail section, and other clear evidence that the aircraft had been left exposed to the full force of the gale.

'Why?' Banning, trembling with fury, picked up a stone and hurled it with maximum force at nothing in particular. 'Why are they born with poison in their fucking skulls?'

'Don't waste time, James Herman,' said Allen, moving closer to the plane for a more detailed inspection. 'You should know all the answers by now.'

'I'm going to the office.'

'*No!*'

Allen's unusually emphatic negative halted the pilot in his tracks. He turned, walked back, and stood waiting for an explanation.

'Dunlop won't be at work,' said Allen uneasily, but steadily. 'Gilbert will be busy and unavailable. And the man you spoke to – Sanders – probably doesn't have the authority to flush a toilet.' He stooped and looked carefully under the broken wing. 'Don't go to the office and start trouble. A waste of time. Believe me.'

'What do you suggest, Uncle Thomas?' snarled Banning. 'Want us to put on big toothy grins – and shuffle around this damn field – like nothing happened?'

'I want to fix the airplane and take off for New Mexico.' Allen waggled a loose strut before getting up and facing Banning. 'Not as bad as it looks,' he remarked. 'Let's go find some iodine and bandages in the hangar workshop.'

'On our knees, partner?'

'With a little calm diplomacy, James Herman,' Allen replied. 'Listen, you always do exactly what they like best. And the stage is set. Oh, yeah. Did you see Dunlop's helpers when we arrived?'

'I saw them.'

'Well, don't grab the bait this time,' Allen warned, feeling that Banning was reasonably receptive, at least for the moment. 'There's only one practical way to deal with these bigoted sons of bitches. Land our plane in New York City – and watch them all make long, low, respectful bows.'

Wire, tape, and an assortment of parts, together with necessary tools and accessories, were requisitioned from the hangar workshop, and itemized by Lester Sanders, a tall, thin flunkey with pimply skin and a self-conscious manner. Referring to the damaged Eagle Rock, the airport assistant apologized, citing poor communications and a series of field emergencies, caused by the violent storm. Mr Dunlop and Mr Gilbert, who were unavailable at the present time, had instructed him to pass on the message, with their deepest regrets. He also made another apology for not being able to assign any ground crew members to help repair the neglected aircraft.

Maintaining a polite but cool and detached attitude, Allen and Banning completed their order, accepted the supplies, watched Sanders initial a form, and left the workshop without believing one word.

With ingenuity, determination, and plenty of elbow grease, they proceeded to overhaul the Eagle Rock OXX6. Every once in a while, an airport employee, or a small group of them, would saunter by, pause and grin sardonically, and then rejoin their

83

colleagues. But the aviators knew that some kind of real trouble was brewing. The stockily built, overall-clad Dunlop worker who had been pressing for some hostile action from Banning, moments after they had landed the evening before, was standing with five or six snickering ground crew members outside Hangar Three. Allen saw him gesture in the direction of the Eagle Rock, and he alerted Banning, who glanced over his shoulder, and made a mental note, before returning to his work.

Gasoline was dripping from the carburettor. Believing the float was stuck, Allen tapped on the bowl with a screw-driver handle, and the carburettor flooded. He removed the leaky float. It would have to be taken to the hangar workshop. They needed an air pressure hose to force out the gas and an electric soldering iron to repair the leak.

Inside the hangar, in a quiet corner of the repair section, away from Lester Sanders and his check-out counter, Allen had finished with the air hose. Banning had prepared the soldering iron and was holding it ready for the mechanic's use.

At that moment, the heavy-set Dunlop trouble-maker entered the workshop area, followed by his band of insolent helpers. They circled Allen and Banning and watched in silence. All of them were big and rough and obviously keen to take their cue from the leader. The aviators knew from past experience that the man in charge would soon begin to needle them, until he was given a legitimate opportunity for defensive hell-raising. Knowing the exercise well, they concentrated on the carburettor repair job, uncomfortably aware that some of the intruders were holding crude weapons behind their backs. Parts of a metal bar and a heavy chain were noticeable.

'We understand you've got a bad leak problem,' said the leader, moving closer to Allen. 'Did you grease the valve action and drain the wells on that carburettor?'

Allen looked up from his work and studied the man's face impassively. 'Everything is now under control here,' he finally answered. 'Thanks very much for the interest.'

'I asked you a question.'

Ignoring him, Allen held the carburettor float up to the light, and squinted at it professionally. Banning, ready with the soldering iron, kept his eyes on the mechanic, and his temper in check.

'You have no right to be so damn arrogant,' the leader snarled. 'Where's a thank-you for the floods? And a compliment

84

for our quick action? We saved your asses.' He waited for a response, but Allen and Banning were silent, continuing with the repair job. Angered, the leader took a menacing step forward. 'And what about an apology for landing an unlit wreck in a disgraceful manner? This airport has a proud reputation for orderly flight operations.'

Allen had to smile to the ludicrous statement. 'Orderly flight operations?' he repeated, taking the iron from Banning in order to seal the leak. 'This carburettor problem is minor. You people left our airplane out in a terrible storm. And we had to fix all the damage ourselves – plenty of it – thanks to Mr Dunlop's *orderly* airport.'

'We had poor communications and field emergencies last night,' said the leader, repeating Lester Sanders's excuse. 'And don't get so damn bumptious with me, boy. I demand some thanks and an apology for –'

'Just go away and let us finish our work,' Banning interrupted, coldly. 'We have a take-off scheduled this morning.'

The leader's piercing grey eyes switched instantly to the pilot. This was what he had been waiting for.

'I understand you do stunt flying in a Negro circus,' he said derisively, close to Banning's face, much too close, judging by the pilot's grim expression. 'Does that qualify you to order senior flight attendants around? he asked, stretching a wide mouth, full of crooked yellow teeth. 'This is a municipal airport, not a cottonfield landing patch. You had better show respect. Or you won't take off this morning – or any other morning.'

Banning glared, and Allen was poised to intervene, as the ground crew members gathered behind their leader.

'All I want is a nice thank-you and a humble apology,' the man stressed, poking his finger lightly into Banning's jacket. 'Or –' he moved his finger slowly up to Banning's throat, and slid it across. 'What do you say, ace?'

In a flash, the pilot yanked the soldering iron away from Allen, grabbed the leader by his overall collar, and pulled his face close enough to feel heat.

'I'll burn you black, man,' Banning threatened hoarsely, tightening his grip on the startled trouble-maker. 'Much blacker than I am. And your black will really hurt. Like agony, you bastard. Every day and night of your miserable life. Do you hear me?'

The leader nodded several times in rapid succession, his frightened eyes riveted on the soldering iron a fraction of an inch away from his face.

85

'Now tell your scum pals to leave us alone,' Banning ordered, pressing the iron even closer. 'Or I'll sizzle me some white chicken meat, right now.'

The tension was palpable. For a timeless moment nobody moved.

'Is this some kind of union meeting?!' The peremptory demand came from Jonathan Dunlop, standing in the hangar entrance with the young clerk, Lester Sanders. They were staring at ground crew backs. Nothing else could be seen from their positions. 'What the hell is going on in here?' he shouted. 'Gilbert needs immediate help on the field!'

The workshop came to life at once. Banning lowered the soldering iron and released the heavily breathing leader. A relieved Tom Allen reached for the tool and held it with the carburettor float. The gang of airport employees lowered their weapons to the cement floor very discreetly, and then filed out of the hangar, smiling ingratiatingly at their boss as they passed him. The leader hesitated, adjusted his overall collar, and whispered to Banning, 'I'll get you for this someday, nigger.'

'Explain this irregular behaviour,' Dunlop demanded, crossing the floor towards them and staring at his worker. 'And come straight to the point. Gilbert is waiting.'

'Yes, sir,' the leader responded. 'We've been advising these flyers about a leaky carburettor float.' He glanced in Banning's direction, without meeting his eye. 'And also about some other problems due to the storm.'

'Gilbert's instructions?'

'No, sir,' the leader confessed, glancing sheepishly down at the floor. 'We tried to help because they – well – they're heading for New York City – in a – beat-up death trap – and you saw the landing yesterday, Mr Dunlop.'

'How noble of you,' said Dunlop acidly. 'Report to Gilbert without any further delays. We'll discuss this matter later.'

'Yes, sir.'

The leader made a brisk exit, and Dunlop turned his attention to Allen and Banning. 'Are the repairs nearly completed?' he asked Allen, who had already started using the iron on the float. 'What about the storm damage?'

'Almost finished, Mr Dunlop,' Allen replied, without glancing up. 'We'll be on our way as soon as I seal this piece and get it back in the carburettor.'

'Excellent,' the airport manager snapped back. 'I want that –

blemish – off my field before noon.' He nudged Sanders. 'Keep an eye on them, Lester. And make sure.'

'I will, sir.'

'Speaking of storm damage,' said Banning, 'why was our plane left out in the open all night?'

'The reasons have already been explained by Mr Sanders,' Dunlop answered, ready to leave. 'I have nothing to add. Just get off this field as quickly as possible.'

Banning watched him go, the muscles of his jaw twitching.

To hell with it, James Herman,' said Allen, putting the finishing touches on the sealed float. 'Let's put this back in the carburettor and take off for New Mexico.'

'Before you leave, gentlemen,' Sanders interjected, 'Here's an itemized list of the materials, parts, accessories, and tool rentals I checked out to you this morning.' He handed the paper to Allen. 'The full payment due is in the right-hand corner.'

After paying the requisition clerk's bill – a grossly inflated $26.85 – along with two dollars and twenty-five cents for gasoline, they were left with a balance of one dollar and eighty-six cents in the Eagle Rock treasury.

'We'll have to hustle us some cash in Lordsburgh, James Herman,' said Allen, glancing mean-eyed at Lester Sanders, who was standing near the runway watching the preparations for take-off, by order of his boss. 'Do you know anybody there?'

'Nobody.'

'I don't either.'

'We should grab that snot-nosed pencil-pusher and empty his pockets,' growled Banning, also taking notice of Lester Sanders. 'Get back what they snatched.'

'You'll need better ideas for Lordsburgh, partner,' said Allen, walking to the propeller. 'Let's start the engine, warm it up, and see if that carburettor spits gasoline.'

A curious and impatient Lester Sanders ambled over to the Eagle Rock while the engine was warming up. Allen and Banning, feeling a little more at ease now that the carburettor was functioning normally, ignored the clerk as he practically stood on tiptoe in order to stare inquisitively over their shoulders at the Gold Book.

'I'll write Walter Jessup right here – next to The Greaser – and Pipkin's Hot Spot!' Allen yelled over the engine noise. 'God bless his generous soul!' he added, signing the barber's name for future generations to see. 'And all the others too!'

'What that?' Sanders pointed. 'The names on the wing?'

'People, Mr Sanders!' Allen yelled back. 'A list of good people!'

'I don't understand!'

'Of course not!' Banning blasted, without looking around. 'Now why don't you go find something orderly to do? In other words, Sanders, get the hell away from here!'

'Mr Dunlop instructed me –'

'Ignore the gentleman, James Herman,' Allen advised loudly, while the Eagle Rock engine roared. 'Now what about the cowboy?'

'Who?'

'Our free ride to town – and the dollar bill – and the good luck charm – and his very best wishes. Remember?'

'Yeah.' Banning thought for a moment, and then snapped his head back sharply, indicating the presence of Sanders. 'Considering the circumstances, I don't think the cowboy would want to be involved with us – he might get stomped on – know what I mean?'

'That's a point.' And then, as though drawn by a strong magnet, Allen's eyes moved slowly to the extreme right of the Gold Book, and they stopped there, and lit up, and gleamed like diamonds.

'Well, well, and what d'ya know!' he exclaimed, motioning for Banning's attention. 'Take a happy peak at this, James Herman!'

Lester Sanders's pimpled face pushed forward, straining for a better view.

Close to the wing tip, printed neatly in thick black ink, was an inscription:

LA TO NYC

ALL THE BEST FROM ENVIOUS ME

•

RANDOLPH SCOTT DUNLOP

After leaving Tucson, they flew south-east to Edmond, and then swung left through Rincon Valley – all desert, and heat, but they kept their clothes on this time. Banning managed to hold the old, rattling wreck on course over the Rincon and Dragoon Mountains to Cochise, by checking the Southern Pacific and Arizona-Eastern and El Paso Railways, and the Alkali Flat. Appearing to be a giant lake, a mirage in desert country, the Flat was about twenty miles long, and eight or nine miles wide and, on this particular day, every inch could be seen clearly, white as snow.

After flying past Cochise, they wavered dangerously through

the Apache Pass of the Dos Cabezeas Range, and over some level country, a few miles to the left of Pyramid Mountains.

Just before noon, Banning spotted an airport, about a half-mile from Lordsburgh, New Mexico. The air was light, and the machine came down like a greased bullet, taxiing across most of the field, before coming to a jerky, whip-lashing stop. Banning kept the engine running, so that it would cool down slowly, while they sat for a moment, and did the same.

A Deputy United States Marshal and a Mexican immigration officer were standing near the airport's gas pumps. They had been observing all incoming flights, on the look-out for an escaped convict, who might have stowed away aboard a flight from Tucson. Allen, Banning, and the two-seater Eagle Rock were obviously not credible suspects, but the Deputy Marshal, a big man with a large head, and a revolver on each hip, appeared fascinated by the aircraft, and by its crew – a curious, rather unsettling situation, which caught the new arrivals completely by surprise.

After being ridiculed and pushed round so many times at the other airports, they found it difficult to believe that the Marshal, a man called Jimmy Quayle, was actually studying the Eagle Rock with curiosity and signs of admiration.

Always suspicious of white motives, especially where law men carrying loaded revolvers were concerned, Allen and Banning watched his every move, and listened to every pause and inflexion, searching for signs of insincerity – but could find none. He seemed genuinely interested in the purpose of their flight and its wider aims.

While the Mexican immigration officer strolled back to the small administration building, Jimmy Quayle stared at the wary aviators, scratched his chin thoughtfully, and came up with an extraordinary proposition.

'We've got a luncheon meeting of the Lordsburgh Chamber of Commerce in about an hour,' he announced, evidently still mulling over his idea and the practicalities. 'How about coming along and speaking about the flight to our members? I think everyone would be mighty interested.'

Allen glanced at Banning with a look of panic in his eyes. But the pilot was staring right back at Quayle, without a trace of concern. He apparently like the idea.

'The Chamber won't be able to pay you more than a five dollar fee,' Quayle continued apologetically. 'All the mines are closed around here. Lots of unemployment. Business is terrible in

Lordsburgh – worse than El Paso. Will five dollars be acceptable?'

Banning nodded his approval after a short pause, ignoring Allen's nervous fidgeting and obvious desire to discuss the invitation before acceptance.

Quayle explained that the speech would be delivered from the conference room dais after the members had finished eating – about 2:30 pm. He suggested a table at one of Lordsburgh's most popular Negro restaurants, on the house. All transportation would be arranged by the Chamber. Quayle also offered to speak to the airport manager about using the wash-room and changing facilities so the flyers could shower and dress for the occasion. In addition, the Deputy Marshal would contact the *Lordsburgh Herald* and, if possible, arrange to have a reporter and photographer present.

'You understand that I don't have a prepared speech, Mr Quayle,' said Banning. 'We're aviators not orators.'

'Just tell our members exactly what you told me, and they'll be impressed, for sure,' Quayle said, checking his watch, and then looking up fast, a man in a hurry now. 'You'll probably have to field some questions afterwards,' he added. 'From the reporter, too – if he shows up.'

'No problem, Mr Quayle.' Allen decided to contribute to the conversation, but his voice cracked, and nearly broke completely. 'This will be good training before the big one in New York City.' He paused and winced, realizing his blunder. 'I don't mean to belittle the Lordsburgh Chamber of Commerce, sir.'

'I know that. Well, I'd better phone, make arrangements, and let you men get ready. My car will be in front of the administration building entrance. Sorry, but it's a marked police vehicle. I'll make arrangements for something more suitable later. See you in a few minutes. And thanks.'

As Quayle was about to leave, the Mexican immigration officer hailed him.

'What's up, Hector?'

'Diego Arraya,' the Mexican answered. 'You were right. A waste of time. He never left the Tucson airport.'

'They picked him up?'

'Shot him dead.'

'Good,' Quayle said, matter-of-factly. 'He killed a cop,' he added by way of explanation to Allen and Banning before swaggering off to join the Immigration Officer. The flyers watched them turn a corner and disappear.

*

90

After a fast ride through town in Jimmy Quayle's police car, Allen and Banning were deposited in the Grand Fiesta Restaurant, where the Marshal had arranged for a choice table, a special welcome from the owner, and a free lunch. The food was delicious. Later, after a quiet discussion with the waiter, two large teapots were placed before them.

'No more than a few sips, James Herman,' said Allen, faking a clogged nose, as he pointed to the concealed whisky. The mechanic, blaming a sudden sinus attack, had agreed to participate only in the question and answer session. 'Just enough to loosen your nerves and tongue – and generate some courage.'

'Who appointed you my theatrical agent?' Banning poured some of the special tea into Allen's cup and then filled his own to the brim. 'I'll give them a performance they will never forget, partner.'

'That's exactly what's bothering me,' said Allen. 'Can you really gave a speech from a dais – to a group of Chamber of Commerce types – in a strange town – without anything written down – and with a big policeman leaning over your shoulder?'

'Absolutely.'

They both took a large swig of booze, and sat quietly for a moment, while Allen inspected the cool, composed, almost arrogantly confident pilot, looking without success for signs that it was a façade, camouflaging a jumpy stomach, or shaky legs.

'I have to give you credit,' said Allen sincerely. 'How could you possibly have developed such giant balls?'

'Nothing to it, Thomas,' Banning replied, finishing his cup of knock-out brew, and serving himself another. 'Think of the old Eagle Rock and the two of us, and what we're doing, and why, and – hell, man – I could talk about it straight out to anyone – anywhere – for hours and hours – and I don't need paper to remind me about anything – not anything.'

Both men were silent again, drinking teapot whisky, too much of it, and they knew it, and realized they would regret it, but for the moment they didn't care.

'Know what happens if your speech is bad, James Herman?'

'They keep the five dollars.'

'Wrong,' slurred Allen, pushing his cup aside. 'That huge Deputy United States Marshal will blow our fucking brains out on the spot. And please keep that fact in mind.'

9

In the ballroom of the Hotel Meridian, a first class establishment by Lordsburgh, New Mexico, standards, James Herman Banning was standing on the formally decorated speaker's platform, completing his address to the Chamber of Commerce members. Thomas C. Allen, Marshal Quayle, and three elderly, distinguished-looking gentlemen, were also on the rostrum, seated beside the Negro pilot, listening attentively.

Allen and Banning were neatly dressed in conservative business suits, with white shirts and ties, clothing they had reserved for fancy occasions along the way, and after the New York landing, God willing. Fortunately, Jimmy Quayle had arranged for the hotel laundry staff to do a fast, emergency ironing job on the badly creased, hardly recognizable Sunday best garments. To their slight embarrassment, the aviators ended up being more conventionally attired than anyone else present, the Lordsburgh residents being mostly in casual dress.

Allen and Banning had had to swallow what seemed like gallons of black coffee before staggering out of the Grand Fiesta Restaurant and entering a waiting taxi, which had been ordered by the Marshal. Even so, after their arrival at the Meridian, Allen had smiled too much, and always at the wrong things, while Banning's nerves had gone completely dead, his tongue had loosened to the point of disconnection, and his courage knew no bounds. However, in time, the effects of the teapot hooch had levelled off, without abandoning them entirely, and both men felt able to cope with the unusual challenge facing them.

After a dramatic and commendatory introduction by Quayle, Banning had assumed command with ease and surprising authority. He recounted the details of their flight so far, without attempting to minimize either their continuing financial problems or the spirit-draining effects of the bigoted racialist attitudes they had met with. However, he countered this by emphasizing the kindness and generosity shown by so many others.

The Chamber of Commerce members listened in absolute silence. It was impossible to gauge their feelings.

After a short pause, Banning surveyed the gathering very solemnly and lowered his voice.

'I'm not a particularly religious man,' he admitted. 'But I figure – maybe the name of this town – has something to do with the way Marshal Quayle – and all of you – have treated us. We thank you very much – for everything.'

Banning sat down looking straight ahead. The Lordsburgh Chamber of Commerce members still appeared to be deaf and dumb, curiously unresponsive. Even Tom Allen and Jimmy Quayle stared at the pilot without attempting to utter a sound.

Then, a man and a woman at a front table began to clap, and another table joined in, and another, and another, and in a few minutes the entire room was filled with enthusiastic applause. Quayle was beaming and shouting congratulations, pounding his hands together like everyone else. And Tom Allen, also clapping wildly, had a few proud tears in his eyes as he yelled over the hubbub, 'Take a bow, partner! You big ham-bone!'

The question and answer session went extremely well, and Allen made a significant contribution of his own, especially when several of the audience showed an interest in aircraft mechanics. He also received a fair share of laughs when relating a carefully laundered version of their striptease over the desert, and the unexpected appearance of a woman field attendant at Yuma.

Later, a young lady from the *Lordsburgh Herald* conducted a brief interview with the aviators, while an incredibly tall and gangling photographer knelt on both knees in order to take pictures from various angles. Allen and Banning grinned and posed and thoroughly enjoyed the attention.

As promised, they received five dollars from the Marshal, along with many thanks, compliments, and expressions of appreciation. There was also a very welcome and completely unexpected gift: Quayle had arranged for Allen and Banning to use the hotel telephones in the executive suite. Each man would be allowed one long distance call on the house, providing the conversation did not exceed five minutes.

Allen, of course, phoned Celene. Banning phoned Little Dandy to inquire about publicity and fund raising.

It was a depressing contact. According to Little Dandy, people were concerned about eating and keeping a roof over their heads, and to hell with a couple of special black faces getting into history books by flying an old machine across the United States. Nobody on the Avenue was interested. In the white neighbourhoods, Phil

Nash had picked up laughs and gibes, nothing else. His odd-jobbing had tapered off to dire emergency repairs, on credit, and all his boarders were far behind with their rent. Conditions had become even worse for the Mosby brothers. Floyd and Booker T. fixed an occasional car, bikes, and all kinds of mechanical devices, but everything was pay later, much later, if at all.

'Things are real bad around here, James Herman,' Little Dandy moaned. 'You boys live mostly up in the clouds – far away from the Depression.'

Eventually, after more pressure from Banning, Little Dandy admitted that two Eagle Rock fund-raising drives had been conducted on Central Avenue, with the help of Phil Nash. Thirty-five dollars and eighty cents had been collected. But Little Dandy had a long-standing debt on the books of Mr Charles 'Pigmeat' Hughes, a Vice-President of the Good Samaritan Credit Bureau, and word was circulating that the six-foot three-inch former heavyweight boxer had decided to demand immediate payment, in his own persuasive way.

'I had no choice, James Herman,' Little Dandy explained apologetically. 'That ape would have torn me apart and scattered the pieces all over the Avenue. You know that. But don't write us off. We'll keep trying to –'

'Do me a favour,' Banning interrupted gruffly as the final seconds ticked away. 'Call my father and tell him everything is fine. I'll be in touch soon.'

'Of course, James Herman.'

'And get off your ass.'

At the Airport, Deputy United States Marshal James Quayle signed the Gold Book, and added best wishes from the Lordsburgh Chamber of Commerce.

An attendant pulling a dolly approached the aviators. He explained that he had worked the field for over eight years, and knew exactly what they would be up against, attempting a take-off in the crippled Eagle Rock, at midday, five thousand one hundred feet above sea level. In addition, the mile and a quarter square airfield had soft sand on the runway, a real hazard for an old, sluggish, patched-together contraption. Luckily, there were no high lines or trees to clear, and the wind was nothing more than a breeze. And their direction eliminated the need for a turn. Even so, getting the plane up and away from Lordsburgh was certain to be tricky, and dangerous.

94

Following his advice, Allen and Banning helped the attendant operate the dolly and pull the plane off the runway, all the way back against the fence, to get as much take-off distance as possible.

With Banning at the controls, the Eagle Rock rumbled and shuddered diagonally across the field, taking the long route. Half-way down the runway, the plane continued to roll heavily, as the wheels were still supporting its weight. At the three-quarter mark, about two hundred feet from the New Mexican sagebrush, the Eagle Rock began to break loose. It rose and flew a hundred feet, then settled to the ground, hard on the wheels. After bouncing, and rising up nearly fifty feet, the plane started to settle again. But by pushing the stick forward, Banning forced the aircraft to slam down roughly and rebound high enough for him to snatch control – less than thirty feet from the sagebrush.

For fifty miles, flying east and slightly south from Lordsburgh, the machine was never more than two hundred feet off the top of the brush – a worry, but Banning managed to hold the wreck on a level run, and eventually gained altitude. Within a short while, they crossed the Southern Pacific Railway at Gage, just north of the Victoria Mountains. The course had been set over Rattle Snake Hills, to the Capitol Dome of the Florida Mountains, then above desert country to the right of Providence Cone, and left of Mount Riley, on the approach to the Extinct Volcano. The final leg of this rugged flight plan would give them a view of Strauss, a few miles from their destination, El Paso, Texas.

But while bumping violently in a blinding patch of clouds and heavy turbulence, Banning heard the engine grind, and knock, and vibrate, and then run smoothly again. Minutes later, the pattern was repeated, as they looked down anxiously at a particularly rough and isolated stretch of mountains and desert. Tom Allen was even more concerned than Banning. He knew the exact meaning of each sound, and realized that when engines alternated from good to bad, back and forth, anything could be expected, at any time.

They did not have long to wait. The grinds and knocks and vibrations started again, louder than before, and the engine was now missing and revving down. Banning struggled, and Allen prayed, but they were unable to prevent the Eagle Rock from losing altitude fast.

As they dropped uncontrollably, Allen and Banning checked the terrain below, searching vainly for a place to set the plane down, while the engine lost more and more revs, leaving hardly enough to sustain level flight. Seconds later, after the rpm's had fallen below twelve hundred, and the mountains were looming up ominously, Banning had no choice: the Eagle Rock would have to be emergency ditched, at once, on a slope, in a ravine, somewhere, anywhere.

A rocky knoll came into view, just ahead and below them, and both men knew that this had to be it. After buckling their seat belts tightly, and bracing themselves for the worst, Banning cut the switches, and pulled back hard on the stick, all the way, until the Eagle Rock rattled and quivered and nearly broke apart, before making a spectacular, last second, stall-landing on the mountain top.

But without enough space to roll, a wheel slammed against a large boulder, and the plane lurched, spun in a complete circle, skidded to the summit's edge, and fell nose first part of the way down a slope, landing bottom side up.

Strapped in the cockpits, with their heads dangling towards the ground, Allen and Banning felt the blood rush, and knew that, if nothing else, they were conscious, and survivors, at least for the moment. But the shock of the crash had dazed them, and they stayed put, with eyes closed and mouths shut, waiting for the dust to settle.

The Eagle Rock had taken another beating. Already weakened by the storm damage in Tucson, the wings had buckled completely, and the tail section was unrecognizable. Both landing gears had collapsed. Something had put a hole in the fuselage. And, among other problems, there were two broken push rods, both an intake, and exhaust.

'Hey, James Herman!' Allen suddenly yelled, coming to life. 'We'd better get the hell away from his wreck, man! Right now!'

Frantically, the mechanic unfastened his seat belt and dropped to the ground, where he rested for a moment, light-headed and shaken.

'What's your rush?' Banning asked calmly, lowering himself to a firm-footed standing position, the movement of an athlete, or a professional acrobat. 'I want to check the plane. Look at the goddamn wings.'

'Forget the wings,' Allen snapped back, with his eyes focused on the upside-down nose of the aircraft. 'I hear funny noises in there. She might catch fire and explode. Let's go! Now!'

'Clock me, baby! Banning shouted, as he raced behind Allen,

and quickly overtook him on the way up the slope towards the summit. 'Jazz your throttle, lead-ass!' he whooped over his shoulder. 'I'll be waiting on top!'

They sat dejectedly on the knoll, and peered around at a barren landscape of steep hills, deep ravines, and miles of desert. Allen's warning about fire and an explosion had proved to be a false alarm. One piece of good fortune. But, the Eagle Rock was on her back, grounded, in need of major surgery. And the aviators were stranded, hopelessly lost in wild, unfamiliar surroundings, without any sense of direction, and with hardly a chance of being spotted and rescued.

'We can't sit up here forever,' Allen said, tossing a small rock over the summit's edge. 'Let's make some kind of a move. Better than doing nothing.'

'Go ahead.' Banning leaned back, rested on both elbows, and nibbled his lower lip, a sign that he was pondering an idea. 'I'm staying on this hill until dark.'

'Until dark?' Allen stared at the pilot curiously. 'And then what?' he asked. 'Roam around this wilderness like blind men? Go in circles? Fall down holes and break our damn necks? Why? That's crazy talk, James Herman.'

Banning lifted one arm and pointed to an area in the distance, to their right, beyond some desert sand, and just before a range of low hills. 'There's a farmhouse out that way,' he announced. 'About ten or twelve hiking miles from here.'

'How do you know?'

'I spotted it when we were coming down.'

'Well, let's go find the damn place.'

'After dark.'

'You don't make any sense.'

'Thomas.' Banning sat up irritably. 'We won't have a chance out there now. That goddamn farmhouse could be anywhere. Want to flip a coin and pick a direction?'

'You pointed.'

'To a big chunk of desert and mountains,' he retorted. 'A needle in a scary haystack, brother. Drop dead in that neighbourhood and only the vultures will find you.'

'And at night?'

'The odds are better.'

'Why, old wise man?'

'Our farmhouse will obviously put on a light,' he replied, ignoring Allen's sarcasm. 'In fact, if I saw one farmhouse in that area, there must be others. And they will all light up at night. And lights can be seen for miles in country like this. Especially from up here.'

Allen stood, brushed dirt off his flying suit, and started moving cautiously over the summit's edge.

'Hey!' Banning pulled himself up fast, and watched Allen begin to descend the mountain, one careful step at a time. 'Where the hell are you going, Tom Allen?'

'To inspect the Eagle Rock!' he whooped over his shoulder, copying Banning. 'I might fly the old bastard to your farmhouse when night-time comes!'

Before fading, the last of the day's sun put a brilliant shine on the jagged rock formations, deep canyons, and stretches of desert sand. The vivid colours were accentuated, and the glorious sight bedazzled the aviators, at the same time reminding them that they were alone and lost in this primitive, desolate region of the country.

Earlier, after a close inspection, Allen had left the damaged aircraft in place, realizing that parts and special tools would be needed, and this realistic assessment had added to his concern and frustration. He kicked angrily at pebbles on the way back up the mountain slope.

Dusk created weird shadow patterns, transforming the colourful hills, sand, and wild stone carvings into a frightening montage, straight out of a bad dream, or a drunken binge, thought Allen, as Banning snoozed peacefully on his back.

A short time later, it was dark, with the moon hidden behind a sudden grouping of thick, low-hanging clouds. Suddenly, his eyes were glued on a spot a long way off, to the right of their position, and he sat in a trance for an instant, until he was able to whisper excitedly to himself, 'I do not believe this.'

Seconds passed, and the mechanic finally blinked repeatedly, and then jumped to his feet, and screamed, 'JAMES HERMAN!' A powerful echo bounced the name off hills and mountains, and rolled it across the valleys, and over the desert sand.

The pilot sprang up like a jack-in-the-box, and sat stunned, waiting to get his bearings, and an explanation from Allen.

'You called the shot!' the mechanic exclaimed. 'We've got a light over there! It must be your farmhouse, James Herman!'

'Must be,' Banning agreed, wide awake now, and smiling broadly. 'Prepare yourself for a rugged expedition,' he advised, staring into the distance. 'Like I said, that place is about ten or twelve miles away from here. Past the stretch of desert. Just before the hills. Quite a hike.'

'And it's dark as hell,' said Allen, beginning to deflate. 'We'll bust our asses for sure.'

'Not if we're careful.' Banning peered up at the sky. 'The clouds are scattering,' he declared. 'I expect a big, bright moon, any time now, Thomas.'

At that moment, from somewhere just below the summit's edge, a long, loud, spine-tingling howl broke the silence around them, and Tom Allen reacted at once. 'Oh, dear God, no, no, no! I just can't take them – absolutely not – they goose-pimple me, man – especially at night – and that's a fact.'

'A coyote?' Banning was laughing. 'A poor old prairie wolf wailing for his mate? You have to be joking.'

'I'll build a large fire and stay right here,' said Allen. 'Call me when you reach the farmhouse.'

'Know how to handle these dogs properly, Thomas?' Banning asked, filling a sack with items brought from the plane by Allen, odds and ends useful for the night-time safari. 'An old black California prospector taught me years ago,' he continued, as the mechanic began helping with the preparations. 'Want to know the secret?'

'I have my own.' Allen was busy putting matches, a pen-knife, and other articles into the travelling bag. 'You blast them with a double-barrelled shotgun.'

Another howl cut through the quiet and reverberated until Allen shivered and cursed under his breath. Banning suddenly placed the sack on the ground and said, 'Listen to this, partner.'

He moved a few steps closer to the ridge, cupped his hands around his mouth and, in an unusually high pitch, howled longer and louder than the coyote. A few seconds after Banning's echo had died away, another howl came from somewhere down the slope, and the pilot walked back to Allen, smiling with satisfaction.

'That old black California prospector was right,' he said, watching Allen pick up the sack and finish the packing. 'It works every time.'

'What works every time?'

'That mating call.'

'You are definitely a fruit-cake, James Herman.'

'Our friend on the hill now thinks I'm a hot lover,' Banning explained, checking the contents of his flight jacket pockets.

'Male or bitch – they fall for it every time. Why use a shotgun, Thomas?'

'That old black California prospector was crazier than you are.' Allen closed the bag and hung it over his shoulder. 'Wouldn't the howling wolves want to meet this hot piece of prairie tail?'

'They might,' Banning answered, ready for the hike. 'But never in order to attack. The special mating call reduces their natural aggression and makes them docile and easy to handle.'

Allen stared at the pilot for a long moment, before shaking his head sadly. He turned and moved towards the edge of the ridge. 'So,' he said, 'we'll either get fucked by the elements – or a pack of horny coyotes.'

After navigating past the Eagle Rock, and stumbling the rest of the way down the mountain slope, Allen and Banning, with their eyes fixed on the light in the distance, started a cautious inch-at-a-time walk and crawl through a vast wilderness of rocky highs and lows and spectacular stone formations. As Banning had predicted, the thick, low-hanging clouds soon scattered, and the moon came out, big and bright, with a clear sky full of stars. At least they were able to find their way, and move faster and more confidently.

Both men had cuts and bruises from tumbles on jagged rock. And, along with the unsettling coyote howls, and other eerie sounds, they had to watch out for stones falling from over-hanging slabs, ankle-snapping crevices, and knife-like thorns on cactus bushes. And all the time, Banning repeated the same instructions, a reminder, over and over again. 'Let's keep our eyes on the light and run a steady course, no matter what. This is a beacon flight, partner.'

Time passed, and their concern mounted, because the distant light never seemed to get any closer. And they were becoming hungry, and weary, and ready for sleep. Just before they reached the stretch of desert, a very deep ravine appeared, a long trench, a gully full of powdery black chalk, cutting straight across their path. There was no way around it.

The dust swirled in all directions as the aviators made a descent, unwillingly gaining momentum, until they lost their balance, tripped, and rolled to a stop at the bottom, uninjured, but coloured a darker shade of black. They sat up, looked at each other, and roared with laughter. Brushing failed to remove the thick chalk from their hair, faces, and clothing.

Banning searched the travelling sack for rags, while Allen raised his black minstrel face to the sky, and pleaded in a theatrically reverent manner, 'Oh, dear Lord, please don't rub it in – things were bad enough the way you had them.'

And then his entire body turned into instant granite. 'Holy, shit,' he whispered through clenched teeth. 'It can't be real.'

'What's the problem?'

'Don't speak – or move,' Allen breathed, still paralysed, and staring up wide-eyed. 'Lift your head – take a peek – and freeze.'

Banning followed the direction of Allen's gaze. 'Holy shit,' he repeated. 'It is real, man.'

Just above them, with the moon and stars as a backdrop, five large and savage-looking coyotes were standing quietly in a line, glaring down at them from the rim of the gully. They seemed to be debating their next move. Allen and Banning did the same.

'No mating calls, James Herman.'

'That old prospector –'

'Screw him.'

'We've got some heavy rocks down here to throw.'

'They'll become meaner.'

'I still think the old prospector's trick is –'

'Want to get raped and eaten by five wild dogs?'

'How about a knife and a hammer?'

'Forget the Tarzan crap, James Herman.'

'Kill the leader – the big one in the middle – and they'll all run.'

'More tips from the old prospector?'

'A jungle fact, Thomas.'

Suddenly, a long, loud howl from the leader silenced both men, and Allen's goose-pimples returned at once.

'I'll see you later, James Herman.'

'*What?*'

Allen reached into his jacket pocket with care, removed his goggles, and put them on. The other dogs joined their leader in a howling chorus, accompanied by echoes.

'Have you lost your marbles, Thomas?'

'Some of them.' Allen bent over, grabbed two handfuls of chalk, and with both dirt-filled fists high above his head, he took a few bold steps up the ravine towards the howling coyotes. His partner looked on, mesmerized. The mechanic resembled a weird and clumsily constructed robot, and the shrill pitch of his voice matched his appearance.

'SHUT UP, DOG!' he screamed, moving faster up the side of the pit, with his arms still raised and barely visible in a cloud of chalky black dust. 'AND GET THE HELL OUT OF MY WAY! RIGHT NOW!

Unexpectedly, the howling stopped at once, and so did Allen, just before reaching the coyotes' position at the top of the slope. The five animals examined the strange, powdery black creature with suspicion and with what appeared to be a touch of fear. Holding his arms even higher above his head, Allen took a few more steps forward, in the style of a mechanical monster. Eventually, he confronted the pack's leader, a heavy-boned, muscular prairie wolf, with menacing jaws and razor-sharp fangs. They eyed each other, while the rest of the pack stood quietly, apparently waiting for a signal to attack or retreat.

As the seconds passed, Allen felt his legs, lips, eyelids, and right fist begin to tremble, and the realization that he was now hopelessly trapped, unable to back off or admit defeat, forced him to take action. He suddenly growled, an animal's growl, deep in his throat. Contorting his face grotesquely, he pulled back his arm in the manner of a professional baseball pitcher, shrieked 'GO' and then threw a handful of blinding chalk into the leader's face. Before the coyote was able to react, Allen repeated the procedure with his other arm, and this time, on the word 'GO!' and as the black dust flew, the lead dog yelped, whined, turned abruptly, and fled, with the rest of the pack right behind him. 'AND DON'T COME BACK!' Allen yelled, mainly for Banning's benefit, although his voice was now shaking as much as the other parts of his body. 'YOU GODDAMN SAVAGES!'

Banning roused himself out of his hypnotic state, scrambled up the pit side, stood beside Allen, and watched the animals disappear over the moonlit rocks and hills.

'How about that clever trick, James Herman?' Allen asked, with his vocal cords quivering even more than the Eagle Rock's wings. 'Taught to me by an old black Oklahoma preacher-man, who said, "Whenever the devil rears his ugly head – pump yourself up with God's gift of courage – grab old Satan by the horns – and scare the wicked shit out of him."'

'A real fine job, Thomas,' said Banning, looking over the mechanic's dust-covered and twitching features. 'But I could have used that mating call and produced the same results. As we saw, no self-respecting coyote would ever lay a paw on you – especially for romantic purposes. I have never seen anything so damn black and ugly in all of my life.'

10

With their eyes on the light in the distance, Allen and Banning trudged over the desert sand, a longer stretch than anticipated, with giant dunes and level, monotonous patches, a dreamlike wasteland, glistening under a perfect moon.

By eleven o'clock that night, after conquering over half the desert, both men were utterly weary and unable to continue without taking a short rest. At the foot of a large dune they settled the sack beside them, and leaned back against the soft sand. Neither man spoke a word. Gradually their eyes closed. Allen dozed first, followed by Banning, and they slept until nearly one o'clock in the morning. When they awoke, and searched frantically for the farmhouse light, it was gone, obviously turned off by the occupants before retiring for the night.

'No use cursing ourselves, James Herman,' Allen advised despondently. 'A man's body can only take a certain amount of punishment.' He hauled himself to his feet, lifted the sack, and threw it over his shoulder. 'We just reached our limits.'

'I should have known better.' Banning was already up, waiting, in no mood for consolation.

'What now?'

'No choice,' Banning replied gruffly, pointing into the distance slightly to the right of them. 'We know the general direction. Let's head that way and take our chances.'

With a firm grip on the sack, Allen fell into step beside Banning, lowered his head, and whispered intensely, 'Do it for us, baby.' He was kissing something in the palm of his free hand. 'Take us straight to the front door without a pause or a detour.'

'A pocket compass won't guarantee anything.'

'This is not a pocket compass, James Herman,' Allen corrected at once. 'I am kissing a prairie wolf's tooth on a cowhide key-ring.' He dangled the object in front of the pilot, as they tramped heavily over the sand. 'A good luck charm from Randolph Scott Dunlop. Remember?'

'Dunlop.' Banning spat out the name and made a sour face. 'That sure as hell won't guarantee anything but trouble.'

'He was a nice kid.'

'Daddy probably put a curse on his tooth.'

'Now just loosen up, James Herman.'

'I had no right to fall asleep with a beacon in my sights,' he said bitterly. 'No amount of good luck charms will ever change that fact. It's on my record now.'

'We both fell asleep, partner.' Allen stuffed the trinket into his flight jacket pocket. 'You can't crumble over one error.'

'It only takes one in this business, man.'

By two thirty in the morning, after covering what they knew should have been the end of the sandy stretch, the aviators realized that Dunlop's charm had failed to work. There was no sign of the farmhouse on the course they had first taken, or on four others they had tried. Both men were now physically and mentally exhausted and, for the first time, seriously concerned about their chances of survival.

After one last knee-buckling, heart-pounding climb over a high and particularly soft-grained dune, they stopped at the bottom and collapsed. All responsibilities forgotten, they gave themselves up to sleep without any feelings of guilt.

Allen heard the voice first, thought he was dreaming, and settled back against the sand dune, finding a more comfortable position. But the husky drawl seemed to grow louder, and more insistent, and the mechanic gradually realized that the sound was not coming from inside his own head.

'I've said good-morning five times.' The voice paused, while Allen sat up, shook away cobwebs, and poked Banning with an elbow. 'Will you gentlemen please give me the courtesy of a reply?'

Allen opened his eyes, and found himself staring into the barrel of a shotgun. He blinked, focused on a badge, blinked again. The uniformed stranger at the other end of the barrel had a narrow, grim face marked by a prominent nose, pale blue eyes, and unusually thin lips. His complexion was dark and leathery, and he needed a shave.

'Good-morning, sir.' Allen beamed moronically at the lawman, while Banning propped himself up, and took in the scene without saying a word.

'My name is Dexter Winthrop, Junior,' the lawman drawled, keeping his weapon pointed at the aviators. 'I'm a Texas Ranger. Now who the hell are you?'

'My name is Thomas C. Allen,' the mechanic replied, forcing his eyes to avoid the shotgun. 'And this is James Herman Banning. We're aviators – who must have overflown our mark – because of clouds.'

'Aviators?'

'That's right, sir.'

'What are you doing here?'

'Our plane crash-landed on that mountain-top.' Allen pointed to a range in the distance. 'So we hiked down here to find a house and get some help. But we got lost, and fell asleep on the sand.'

'How come you're not dead?' Dexter Winthrop, Junior, looked both men over suspiciously. 'How come you don't have wounds, and blood, and busted-up bones?'

'Mr Banning stall-landed our plane expertly, sir,' Allen explained with pride, before shrugging his shoulders, and adding, 'I guess we were also very lucky.'

'You are also full of pig shit.' The Texas Ranger moved the shotgun closer to Allen's head. 'Nobody can land an airplane in those mountains and walk away without a scratch.' He glared at Banning, noted the pilot's hostile expression, and returned his attention to Allen. 'And I never did hear of a nigger flyer, anyway. So explain what you people are doing in these parts at five o'clock in the morning. And understand that I'm not a patient or tolerant man.'

'My partner has already told you,' Banning answered. 'Is it a crime to fall asleep in the desert?'

'No,' the Ranger replied acidly, his eyes burning into Banning. 'But it's a crime to kill a postman in El Paso.'

'*What*?' Tom Allen looked shocked for a moment, but a smile returned, after he had exchanged a quick glance with Banning. 'I'm afraid you are on the wrong trail, Mr Winthrop.'

'Ranger Winthrop.'

'Sorry,' said Allen, nodding respectfully. 'Ranger Winthrop. Please understand that we never reached El Paso. Our plane was forced down on the mountain and –'

'Shut your mouth, boy,' the Ranger interrupted. 'A special transport postman was bashed over the head and robbed last night, at precisely seven-twenty, on Post Road, just off Rancho Drive, El Paso. He died from his injuries in Barksdale General. Two reliable witnesses saw a nigger, of medium height and build, running from the scene. The suspect jumped into the back seat of a car with another nigger at the wheel.' The Ranger took a short step forward, and pressed the shotgun barrel against

105

Banning's forehead, failing to make him flinch. 'Now ain't this a coincidence?' he asked mockingly. 'At ten after five the next morning, I find me two niggers fast asleep in the desert – sixty-two miles east of El Paso – claiming they crash-landed an airplane on top of the ruggedest mountains in the area – and there ain't one harmful mark on them.'

'You're making a terrible mistake, Mr – I mean – Ranger Winthrop,' said Allen, desperately. 'We can prove everything – if you just give us a chance.'

'That you'll get soon enough, boy.' Without moving the shot-gun, Winthrop took a closer look at the aviators' flying suits, as though he were noticing them for the first time. 'Craziest goddamn disguises I ever did see.'

'Can we please explain –'

'Get up!' the Texas Ranger ordered, cutting Allen off in mid-sentence.

Allen stood first, and Banning followed, as Winthrop stepped back with the shotgun covering both men. 'When I say move – start walking slowly in front of me,' he commanded. 'Go around that next big sand dune and you'll see my car. Can you drive?' he asked Allen.

Allen nodded.

'Get in behind the wheel.' He looked fiercely at Banning. 'You sit next to him up front. I'll be on the back seat directing with this shotgun right behind your heads. One funny move and you'll be black pulp. Understand?'

Allen hesitated, scowled, and then gave the hint of another nod.

'Are we going to El Paso?' asked Banning.

The Ranger seemed to be debating whether or not to answer. 'No,' he said finally. 'Jeff Hunter's place at the end of the sand. He's a very influential man in these parts. I'll use his phone and call the El Paso Ranger station. They'll advise me in this case. With luck I'll get to shoot you both dead without trial.'

'Do you work out of El Paso, Ranger Winthrop?' Allen asked, ignoring the man's threats. 'You seem to patrol an awful lot of territory.'

'My base is Fort Tucker,' he answered, showing by voice and expression that the interview was about to be concluded. 'I've been visiting my good friend Jeff Hunter and his family. We heard quite a bit of unusual coyote noise out here all night. And God bless those dogs for leadin' me to you. Now get moving.' He motioned with the shotgun.

106

The aviators plodded ahead of him over the sand.

'Dunlop's charm really worked miracles,' Banning remarked bitterly. 'Five attempts at that damn farmhouse and we even missed the road.'

'Come now, James Herman,' said Allen, trying to be positive, 'We're finally back on course with your beacon, ain't we?'

Some while later, feeling extremely humiliated, angry, and out-of-place, the aviators were in the spacious, wooden-beamed living-room of Jeff Hunter's ranch-house, perching stiffly on the edge of a sofa while the Ranger stood leaning against a fireplace wall, facing them with an arrogant smirk, and his shotgun aimed for maximum destruction. The seemingly ineradicable black chalk which covered them contributed to their embarrassment and demoralization as they waited for the Hunter family to come downstairs. Ten minutes earlier, Winthrop had shouted loudly that he had returned from the desert with guests, two very special ones.

'Now you'd better act with great humility and respect,' the Ranger warned, as descending footsteps were heard on the stairs. 'These folks are high class and very important around here. Stand up when you see them.'

Jeff Hunter entered the room first, then his wife, and then a young son and daughter. The entire family came to an abrupt halt and stood with shocked expressions the moment they saw Winthrop, his gun, and their two special guests. Much to the Ranger's annoyance, Allen and Banning had remained seated, although they had turned their heads towards the new arrivals. Instead of the swaggering, rednecked, mean-faced, Ku Klux Klanish types they had expected, they saw a kindly-looking, handsome-featured family. Judging by their eyes and mouths, they were all accustomed to smiling on most occasions.

'The coyotes had a right to be disturbed last night, Jefferson,' the Ranger drawled. 'I've got myself two dangerous niggers here.'

'What did they do?' Hunter asked, moving over to Winthrop's side of the room, with the others following. 'I really don't like pointed weapons in this house, Dexter,' he said, turning and inspecting the aviators. 'Unless there is an extremely important reason.'

'How about murder?' the Ranger asked dramatically. 'You heard the radio last night. I found them asleep near the Eldorado dunes at five o'clock. A lucky break – thanks to the wolves and some professional gun handling.'

'Why are they dressed like that?' asked Mrs Hunter. 'These men are wearing flying outfits.'

'Now that's the crazy part, Amelia. Your guests claim they crash-landed an airplane on the peaks, and walked away without a scratch on their putrid black bodies.'

The Hunter family continued to study Allen and Banning, and the aviators stared back at them, feeling like animals in a zoo. They waited for an opportune moment to speak, without losing their pride, or control, or the remote possibility of support from the Hunters.

'What's your next move, Dexter?' Jeff Hunter asked the Ranger. 'I don't want my place used as a jailhouse. Are you driving them to the Fort?'

'I'd like to call El Paso and get instructions, Jefferson,' the Ranger answered. 'This is a murder case and these niggers are very dangerous. Will you cover them while I phone?'

'Is the shotgun really necessary?'

'Absolutely,' Winthrop replied without a hesitation. 'For your family's safety and because this is an official police matter. Please cover them, and shoot to kill if they wiggle a little finger.'

With a curious expression on his face, Jeff Hunter stood near the fireplace wall, pointing the shotgun at the aviators, as instructed. The other members of the family had taken seats close to Hunter, and they also had inquisitive eyes riveted on the two men, who could do nothing, at the moment, but return their gazes.

'How did you get so black?' The young girl finally broke the silence, then realized that her question was badly worded. 'I mean, all that powder on your hair and faces?'

'We fell into a ravine full of chalk last night,' Allen explained, venturing a smile at the Hunter girl. 'And that's how we got so black,' he added, pleased to see her return the smile.

Jeff Hunter had lowered the shotgun a little, although it was still on target, and ready for trouble. 'I would like a truthful statement before Winthrop returns,' he demanded. 'Did you men crash-land an airplane in the mountains yesterday?'

'Yes, sir,' Allen replied. 'We did.'

'What about El Paso?' Mrs Hunter asked. 'Ranger Winthrop claims that you robbed and killed a postman. Are you denying his allegations?'

'Yes, ma'am,' Allen replied again, while Banning stared directly into the eyes of Jefferson Hunter. 'Engine trouble brought us down after we missed El Paso. We don't know anything about the murder of a postman.' He paused, looked away from Mrs Hunter, and addressed her husband. 'Will you please give us a chance to tell our story?'

'Go ahead,' Hunter answered, shifting his attention from one man to the other. 'But we're not the police,' he reminded. 'You'll have to convince Dexter Winthrop and the Rangers in El Paso.'

'That's fair enough,' said Allen, relaxing a little. 'We've got the truth on our side, Mr Hunter. And that gives us the advantage,' and he swiftly recounted the story of their flight, showing their credentials, and flight documents. 'Ranger Winthrop has detained the wrong men,' he finally concluded.

The room was quiet for a moment as the Hunters digested the information. They continued to stare at the two black aviators, though in a different way now.

'Let's go find the plane, Dad,' the young man suddenly blurted. 'We can use the pick-up and then do some climbing.'

A strangely dejected Dexter Winthrop entered the room before Jefferson Hunter could respond to his son's proposition. He seated himself into a chair near the family, stretched his long legs out full length, and rested the heels of his polished boots on a low footstool.

'What's the problem, Dexter?' Hunter asked, aware that he had lowered the shotgun completely without being reprimanded by the Ranger. 'Did you get through to El Paso?'

'I did,' Winthrop answered, apparently absorbed in the colourful pattern of a Mexican rug in the centre of the floor. 'State Police grabbed three niggers on the outskirts of town about four o'clock this morning. Witnesses identified the killer positively and all three men finally confessed. They have been formally charged, booked, and are now behind bars without bail.'

Mrs Hunter smiled first, followed by her children, then Tom Allen, then Jefferson Hunter, as he handed the shotgun back to Winthrop.

'You treated us like scum without any justification, Winthrop,' rasped Banning. 'How about an apology? That's the least you can do.'

With all eyes on him, the Ranger glared at Banning, and raised the shotgun again. 'Apology?' He twisted his thin, weather-creased face into a parody of a smile. 'We're driving to Fort Tucker, nigger. You and your monkey have a lot of questions to answer – starting with a fantasy plane crash in the mountains.'

'Dexter.' Mrs Hunter seemed upset. 'These two men have told us their story. And we believe them. Daniel and Jefferson will try to locate the aircraft. Why not wait and see if they find it?'

'A complete waste of time, Amelia,' Winthrop answered, keeping his eyes on Banning. 'I've had enough police experience with liars to know –'

'Dexter.' Jefferson Hunter interrupted with an unexpected touch of anger. 'We'll go back to the mountain with them and search for the plane. I'll phone your superiors at the Fort and get clearance, if you think it's necessary.'

'Don't put yourself out, Jefferson,' the Ranger stuttered, obviously backing down from a man who had a great deal of local influence. 'I believe that a search is in order. When are you starting?'

'After I rustle up a good breakfast for these two men.' Mrs Hunter looked at the aviators and smiled pleasantly. 'I have a feeling they need some home-cooked food and hot coffee very badly.'

With an appreciative expression on his face, Tom Allen smiled back, and for the first time in a long while, James Herman Banning did the same.

Later in the day, after the plane had been located and Dexter Winthrop had been put in his place once and for all by Jefferson Hunter, Allen and Banning discussed their problems with the family. Realistically, the plane should be dismantled, carted sixty-two miles to El Paso for professional work, reassembled there, and flown out of a proper airport for the next hop. But the aviators certainly could not afford an elaborate operation of this kind, and Jefferson Hunter had explained very honestly, and sadly, that the Depression had nearly ruined him, and things were getting worse on the ranch every day.

An emergency, low-budget plan was devised. The aviators were to make a list of the absolutely essential parts needed, then Banning would call the El Paso Airport and order the parts in the name of Jefferson Hunter, explaining that he would arrive with Mr Hunter in the early evening to settle the bill and make the collection. Once there, Hunter would pay what he could afford and, if necessary, arrange for credit for the rest. He would also, through his contacts, get permission for Allen and Banning to requisition the appropriate tools, and scrounge around the airport's hangars for any throw-away material – airplane junk – that might be useful for this latest patch-up operation.

The first phase of the almost impossible rescue mission worked perfectly and, after returning from El Paso with the parts, tools, and selected bits and pieces, the aviators were invited to clean up, eat, and stay the night in one of the vacant ranch-hand dwellings near the main house. They were brought food and coffee from Mrs Hunter's kitchen, and reminded to be up and ready for a quick breakfast at five-thirty in the morning. Phase two of the Eagle Rock restoration plan was scheduled for six on the dot. It was to involve both Banning and Allen, Jefferson Hunter and his son, and their two ranch workers.

After detaching the damaged wings and a few other sections, the rescue team laboriously carried the pathetic contraption – which no longer resembled an airplane – down the slope, slipping, tripping, always off-balance. After much effort, and a lot of cursing and groaning, the thing was carefully chained on to a large and powerful timber-hauling truck waiting at the foot of the mountain. It was then brought back to the ranch, unloaded, and laid out on grazing land near the main house.

By five-thirty that afternoon, the knocked-together, born-yet-again airplane was sitting right side up on the grass, with her wings in place, and her tail section recognizable. Both landing gears were fixed and steady and there was no sign that there had ever been a hole in the fuselage. Along with the other repairs, the two broken push rods, intake and exhaust, had been replaced successfully. Finally, the old Eagle Rock had been scrubbed, polished and touched up with paint, where needed.

'You know something, Thomas?' Standing beside Allen, a short distance away from the others, Banning was ogling the finished product. 'I'm madly in love with that airplane.'

'Me too, partner.'

'She's ugly-beautiful – loyal – stubborn as an ox – and unique.' Banning smiled at the Eagle Rock. 'That plane sits out there like she can't wait for us to get in and move on. What a gutsy little bitch!'

'Why don't you marry her, James Herman?' Allen smiled and ogled with him. 'She's better-looking and has more class than any of the gals I've seen you hustle.'

'*Marriage?*' Banning was still gazing at the plane. 'I don't love her that much, Thomas. Life's too short for marriage. Because the world is full of airplanes – all shapes and sizes – and I want to get acquainted with as many as possible before my number is up.' He

111

turned, punched Allen playfully on the arm, and smiled again, as they walked over to the rest of the onlookers. 'And besides,' he joked. 'You covered up her goddamn hole.'

At six-thirty in the evening, after the aviators had expressed their heartfelt gratitude to the Hunters – who in addition to all their help had boosted the treasury balance with a ten dollar bill – and after the Gold Book had been signed by all, Banning gunned the motor, taxied across the grass, picked up speed, and at the last possible moment, left the ground, nearly ripping a piece of adobe tile off Hunter's ranch-house. On the steep climb, a wheel actually clipped the edge of a rocky hill, and kicked up dust. But they were airborne, overjoyed, and on their way again.

The Eagle Rock made the sixty-two mile flight in clear skies, without incident, landing safely at the El Paso Airport, Texas where a senior field attendant named Owens, whom they had met the day before when collecting the parts with Hunter, ensured co-operative service. While taking gas and water, Banning explained that they had planned to take-off immediately for Sweetwater, even though it might mean risking some night flying. However, a late weather report changed the pilot's thinking at once. Thick fog was expected to block out the Guadalupe Mountains within an hour. The slow-moving Eagle Rock would never make the one hundred and ten mile flight before the pea-soup descended.

Mr Owens offered to hangar the plane for the night without charge, and make the airport lounge available for sleeping. They could also use the toilets and wash-room, provided they did so discreetly. There was an Army Base a short distance away, Owens told them, which had a public dining-room and a corner section reserved for Negroes.

They were up early the next morning, after a reasonably good sleep on comfortable leather benches. But once again, the weather reports delayed them, although an attendant said that the low clouds had started lifting, and they might be able to take off at one o'clock in the afternoon and head for Midland, not Sweetwater.

At exactly two-thirty, with Banning at the controls, the Eagle Rock was in the air, flying due east of El Paso over the Hueco Mountains. The desert was next, and then Tinoja Pinto, to the right of Cerro Diablo, which is five thousand five hundred feet high. After ten miles of looking down at the Salt Basin, and five more miles of rugged country, they approached the Guadalupe Mountains, and heavy fog. When they finally pulled out of it, the rains came, and the engine revs dropped to 1300, and the vibrations started again. Luckily, Banning spotted an emergency field near a town called Porterville. Without time to circle and check for direction, Banning made a cross-wind landing, and the plane was tossed and bounced, but she finally straightened out without dragging a wing.

Allen found the trouble, fixed the engine, and ordered five dollars' worth of gas – a safety measure, because they should have had enough for the forty-mile flight to Wink, Texas, provided there was no change in the wind from cross to head.

After they crossed the Pecos River at Arla, the rain started again. Oil derricks began to appear, and the smell of crude rose unpleasantly. The tops of wet storage tanks glistened. Wink, Texas was directly below them. Banning circled the field and throttled the engine for a landing. It was 4:15 pm. Still time to reach Midland before nightfall.

11

At the small airport in Wink, the aviators ordered gasoline for the hop to Midland, but the slow-moving, droopy-jawed attendant just gaped at them and the plane, with an idiotic look of amazement on his face. Again the order was placed, and the attendant finally responded, a halting word at a time.

'We don't keep gas on this field,' he explained, still astonished by the new arrivals. 'It has to be brought in from town about seven miles away.'

'Damn.' Banning was concerned about facing another delay after the mountain-top crash-landing. 'We're trying to make Midland before dark,' he explained. 'Can you get things moving right now?'

'No, I can't,' the attendant replied bluntly. 'Aviation gas ain't kept on hand anywhere. Don't you know that aviation gas is refined to order around here?'

'First time we've heard about it,' Allen replied, attempting to move the conversation along. 'Now how do we get some gasoline for our airplane?'

'There's only one way,' the attendant answered. 'You have to give the refiner four or five hours' notice.'

'Shit.' Banning glanced at Allen and his feelings were obvious. 'That takes care of Midland today.' He returned his attention to the attendant. 'How about putting us up for the night?'

'We'll take care of the – plane,' he replied, giving the Eagle Rock a curious look. 'But, remember – this is an emergency field. We don't have hangars or any fancy stuff.'

'Understood.' Banning looked around for a road or some signs of civilization. 'You say that town is about seven miles away?'

'That's what I said.'

'Can we hitch a ride?'

'I'll take you in,' the attendant answered, motioning for the aviators to follow him as he started a slow and lazy walk towards a dilapidated hut, presumably the field's office. 'We can't leave now,' he explained, as they ambled along. 'My night man comes on duty at six, and then we'll go.'.

*

Before leaving the airport, Allen and Banning watched the Eagle Rock being settled for the night with three stakes, some ropes, and four lanterns to protect her in case a pilot was forced to land on the darkened field. The aviators were very pleased both with the arrangements, and the attendant's unexpected helpfulness, although his long, curious stares and amused expression had become a damn nuisance.

About a quarter of a mile from Wink proper, at the start of Main Street, they came to the coloured section of town. The driver stopped in front of a café and the aviators climbed out.

'I'll pick you up here at five-thirty tomorrow morning,' the attendant called out.' 'My night man already placed an order with the Humble Oil Service Station,' he added, taking his time, as usual. 'The refiner should have your gasoline finished and on the field by seven am.'

Both men thank him.

'You are the very first coloured pilots I have ever seen,' he announced, finally saying what was on his mind. 'Do you all fly crazy-looking planes like the one I staked down at the field?'

'No,' Banning replied, with a broad smile on his face. 'Only the rich and lucky ones like Tom Allen and myself. All the others fly water-melons.'

The attendant laughed heartily and drove away.

There were only a few people in the stuffy, box-like, sparsely furnished café as Allen and Banning entered. Four shabbily dressed black men and a stout black woman were sitting at separate tables, bare tables, without cloths, or plates, or food, or drink. They all looked up, stared inquisitively, but said nothing, as the aviators took a table of their own against a drab, paint-chipped wall.

After staring back for several moments, and receiving no greeting of any kind, Banning asked the woman, 'Is this place open?'

'Of course it's open,' she answered, in a deep, husky voice, boldly surveying the aviators' flying suits, and Banning's smooth good looks. 'You boys are in here, aren't you?'

'We're in here, true enough,' said Allen, grinning amiably at her. 'But is anybody serving food and drink?'

'I'm the anybody,' the woman answered, acknowledging that she was the owner. 'And I can tell you that no meals have been served in this place for over thirty days. Because this town is flat broke, stranger. Especially the coloured section.'

'You should close the doors and take down the sign.' Allen glanced around at the four men, who were still silently staring. 'What do they do in here?' he asked. 'Pray and take shelter?'

'Sit – and talk sometimes – and commiserate.' The stout woman's round, fleshy face, which might have been jolly once, was now downright forlorn. 'Wink used to be a booming oil town, you know. And we all lived pretty well. There must have been around three hundred shacks in the coloured section. And now we've got about forty or fifty.' Abruptly, she leaned forward, resting her elbows and huge bosom on the table. 'But you boys didn't come in here for a history lesson, that's for sure.' She pointed to their flying suits. 'Is that some kind of military get-up?'

'We're aviators,' Allen replied simply. 'Our plane is on the field waiting for gasoline. We'll be leaving for Midland early in the morning.'

'Well, I declare,' the woman remarked, very much impressed. 'But I figured you boys were big city, and doing something special.' She glanced at Banning and smiled flirtatiously. 'There ain't nobody around here who looks like you, handsome. Can I fix you a nice meal?'

'That would be just great, beautiful,' Banning replied, switching on the charm. 'But I thought your kitchen was closed.'

'Tell you what, send out for some things and I'll prepare them for you. We've got a stocked grocery store down the block.'

'A butcher too.' One of the men finally spoke up. 'There were some fresh chicken parts in the window yesterday. Want me to go, Florence?'

'Now that's strictly up to these gentlemen, Tyrone,' the woman called Florence answered, her admiring eyes still on Banning. 'You don't have to buy for the house, handsome. I'll be cooking just for you and your friend. And it will be my pleasure.'

Allen took a quick look at Banning, saw indecision, and turned back to the stout woman. 'We don't really want you slaving away in the kitchen, ma'am,' he said pleasantly. 'I suggest we pick up a salami, some crackers, and apples, and have ourselves a fine snack, without any trouble or mess. Do you have coffee and a can of milk?'

'Not even that.'

'Well, add it to the shopping list, Tyrone,' said Allen, reaching into his flight jacket for the money. 'Here's a one dollar bill. You can bring us the change.'

116

The man stood up and the aviators had their first full length glimpse of him. Tyrone was about forty, a tall, skinny, round-shouldered character, with greying hair, and large, sad eyes. His dark, baggy trousers were frayed, and creased, and much too short, exposing grubby ankle socks, and worn-out shoes. A tattered blue sweater covered the top part of him.

'I'm buying the dessert with my own cash,' Tyrone announced proudly, in a voice which lacked volume and resonance. 'Sure hope you folks enjoy liquorice as much as I do.'

'Enjoy what?' Banning grimaced, but then caught himself, when he realized how serious the tall man was. 'Great idea,' he said, as Tyrone moved to the door. 'But it's our treat. Don't touch your money.'

'This one is definitely on me,' said Tyrone, beaming at the aviators. 'I'm proud that gentlemen like you appreciate my taste.'

He went out the door.

'And why not?' Banning looked directly at Allen, straight-faced. 'Name one person on this earth who doesn't enjoy liquorice – especially with salami.'

By the time Tyrone returned with the snack, Florence's oil stove was ready to start heating the coffee. He had brought back the exact change, with a proper accounting, and he had paid for the liquorice himself. The salami, crackers, and apples were enjoyed by all. Only Banning refused the dessert, claiming politely that a back tooth had been giving him trouble, and there was no time for dentistry on a tightly scheduled flight to New York City. The three other men, who were never introduced, remained silent, except for a variety of noisy eating sounds, and an occasional belch.

'Where are you boys sleeping tonight?' Florence asked, with her gaze fixed on Banning. 'Sadly, I don't have an apartment of my own anymore – just this café – and a drag-out bed.' She sat up straight, either to ease her back, or show off her enormous figure. 'But,' she went on, continuing to gaze at Banning, 'you are perfectly welcome to stay and squeeze in – any way you can.'

'How sweet and gracious of you, Florence, my dear,' said Allen, enjoying the prospect of Banning's predicament. 'If it's really not too much bother, we would be delighted to stay – and squeeze in somewhere.'

'Now, Thomas.' Banning was on the spot. 'We've put Florence out enough already.' There was an unfamiliar bead of nervous

117

perspiration on his forehead. 'I truly believe that we should not impose on her any further.'

'You can both stay at my place tonight,' said Tyrone, coming to the pilot's rescue. 'I've got two spare floor mattresses, nothing fancy. And it might also be a tight squeeze. But you're sure welcome.'

'Tyrone.' Banning turned to him with relief. 'You are proving to be a man of honesty – good taste – generosity – and impeccable timing.'

Tyrone gawked dumbly at the pilot for several moments, and then scratched his head, blinked his eyes, and mumbled, 'Thank you kindly.'

After traipsing through a smelly, depressing, ramshackle tenement neighbourhood, Allen, Banning and Tyrone moved in single file down a rat-infested, garbage-strewn alley behind rows of broken-down wooden shacks. At the end, and just around the corner, they arrived at their destination.

Tyrone had one very large room, with a low ceiling, a high window, a slightly tilted floor of warped planks, a table, three chairs, a water bucket, an oil stove, and a bed, which was just as skinny and untidy as the owner. The room also had an extremely unpleasant odour. For some reason, a worn blanket, which hung from rusty hooks on the ceiling, veiled something mysterious in a corner.

Fully clothed, Allen stretched out on one of the floor mattresses, close to the hanging blanket; Banning had the other, under the window; and Tyrone was on the bed, with his legs, from the knees down, dangling over the end.

Although their eyes refused to open, and their bodies had become uncontrollably limp, the aviators remained awake, unable to drift away mainly because of the unbearable stench in the room.

About ten minutes later, a very odd noise was heard, coming from behind the blanket. Tom Allen sat bolt upright, heard the sound again, and yelled, 'What the hell is that?'

Tyrone, who was already fast asleep, and just beginning to snore, raised his head, groped for a flashlight, and asked sleepily, 'Did somebody call?'

'I called,' Allen replied irritably. 'What the hell is going on over there, behind that blanket?'

Awake now, Tyrone lit up the corner, and made a high-pitched clucking sound, evidently his version of a laugh. 'Oh, that's probably Gladys, or Elmo,' he explained, with affection. 'Most probably Gladys, at this time of night, although it might be Elmo too.'

'That's enough, man.' Banning was also sitting up now and in a very bad mood. 'Just who the hell are Gladys and Elmo?'

'Lord's sake, gentlemen,' Tyrone answered cordially. 'You must know that Gladys and Elmo are my prize hogs. And they've got a real nice pen in that corner.'

Tyrone clucked a few times more, switched off the flashlight, leaned his head back on a greasy pillow, and appeared to fall instantly into a deep sleep.

As the minutes passed, and the snorts and squeals grew louder, Allen and Banning, sitting on their mattresses in the dark, considered their situation. 'Are you there, James Herman?'

'I'm here.'

'You made a terrible blunder,' said Allen, trying not to inhale deeply. 'Squeezing in with Florence was the right move – and I did call the shot. Remember? A much better deal.'

'Only for you, man,' Banning replied, yawning, in spite of the farmyard atmosphere. 'I would have had the same smells and noises,' he added, easing back on his mattress. 'Along with crushed balls and a serious hernia. Good night, Thomas.'

It was raining hard the next morning when the refinery truck arrived with thirty gallons of gasoline. The rain made it difficult to transfer the fuel from the cans to the tank. Allen used his flight jacket to make a tent over the containers to prevent the water from mixing with the fuel. Ten minutes after every hour, weather reports were received from points east – Midland, Sweetwater, and Abilene. Between showers they tuned up the engine, and when the downpour eased off for a while about 10 am, the Eagle Rock took off with Banning at the controls, heading for Midland, Texas.

Mary Beth Wells, a twenty-five year old blonde, who could have passed for a fashion model or a movie star, was actually a very sharp and experienced news reporter, working in Oklahoma for the *Wichita Falls Daily Gazette*. Along with looks, intelligence and ability, she had a quick wit and a dirty mouth. With a photographer, and another, male reporter, she had been assigned to cover the arrival at the airport of Congressman Paul Taubman and his party, due in from Washington, DC for a conference with city Democratic leaders. Reports had been received that the Congressman's plane had been delayed in Louisville, Kentucky. Mary Beth and her colleagues, and reporters from other newspapers, were in the glass-enclosed Terminal Lounge, killing time watching the incoming and outgoing air traffic.

After flying through heavy rain storms, and making brief landings for gas, oil, water, tune-ups, and weather reports at Midland and Sweetwater, Texas, Banning controlled the Eagle Rock, as she dipped and lifted and rattled her way over Hamlin, and Stamford, and Sycamore, until the Wichita Falls Airport could be seen below, and to the right.

Just as daylight was beginning to fade, the plane rammed down unusually hard, swayed dangerously, and nearly nosed over, before she settled and came to a stop, not far from the Terminal Lounge's observation glass.

'Hoover's campaign needs some urgent funding,' Mary Beth Wells remarked, with her blue eyes on the Eagle Rock. 'Is that damn thing really an airplane, Marvin?'

'It was up and it came down, Mary Beth,' said one of the reporters, watching as the aviators started a slow climb out of the cockpits. 'But I've never seen anything like it in all my days.'

'That has to be a home-built job.' The other newsman was also studying the plane, the helmeted and goggled flyers, and the crowd of curious ground crew members who had gathered around. 'It's a stunt or a gag or a commercial promotion.'

'What are they advertising – Uncle Tom's Cabin?' Mary Beth Wells gazed at the aviators, who had removed their head gear and were walking towards the airport office. 'I wonder if they did build that plane themselves?' she said thoughtfully. 'Would it be possible, Marvin?'

'Damned if I know,' the reporter answered. 'Quite a few coloured people are fooling around with aviation these days. Air circus performers and – '

'I'll bet there's a good little human interest piece out there,' Mary Beth Wells interrupted, turning away from the glass. 'Keep me posted on fat-ass Taubman,' she instructed, preparing to leave. 'Buzz the airport office if you get an arrival time.'

'Should I put Stoker through if he calls you?' the reporter named Marvin asked, watching Mary Beth prepare to leave. 'The big man doesn't like assignment changes without his permission. Remember last week's memo?'

'Every pompous line of it.'

'Well?'

'Give him extension 549,' she replied, checking her exquisite features in a hand-mirror. 'The ladies' toilet. Ask him to wait for a loud flush.'

'I'm serious.'

'Don't put him through, Marvin.' Mary Beth Wells stood up, and the reporters did the same, in a gentlemanly fashion. 'My cub days were over a long time ago,' she added, haughtily. 'I'm sick and tired of being monitored. I'll see you guys later.'

After logging in, freshening up, and swallowing the usual dose of curious looks, amused expressions, and ridicule, Allen and Banning were told by an office clerk that a reporter from a local paper was waiting for them in a small room used by the press for interviewing visiting dignitaries. The aviators were surprised, and a little confused. They had never heard of a Negro publication in Wichita Falls, Oklahoma. And if a white man was waiting, where did he pick up news about the flight? Even if the Wichita Falls man had somehow found out about the transcontinental attempt, would he really be interested and unprejudiced enough to investigate and report it, before a successful landing in New York City? Banning supposed that they were facing another malicious exercise in humiliation and mockery.

'My name is Mary Beth Wells,' the beautiful blonde purred, as Allen and Banning entered the interview room. 'I'm a journalist on the staff of the *Daily Gazette*.' She waited patiently while the aviators recovered from their initial jolt, and took seats, facing her elegant pose on a sofa. 'The office gave your names as Thomas C. Allen and James Herman Banning. Correct?'

'Yes, ma'am.' Allen fidgeted in the chair, cleared his throat nervously, and added, 'I'm Allen and this is Banning next to me.'

Mary Beth Wells nodded, and wrote something on a pad she was holding, without bothering to take a proper look at either man.

'All right, gentlemen,' she said, glancing up at Allen. 'Tell me about the – unusual – airplane you landed here this evening. Did you build it yourselves? And why?'

'Excuse me, ma'am.' Allen was careful about his wording, tone of voice, and general attitude. 'Can we ask you how you knew about our flight and arrival time at Wichita Falls?'

'I didn't,' Mary Beth Wells replied bluntly. 'I'm here to meet Congressman Paul Taubman and his party. Their flight from

121

Washington has been delayed.'

'So what put you on to us?' Banning asked, staring hard at her, until she turned his way. 'Do you know anything about our intentions and schedule?'

The reporter seemed to notice Banning for the first time, and it was obvious that she was struck by his unusually handsome features, and straight-shouldered, slim, athletic build.

'I know nothing about your intentions or schedule. I didn't even know of your existence,' Mary Beth Wells finally answered coolly, her alert blue eyes still examining Banning. 'I happened to be in the lounge and I saw a strange craft fall out of the sky. And who the hell is conducting this interview anyway?'

'Just one more question,' Banning persisted, trying to be as polite as possible. 'Were you attracted by the unusual airplane – or the unusual flyers?'

'Both,' the reporter, answered, beginning to show impatience. 'And, at this precise moment, I'm wondering why.' She switched her attention abruptly from Banning to Tom Allen. 'Ever heard of a human interest story?'

'Yes, ma'am.'

'Something resembling a home-built airplane was dumped down on this field by two Negroes a while ago,' Mary Beth Wells lectured. 'My colleagues thought it was a gag, a stunt, or a commercial promotion. I was curious. I decided to dig for some possible human interest. And that's the only reason I'm here. So don't smear your racial shit in my face.'

'You were right,' said Tom Allen, pretending not to hear her last remark. 'We do have a story for your paper. Want us to tell you about it, ma'am?'

Mary Beth Wells stared at him for a moment, thoughtfully tapping her gold pencil on her lower lip. 'Go ahead, Mr Allen,' she said finally. 'And excuse me for blasting off like a slut.'

'My fault.' Banning had been sitting quietly, an interested spectator. 'Certain situations arouse my suspicions and switchblade instincts. This happened to be one of them. Sorry, Mrs Wells.'

'Miss,' the reporter corrected, without looking at him. 'And we had better get to your story,' she said to Allen. 'I might have to cut it short if they confirm Taubman's arrival time.'

'Yes, ma'am.'

Mary Beth Wells took notes – a lot of them – and asked a great many questions, as Allen recounted their story. It seemed to be making a great impression on her.

As Allen was concluding, an airport attendant knocked and informed the aviators that there was a minor problem with the plane's gas tank. The mechanic asked Mary Beth Wells if she had been given enough information. She replied that she wanted some additional facts about the flight plan from Wichita Falls to New York City.

'Mr Banning can handle that for you, ma'am,' said Allen, getting to his feet. 'I'll go check out the plane and organize the hangar for tonight. James Herman,' he informed the pilot as he left. 'We'll meet in the office later.'

'How about the flight plan from here, Mr Banning?' With her shapely legs crossed, and plenty showing, the beautiful young blonde sat poised on the sofa. 'I would like each town and an approximate time schedule,' she said, with her eyes on her notepad. 'Also, give me your thoughts about the problems you anticipate along the way. Funding, weather, mechanical trouble, anything that – '

'We'll go Wichita Falls to El Reno to Oklahoma City to Tulsa,' Banning interrupted. 'And that's all I can tell you now with any certainty.'

'You don't have a formal flight plan?' She looked up, met his eyes, and teased him with a seductive smile. 'What the hell kind of a pilot are you?'

'A very good one,' Banning replied, maintaining his composure, as he had promised himself he would do. 'My plan has to be tentative and flexible,' he explained, ignoring the way she leaned back, allowing her skirt to expose even more flesh. 'You saw the aircraft. We'll probably change course many times, and make stops for all kinds of emergencies. So I don't have a time schedule. And who knows what kind of problems we'll face along the way?' He paused for a moment, refusing to be provoked by her taunts and posturing. 'Sorry I can't be more useful.'

'Try.' Mary Beth Wells placed the notepad on the sofa, and rested her outstretched arms on the back cushions, giving Banning an unobstructed view of a silky blouse, which was now pulled tight across her full breasts. 'Allen tiptoed around one of the biggest problems you face on this flight,' she went on seriously. 'The key to the story: racial discrimination. How have you been coping with it, Banning?'

'We cope.'

'But there must be all kinds to handle on a coast to coast trip,' she persisted. 'Especially for a guy like you, with a chip the size of a boulder perched next to his good-looking head. You almost switchbladed me at the start. And for no reason. And look at you now.'

'I'm fine now.'

'Like hell you are,' she mocked, stretching the blouse even tighter, and allowing the skirt to slide further up her legs. 'I don't know one normal white man who would have kept his eyes off my body for so long. You really do know how to cope, Banning.'

'It just takes practice, Miss Wells.'

'Want to discuss a special arrangement for tonight?' she asked, in a low, tempting voice. 'I might like to experiment with a type like you.'

'Thank you very much for the kind offer,' said Banning, concentrating on her face only. 'But I honestly don't want to finish this flight dangling on the end of a rope in Wichita Falls, Oklahoma.'

'No one would know.'

'They'd smell it on your breath, lady.'

'Did you ever lay a white girl?'

'A few.'

'How was it?'

'All female parts function in the same manner.'

'But you prefer black ass.'

'I would like to have the *right* to lay you – and any other consenting woman I fancy – without being strung up – or shot dead.' Banning watched her stand up and begin straightening her skirt. 'But that doesn't mean that I *want* to lay you – I just want the *right* to do it – like all the normal white men who can't take their eyes off your body.'

'This is truly rich.' Mary Beth Wells laughed, huskily. 'You've become a first for me anyway,' she continued, looking away from Banning. 'No other man has ever turned his back on my equipment – and I have damn seldom offered it to a stranger – until very recently.'

'Chalk it up to fear on my part, Miss Wells, said Banning, feeling uncomfortable about humiliating her. 'You're the one who said – the key to this story is – racial discrimination.'

The phone rang, and Mary Beth Wells was told by her assistant that Congressman Paul Taubman's flight was due in twenty minutes. He also asked if she had picked up any human interest. 'Yes,' she replied. 'Quite a bit.'

After the call, the reporter explained that she intended to contact the office right away, and make certain that the Eagle Rock story appeared in the early edition of the *Gazette*. Banning and Allen would be able to read about themselves in the morning before take-off. She wished the pilot good luck and success and told him to pass her sentiments on to Thomas Allen.

'By the way, where are you sleeping tonight, Banning?' she asked, inspecting her appearance again in the hand-mirror. 'Do you have accommodation in town?'

'Not yet.' Banning studied the woman's face as she applied fresh lipstick. 'But I'm sure we'll organize something.'

'Do you have enough money?' Business-like, and in a hurry now, Mary Beth Wells put the lipstick and mirror back into an expensive-looking bag, and adjusted the strap on her shoulder. 'Forget your goddamn pride and arrogance. You'll be hungry and on the streets tonight.'

'I won't take a dime from you.'

'You didn't get the offer of one.' She picked up the notepad, scribbled something, and handed the paper to Banning. 'Go to this address around nine o'clock tonight. You'll have a home-cooked meal, booze, friendly conversation, a comfortable bed, breakfast, maybe even a few bucks for the road. Be there. I'll have everything arranged.'

'Miss Wells.' Banning stopped her abruptly as she reached the door.' 'I certainly appreciate everything you're doing for us,' he said, sincerely. 'But spending the night at your place – even on a strictly charitable basis – might end up being troublesome for you – and disastrous for us.'

'*What?*' The reporter glared at him over her shoulder. 'Don't flatter yourself,' she advised, icily. 'The house belongs to Mr and Mrs Isaac Ovington. He's been a janitor in our newspaper building for years. The family is black. And I won't be there. So relax, Mr Banning. You won't be strung up or shot dead. Have a safe flight.'

She left the room.

All of the reporter's promises were fulfilled. Allen and Banning had a sumptuous dinner, with high quality hooch, and friendly conversation. The beds were comfortable, the breakfast superb, and they had been handed an envelope containing two five dollar bills. Everything, according to the Ovington, had been arranged and paid for by Miss Mary Beth Wells, who hd told them that it was a token of her appreciation for an interesting newspaper story she had received from the aviators. And, as promised, just before they left for the airport in Mr Ovington's car, the *Daily Gazette* arrived.

At first, they glanced at each heading, on every page, and saw nothing. And then, after starting again, Allen spotted a very brief item on page two, headed:

CONGRESSMAN PAUL TAUBMAN ARRIVES

Congressman Taubman, and his party, arrived here last night, after their flight from Washington, DC was delayed by poor weather conditions and engine trouble. The four-man political task force will meet later today with Mr Keith Cates and other local Democratic leaders. Mr Cates, his colleagues, and many others at the airport, were unexpectedly entertained during the waiting period by two Negro air circus performers, who landed a comical, home-made aircraft in a bizarre, almost suicidal fashion. When questioned by *Gazette* reporter Mary Beth Wells, the men, Thomas C. Allen and James Herman Banning, stated that they were attempting to become the first Negroes to fly coast-to-coast. The winged contraption, reportedly salvaged from a wreck, left Los Angeles on Monday, 19 September, and has already made eleven scheduled and unscheduled landings. The pilot told our reporter that he had no idea when or how the 'plane' would arrive in New York City. If nothing else, according to Miss Wells, they are personable and amusing Negroes, and should be hired by the airport as a permanent attraction.

Just before take-off from Wichita Falls on Saturday morning, 24 September 1932, Banning was called to the office phone by an airport attendant. Mr Marvin Greenbaum, a journalist on the staff of the *Daily Gazette*, had a personal message for the Eagle Rock pilot. After introducing himself, he moved directly to the point, before Banning could respond.

'Mary Beth Wells filed a beautiful story about you and Mr Allen,' Greenbaum said. 'All about courage – and ability – and determination – and a battle against the odds. But we have a bigoted publisher here named Stoker. He asked a junior punk to do a rewrite for him. And that's what you read. Mary Beth Wells resigned from the *Daily Gazette* this morning.'

Marvin Greenbaum hung up.

12

The Eagle Rock took off from Wichita Falls at ten o'clock in the morning, and Banning flew her slightly east of north. After checking the course at Red River, they rumbled over Walters, Oklahoma, passing east of Lawton, above the Keech Hills, a little west of Chickasha. A short time later, while Banning was trying to identify a new and worrisome knocking sound under the fuselage, he manoeuvred the ship across the South Canadian River and swung slightly to the left, around the town of El Reno, Oklahoma. They descended three miles west of the city limits, and made a tricky and very fortunate landing on a field obstructed by deep, grass-covered holes, created years ago by wallowing herds of buffalo.

During the brief El Reno stop, the aviators got their hair cut, made phone calls, and prepared friends and relatives for a joyous reunion in Oklahoma City, just forty miles away. Tom Allen hadn't seen his mother since 1929. And, along with other friends, Banning was anxious to see a girl he used to date frequently, years back, a former beauty-contest winner. Both men were excited and happy, so much so that Banning accepted Allen's proposal to flip a coin to decide who would pilot the Eagle Rock, and make the ceremonious landing in Oklahoma City. Tom Allen won. Banning crossed himself and mumbled, 'Oh, shit.'

At the same time that Allen and Banning were hitching a ride from the airfield into El Reno, Lieutenant Craig Meredith, the black pilot's former instructor, was having lunch at home in Des Moines, Iowa, with his pretty Southern wife, his two young sons, and one of the mechanics who worked at his flying school.

The conversation around the luncheon table centred on politics, the Presidential campaign, the respective merits and weaknesses of Roosevelt and Hoover.

'I can't understand why Lindbergh is supporting him,' said the mechanic, referring to Herbert Hoover, who was running for re-election. 'You know he's doing a transcontinental for his campaign?'

'So I heard.' Lieutenant Meredith glanced up from his soup and addressed Mark, the eldest son. 'What do you think, champ? Roosevelt or Hoover?'

'Roosevelt without a doubt,' the youngster answered confidently. 'Everybody in school says the country needs a change. And a change is Roosevelt. A New Deal.'

'Speaking of transcontinentals,' said the mechanic, 'I heard two niggers are attempting one in a very strange way.'

'We say Negroes in this house, Clancy,' said Meredith mildly. 'At least I do, and I expect my children to do the same.'

'Sorry, Craig.' The mechanic took a quick look at Mrs Meredith, who was known to use the word frequently around the school, despite her husband's objections. 'Anyway, I heard from a friend in Lordsburgh, New Mexico, that two – Negroes – are flying coast-to-coast in a wrecked OXX6 Eagle Rock with an ancient motor.' He shook his head and laughed. 'A couple of black clowns from an air circus. They plop down every couple of miles and beg for gas, food, hangars, parts, and God knows what else. Another mechanic I know spotted them in Sweetwater, Texas. And they are still on the move. Los Angeles to New York City – the hard way.'

'Why are they doing such a dumb thing, Dad?' Mark Meredith asked his father, with a look of exaggerated bewilderment on his face. 'Think it's another crazy stunt for the election?'

'It probably has something to do with the NAACP,' said Mrs Meredith, beginning to collect the soup bowls. 'Those people are forever crusading in some outlandish way.'

'What's the NAACP, Mom?'

'The National Association for the Advancement of Colored People, Mark,' she answered, on her way to the kitchen. 'And I personally believe that they have advanced a little too far already.'

'Please, Julia,' Meredith snapped irritably, his attention still focused on the mechanic. 'Did anybody give you the names of the Negro aviators, Clancy?'

'One is called Allen, I know that for sure.' The mechanic thought for a moment, as Julia Meredith brought in a large glass bowl of salad. 'The other one might be Denning, or Benning, or something like that.'

'Banning,' said Meredith, with a broad smile on his face. 'It would have to be James Herman Banning.'

'That's it,' the mechanic confirmed. 'Banning is the other one.'
He accepted a serving of salad from Mrs Meredith, thanked her,
and then asked his boss, 'Do you know the man, Ray?'
'I taught him to fly,' Meredith replied proudly, glancing at his
wife, who was busy filling plates. 'He's an excellent pilot – the
first Negro to be licensed – and a damn good man. Remember
him, Julia?'
'I certainly do,' Mrs Meredith answered, acidly. 'He walked
around the school like he owned the place. And you encouraged
him.'
'He thought he was a big shot,' Mark Meredith joined in. 'Dad
should have made him sweep out the hangars like all the other
black workers. Everybody said so.'
'These two flyers probably need a lot of support by now.' Craig
Meredith, in a pensive mood, picked at his food, and ignored
his family's comments. 'Help me track them down, Clancy,' he
instructed. 'Maybe I can arrange some kind of assistance.'

Tom Allen sang loudly and ecstatically over the uneven roar of
the engine as he piloted the Eagle Rock over familiar territory,
on the way to Oklahoma City, where he had spent his youth. He
landed the plane heavily again, but this time in full view of family
and friends: a heart-warming reception for a change.
Allen's mother and younger brother had light housekeeping
rooms in a house owned by a Mr and Mrs Badger. The aviators
and the welcoming committee congregated there amid more hugs
and kisses and talk of old times, and hospitality. A phone call
was received from Mr Langston Wright of the *Oklahoma Black
Dispatch*. The editor wanted a detailed report about the flight, and
both men knew that this was genuine – straight business – unlike
the humiliating episode with the *Wichita Falls Gazette*.
After bathing and dressing up, the aviators went to see Mr
Wright in his office in the coloured business district. They
presented the complete story of the transcontinental record
attempt, photographs were taken, and the editor promised that a
Sunday feature would definitely appear.
Later, in the evening, calls were made to Celene Allen and
the Mosby brothers in Los Angeles. The mechanic's wife was
cheerful, and doing well, although she missed him very much.
As expected, the Mosby brothers, representing the promoters
and fund-raisers, reported that nothing, as yet, had actually been
promoted or raised. After issuing a grim warning, Banning hung
up in the middle of Booker T.'s moaning excuses.

On Sunday morning, Banning went to visit old friends, and Allen, for old times' sake, attended Sunday school. Then, again for old times' sake, he took his mother's arm, and escorted her to church for morning service. He spent the rest of the day and evening getting together with former teachers, school and neighbourhood pals, and distant relatives. The Oklahoma City reunion touched him more than he had expected. Banning returned to the Badgers' house very late, slightly drunk, and in a pensive mood.

The aviators were awake early on Monday morning with the problem of money uppermost in their minds. Hangar rent, gasoline, oil, a tune-up, plugs, and a few engine parts would drastically reduce the kitty, or damn nearly wipe it out. Oklahoma City was the obvious place for a fund-raising campaign. But after the newspaper article and photographs had appeared on the Sunday *Black Dispatch* feature page, they found themselves minor celebrities in the coloured sections of the city, and begging on the streets and in the shops would be awkward and demeaning. It was no use approaching relatives or old friends – they were broke because of the Depression. However, the publicity about the flight had caught the attention of the black owner of a large drug store, who presented the aviators with a legitimate opportunity to raise money.

Mr R.B. Hayman, of Hayman's Drug Store, invited them to address the Oklahoma City Negro Business League, at Jackson's Tenderloin Café, in the Elks' Building on North-east Second Street. The two men agreed to appear at one pm with great pleasure.

Allen was proudly introduced as a local, and Banning as a dear friend of the black Oklahoma City Community. Both excelled themselves describing the flight and its purpose, the rewards and the dangers, and the financial problems, hoping to extract a few desperately needed dollars from the prosperous-looking Negro businessmen. Their audience seemed engrossed – in fact, Banning, who spoke second, had winked at the mechanic after completing his turn, sure that they had put their story across with all cylinders firing.

However, moments later the aviators were shocked and cha-grined when Mr Fletcher Braithwaite, president of the Business League, commended their bravery, skill, and determination, but refused to help financially, and advised the members to follow his example. He argued that monetary aid was needed for more important purposes in the poverty-stricken black communities;

and that it was futile to try to compete in such white spheres of achievement as aviation.

'All efforts,' he said, 'should be directed towards securing the basics of life for Negro people – food, clothing, shelter, and the right to move about freely and unmolested, in places of their own choosing.'

Later that afternoon, as Allen was sitting dejectedly beside the phone in Mr and Mrs Badger's house, an equally dejected James Herman Banning entered, flopped on a sofa, and stared up at a spot on the ceiling.

'I'm disillusioned,' said the pilot. 'Flabbergasted.'

'To say the least,' Allen responded at once. 'My oldest and dearest school buddy just wriggled away from a five buck loan.' He shoved the telephone aside. 'And as for Fletcher Braithwaite – even the Chinese at Pipkin's Hot Spot dug into their pockets for us. How could our own brothers not –'

'Braithwaite is old news to me at the moment, Thomas,' Banning interrupted sadly, without looking at his partner. 'I've been disillusioned and flabbergasted by Hannah Templeton.'

'Who?'

'Remember the gal I told you about?' he asked, still observing the spot above his head. 'My old flame?' She was Miss Black Oklahoma City a few years ago. A truly gorgeous creature. A friend of mine just told me what happened to her.'

'She passed away?'

'As far as I'm concerned she did. Hannah Templeton got mixed up with a crooked dude and became a whore. She lost her looks, her ass, her mind, and her freedom, for a while, poor soul. Then another big-time pimp came on the scene and now she runs her own house. Hannah Templeton,' he said, almost reverently. 'A goddamn brothel keeper.'

'You might have saved her, James Herman.'

'That's not so funny, man,' said Banning. 'My friend says she still has a hot thing going for me. Keeps our picture in her family album.'

'A free piece of commercial tail for you, partner.'

'Never,' Banning fired back emphatically. 'Once they put it up for sale, I hang soft, and run the other way.'

'Good for you.' Allen's thoughts were elsewhere, as he gazed at the phone, and debated lifting the receiver. 'I don't have the guts to beg my cousin Ralph,' he went on, almost to himself. 'They had a recent death in the family and a lot of doctor's bills. But we have to put our hands on some cash for that airport – today.'

'Hey, wait a minute!' Banning sat up immediately. 'I've got a smart idea. We were turned down by the black Oklahoma City businessmen, right?'

'Right.'

'But what about the black Oklahoma City business*women?*'

'I don't get you.'

'Hannah Templeton and her girls.'

'Are you selling your body?'

'Fund raising, Thomas,' said Banning excitedly. 'I'll pay Hannah a shock visit. Play her along for a while with the olden days, but keep my distance, then pitch the flight – and ask for donations.'

'From Hannah Templeton?'

'And the girls, too.'

'How about the customers?'

'If I catch them with their pants down.'

'They'll never sign the Gold Book.'

'What do you think, Thomas?'

'Are you serious?'

'Never more so.'

As planned, Banning visited Hannah Templeton. He was shocked to discover that his old flame, the former beauty contest winner, the gorgeous creature of his memory, had shrivelled into a frail, mousy little character, with short, kinky hair, flat breasts, and nervous twitches on every visible part of her body. She smoked constantly, wept several times, and it was clear to Banning that his friend had been absolutely correct about the Madam's feelings. Hannah Templeton still had love and passion for him in her glassy, blood-shot eyes.

After Banning's fervent appeal for donations, Hannah at once instructed her receptionist and housekeeper – a very black teenage girl, who had what appeared to be a long razor scar on her forehead – to signal each of the six working whores that Miss Templeton wanted to see them in the upstairs room the moment they pulled out from under their present clients. The next mongers in line would have to wait and bear the heat until the meeting was over.

In a short time, James Herman Banning, sitting on a couch next to Hannah Templeton, found himself staring wide-eyed at six half-naked dark women. Hannah introduced him to her girls, repeated his story, and explained his financial problems. The girls were impressed with the information – and with the handsome visitor. Banning smiled back at them awkwardly, and added a few lines to the Madam's narration, but without his usual conviction and flair. However, all the girls consented to make a contribution from their hard earned wages to help him on his way.

'One more thing,' the Madam added, before her whores left the room. 'Tell your next client about this fantastic venture. Give them extra time and a couple of fancy tricks in exchange for a donation.'

The prostitutes nodded agreement.

'And Goldie.' The Madam addressed a tall, big-busted young woman. 'Make sure that Bert Mills co-operates. Or inform him that Miss Hannah will contact his loving wife Irene later tonight.'

Goldie smiled and mumbled her consent.

'You girls are helping to make history today,' the Madam went on. 'Go downstairs and use all of your talents for a very worthy cause. We'll tally up the proceeds before Mr Banning leaves.'

Again the prostitutes nodded, smiled at the pilot, and started to leave the room.

'Oh, ladies.' Banning stopped them, and they turned, apparently oblivious to the nakedness revealed by their gaudy, unfastened dressing-gowns. 'Please accept my thanks and deep appreciation in advance for any help you can give us,' he said, sincerely, glancing from face to face. 'We'll never forget your kindness.'

'Maybe you'd like a special donation from me, good looking,' said a pretty, light-skinned prostitute. 'Come downstairs after my next session,' she added temptingly. 'I won't deduct anything from the pot.'

'That should really make me feel jealous, Valerie,' said the Madam, before Banning had a chance to reply, a wistful expression on her face. 'Our famous airplane pilot used to be my guy. But, that was a long time ago.' Hannah looked at Banning. 'Valerie is a winner in every department, James Herman. And she is very clean. Like the others. Why not take all six and have a ball on the house? A Templeton good-luck send-off.'

'Damn,' said Banning, charming the women with a broad, even-toothed grin. 'Here I finally get the proposition of a lifetime and have to turn it down.' He shook his head in an over-acted gesture of disappointment. 'I would never be able to manage six knock-outs like you gals and get the plane up too – on the same day. And besides – as inviting as you all are – my old flame is here – and I do owe her some respect, for old times' sake. Do you ladies know what I mean?'

133

They did.

When Banning left Hannah Templeton's whorehouse, the Eagle Rock treasury balance had been increased by thirty-eight dollars and forty cents, with contributions from the Madam, her girls, a black customer named Bert Mills, and a white one, who called himself Mr John Smith. Even the young, razor-scarred receptionist-housekeeper had donated a twenty-five cent coin.

At the Oklahoma City airport, the aviators discovered just how important the unorthodox fund-raising campaign had been, because they were presented with a thirty-two dollar and fifty cent bill for hangar rent, gas, oil, servicing, and a few engine parts. Once again they were taking off nearly broke.

Family, friends and, probably because of the newspaper article, some curious spectators from the town's coloured sections, were gathered to watch the departure. Even Mr Fletcher Braithwaite, and members of the Oklahoma City Negro Business League, had made an appearance.

Allen promised his mother and younger brother that he would find some way for them to visit him in Los Angeles, as soon as Celene had given birth. Banning moved around for a couple of minutes, speaking briefly to old friends, male and female, but his mind was on the flight preparations.

While the engine was warming, the two men discussed the Gold Book, and whether or not to inscribe all the whorehouse names, including the two clients. It was finally decided that only Hannah Templeton should be listed, as the official representative for them all, but even this compromise did not please Allen.

'She did a lot for us, I know,' he said. 'But should a prostitute end up in the Smithsonian Institute?'

'Why not?'

'Hey!' Allen snapped his fingers. 'I've got a brilliant twist. We don't put her name in the regular place. Let's make a very appropriate change and put her on the tail section. Right?'

'Wrong.'

Banning printed Hannah's name carefully in the Gold Book.

Just as they were about to climb into the cockpits, a Negro ran towards the plane shouting, and waving a sheet of paper.

'I'm from the *Black Dispatch*,' he yelled breathlessly, over the engine noise. 'We received a telegram with an urgent message for you.' He handed the paper to Banning. 'Contact Mr W.B. Skelly of Skelly's Tagolene Gasoline Company in Tulsa.'

134

Before the confused aviators were able to question the messenger, he had rushed away. Banning shoved the paper into his flight jacket, as both men boarded the aircraft, and prepared to leave.

With Banning piloting, the Eagle Rock took off at 4:30 pm, lumbered past the southern part of Oklahoma City, crossed the North Canadian River, and then headed over the oilfields, swinging north-east to the right of the State Fair Grounds, which were crowded during this last week in September.

Signalling from time to time that all was in order, Banning controlled the plane over farm and Blackjack timberlands, then more oilfields, as they passed to the left of Cushing, and over Oilton. Several miles of tank farms came into view next. It was a smooth flight, without problems. Both men were enjoying the ride.

After crossing the Arkansas River, Banning flew to the south, around Tulsa, Oklahoma, to Sparton Field, the Municipal Airport. The Eagle Rock landed at six o'clock in the evening.

As they checked in and arranged for hangar space, a clerk in the airport office, who stared at them in the same amused and bewildered way as almost every other clerk in almost every other airport office along the way, finally discovered his tongue.

'Allen and Banning,' the clerk monotoned, gazing down at a scribbled note and rubbing his baby-smooth chin with a manicured finger. 'I can't figure why, but Mr Skelly wants to see you people tomorrow. We have a message here.'

'So have we,' said Banning, waiting for the clerk to lift his eyes. 'Did he give you a telephone number? We're supposed to contact the gentleman here in Tulsa.'

'There are four telephone numbers on this pad for Mr Skelly's assistants,' the clerk replied, smiling unpleasantly. 'I'm sure that one of them will make the necessary arrangements.' Again he inspected the aviators' faces in disbelief. 'Why would Mr Skelly want to have anything to do with characters like you?'

'Mr Banning is his adopted son returning from the African jungles,' said Allen, signing an airport hangar rental slip. 'Do you have a public telephone in the building?'

'Over by the side entrance, comedian,' said the clerk testily, handing Allen the telephone numbers. 'And conduct yourselves in a civilized fashion on these premises,' he ordered as the aviators moved away from the counter. 'This is Tulsa, Oklahoma, USA – where baboons are normally caged.'

*

135

Allen and Banning were leaning against a hangar wall, sipping coffee in paper cups, and discussing two phone calls they had made a short time earlier. The first, to one of Banning's former school chums at Iowa State College, now living and working in Tulsa, had been unexpectedly productive. An electrician by the name of Clarence Patterson, who was now out of necessity doing freelance jobs in coloured neighbourhoods, and had offered transportation, dinner, and sleeping accommodation at his place, a basement apartment on a busy commercial street. Patterson, who was a bachelor, had already left to pick them up.

The second call, to one of Mr W.B. Skelly's assistants, had stunned and mystified them. They had discovered that Skelly, the owner of Skelly's Tagolene Gasoline Company, was an extremely wealthy, white Tulsa industrialist, who had personal and business interests in aviation, nationally and worldwide.

According to the assistant, a brusque, no-nonsense type, Mr Skelly wished to invite the aviators to his mansion on the outskirts of Tulsa, where some close friends would be gathering for lunch the next day. He had heard reports about the Negro transcontinental flight attempt, and wanted Allen and Banning to appear and entertain his guests by giving a first-hand account of the journey so far. A limousine would pick them up at 3:15 pm, after luncheon had been served. In a lofty manner, Skelly's assistant suggested that, for the sake of authenticity and dramatic effect, the aviators should wear their flying gear, and bring all their maps, documents, and other relevant paraphernalia.

And then, much to Banning's disgust, the man had carefully spelled out a set of rules for social behaviour in the presence of Mr Skelly and his guests. When to speak, when to be silent, when to move, when to stand still, and where and when to sit, and there had been more, but Banning had tuned him out until just before the final click.

'I should never have given him Clarence Patterson's address for the pick-up tomorrow.' Banning eased himself down to a squatting position against the hangar wall. 'That bastard deserved a straight refusal and a screw Skelly,' he lamented, taking a sip of coffee. 'We'll be treated like nigger clowns by these high-class society freaks.'

'But there might be something in it for us, James Herman,' said Allen, sliding down to join his partner. 'We could use a few bucks right now. And we did agree at the start – to hell with pride – just get the plane down in New York.'

'This one is too damn humiliating for me.'

'What about collecting money in a whorehouse?'

'Nobody ridiculed,' the pilot replied, finishing his coffee, and tossing the paper cup into a nearby dustbin, with a perfect basketball shot. 'I am sick and tired of being a comic figure for the white population.'

'The blacks turned us down in Oklahoma City,' Allen reminded him, undecided himself about the wisdom of accepting Skelly's invitation, mainly because of Banning's temper. 'Did you forget about Fletcher Braithwaite?'

'But nobody ridiculed,' Banning repeated soberly. 'And they did have a few legitimate excuses,' he added. 'These rich whites want some black entertainment. Right down to costumes and props. They'll expect a banjo along with the maps and documents. A little afternoon diversion to help them digest their caviar and fine –'

The pilot suddenly broke off, and leaned his head back against the hangar wall, apparently struck by a new thought, or an idea, or a plan. Allen looked at him with concern, and decided to ease the situation, before it became worse.

'No sense in getting all upset, James Herman,' he advised sympathetically. 'Why don't we call Skelly's man and politely decline to attend because of some unexpected flight problems?'

'I have a better proposition.' A slow, sly, smile softened Banning's features, and made his eyes twinkle with devilment. 'Skelly and his guests are waiting for two shuffling niggers dressed up as airplane pilots,' he said, enjoying whatever was on his mind. 'The fact that they spelled out rules of behaviour makes it clear that they are expecting two ignorant black street urchins. Do you agree, Thomas?'

'Possibly,' Allen replied, staring at his partner even more uneasily. 'Just what do you have in mind, old buddy?'

'We get picked up by limousine and make an appearance at the mansion as promised.' Excited now, Banning stood, rubbed the muscles in his legs, and chuckled with delight. 'Only Mr W.B. Skelly and his socialites get fooled and we end up having the last laugh.'

'I smell *real* trouble.' Allen also stood, crumpled his paper cup, tossed it at the bin, missed, and was forced to walk over, pick it up and drop it in. 'Do tell me how we fool the socialites and get a laugh, James Herman.'

'With pleasure, Thomas,' said Banning, grinning broadly. 'Instead of bowing and scraping nigger clowns in flying costumes, the Skelly limousine will collect two of the most sophisticated, stylishly attired, well spoken, and socially acceptable black men on the face of God's earth.'

Allen gaped open-mouthed at his partner before he could utter a sound. 'And who are these two highly privileged Negroes, may I ask?'

'Us.'

'Us, Allen repeated, continuing to stare at the pilot, as though he had lost his mind. 'Stylishly attired?' His quick laugh came out as a cough. 'A store heist is out of the question, James Herman. I always have trouble finding the right fit.'

'No theft, man.' Banning was now prepared to reveal his strategy. 'We are going to be outfitted fashionably, and without charge, by an old friend of mine here in Tulsa. Mr Hubert Lloyd Fish.'

'A tailor or a clothing shop owner?'

'He's an undertaker.'

'A *what*?'

'Mr Hubert Lloyd Fish operates this city's largest black funeral parlour,' Banning stated with a touch of pride. 'We met a few years ago when I performed here with the Bessie Coleman troupe,' he added. 'Hubert is a loyal fan of mine.'

'That's all very interesting, James Herman,' said Allen, still confused. 'But what the hell has it got to do with stylish attire? Does Hubert strip the cadavers?'

'Hubert has a special deal with J.D. Flemington and Sons,' Banning answered. 'They rent tuxedos and all kinds of fancy gear for weddings, burials, and other special occasions. Hubert Fish will arrange for us to borrow the best and latest trappings. And one of the Flemington boys has a reputation for being the best-dressed coloured man in Tulsa. I'm sure he'll help us bedazzle Skelly and his highfalutin' guests.'

'In a rented tuxedo for black funerals?'

'Nobody will know they're rented, and not all of Flemington's clothes are for funerals,' Banning replied. 'And remember something else, Thomas, we'll be dressing as high class Negroes. Not big shot whites. Hubert will give us some style of our own.'

'You know something?' Allen smoothed the wrinkles on his flight jacket sleeves. 'It might be fun.' His expression sobered for a moment. 'Your undertaker gets us dressed up,' he went on. 'That's a start. But what about the rest of our performance?'

'Who said it was a performance?' Banning squared his shoulders and adopted a superior pose. 'I believe that we're sophisticated – well spoken – and socially acceptable,' he declared confidently.

'All we have to do is use our natural attributes and exaggerate them a little. And Hubert Lloyd Fish's wardrobe will take care of the rest.'

'Is it really worth all the trouble?' Allen was still undecided. 'So they expect two shuffling niggers in flying costumes to entertain them,' he rationalized. 'Maybe we should give them what they want and to hell with it. Who cares how we pick up a few necessary bucks?'

'I do,' said Banning adamantly. 'I draw the line on this one, Thomas. Skelly's man turned my stomach inside out. His rules and regulations were obscene. I'm an educated man. A licensed pilot. And you're the best damn aviation mechanic in the business. Let's go to that mansion and get the last laugh.'

Allen's slow-developing grin said it all, but still he added, in a mock British accent, 'I am certainly with you all the way, dear boy. But do remember: two sophisticated – well spoken – and socially acceptable gentlemen – who happen to be black – and dressed by a local undertaker – stand a bloody good chance of being called rather eccentric – or a couple of entertaining nigger clowns.'

Hubert Lloyd Fish, a towering, pot-bellied individual with a gorilla's head and a bloated face, resembled a second-rate club wrestler rather than a first-class funeral parlour proprietor. But he had a pleasant voice and a gentle manner, and his respect for Banning was obvious. The undertaker would, of course, do everything possible for the pilot and his friend, except donate money, because business was bad these days even though everybody had to die. According to Fish, most folks nowadays just wanted their kin to be laid out plain, wooden-planked, and flung under as quickly and as cheaply as possible. And he had a wife, three children, and a sickly mother to support.

But, as Banning had known, the undertaker did have a special arrangement with J.D. Flemington and Sons, and the aviators were escorted to the large shop shortly after breakfast with Clarence Patterson the following morning.

139

13

While Allen and Banning stood stiffly and awkwardly in front of him, Lewis Flemington, the plump eldest of the Flemington sons, and reportedly the best-dressed coloured man in town, observed and touched and knelt and measured and rose, and measured and pondered and observed once again, without speaking a word. And then he stepped away, and with his eyes darting expertly from garment to customer, and back again, he selected shirts, trousers and jackets from a rack. Finally, whistling, he began the search for stylish shoes and other accessories.

With mounting apprehension, Allen and Banning watched the performance. At last, satisfied with his selection, the young man approached, his head concealed behind a pile of Flemington rentals . . .

For a long, silent moment, the aviators gaped at their unfamiliar reflections in the mirror, while the quiet fashion consultant admired his work from a short distance away. Lewis Flemington's meticulously arranged costumes consisted of polka-dot bow ties, starchy, high-collar white shirts, brightly coloured braces, and dark, velvety trousers, hung much too long over grey spats and glossy patent leather shoes. He had also selected white double-breasted jackets, with unusually wide black lapels, and heavily padded shoulders. And there were gold-plated links, on exposed French cuffs, and a fake carnation in each lapel. To complete the flashy picture, Flemington had provided each man with a slim, brass-handled walking stick.

'Don't you think we look a little too – spectacular, Mr Flemington?' Banning asked, gazing at himself, with stick in hand. 'These outfits are very – theatrical,' he added, choosing his words tactfully. 'Maybe we could tone them down just a bit.'

'It might be wise, Mr Flemington,' said Allen, also grimacing at the figures in the glass. 'You know, we're visiting some very, very rich white folks. I don't think we should try to outclass our hosts. That wouldn't be smart or proper.'

'You won't outclass the rich white folks, Mr Allen,' said

Lewis Flemington, speaking for the first time in a surprisingly deep voice. 'There ain't no competition, really,' he continued, walking over and straightening Allen's bow tie. 'All rich white folks nowadays copy Paree. And you gentlemen are wearing the best and latest from Harlem. So everybody will be in fashion.'

'Is this really how people are dressing in Harlem today, Mr Flemington?' Banning asked, still being cautious. 'We do have a Depression and a lot of poor on the streets.'

'I'm referring to the ones who still have some money and good taste,' said Flemington, with a touch of annoyance. 'Like merchants – bootleggers – number runners – and union stevedores on the piers.'

'They sure do spruce themselves up,' Allen remarked, keeping a friendly smile on his face. 'Have you ever been to Harlem, Mr Flemington?'

'No,' the fashion expert answered. 'But my Daddy has. And I've seen a lot of pictures.' Suddenly, and rather unexpectedly, his indignation surfaced. 'If you don't like the clothes – take them off,' he ordered. 'We're doing a favour for Mr Hubert Lloyd Fish. These outfits and my personal services would normally cost you men a fortune. If you don't appreciate –'

'Mr Flemington.' Allen held up his hand to keep the peace. 'We are both deeply grateful for what you and Mr Fish are doing for us.' After glancing at a troubled and uncomfortable-looking Banning, the mechanic faced the mirror again, leaned on his stick, and postured like a fashion model. 'But you have to understand, we're just a couple of slobs – and all this – elegance – has thrown us, temporarily.' He turned back to Lewis Flemington. 'We'll be honoured to wear your apparel to the Skelly mansion today.'

In view of the fact that they were so fancily dressed, and that Clarence Patterson's basement apartment was under a run-down billiard parlour, and that a limousine had been instructed to collect them, Banning had called Mr Skelly's assistant in order to give their address as the Royal Majestic, a high-class coloured hotel located a few blocks away from Clarence's dingy quarters. By tipping the uniformed doorman fifteen cents, the aviators were able to wait for the limousine outside the hotel's impressive entrance.

Sitting stiffly on the plush upholstery of Mr W.B. Skelly's grand automobile as it sped through Tulsa, Allen and Banning tried not to move too much in order not to wrinkle their Flemington rentals before making their grand entrance at the mansion. They were already uncomfortably aware of the impression they had made on the chauffeur, who had stood holding the door and gawking at the aviators for some minutes after they had entered the vehicle. Finally Banning had said, airily, 'To the Skelly residence, please – we have an appointment – and we do not wish to be late.'

The limousine drove slowly through magnificent grounds. Moments later, it moved down a slight incline towards massive iron gates, and the aviators peered out silently, and in subdued wonder, at a golf course and tennis courts. And then the mansion loomed up, a sprawling, eye-popping, Western-styled extravaganza, unlike anything they had ever seen.

Skelly's chauffeur, who had not uttered a sound during the journey, brought the car to a smooth halt at the foot of the stone steps leading up to the entrance. A waiting butler, in uniform, opened the door of the limousine as it came to a stop. Allen and Banning remained seated for a moment, without moving, speaking, or breathing.

'Good afternoon, gentlemen.' The butler, smiling mechanically at first, bent low, looked into the car, and gasped when he caught a glimpse of the visitors. 'Welcome to the Skelly residence,' he spluttered, trying desperately to recover himself. 'Mr Skelly and his guests will meet you in the den. Please follow me.'

Taking his time, Banning climbed out of the limousine, and stood upright and confidently in front of the bemused butler. He smoothed the lapels on his jacket, adjusted the polka-dot bow tie, and then tapped the ground rhythmically with his stick, while waiting for Allen to join him. When he had, Banning smiled at the butler, bowed slightly, made a wide sweeping gesture with his free hand, and ordered in a firm, clear voice, 'Lead on, my good man.'

The aviators slowly followed the butler through the elaborate front entrance, up a grand circular staircase, and down a long corridor on the second floor. They took their time studying each painting, touching every vase, and allowing their patent-leather shoes to linger in the richness of the carpeting. The butler, still gazing doubtfully at their eccentric Flemington rentals, waited for them to approach.

'The den, gentlemen,' he said, opening a heavy mahogany door. 'Mr Skelly and his guests will join you in a few moments.' He ushered them in. 'Please make yourselves comfortable.'

The door closed quietly behind them and, once again, the aviators were impressed by the luxuriousness of their surroundings. Although the room was spacious, the colours, wood panelling, and furnishings gave it warmth. Almost everything was built into the walls, including an ornate bar, a motion picture screen, and numerous, well-stocked bookcases.

Rehearsing his act, Banning strutted around the room, examining everything like a connoisseur. Allen, feeling ill at ease, foolish and apprehensive, stood rooted to the spot, watching his partner perform. Quiet male voices could be heard coming from somewhere beyond a side door. Skelly and his guests, the aviators assumed.

'Exquisitely furnished, and practical too,' said Banning, in a loud, affected tone as he moved close enough to the side door to be heard. 'Don't you agree, Thomas?' He beckoned Allen to join him.

'I do, indeed, James Herman,' Allen replied, obeying rather reluctantly. 'A magnificent room.'

The voices beyond the door were silenced.

'I was most impressed with that Mo-Nay hanging in the corridor,' Banning continued, knowing that they had an attentive audience. 'One of my favourites.'

'Oh, yes – that Mo-Nay,' said Allen, looking completely baffled. 'It is probably the very best – Mo-Nay – I have seen in a long while.'

Banning glared at him, walked to a nearby sofa, and sat, majestically. 'Was that a Ming on the shelf near the window in the corridor?' he asked, aware that he could still be heard by the quiet socialites next door. 'The butler moved us past it a bit too hastily.'

'Difficult to ascertain, James Herman.' Allen, with the same confused expression on his face, moved to the sofa and took a seat beside Banning. 'One must have time for a careful inspection – before – before – calling a Ming – a Ming. And that is a proven fact.'

As Banning glared sourly at Allen again, the side door opened, and four men appeared. The aviators rose to their feet and stared. They could not believe their eyes. It was apparent that the wealthy white socialites were experiencing the same surprise. Much to the consternation and embarrassment of the aviators, Skelly's guests were neither monocled, nor aristocratic, nor dressed in the latest Paris fashions. All four men were conservatively dressed in plain sports shirts, ranch-hand type trousers, and casual shoes. They were patently not interested in scoring sartorial points over their black visitors. With sinking hearts, Allen and Banning realized they had truly managed to become the couple of nigger clowns – comically over-dressed street urchins – that the pilot had imagined the whites were expecting to see.

'My name is Walt Skelly.' A middle-aged man stepped forward, smiling in a genuine way, and shook hands vigorously with each aviator. 'Are you Banning?' he asked, picking the right man. 'The pilot?'

'That's right,' Banning replied, getting a sudden wild urge to rip off the Flemington rentals and heave the stick far out of sight. 'And this is Thomas Allen, my co-pilot, and mechanic.'

'A pleasure to meet you,' said Skelly sincerely, motioning to the sofa. 'Have a seat and I'll pour us all a drink.' He walked to the bar. 'We take straight bourbon. Any preference?'

'Bourbon is fine,' Banning answered, wondering how to limit the damage his ill-conceived and reckless plot had caused. 'And Thomas likes the same.'

'Good,' said Skelly, pouring the drinks. 'You boys are sitting across from Cliff Powers, Ned Gould, and Robbie Culbertson. Aviation nuts like me.'

They all smiled and shook hands.

After distributing the illegal alcohol, Skelly took a seat and raised his glass. 'To a successful transcontinental flight,' he said. 'Go all the way safely and make the record books.'

His guests echoed the toast. Allen and Banning thanked them, and everybody took a large gulp of high quality bourbon. Mr Skelly settled back comfortably, and so did his friends. Trapped in their finery, the aviators were forced to sit awkwardly on the edge of their seats.

'You gentlemen didn't have to dress for the occasion,' Skelly remarked, looking them over without a trace of ridicule. 'Cliff, Ned, and Robbie were coming over for an informal business lunch and I had heard about your flight attempt. We thought it would be great to meet you and have a chat.'

Suddenly, Tom Allen began smiling, and then grinning, and then chuckling, and then laughing out loud, and only the stunned Banning could detect that his actions were forced and phoney.

'Please excuse me,' said Allen, when his outburst had been controlled. 'But I honestly can't continue with this stupid escapade.' While Banning stared at him as though he had gone mad, Allen reached into the inside pocket of his white jacket, removed

144

a wallet, and took out a one dollar bill, which he held up for the dumb founded pilot. 'You win, James Herman,' he declared, shoving the money at him, and staring him in the eye until he accepted it. 'I broke first, like you predicted.'

And then, placing his walking stick on the sofa beside him, Allen unfastened his polka-dot bow tie, and turned to Skelly and his guests. 'We owe you gentlemen an explanation,' he said, apologetically. 'Mr Skelly – your assistant asked us to come over and entertain – and that is the exact word he used – *entertain* – you and your guests. And, "for authenticity and dramatic effect", as he put it, he wanted us to perform in our flying gear – with maps, documents, and other relevant paraphernalia.'

'I'll be damned.' Skelly frowned. 'Go ahead with the rest, Allen,' he ordered soberly. 'This is outrageous.'

'We were also given a run-down on how to behave,' the mechanic continued, without sounding resentful in any way. 'When to sit – stand – speak – and so forth.'

'Carl Thurman,' Skelly blurted angrily, glancing at his three friends. 'Looking for another raise and a bonus. Pompous damn fool. All he rates is a swift kick in the ass. And that's what he'll get this evening.'

'Mr Skelly, we don't want to cause any trouble for the man –'

'Nonsense,' the industrialist interrupted with a quick wave of his hand. 'I've had problems with Thurman before. Get on with your story, Allen.' He smiled.

'Well.' The mechanic looked at Banning, who was still staring at him with a curious expression on his face. 'Frankly, I have to admit, we didn't take too kindly to your assistant's proposition. So I bet my partner one dollar that he wouldn't have the nerve to get dressed up like clowns – visit your place – and entertain you real good.'

'Absolutely beautiful.' Skelly laughed heartily. 'And you probably expected to face some real stuffed shirts – after what Carl Thurman said.'

'Yes, sir,' Allen admitted. 'We sure did.'

'Say,' the man called Ned Gould interjected, 'why don't you guys bust out of those jackets and ties, rest easy, and tell us about the flight?'

'Good idea,' said Skelly, with his eyes on Banning. 'And by the way, that Monet in the corridor is one of my favourites, too. And you did indeed pass a very rare Ming vase on the shelf near the window. You gentlemen have extremely smart taste.' The wealthy Tulsa industrialist leaned back in his chair. 'Now, about your flight,' he said to Banning. 'Start at the beginning in Los Angeles.'

Later that day, after Powers, Gould and Culbertson had left, Skelly had a private talk with the aviators. Mainly, he wanted to discuss financial assistance. He explained that an old friend of his, Lieutenant Craig Meredith, of Des Moines, Iowa, had contacted him and asked him to give them as much help as possible. He was accordingly offering to pay all of their flight expenses from Tulsa, Oklahoma to St Louis, Missouri. Every airport along the way would be instructed to service the Eagle Rock, provide anything else they needed, and bill Mr W.B. Skelly personally.

In the limousine on the return trip – to Clarence Patterson's basement apartment, instead of the Royal Majestic Hotel entrance – Allen and Banning were resting thoughtfully against the plush cushions, having discarded Flemington's links and spats, along with the jackets and ties.

'And we expected high-class society freaks and expensive Paris fashions,' said Allen quietly, in a philosophical mood. 'How wrong can you get? And I do mean *you*, James Herman.'

'Both of us.'

'You started all this,' said Allen, looking out of the window as they entered Tulsa proper. 'Who referred to nigger clowns and shuffling street urchins?'

'I was justified after listening to that damn assistant,' Banning answered, refusing to accept the full blame. 'Even Skelly thought we did the right thing.'

'Well, it's over – and what results, eh, partner?'

'Beautiful.'

'A free ride from here to St Louis.'

'I can't believe it.'

'You should.' Allen turned to the pilot. 'When will James Herman Banning accept the fact that this world is full of good and bad types – and it has absolutely nothing to do with skin colour – or the size of a man's bank account. We saw that today. And –'

'Clam up, Thomas,' Banning interrupted, leaning his head back and closing his eyes. 'When I need a preacher I'll go to church.'

'Did Mr Skelly do a marvellous thing for us?'

'He certainly did.'

'A white man.'

'So?'

'What about your chip?'

146

'Any friend of Craig Meredith has got to be quality stuff.'

'Another white man.'

'No, Thomas,' said Banning, opening his eyes slightly. 'Lieutenant Craig Meredith doesn't have any colour. He is something very special. And this world won't be worth a shit until a lot more people like him begin to populate it.'

Overcome with euphoria, Banning allowed Allen to take the controls for the short hop to Miami, Oklahoma. He got up reasonably well and flew north-east over forests of Blackjack timber to Claremore, over Claremore to the right of the Military Academy, then over more dense Blackjack forests, and then over Vinita, where there are some meadows and farmlands, and finally, Miami. Allen circled the dirt field and made a side-slip landing.

Because there were no coloured people living in this small Oklahoma town, always a worrying situation, the aviators felt that the port would be a reliable test, as far as Mr W.B. Skelly's promised assistance was concerned.

Allen instructed the attendant to fill the gas tank. It only needed ten gallons, and a little oil and water. When the servicing had been completed, the aviators waited for a bill. Moments later, the unsmiling employee returned from the office and muttered that the account would be settled by Mr Skelly, of Skelly's Tagolene Gasoline Company, Tulsa.

Concerned about Miami's proximity to the Ozark Mountains, Banning asked the attendant about any problems he was likely to encounter when flying over this rugged strip of country to St Louis. Listlessly, and with his dead eyes on the unusual aircraft, the man suggested that the pilot swing north a bit at Carthage, Missouri, in order to avoid the Springfield district – a very bad patch.

Banning flew over the lead and zinc mines of north-eastern Oklahoma and south-western Missouri. Passing to the right of Joplin, leaving the mines, the aviators saw a few wheatfields as they approached Carthage, Missouri.

Once again, all expenses on the field, including hamburgers, coleslaw, ginger ale, and two jelly doughnuts were, according to the office, covered by Mr W.B. Skelly, of Tulsa, Oklahoma.

With Banning at the controls on take-off, the Eagle Rock suddenly became more sluggish than usual, gaining hardly any altitude.

147

The old crate just mushed through the air in a climbing position. Finally she rose to two thousand feet. Wheatfields stretched in all directions below them. And they had a clear view of the distant Ozarks.

When the plane was east and slightly north of Carthage, twelve miles out, Allen listened carefully and decided that they definitely had an engine problem – no misses – but not enough power. He wrote a note and positioned it so that Banning could read, 'Left bank sounds bad.'

Believing that he was capable of executing a safe forced landing in the wheatfields, Banning remained calm, waved to Allen, made a descent, whacked the airplane down, and ploughed wildly and uncontrollably through a maze of tall stalks, until they came to a shuddering halt. Both men gazed up at the sky, and grinned, breathing a humble thank-you for having the Dear Lord's guiding hand on their shoulders, yet again.

News of the landing spread rapidly and, in a short time, nine inquisitive local farmers had gathered around the plane, while the aviators checked the engine. The intake valve was holding open. Allen adjusted the tappet, and put in a new spark plug, the best he could do for the moment.

When the Eagle Rock was ready, several of the more courageous farmers begged for a short ride, and they were willing to pay for the experience but, remembering their pledge about no passengers or circus stunts en route, not to mention the fact that they had to reach St Louis by nightfall, the flyers politely declined.

Because of the thick weeds and wheat stubble, Banning would need the entire field to gain speed, and get up. They braced themselves, and held up crossed fingers to each other. The Eagle Rock rolled, and bounced, and shook, and rocked, and moved faster and faster over the stubborn Missouri cereal crops. And, as so many times before, at the very last moment, the shuddering wreck shot up through an opening between some trees, dived down sharply over cornstalks to get more acceleration, and then flew away.

The farmers watched in amazement.

Lambert Field in St Louis, Missouri was one of the country's finest airports; so large, that planes had to land near the middle, or be forced to taxi about a mile to the hangars. Because it was a big-city terminal, with a large staff, and a stream of incoming and outgoing passengers and visitors, Banning flopped the Eagle

148

Rock down at the far end of the field, on purpose, hoping to minimize the familiar and quite exasperating reactions to their arrival anywhere.

'I've never seen anything like it,' mumbled a Lambert clerk, filling out a rental and service form for the aviators. 'Must be about thirty or forty coloured people jammed in that terminal press room,' he continued, without looking up. 'Police, too, and black newspaper reporters, photographers, and even a couple of preachers.'

'What's going on?' Allen asked, giving Banning a fast look, full of interest. 'Only something mighty important could drag thirty or forty coloured people to an airport.'

'Beats me,' the clerk remarked, still concentrating on his writing. 'They've been waiting for almost an hour,' he added. 'And we don't have anything special on the books – coming or going.'

'You must have heard a few rumours,' probed Banning, as the clerk finally looked up. 'That kind of commotion has to be organized. What's your guess?'

'A grease monkey said that two black celebrities would be turning up,' the clerk replied, handing the form to Allen for signature. 'And they were flying on to New York City – to make some kind of history. These people are gathered here to give them a surprise send-off. Anyway, that's the rumour – according to the grease monkey.'

'Well, well, well.' Allen scribbled his name, grinned, and shoved the paper back to the Lambert Field employee. 'I think we'll just mosey over there and look for ourselves. Are you with me, James Herman?'

The aviators, standing partially hidden at the side of the administration building, watched several blacks, a policeman, and a photographer, rush towards the terminal press room. A tall Negro and his female companion walked quickly past them, talking about a record, and something being an inspiration for coloured youth. Allen and Banning were thrilled, as they prepared themselves for true celebrity status, in a big city – St Louis, Missouri.

'How did the word get out so completely?' Allen asked his partner, who had his eyes on more coloured pedestrian traffic, moving hurriedly to the same area. 'The *Oklahoma Black Dispatch*?'

'And probably Skelly in Tulsa and Craig Meredith in Des Moines,' Banning replied, nibbling his lower lip. 'Lordsburgh, New Mexico, too,' he added. 'And there must have been many

149

other leaks along the way – from ground crews – and Gold Book contributors.'

'Hot damn!' Allen blurted happily, as they lingered in the shadow of the building's jutting roof. 'My boy will have a thick scrapbook about his daddy to show his friends someday.'

'To hell with that now,' said Banning. 'We've got to be on our toes and ready for some high-powered action this time. A true dress rehearsal for New York City.'

'And that is point one,' said Allen, becoming as serious as his partner. 'Do we put on our Sunday suits for the occasion?'

'Not a chance,' Banning fired back. 'I did enough damage with Lester Flemington. We'll do a quick wash-up and appear in our working clothes. That's what the good people of St Louis are expecting.'

'Who talks first?'

'I do.'

'You do every time.'

'Right.'

'Why?'

'Because I am the pilot.'

'And who keeps that wreck in shape for you?'

'Don't be petty, Thomas,' said Banning firmly, staring at the terminal's press section. 'We've got more important things to discuss right now – and fast, too – because that congregation has been waiting a long time for us.'

'Well, let's go.'

'Hold it,' said Banning, restraining him. 'Stragglers are still arriving. We'll clean up while we wait until the press room is full – and then make a proper entrance.'

'Do we sign autographs, James Herman?'

'We'll do anything to make these people feel proud and self-respecting,' Banning answered seriously. 'The spirit of St Louis is being aroused by coloured folks this time, Thomas.'

Allen and Banning entered a packed press room behind the backs of about fifty spectators. Negro men, women and children were sitting crowded together in front of an empty, raised platform. The setting excited the aviators – the element of surprise – an introduction from the audience – it was as it should be.

Several mean-faced white police officers were monitoring the proceedings from strategic positions along the walls. A small, busy Negro attendant, who was evidently in charge of seating arrangements, rushed to the aviators and led them to two empty

150

chairs at the back of the large room. He then moved swiftly to the doors, closed them, and stood guard inside. It appeared that the room was now full and ready for the eagerly awaited ceremonial.

Moments later, a pudgy, smartly dressed black man strode briskly and confidently to the centre of the platform, and faced the gathering.

'Ladies and gentlemen,' the host announced, using his hands and arms in a broad, stagey manner. 'We're here at this airport to say Godspeed – and God bless you – to two members of our race who are on the way to New York City – to make us stand taller – with dignity – and pride.'

The spectators applauded wildly, and some shouted 'Amen!' and 'Hallelujah!' Banning, who was silently rehearsing his opening remarks, glanced at Allen, and they exchanged knowing winks and secret smiles.

'In a short time,' the host continued, with even more theatrical gestures, 'their names will be known and honoured throughout this land – and possibly throughout the world. I know – and God knows – they are going to succeed, and their success is sure to be an inspiration for all Negro people – young and old.'

Again the spectators applauded loudly, enthusiastically, and there were more shouts of 'Amen!' and 'Hallelujah!' Allen leaned close to Banning's ear, cupped his hand and yelled, 'This man is a bigger ham-bone than you are, James Herman.'

'And now,' the host continued, playing with every word. 'It is time for us to welcome – our two distinguished guests – and I ask – that when I call their names – you stand with me – and demonstrate – how deeply we feel about their mission – and how passionately we want them to succeed.'

As the host paused for the big moment, Allen and Banning, feeling awkward, and slightly embarrassed straightened their flight jackets, cleared their throats quietly, and prepared to stand.

'Ladies and gentlemen,' said the host, with his eyes on the black photographers, who were already standing in position, focusing their cameras on the raised platform, 'Please welcome – and give a heartfelt St Louis send-off – to – Miss Elvira Washington – and Miss Augusta Bradshaw!'

With the exception of the dumbfounded aviators, the entire congregation rose to its feet, cheering and applauding, as two fat-faced, heavy-set, middle-aged Negro women left their seats, climbed a few steps, and stood beside the host, smilingly accepting the noisy, enthusiastic acclaim.

Moments later, while the standing ovation was still in progress, Allen looked at Banning, and allowed a slow, rueful grin to take shape, and remain fixed in place. Banning just stared blankly at his partner. Finally, the mechanic shrugged his shoulders, stood up and screamed his approval of Elvira Washington and Augusta Bradshaw with the rest of the audience. He had never heard of either of them, and still didn't know what their mission was in New York City.

Banning, glued to his chair, happened to glance over at the wall, and meet the cold eyes of a white policeman. 'And fuck you too, pig head,' he muttered.

14

Swallowing their pride, Allen and Banning had successfully begged a ride from an airport employee, who had deposited them at the Red Bird Café on Market Street, in a coloured section of St Louis. It was 7:30 pm.

The aviators sipped coffee and examined their situation. As usual, they were nearly broke, unable to buy a decent meal or find a room for the night. Luckily, the airport bill would be picked up by Mr Skelly – his last – and this was going to be a hefty one because, along with gas, oil, hangar rent, and engine servicing, the valves had to be ground.

They were still feeling foolish and rueful after the reception in the terminal press room. They had discovered that Elvira Washington and Augusta Bradshaw were two of the city's best-known gospel singers, idols of the black communities. The women had been invited to New York City by Gordon Henry Cullen, a prominent Negro writer, who had been recruited by state officials to co-ordinate a major relief programme for the black population. Cullen was forming a choir to give concerts and make a phonograph recording, courtesy of RCA Victor, revenue from the sales of which would go to the central relief fund, and Elvira Washington and Augusta Bradshaw had been selected as soloists. The black residents of St Louis were excited and very proud.

Just before 8:00 pm, Allen and Banning were astonished to see the pudgy, smartly dressed press room host approaching them at the counter.

'It took me damn nearly an hour to find you boys,' the man said, a bit breathlessly, adjusting the knot of his tie with great precision. 'Let's move to that corner table,' he added. 'I want to talk some important business.'

The host, Mr Eugene 'Lippy' Hapgood, explained in a sharp-talking, big-city way, that he was a publicity man, an experienced professional, who had handled Negro celebrities from all walks of life. Although his office was in Harlem, he had travelled to St Louis because of his contract with Elvira Washington and Augusta Bradshaw.

'I heard about you boys earlier today, from a contact at the *Oklahoma Black Dispatch*,' he said, flashing a diamond-studded pinky ring. 'I had no idea you landed in St Louis and were out there in my press audience.'

The aviators, still surprised by his sudden and unexpected appearance, sat quietly waiting for him to get to the point.

'I like the project very much,' said Hapgood, leaning forward on his elbows. 'We have a chance to create a couple of black action heroes – if things are organized properly in New York City – and that's my speciality.'

'What are you talking about exactly, Mr Hapgood?' Allen asked, courteously. 'You mean arranging for newspaper interviews and stuff like that?'

'I mean a whole lot more, Allen,' Lippy Hapgood replied, using his hands and arms again, as he had done at the airport. 'We need a Harlem parade, with crowds and confetti, and dinners – with stars of stage and screen – meetings with business and civic leaders – and the public – don't ever forget that great black public, so needful of inspiration and –'

'Mr Hapgood.' Banning cut the publicity man off in midsentence, causing him to sit back, and deflate a little. 'Do you understand what our flight is all about?' He did not wait for a response. 'This is not a stunt. We are not gospel singers or vaudeville performers. Allen and myself are qualified and experienced aviators – attempting to complete the first Negro transcontinental flight.'

'And if you do?' Hapgood was back fast. 'Want to keep it a secret?' The publicity man knew by Banning's expression that his point had been scored. 'The public must be made aware,' he continued, less animated than before. 'Or your landing in New York City will go unnoticed. Is that really what you boys want?'

'Of course not,' Allen answered at once. 'If the Eagle Rock comes down safely on New York soil we want the whole damn world to know – white and black. Right, James Herman?'

'Right,' Banning admitted, keeping his eyes on Lippy Hapgood. 'But I also worry about cheap publicity angles. Everything about this mission has to be kept at the highest possible level. We're going for the history books and the Smithsonian in Washington, DC.'

'My office only works at the highest possible levels, Mr Banning,' said Hapgood with a trace of irritation. 'And we're very selective about the clients we represent.'

'What do you charge?' Allen asked bluntly.

'You can't afford me,' Hapgood replied, meaning it. 'I only work on a percentage basis – a percentage of every penny you earn on this venture.'

'How much of a percentage?' Banning inquired, still keeping the publicity man under constant observation. 'And when do you stop collecting?'

'I get ten per cent,' Hapgood replied. 'And my contracts run for three years – with options.'

'We have a problem, Mr Hapgood,' said Allen, breaking in again. 'You see, we took on partners. All of us have a split of the one thousand dollar prize money. But, we could lower their takes, or even cut a few of them out, because –'

'That's your business, Allen,' Hapgood interrupted. 'I get ten per cent of everything – off the top – and your one thousand dollar reward is a drop in the bucket. My ideas generate real money. Want to draw up papers?'

'Yes,' Banning answered instantly, surprising his partner. 'You receive five per cent – and the contract runs for one year – without options.'

'No deal.'

'Fine with me.'

'Wait a minute.' Lippy Hapgood smiled, and it made his forty year-old face look boyish, almost innocent. 'A deal,' he said, finally. 'Five per cent for one year without options. And do you know why? This guy Banning's looks might pull in a big advance from a movie company.'

'Oh, damn.' Allen suddenly laughed out loud. 'James Herman – a motion picture star. I am truly glad and thankful that we'll be doing business together, Mr Hapgood,' he said cordially. 'Because you are the most persuasive bullshitter I have ever met.'

After they had clasped hands on an agreement, which was to be followed by a formal contract signing in New York City – God willing – Hapgood booked the aviators into a fine room on the top floor of the best coloured hotel in town. Their late meal was delicious. And a full bottle of high quality whisky was delivered by the night manager. Banning opened it while Allen called Los Angeles and spoke to Celene for over five minutes. She was fine, but missing him more each day, she said. 'I miss you, too, honey,' said Allen, and blew kisses into the receiver to prove it. Banning poked fun, and gulped whisky, until Allen clicked off and snatched the bottle.

Everything, including tips and a ten dollar bill for pocket money, had been arranged by their new publicity man. And, when Lippy Hapgood made arrangements, Lippy Hapgood made arrangements, as the aviators discovered at one o'clock in the morning, when Banning answered a quiet knock on the door.

Two young and beautiful coloured girls entered, mentioned Lippy's name, and immediately stripped off all their clothes and sprawled on the bed. It was quickly established that they were not whores, but dancers from the Bamboo Room who had been promised a job in the Lafayette Theatre in Harlem by Mr Hapgood.

Fortunately for Tom Allen's conscience, after singing a loud chorus of 'Hard Hearted Hannah,' and a few lines of 'Lovin' Sam,' he collapsed on a sofa, out cold. What Banning got up to with the two enticing young ladies, he could only surmise from the pilot's blissful and smug expression the next day.

Banning called Lambert Field in the morning and was told that the mechanics had not had the time to complete their work on the Eagle Rock. It would be ready about 1:00 pm. The aviators had a large breakfast at the hotel on Hapgood, enjoyed a short sight-seeing walk around town, had an early lunch at the hotel on Hapgood, and then checked out, splurging a little of their pocket money on a taxi ride to the airport.

Along with a copy of the bill, which was being sent to Mr W.B. Skelly of Tulsa, Oklahoma, as per his instructions, the aviators were surprised by a formal note that had been left for them in the administration building.

Mr Eugene Hapgood sincerely hoped that Allen and Banning had enjoyed their contract signing celebration in St Louis, but he wanted to go on record that this was his standard operating procedure with every new client, and they had now seen the end of his generosity. Hapgood was a publicity man and not a banker. He never gave loans, advances, or gratuities to his clients, no matter how serious or urgent the problem; a strict policy, never altered. After St Louis, Allen and Banning would have to make their own way, without depending on any financial assistance from Hapgood. His lessons had been learned the hard way over the years. The publicity man asked for progress reports

156

en route, so that the welcoming arrangements in New York City could be made in good time. He wished them both a safe and successful journey.

Listening to the engine being warmed up, Allen was instinctively not too pleased with the Lambert Field workmanship. However, with Banning in command, the Eagle Rock took off at 2:15 pm, and flew in a north-easterly direction. They crossed the Mississippi River within a few minutes.

In time, they were bumping, and bouncing, and praying over the farms of Illinois. For about an hour, the aviators had high hopes of spending the night in Indianapolis, a good jump for them. But, as Allen had feared, the engine started to sound erratic. It became worse at Effingham. Even so, the pilot decided to keep going, because they were flying at a high altitude.

Passing a little to the right of Marshall, Illinois, and after crossing the Wabash River, Banning finally gave up, and whacked the plane down extra hard on a small field in Terre Haute, Indiana.

After the landing, Allen raised the hood, shook his head sadly, and cursed until he ran out of appropriate words. The Eagle Rock had another broken push rod, and the whole overhead valve action, and everything else that had given them trouble in St Louis, was loose, and ready to drop off. A closer inspection revealed that a few parts had actually disappeared already.

Even though they could do most of their repair work themselves, it meant an overnight stay in a strange town, without enough money for parts, hangar rent, accommodation, food, and other necessities. And they could not fall back on either Skelly or Hapgood. It was a real pity, the aviators agreed, because Banning had a few friends in Indianapolis, their long-shot destination. Here in Terre Haute, they didn't know a soul.

In the airport office, an unusually friendly and co-operative young man handled their paperwork, and listened with interest to Tom Allen's hard luck story, and questions about possible assistance. He made it very clear, at once, that the field's management would never consider giving credit to anyone, especially – unfamiliar – people, just passing through Terre Haute. But the pleasant clerk remembered that a coloured man by the name of Willie Greer used to work at the airport, doing odd jobs. According to the clerk, Willie was a real nice guy, always smiling, and very popular on the field and in the Negro community.

'We all had a lot of fun with Silly Willie,' said the young man. 'I'm sure he'll be able to organize something for you. All things considered Willie is definitely your best bet – maybe your only bet – in this town.'

'Now that's very kind and helpful of you,' said Tom Allen, sincerely. 'Do you know where we can find him?'

'He works as a handyman part time at Slugger McCoy's gymnasium downtown,' the young man replied, scribbling the address on a slip of paper. 'You'll probably find him there around seven this evening. And – for your information – Newton Street is in a very rough, white neighbourhood.'

'No problem,' said Banning, accepting the paper, and shoving it into his flight jacket pocket. 'We'll both smile a lot,' he added, not bothering to disguise the sarcasm. 'Just like old Silly Willie.'

Allen and Banning walked about a mile, waited nearly an hour for a streetcar, and finally arrived on Newton Street, which might have been rough and white, but there were no problems of any kind. In fact, a couple of swaggering gang types had passed them almost shoulder to shoulder, with total indifference. Minutes later, the aviators reached a sign-posted doorway, and a flight of wooden steps.

Slugger McCoy's gymnasium, an upstairs training facility, was large, busy, and professionally equipped. The regulation-sized ring was the centre-piece, and around it, at various locations, sweaty, white musclemen in boxing gear were punching bags, skipping rope, shadow boxing, and working out with dumbbells, pedal-pushers, and other conditioning devices.

Slugger's customers, mainly local club fighters and a few physical fitness addicts, were too caught up in what they were doing to pay much attention to the Negro aviators, as they moved uneasily through the gym. The loud grunting noises and heavy body odours eased off a bit at the far end, where a corner had been glass-partitioned and marked, 'Office.'

Allen and Banning knocked on the door, entered, and faced a big, rough-looking character in his late fifties, with a balding head, a flat, seemingly boneless nose, and two cauliflower ears. Obviously a former palooka, the man was seated at a small desk, under autographed photos of Jack Dempsey and Gene Tunney. His shirt-sleeves were rolled up above his elbows, revealing a thick growth of dark hair which nearly covered a tattoo on each arm. The mangled butt of a cigar was lodged in the corner of his wide mouth.

'What the hell did you do – land on my roof?' the man growled, inspecting Allen and Banning's flying suits. 'You missed the airport by about twenty miles.'

'No, sir,' said Allen, taking the remark good-naturedly. 'We're looking for a Negro who works here as a handyman. Do you know Willie Greer?'

'Of course I know Willie Greer,' the man replied, still checking the aviators over very carefully. 'How come you bums are dressed up like flyers?'

'Because we are,' Allen answered before his partner could respond. 'We came in from Los Angeles, and we're heading for New York City – a transcontinental flight attempt – the first by Negroes.'

The ageing gorilla continued to stare at Allen, and then focused his curious gaze on Banning. 'Are you bums trying to be cute with me?' he asked gruffly. 'I don't appreciate jokes.'

'We were forced down here because of engine trouble.' Banning's authoritative voice and confident manner added credibility to Allen's story. 'And,' he continued, tugging on his leather flight jacket, 'we didn't have a chance to check our wardrobes for proper visiting clothes.'

'Are you Slugger McCoy?' Allen asked.

'What's left of him,' the man replied. 'Black transcontinental pilots,' he went on with a trace of admiration. 'All kinds of bums have stumbled up and down my steps, but this is a first. Is Willie Greer a friend of yours?'

'No, sir,' Allen replied, watching McCoy lean back, and fold his arms across a barrel chest. 'You see, we have some problems, and the airport clerk thought that Willie Greer might be helpful.'

'What problems?'

'Money,' Allen answered bluntly. 'We'll have a large bill at the airport – and we need food – a place to stay for the night – and things like that.'

'You might get a bed and a can of beans through Willie,' the frog-voiced McCoy commented. 'But don't expect money. He's broke – just like most other people in this town – especially the coloured people.'

'Even a bed and a can of beans would be very much appreciated,' said Allen. 'Do you know where we can find him?'

'He'll be sweeping out the front hallway in about an hour,' McCoy answered, staring at Banning again, with something obviously on his mind. 'You can go and come back, or wait in the ringside chairs. It's up to you.'

159

'Anything special going on in the gym tonight, Mr McCoy?' Allen asked, glancing through the glass partition at the vigorous training activity. 'I love to watch boxing.'

'Ever do any yourself?'

'Just a few neighbourhood contests.'

'What about you?'

'I was on the team at Iowa State for a while,' Banning answered. 'Five wins – three defeats – and a draw. Nothing spectacular. Why did you ask?'

The big man got up, moved his overweight frame to the glass, and waved at a few of the bag-punching fighters. 'I had a crazy thought when you bums mentioned needing some money,' he finally replied, with his eyes still on the perspiring clients. 'But now that I think about it – forget it – too crazy – too dangerous.'

'Go ahead, Mr McCoy,' said Banning. 'We're listening.'

Still chomping on the saliva-soaked cigar butt, Slugger McCoy explained that he was currently managing a bright new welter-weight prospect, a potential world champion named Eddie Lyons. The former Terre Haute amateur sensation had a record of twenty-two straight professional wins, without a defeat, eighteen by knock-out before the sixth round. Lyons could box, and punch, and take them too, a rare combination. His biggest test was coming up in ten days – a world class fight in the Indianapolis Stadium against Young Joe Gayle, a highly rated Negro contender. An impressive win over Gayle would put Lyons within striking distance of the welterweight crown.

'Eddie will be here in a few minutes to work out and do some heavy sparring,' McCoy continued, hoarsely. 'He's never fought a black man before. Gayle will be the first.'

'Why not put it on the line, Mr McCoy?' said Banning. 'You want us to climb into the ring with your Eddie Lyons – and get him used to punching at black flesh, before the Gayle fight.'

'Something like that.'

'What exactly were you going to propose?' Banning pressed on, much to the consternation of his partner.

'OK.' Slugger McCoy spoke on the way back to his desk. 'You bums need a little cash urgently,' he growled, taking a seat, and glaring up at the attentive aviators. 'I want a couple of black sparring partners for Eddie Lyons. My payment will be fifty cents for every round you stay with him. And I don't care how many rounds you go. That is – if you get a chance to raise your gloves in the first – which is doubtful. Because – this close to fight time – I always let him cut loose – so

160

he won't be holding anything back. You bums will be Young
Joe Gayle – ten days from now – as far as Eddie Lyons is
concerned.'

'What about a referee?' Banning asked.

'That's me,' McCoy replied. 'And there's something else. We
won't be responsible for any injuries or death. You'll have to sign
a paper with a couple of witnesses.'

'How charming,' Allen remarked, gazing at the side of Banning's head, until he turned and faced him. 'You can't really
be serious about this, James Herman,' he prodded. 'Mr McCoy
just wants his protégé to get the feel of beating the shit out of a
black man in less than twenty seconds – a psychological exercise
– a morale booster – ten days before his fight with Gayle. And it
won't cost him a goddamn penny.'

'You get the fifty cents no matter when he stops you in the
first,' said McCoy. 'In fact I'll pay you a dollar – no matter
when he stops you in the first – and believe me, Eddie will stop
you in the first.'

'Mr McCoy.' Banning had a crafty smile on his face. 'You've
got a champion and all the odds on your side. Why don't you
make this interesting for everybody? We'll spar with Eddie Lyons
– if you pay us two dollars a round – and twenty-five dollars if we
take this guy past the fourth. As you just said, he'll get us in the
first – without a doubt. So how can you lose?'

'The twenty-five is no worry,' said McCoy, thinking out loud.
'Because you'd need a machine gun to earn it. I just don't like
paying two dollars a round. Four bucks for you bums to go
out in the first? Highway robbery. I usually pay fifty cents a
round. And to spar with Eddie Lyons? The next welterweight
champ? I've got six pros out there who'll do it for nothing – and
with pleasure.'

'Then why don't you use them?' Banning asked, tiring of the
negotiations. 'I'll tell you. You want a different look and smell
for Eddie Lyons tonight. A little nibble at Young Joe Gayle.
Well, you'll have to pay extra for the black meat – or forget
it, Mr McCoy.'

The Slugger checked Banning's expression, saw the unyielding
determination, and came up with a prompt decision. 'All right,'
he grunted, standing up and moving to the door. 'You've got a
deal.'

'Just a goddamn minute,' said Allen, holding one finger aloft
in a vain attempt to halt the proceedings. 'Nobody has a formal
decision from me.'

'Hey, Tubby!' McCoy yelled to someone in the gymnasium. 'Get these two bums rigged up for a sparring session! Eddie Lyons will be here in a few minutes!'

A fascinated crowd had gathered around Slugger McCoy's regulation-sized ring. All the club fighters, health freaks and employees, and quite a few newly-arrived spectators, were excitedly waiting for the start of an unexpected special event.

Eddie Lyons, a powerfully built, crew-cut blond, with a menacing, stone-faced expression, was prancing around his corner, throwing devastating punches at imaginary targets. Across the ring, the audience inspected the trim, solid frame of a good-looking Negro. The borrowed trunks, shoes, and gloves fitted him perfectly. James Herman looked like a boxer. His corner man, another Negro, appeared to be very nervous, and completely out of place, as he watched Banning grip the ropes, and do a few deep knee bends. Tubby Calhoun had briefed him about seconding his fighter, but Allen seemed to have forgotten most of the advice already.

Slugger McCoy was standing in the centre of the ring, ready to begin. He had already explained the arrangements to the curious onlookers – two dollars for each completed round except the first, which was an automatic pay-out no matter when it ended, and twenty-five dollars if the impossible happened and Eddie Lyons was taken past four rounds. No judges were needed, for obvious reasons. Just a timekeeper and a man on the bell.

The fighters, with mouthpieces in place, were brought together in the centre of the ring by McCoy. As they touched gloves, the bell sounded, the stools were quickly removed from each corner, and round one was under way.

The boxers were both right-handers. At the start, Banning stayed in close, but Lyons's left jabs were coming fast and with deadly accuracy, one after the other, and each one connected – on his nose, chin, and forehead. If he crouched, the stinging blows still found their marks, peppering him until he felt sore, welted, and slightly groggy. Upright, his defence was useless against the sharp and constant poking of the outstretched left glove, a lethal weapon. And all the while, Banning could see the knock-out tool, Lyons's right hand, cocked and ready to be unloaded, at the opportune moment.

Banning set himself, and threw a few badly timed lefts of his own, missing completely. And then, using fairly respectable footwork, he backed off, just in time to avoid a swinging left

162

hook. But he was open, and Lyons connected with a crushing right to the body which doubled him over, and exposed his head to a barrage of heavy punches from the dangerous professional. A left, a right, a left, a right, a left, a right, and Banning heard crowd noises, and felt warm blood oozing from his nose, as he went down on one knee.

McCoy shoved Lyons away, and started counting. Banning, with his head spinning, waited until nine, stood, brought up his gloves, and back-pedalled, while Lyons punched just short, until they hit the ropes. After tying Lyons up, in a clumsy, amateurish fashion, Banning took a few more body shots, but was able to hold on, and frustrate the professional, by preventing him from landing the clean wallops he needed for a knock-out.

A moment after McCoy broke them on the ropes, Banning unexpectedly caught Lyons with a short, jolting upper-cut, and this affront infuriated the future champion. He lashed out with a hard left to Banning's temple, followed by a punishing right to the chin, which knocked his mouthpiece out, and on to the canvas. But as the Negro staggered back towards the ropes, legs buckling, the bell sounded, ending one complete round. Banning, who should have rolled over during Slugger McCoy's count, had earned his guaranteed two dollars the hard way, along with a chance to absorb more punishment in round two, unless he stayed put on the stool and ignored the next bell.

'Just keep moving away from him, James Herman!' Allen shouted over the noise, after replacing Banning's mouthpiece, and clamping the towel under his bleeding nose. 'Don't throw a punch unless –'

'Shut up, Thomas!' Banning yelled, breathing heavily. 'I'm still debating whether to go out there again! That guy might kill me!'

'Want to quit?'

The bell rang for the second round before Banning could answer. Lyons was on his feet, McCoy stood ready, and the excited ringside crowd had increased. Banning got up automatically and moved towards his opponent.

Again, Lyons's fast, snapping left jabs hit their targets, each time the Negro stepped into range. And he was using his bone-crushing right hand more frequently, and with greater effect, in this second round. Banning's eyes were puffed, and nearly closed, and the rest of his face had become swollen. Blood still trickled from his nose, covering his lips, and chin. He felt light-headed and weary.

But he continued to duck and bob, and weave and clinch, and luckily avoid the one big punch which would have ended the lopsided contest.

Just before the second round ended, Lyons caught his man with a short left hook, dazed him, and then pounded a scorching right to the mid-section which took the breath away from Banning and, for some unknown reason, gave him a brief moment of wild, uncontrollable aggression. Forgetting his guard, and the brutal consequences, he waded into Lyons, swinging long, looping rights and lefts until the professional was leaning against the ropes, using his gloves for protection.

When the bell sounded, Banning had picked up four dollars, a battered face and body, a strange look from Slugger McCoy, and another opportunity to go again, or quit and walk away.

'I just don't believe you, James Herman!' yelled Allen, using the towel to wipe away blood and perspiration, while his partner slumped on the stool with eyes closed and chest heaving. 'We've got four bucks and a chance for twenty-five!'

'Where-do-you-get-this-*we*-shit, ass-hole?'

'Sorry, James Herman!' Allen, with the towel now around his neck, sponged cool water over Banning's head, glanced over at Eddie Lyons, and winced. The professional, who had just been whispered to by Slugger McCoy, was already standing in his corner, hopping from one foot to the other, and Tom Allen had never seen such an evil and threatening expression on any man's face, white or black. 'Maybe we – excuse me – maybe *you* should stop right now, partner!' he shouted into Banning's ear. 'That man looks awful mean and vengeful!'

'One more time, Thomas!' Banning yelled back, opening his eyes, and straightening up to wait for the bell. 'And then he's all yours!'

Eddie Lyons, resembling a vicious jungle animal, attacked the instant the bell clanged for the third round, and Banning realized that he should never have humiliated the professional by lashing out at the end of the second – a costly tactical blunder.

All Banning could see for the next few agonizing minutes were flashes of bloody leather, a spinning gymnasium, close-up specks of dust on the canvas and, every once in a while, Eddie Lyons's twisted smile, a fuzzy, grotesque image, which usually preceded a punishing assault.

Without landing one punch of his own, Banning was hit consistently by stunning rights and lefts, and Lyons refused to tolerate clinching, or backing off. Dazed, and on automatic, Banning went down four times, but somehow managed to haul himself up each time, before the count had ended. Slugger McCoy and Eddie Lyons showed their amazement and frustration. The ringside onlookers were delighted. Tom Allen, thinking of his partner and himself, was grappling with a mixture of emotions, including admiration, concern, fear, and trepidation. And, mercifully, for the moment, Banning was too numb to feel the swelling, cuts and bruises inflicted by his opponent.

The bell rang. Banning, almost blind, staggered crazily around the ring, until Slugger McCoy led the badly beaten Negro to his corner, where he was grabbed by a very worried Tom Allen.

Banning flopped on the stool, crumpled, and knew, as everyone else did, that he would not be up and ready at the bell to start the fourth.

After hustling Tubby Calhoun over to work on Banning's wounds, Slugger McCoy stood in the centre of the ring and addressed the excited spectators.

'This bum Banning has a lot of guts,' the former boxer announced, after the crowd had settled down. 'He stayed with Eddie Lyons for three full rounds and took one hell of a beating. So instead of getting the agreed six dollars, I'm handing over ten.'

McCoy's audience cheered, whistled, and applauded loudly.

'A few other things,' he went on, holding up his hand for silence. 'Let's not forget about Eddie's performance. Another black man called Young Joe Gayle will finish the same way – or worse – ten days from now, in Indianapolis.'

Again a spirited response was quickly silenced.

'We have another bum coming up in about fifteen minutes,' McCoy continued. 'The same pay-off rules apply. Two dollars a round – the first guaranteed – and twenty-five bucks if Eddie is taken past the fourth. He waited for the merriment to subside. 'Anyway, I won't have to be so generous with this next bum – a real stiff. Don't blink or you'll miss the action. I might give him his two bucks before the first bell. Are you all being entertained this evening?'

The audience shouted affirmatively.

'Good,' said McCoy. 'Tubby Calhoun will be moving around with our collection box – as soon as he finishes patching up Eddie's first victim. Drop a few pennies in. Whatever you can spare. This show would have cost plenty down at the Palace Theatre. Why should I give things away like a punch-drunk?'

*

165

Banning's injuries had been efficiently treated, bandaged, and massaged, but he looked and felt like a man who had just finished being kicked repeatedly by a runaway mule.

Willie Greer, an exceptionally tall and thin Negro, had arrived at the gymnasium during the interval. The Terre Haute airfield clerk's description of Greer was accurate. He appeared to be a real nice guy, always smiling, popular with blacks and whites, full of fun, good old Silly Willie. And McCoy had been right, too. The aviators had arranged for a bed and a can of beans through Willie – but no money.

So, Banning was depending on Tom Allen to collect as much as possible in the ring with Eddie Lyons. Based on his own frightful experience, he advised Allen to clinch, hang on, duck, bob, weave, run, fall, and take full counts, something he had stupidly failed to do.

'Don't box him or throw a punch,' said Banning, through puffed lips. 'If you try clever footwork – he'll nail you. Swing – and you'll miss and be wide open – or you might get lucky and connect – and that's even worse.' Banning touched the bandages on his chopped-up face. 'That rough boy hates being hit. He roars back like a mad bull. So don't make my mistakes and try to go for him.'

Allen listened to Banning's advice in a speechless, mummified state. Unlike Banning, who had been perfectly fitted, Allen's boxing gear must have been borrowed from an oversized heavyweight. The trunks were baggy and much too long, the white socks almost knee high and sagging, and the shoes, like two long skis, with dangling laces, seemed to turn up slightly at the toes, clown-style. He did not look like a boxer.

'We need money, Thomas Allen,' Banning reminded him sombrely, as he opened the door of the glass-partitioned room, and let in the crowd noises. 'Get past the first round and stay with that bastard as long as you can. Remember – take Lyons past the fourth and we've got twenty-five dollars – thirty-five for the night. Worth a few bumps and lumps, right? We can do it, partner.'

'Where-do-you-get-this-*we*-shit, ass-hole?'

Thomas C. Allen's encounter with Eddie Lyons, the future welterweight champion of the world, ended abruptly, seconds after the opening bell.

After the procedural touching of gloves, Allen had suddenly jumped to the side, grinned broadly, and performed a funny little shuffling dance step, which looked completely ridiculous because of his drooping trunks, knee-high socks, and turned-up shoes.

And then, as Eddie Lyons moved towards him, with left jab set, and knock-out punch loaded, Allen, now standing upright and flat-footed, brought his right arm back full, like a football player about to pass a long one.

And then, in what appeared to be a slow motion sequence, Lyons unleashed a left hook, and before it could land, Allen's wide, deliberate overhead swing followed through, and rammed solidly against the side of the professional's head, jarring him into instant unconsciousness. He fell backwards and struck the canvas like a dead man. And there he stayed, arms and legs outstretched, while Banning, McCoy, Willie Greer, Tubby Calhoun and the spectators – and even Tom Allen – stared in stupefied silence, temporarily paralysed.

'You goddamn fool!' Banning finally yelled to his partner in the eerie quiet. 'Now all we get are two lousy bucks! I told you to stay with him for a couple of rounds! Why the hell did you knock him out in the first? You ruined everything! Goddamn fool!'

Allen, still gazing blankly down at Eddie Lyons, appeared not to hear. McCoy was kneeling beside his future champion, talking, slapping, pouring water, and doing everything possible to revive him.

'Hey, Slugger!' someone called from ringside. 'What about the black boy's pay-off?' he demanded. 'You didn't have anything in the rules about Lyons going out.'

'I'll have to think about it,' McCoy replied, finally getting a few blinks from his protégé's glazed eyes. 'This whole damn thing is a mess now – with the big fight ten days away.'

'Give the nigger his twenty-five bucks!' another voice bellowed at McCoy. 'The guy did better than stay with Eddie for four rounds! He put him away, for real!'

Others in the audience took up the point in a rowdy fashion.

'I'll pay him ten – like his buddy,' said McCoy, busy hauling Lyons to his feet. 'Come up with fifteen of your own, instead of feeding Tubby's box.'

The spectators shouted their agreement.

As McCoy dragged Lyons past Tom Allen, the professional glared at him and snarled, 'You dirty black son-of-a-bitch. A lucky punch.'

With his trunks even droopier, and his white socks sagging more than ever, Allen tramped after McCoy and the fighter, nearly tripping over his extra-long laces and turned-up shoes.

'Mr Lyons,' he called out, as McCoy was helping his fighter climb through the ropes. 'You finally had a taste of black meat tonight. And we were just appetizers. Wait until they serve you the main course in Indianapolis. Don't get indigestion, killer!'

Banning laughed and motioned to his partner. 'Come on, he said. 'Let's have a little victory celebration at Willie Greer's place – champ.'

15

Slugger McCoy's fight money was even more necessary than the aviators had anticipated: the Eagle Rock would have been grounded in Terre Haute, because the airport bill came to thirty dollars and sixty cents.

They printed Willie Greer's name in the Gold Book without a hesitation. But they debated Slugger McCoy's inclusion, considering the punishment taken by Banning, and the fact that Allen had certainly earned his pay-off, after knocking out a future welterweight champion. Even so, it was finally decided that McCoy should be listed, because he had given them the opportunity to raise the money they needed so desperately. Allen did the honours.

After getting a weather report, and warming the engine, a patched-up Banning taxied the patched-up aircraft, and they were off the ground and flying, at one-fifteen in the afternoon.

Starting in a south-easterly direction, Banning made a left turn to north-east, and lumbered over farmlands and forests. Passing to the right of the airport in Indianapolis, both men looked down and watched a football game for a couple of moments, and then they saw a very large cemetery, and some factories, which seemed just as dead.

Banning changed to the right, almost due east, and flew over Richmond. Then, down below, Allen pointed to some kind of mines, with pits and tunnel entrances plainly visible.

Crossing the Miami River north of Dayton, Ohio, they passed within a few miles of Springfield, then over the Ohio State Prison Farm, slightly north of London.

The Red Bird Stadium was to their right, as the Eagle Rock approached Columbus, Ohio, where Tom Allen had some friends.

Banning navigated the rumbling wreck across the Scioto River, flying over the city at three thousand feet, before turning left to Port Columbus.

This was an urgent fund-raising stop-over, and Allen took immediate charge, because of his contacts in town. One, a Reverend

R.J. Fulton, pastor of the Second Baptist Church, used to live and hold services in Pasadena, California. The other, Mrs Edna Lunceford, a plump, jovial widow with a big smile and a kind heart, was the mother of an old school friend, and close enough to be called Aunt Edna.

Allen and Banning stayed at the woman's home, enjoyed her food, talked about the flight, and arranged by phone to meet Reverend Fulton at nine the following morning, a Sunday. After Aunt Edna had attended to Banning's wounds, the weary aviators turned in for an early night.

The next morning, after talking to Reverend Fulton, Allen and Banning accompanied him to church, where Banning spoke to the Primary Sunday School Class about their goal, and made a very favourable impression.

The aviators were then introduced to the congregation just before the eleven o'clock service. Each man gave a short talk about the flight, good enough to extract eight dollars and fifty cents from the Sunday School treasury.

After another delicious meal at Aunt Edna's, the Reverend Fulton's son drove them back to the airport, where more names were added to the Gold Book. Their stop-over had boosted the balance to eleven dollars and thirty cents, after the hangar and gasoline bill had been paid.

On Sunday, 2 October 1932, Banning rattled out of Columbus, Ohio, and flew just a little north of east.

Within a half-hour, he had an altitude of three thousand five hundred feet, as they neared the Alleghenies. Crops were being harvested in the valleys and on the sides of the hills.

After passing close to Zanesville, the plane crossed the Muskingun River, and flew north of Cambridge, Ohio.

About ten miles past this point, the engine started vibrating again, and soon it was missing, and revving down. Minutes later, the Eagle Rock began to lose altitude, fast.

Banning struggled, and kept the machine up for another five and a quarter miles, until they saw a small meadow, about two blocks long and a block wide. There was a highway on one side, a haystack near the middle, and trees at both ends.

With Allen pounding his anxiety and encouragement on the fuselage, Banning spiralled around a house, side-slipped over the barn and some trees, and then pulled the stick all the way back, for another stall landing.

There were ridges and deep furrows on the ground, rough

170

enough to make the plane nose up and flop over. But fortunately, when the wheels hit, she bounced high, and Banning was able to bring the tail down, hold her steady, and bump the crate to a jolting halt, near the middle of the field.

Climbing out of the cockpits, the aviators made a quick inspection, and found, once again, that two push rods were broken, both an intake and an exhaust.

'You fucked-up crippled old bastard!' Allen shouted, kicking the plane violently. 'Why the hell can't you stay in one piece?'

'Leave her alone, Thomas,' Banning advised, looking the other way. 'All three of us are about to go on public display.'

People were coming from all directions. And cars were lining up on the highway. Banning was right. The Eagle Rock, and the aviators, had become a suburban Ohio Sunday attraction.

One of the curious spectators, a young white man who introduced himself as Harris, and owned an auto garage in Winterset, a small town just a mile an a quarter away, offered his assistance. After conferring with Allen, Banning asked for a lift to Cambridge, a much larger town about fifteen miles away. They had decided that Banning should send a telegram to the Los Angeles promoters – Little Dandy, Phil Nash, and the Mosby brothers – threatening the cancellation of their percentages unless they wired immediate repair money, at least twenty-five dollars. Allen agreed to stay at the landing site and look after the plane.

During the ride to Cambridge, Harris told Banning that he knew an aviation enthusiast in town, a businessman named Frank Kirchway, who would be fascinated by the pilot's story. He drove Banning to Kirchway's home and introduced him.

Kirchway was a small, quiet, fidgety man who, for some reason, avoided eye contact with Banning, although he appeared to be reasonably friendly and sincere, and certainly enthusiastic about flight in general, and Banning's transcontinental attempt in particular.

After listening to the entire Eagle Rock story, Kirchway explained that he had a plane of his own which was hangared permanently in Columbus. A married son, a licensed pilot, lived there, and made good use of the aircraft. And then Kirchway asked precisely which parts were needed to complete the repairs and get the Eagle Rock on her way again. Banning told him.

Without another word Kirchway went to the phone, called the Columbus airport, ordered the parts, asked for them to be

171

sent by bus, and gave instructions to have everything charged to his account.

'They should be here on the 1:00 pm from Columbus tomorrow,' Kirchway told Banning, now giving the impression that his time was limited. 'I'll notify the station that you have authorization to collect the packages in my name.'

'Thank you very much for everything, Mr Kirchway,' said Banning. 'My partner – Thomas Allen – will be just as grateful – I can assure you.'

'Do you men have accommodation for the night?'

'Not yet.'

'Well, I can't help you with a problem like that,' Kirchway explained, matter-of-factly. 'As a member of the flying fraternity, my only interest is to get your plane off the ground and on its way. I don't give or lend money. And I would certainly not offer you hospitality in my home – or have you impose on my friends or business associates.' He paused, and gazed directly into Banning's eyes for the first time. 'Frankly – like most others in this town – I feel very uncomfortable around coloured people.'

He left before Banning could utter a word.

Without referring to Kirchway's remarks, the pilot asked Harris for a few more favours, and the young man responded sympathetically. He would stop at the Western Union office, wait, drive Banning to a Negro section of Columbus, and then pick him up later in the evening.

Even though the replacement parts had been secured, thanks to Kirchway, Banning decided to send the collect telegram to the Los Angeles promoters anyway, and do his best to organize some additional funding, and a room for the night, courtesy of their Ohio brothers and sisters.

Meanwhile, the Eagle Rock's guardian in the meadow had found himself surrounded by spectators, inquisitive men, women and children, all white, and mostly obnoxious. Many had never seen an airplane on the ground. And, it seemed, most had never heard of a black aviator. They stared, and pointed, and giggled, and touched, with Allen watching out for souvenir hunters, and trouble-makers. A few asked serious questions about aviation, and received polite, professional answers. He dealt with teasing, heckling and, at times, some ugly tormenting in the same way, maintaining a smiling and courteous attitude.

At one point an elderly woman, using a walking stick, hobbled past him to the plane, and began poking, and yanking, and fiddling with everything in sight. When she stepped close to the front cockpit, and started tapping her stick inside, Allen ambled over and proceeded diplomatically.

'Excuse me, ma'am,' he said, pleasantly. 'I can explain anything you want to know about this airplane. May I give you a demonstration?'

'No, you may not,' she answered, in a cracked, imperious voice. 'I find out things for myself. Now go away and pay attention to your own business, or I'll get stomping mad.'

'But, ma'am,' the mechanic said gently. 'This airplane *is* my business. And I have a responsibility to protect it. Please allow me to show you the airplane properly.'

'Go away.'

'No, ma'am,' said Allen firmly, as she took a slow, careful walk towards the Eagle Rock's nose. 'I'll have to ask *you* to go away – this is *our* property.'

'Then get it off *mine* – at once.'

'I beg your pardon?'

'Your airplane is sitting on my field.' She turned her heavily wrinkled face and squinted at him. 'I'm Maude Wilkinson,' she announced. 'All this land belongs to me – and that's my house over there. I just came out to see what all the commotion was about.'

'Please excuse – '

'Watch your step, black boy,' Maude Wilkinson warned, eyeing the spectators, as they circled the plane. 'I'm being right tolerant. One call from me and Sheriff Austin will clear this place at once – and that includes you and that broken-down flying machine of yours. Do you understand?'

'Yes, ma'am.'

'And don't come anywhere near my house,' the woman cautioned strongly, while starting a move away from the plane. 'I have two powerful dogs and three farm-hands with shotguns. Just fix that wreck and get off my land as soon as possible.'

'Yes, ma'am.' Allen watched the old woman totter away, one perilous step at a time. 'Can we use your haystack for sleeping tonight?' he called out. 'In case my partner can't arrange for a room.'

Maude Wilkinson stopped, and took a long time to answer. 'That's acceptable to me,' she finally replied, without looking back. 'Just don't scatter any and cause a mess.'

'Thank you kindly, ma'am.'

*

By eight o'clock it was growing dark, and the spectators abandoned the meadow. Allen made three careful trips to the stack to gather hay and made a comfortable bed under the Eagle Rock's wing. The October night was chilly. He put on his helmet and complete flying suit before settling down.

At nine o'clock, a lanky farm-hand strode over to the mechanic's bed, holding a flashlight, a shotgun, and something tucked under his arm. Without a word, he dropped a heavy bathrobe on Allen, then turned abruptly and vanished.

Thinking of Maude Wilkinson, Allen smiled, wrapped himself in the robe, pulled off his shoes, and curled up in the hay. He slept peacefully until eleven o'clock, when the lights and sound of a car brought him to his feet. Banning had arrived back with Harris, who gave Allen two sandwiches, a Coca Cola, and a jelly doughnut. Banning had already finished the same. Harris promised the aviators that he would return at nine-thirty in the morning to take them into Cambridge to collect the replacement parts, and the money wired from Los Angeles, if any was forthcoming.

After Harris had left, a rather low-spirited and moody Banning told Allen about Mr Frank Kirchway's generous donation, along with the businessman's offensive remarks.

'You are truly a bitter and ungrateful piece of work, James Herman,' said Allen, stretched out on the hay, watching the pilot organize his own bed under the wing. 'A complete stranger puts up his money – and gets us off the ground – and you grumble and moan about hospitality and racial chickenshit. The man was just being honest. Hell, I don't really feel comfortable around white people, all of the time. And neither do you, partner.'

'I'm not upset about Kirchway.' Without a helmet, or a cover, Banning eased back on the hay, and closed his eyes. 'The guy did a wonderful thing, and I told him so – sincerely.' He thought for a moment before continuing. 'And the rest of his crap was so familiar that it bounced off – and that's the truth.'

'So what's your problem?'

'A combination of things, Thomas,' Banning answered, wearily. 'Every once in a while – they get to me – and I lose faith – and become sick inside – and angry too.' He looked up and touched the Eagle Rock's wing. 'I feel that way tonight.'

'Because of Kirchway?'

'Not really,' he answered, in a dejected tone of voice. 'Like I said – it's a combination of things – including the niggers of Cambridge, Ohio.'

'What?'

Banning described his visits to church officials, black civic leaders, influential Negro businessmen, and others in the town's coloured section. He had briefed them all on the flight, its aims and rewards, and the financial problems. Their reactions had been negative – worse even than the response the aviators had received from Fletcher Braithwaite and the Oklahoma City Negro Business League. Donate for a transcontinental airplane ride? Money was needed for more essential purposes in poverty-stricken black communities.

'Can't they understand?' Banning complained bitterly. 'Don't they realize the importance of this flight? The need to demonstrate black ability? Black intelligence? Black determination – pride – equality? Do they really want their children and their children's children to grovel around like fucking lepers in segregated garbage dumps?'

'These people are jobless, homeless, and starving right now, James Herman,' Allen reminded him. 'It's a matter of survival. A transcontinental flight record won't put bread in their stomachs or a roof over their heads.'

'Someday it will.'

'But I guess someday is just too far ahead for the folks you spoke to in Cambridge,' Allen replied, smoothing the hay, and turning on his side. 'We have to be reasonable – and not expect too much from people – these days.'

'You have to make sacrifices – accept challenges – and beat the odds – in order to get ahead – and improve conditions,' Banning persisted. 'That's not the kind of talk I heard in Cambridge tonight. And it makes me sick.' He hesitated, sighed heavily, and continued in a low, intense voice. 'I don't want to be white. But – sometimes – when things go this way – I'd like to be green – or blue – or orange – anything but black – just long enough for me to recruit some gutsy – '

'What the hell are you raving about, James Herman?' Allen interrupted, sitting up, and facing him again. 'Think about us for a minute,' he advised firmly. 'We're crossing the country during lousy times – begging – scrounging – finagling money and services from anybody en route – in order to bring the Eagle Rock down in New York City.'

'So?'

'These people could ask why are we really and truly doing it.' Allen paused to let the statement register. 'Is it for the sake of our race? Or is it for the prize money and other benefits, too? And personal recognition? And excitement? And self-satisfaction? And – '

'Ask Charles Lindbergh the same questions,' Banning broke in, irritated. 'And Hoover. And Roosevelt, And Adam Powell. And Booker T. Washington. And A. Philip Randolph. And anybody else who ever did something important and got some public recognition.'

'You've put us in high-class company, James Herman.' Allen smiled, easing the tension. 'All I'm saying is – don't expect too much from people – and let's be grateful for everything we get along the way. Check the Gold Book again, partner.'

And then unexpectedly, he burst into laughter.

'What's so damn funny?'

'Oh, man.' Allen settled back on the hay, turned away from Banning, and prepared for sleep. 'I just happened to picture you green.'

'Fuck off, Thomas.'

At six in the morning, the same lanky farm-hand strode over to the aviators, and poked them awake with the barrel of his shotgun.

'Miss Wilkinson said you can come over to the barn and have breakfast,' the man announced flatly. 'You'll eat with Bud and Rupert,' he added pointing to a wooden structure, near the main house. 'Better move out right now. She told me to guard the plane until you finish.'

A section of the large barn had been converted to serve as living quarters for Maude Wilkinson's three farm-hands. The aviators were given soap and hot water from a kettle on the stove. After washing, they had eggs, bacon, fried potatoes, and coffee, prepared by a tall, granite-faced character called Rupert. Neither of the two farm-hands spoke a word and, as anticipated, they ate their own food at a separate table. When the unexpected feast was over, Allen and Banning thanked their silent breakfast companions, and asked them to pass their deep appreciation to Maude Wilkinson. Bud, who was wiping his mouth with a large white handkerchief, did not react in any way. Rupert stared for a moment, then nodded his head, and made a strange grunting sound, which the aviators assumed was a yes.

At 9.30 am Banning left for Cambridge with the young and reliable Harris, and Allen stayed to guard the plane.

Later, at the Western Union office, the pilot inquired about but did not find any money wired from Los Angeles, because the Eagle Rock's promoters and fund-raisers had refused to accept the collect telegram. Banning cursed roundly. He toyed with the idea of begging Lippy Hapgood in New York, but decided against it, remembering the publicity man's formal notification that no loans, advances, or gratuities were ever given to his clients. He decided to phone Hapgood from a friend's house in Pittsburgh, Pennsylvania, give him a brief progress report, and ask how arrangements were going in the big town.

Thanks to Frank Kirchway, the replacement parts from Columbus arrived at the Cambridge bus station, on time. As soon as they had collected the shipment Harris bought some sandwiches and Cokes, with extras for Allen, and the two men picnicked in the parked car before driving back to the crippled aircraft.

By four o'clock, all the parts were in place, and the Eagle Rock was ready. But the take-off from the crater-lined meadow presented problems which required the pilot and his mechanic to devise an unorthodox plan.

Large crowds had gathered again, and young Harris, who had brought a camera, took some pictures of the plane, while the engine warmed, revving up to 1400 rpm. Even old Maude Wilkinson, her three farm-hands and two powerful dogs were standing near the house, watching and waiting with the others.

After Allen had removed all the tools and baggage from the plane, he held a wing, while Banning taxied, or rather bumped his way along, avoiding as many ridges and furrows as possible, on the way to the far end of the meadow. The Eagle Rock was finally backed up against Maude Wilkinson's barn. Banning, feeling the exhilaration build, sat in the cockpit, prepared to roll. Allen ran down the field and stood between the haystack and a brush pile. He had begged an old sheet from Maude Wilkinson in which he had cut a hole for his head. He now draped it over his body. With his head and outstretched arms exposed, Allen was Banning's guide for taking off between the haystack and the brush pile, an absolute must, or the plane would never get off the ground. But Banning was in no position to judge the distance accurately, at the far end of the meadow. The plan called for Banning to begin the run from the barn, and accelerate, gaining more and more speed, with his eyes fixed on Allen. At the proper moment, the white-sheeted mechanic would fall flat to the ground, signalling that the Eagle Rock had travelled half the length of the meadow, an essential gauge

177

for the pilot, who could then complete the tricky manoeuvre on his own.

As the spectators gazed in awe, Allen waved, Banning returned the gesture, and the battered aircraft began to move, faster and faster over Maude Wilkinson's dangerously uneven terrain. With his sheet-draped arms outstretched, Allen waited until the last possible second, then belly flopped to the ground as Banning roared and rattled past.

When the Eagle Rock was up about thirty feet, Banning dived her again, and gained enough speed to zoom over the tops of some trees in the way. Then, at about one thousand feet, he broke his pledge and thrilled the crowd with a few stunts before flying off in the direction of the Cambridge airport.

'Goddamn circus clown,' Allen fumed, getting up, and spitting bits of dirt and grass. 'That ham-bone almost snapped the wings up there,' he added, as Harris walked over to help him load the tools and baggage into the car. 'Wait until I kick his precious ass in Cambridge.'

However, there were no arguments at the Cambridge airport, after Allen arrived. Shrewdly, and with his fingers crossed, Banning quickly mollified the mechanic by promising to hand over the Eagle Rock's controls for the next hop.

After the plane had been hangared for the night, Harris drove them to the home of Mr J.B. Dimble, a retired Negro shop owner, one of the more sympathetic black men Banning had encountered the night before. The pilot felt certain that Dimble and his church-going wife would give them a meal and a roof, as long as no flight donations were requested. By flaring up and stomping out of the meeting the previous evening, Banning had missed an opportunity to speak privately with the man. Now he was going to turn on the charm, explain that they were in the neighbourhood visiting a business associate, and hope to extract an instant offer of hospitality.

Feeling confident about the outcome, and remembering that Dimble had a car, Banning thanked Harris very sincerely for his time, help, and extraordinary patience. Allen echoed the sentiments. Along with a listing in the Gold Book, the aviators promised him a signed photograph of the Eagle Rock landing in New York – God and Lippy Hapgood willing.

When Harris had driven away, Allen and Banning knocked politely on the Dimbles' door, switched on unusually wide smiles, and waited to guarantee a meal and a bed for the night.

'Like I was saying, James Herman,' Allen whispered. 'These are lousy times – you can't expect – '

'Shut up, Thomas.'

The door opened.

'Ah, Mr Banning.'

'We just happened to be in the neighbourhood, Mr Dimble,' said the pilot, through exposed white teeth. 'I thought you might like to meet my flying partner – Thomas C. Allen.'

'Come in – come in – what a pleasant surprise.'

At the airport, while attending to the Gold Book before take-off, Allen and Banning pondered over the Harris listing. The young man had only referred to himself as Harris, as though he did not have a first name, or possibly because Harris *was* his first name. Accordingly, they wrote 'Harris', and nothing more, on the lower left wing tip. Maude Wilkinson, Frank Kirchway, and Mr and Mrs J.B. Dimble were also neatly inscribed.

An ecstatic Tom Allen, hauling, as usual, a very worried passenger, flew north-east from Cambridge over mountainous country, practically parallel to State Highway 40. He crossed the Ohio River at Martin's Ferry, Ohio, and Wheeling, West Virginia, with Wheeling on the right of the course.

Ignoring Banning, and the roar of the engine and the wind, Allen screamed a medley of popular songs and, whenever possible, conducted an imaginary orchestra with his left arm.

The drowned-out concert finally ended, and serious business began, when the temporary pilot swung the Eagle Rock a little farther north, passing about five miles north-west of Washington, Pennsylvania, then over Gretna, to the Allegheny Municipal Airport at Pittsburgh, the most expensive in the country.

Allen landed awkwardly, but without a major problem, and for the first time he received a pat on the back from Banning. Later, however, the pilot explained that the pat had been an expression of relief, not a complimentary gesture.

In the airport office, Allen and Banning were quite surprised when a clerk told them that the black *Pittsburgh Courier* had asked to be called, if and when two Negroes landed a weird aircraft.

A short time later, after they had washed and changed, a car from the newspaper arrived, and drove them to the *Courier* offices, in the heart of the Pittsburgh Negro district.

Edmund Drum, the prim little editor, explained that Eugene Lippy Hapgood, of Harlem, New York, had contacted leading black newspapers around the country, alerting them to the story of this first Negro transcontinental flight. The paper wanted a complete story and photographs of the plane and aviators at the Allegheny Municipal Airport before their take-off in the morning. According to Mr Drum, Hapgood had reported that interest was building in Harlem, and in other black New York communities.

'What about white newspapers?' Allen asked, recalling their experience with Mary Beth Wells, and the *Wichita Falls Daily Gazette*. 'Do you think any of them will pick up the story?'

'They'll either ignore it – treat it as comedy – or find some vicious racial angle,' the editor replied. 'You'd have to fly that plane to the moon before getting any legitimate white recognition. Even then, Lindbergh would push you to the back pages, for sure.'

'You probably know that we need money, Mr Drum,' Banning broke in, abruptly. 'Will the *Courier* pay us for this story and a picture layout?'

'The *Courier* doesn't pay for straight news stories, Mr Banning,' Drum answered. 'And we'll probably run one picture – not a layout. Of course, the situation could change – if you land the plane safely in New York.'

'Well, now that figures, doesn't it?' Banning was not impressed with the editor's statement, his pince-nez glasses, or the neatly trimmed moustache under his exceptionally small nose. 'Can I please use your telephone, Mr Drum?'

'Local or long distance?'

'One of each.'

'We have a strict policy about long distance.'

'I want to call Hapgood in New York.'

'That's no problem,' Drum said, pointing to a phone on a desk at the far end of the room. 'He wants you to call him – collect – I was about to tell you.'

'Mr Drum.' Allen waited until Banning had moved over to the desk, lifted the receiver, and started speaking. 'My partner is calling an old friend here in Pittsburgh.'

'Yes?'

'If we can't get hold of him,' the mechanic proceeded carefully, 'do you think the *Courier* could arrange some overnight accommodation for us? Nothing fancy. Just a roof and a bed. As you know, we're a little short on funds – to put it mildly.'

'Oh, yes,' Drum replied, in a surprisingly courteous manner. 'We'd be able to put you up at the YMCA across the street. After all, the paper is obliged to do something in exchange for your story – and the airport photo session tomorrow. And – we do expect some exclusive dispatches – if you land safely in New York.'

'I think that can be arranged.'

'We've already arranged it,' said Drum, glancing at Banning, who had just replaced the receiver. 'The *Courier* has a special understanding with Eugene Hapgood.'

16

Everything, including routine procedures at the Allegheny Municipal Airport the following morning, was beginning to take on a new kind of importance, a real sense of urgency, because New York was now only a few short hops away. Though they performed the weather checks, the gassing up, the paperwork, and the inspections in silence, the glow of excitement and anticipation showed in the aviators' faces.

They had been grateful for Mr Drum's offer of accommodation at the YMCA, because Banning's friend had moved away from Pittsburgh a month before. The rooms were clean, and both meals, dinner and breakfast, had been very acceptable. In addition, the house manager had given them each a packed lunch of bologna sandwiches, pickles and an apple.

Lippy Hapgood had informed Banning that his well-oiled and fast-spinning publicity wheels were now in motion, and the aviators were to call him briefly, collect, from each stop along the way, so that all phases of the spectacular operation could be properly co-ordinated.

Banning and Allen had given Mr Drum, and one of his ace reporters, background on their lives, and the complete story of the flight. A company car had made the early morning pick-up from the YMCA and a swift delivery to Allegheny Municipal.

At 11:00 am, two *Courier* photographers had arrived, and the flyers had posed both formally and informally, beside the plane, inside the cockpits, standing together and standing alone. To their amazement, one of the employees handed over an envelope containing two five dollar bills, and a note from Mr Drum.

The editor had successfully altered company policy by extracting a payment for a straight news story. But, in exchange he wanted two simple requirements to be met: the first, that his name should be displayed prominently in the Gold Book; the second, that they should oblige the newspaper's advertising and promotion department by posing together, beside the plane, holding the latest edition of the black *Pittsburgh Courier*, with the name clearly visible.

Of course, Drum's name was inscribed, but not *so* prominently, and the *Courier* had been held aloft, for all to see. The aviators had no choice really, because of the unexpectedly hefty Allegheny Municipal bill, which gobbled up the extra ten dollars, plus a large chunk of their treasury, leaving a balance of four dollars and eighty cents. With New York in their sights, and the prospect of mean eastern towns on the way, Allen and Banning worried about their financial situation. Fund raising from Pittsburgh on would be difficult, to say the least.

'We'll keep pushing forward, Thomas,' Banning said intensely, as they prepared for departure. 'To hell with food, sleep, and other luxuries. Let's just pray that nothing breaks down or falls off before the finish.'

After exchanging a clenched fist salute with his partner, Banning got the Eagle Rock up and off Pittsburgh's Allegheny Municipal runway at two o'clock in the afternoon, flying slightly south-east. He crossed the Monogahela River within a few minutes.

The flight continued above the mountains all the way to Johnstown, and, swinging further south, they bumped, and quivered, and rattled over more mountains, higher mountains, on a route just north of Shippensburg.

At that point, although neither wanted to believe it, they both heard an unfamiliar knocking sound in the engine and, moments later, every section of the plane began vibrating ominously. And then, without any warning, thick clouds of potent fumes – a mixture of gasoline, oil and burning rubber – drifted back from the nose, clogging their throats, and causing fits of uncontrollable coughing. In minutes, they had left the mountains behind, and Banning pointed to York, Pennsylvania, directly below them.

'I honestly don't know what the hell it could be,' said Tom Allen, wiping his hands with a rag, after inspecting the defective engine. 'We'll have to pull her apart and take a thorough look.'

'Do you think it's serious?'

'Probably.'

'Let's go.'

'What?'

'I'm taking off.'

'You're out of your goddamn mind.'

'We don't have the time or money to mess around here.' Banning's eyes were on fire, the eyes of a man obsessed. 'I say we gamble and head for Philadelphia right now,' he went on, fervently. 'We're just a few hops away from pay dirt, Thomas.'

'Did you hear and smell that motor?'

'I hear and smell New York.'

'You're a suicidal maniac.'

'Trust me, partner.' Banning smiled broadly, and punched Allen on the arm, in his usual charming and persuasive fashion. 'Nothing can stop us now. We're indestructible.'

'Well, if that's the case – let me take the next hop.'

'I'm not that suicidal, man.'

Taking off again, Banning headed south, barely missed the smoke-stack of a power plant, then skimmed along above the tree tops, struggling to gain enough altitude for a turn, due east.

The knocks, vibrations and smells were still causing trouble, but not as much as before. Banning crossed the Susquehanna River, rumbled south of Columbia, and then passed low over Coatesville.

As they banked to the left at Ardmore, the trouble worsened, and the coughing spells began again.

Incapacitated by these spasms, Banning had a very difficult time controlling the shuddering aircraft, as he dropped too close to the Schuylkill River just before making a grotesquely specta-cular landing at Pitcairn Field, Philadelphia.

'Fly solo, you crazy bastard,' Allen yelled, as Banning once again pushed for an immediate take-off after reporting collect to Lippy Hapgood, and gassing up with all but one dollar of their remaining funds. 'I'm going home standing upright.'

'How?'

'With my thumb.'

'Then go.'

'I'm serious, James Herman.'

'Go!'

'Do you really want to kill us?'

Ignoring the question, Banning began to argue the case for going on. He pointed out that the last stop before New York was only twenty-five miles north-east. According to Lippy Hapgood, West Trenton, New Jersey's coloured population, had already heard about the flight, because of a lengthy newspaper story he had planted with the editor of the black *Weekly Times*, a friend of his.

Despite the knocks, vibrations, and odours, the Eagle Rock was still flying, and Banning had a strong feeling that she could make the West Trenton stop-over, and even land in New York the following morning, without the engine blowing completely. Even if the engine pooped out in West Trenton, or if some other emergencies cropped up before the final hop, at least they would be amongst sympathetic brothers and sisters, a definite advantage when fund raising.

They were nearly broke, unable to pay for parts – or anything else – priced at more than one dollar. Why pull the engine apart now, and find themselves begging in the unfamiliar black streets of Philadelphia?

'And why lose our momentum right at the finish?' Banning asked, concluding his sermon. 'Let's get back in that noisy – shaky – smelly heap, and finish the job, Thomas Allen.'

'Suppose Hapgood lied about West Trenton?'

'We assume he didn't.'

'Suppose the coloured folks here also know about the flight?'

'We assume they don't.'

'Suppose the engine blows *on the way* to West Trenton?'

'We bail out.'

'Without chutes?'

'We don't need them, partner,' Banning answered, smiling again, burning with enthusiasm. 'Just hang on to my neck and we'll fly to New York like birds. Believe me – the way I feel now – we'd make it.'

On take-off, they barely cleared the trees, and the engine vibrated so much that the plane's wings fluttered, and nearly ripped apart. However, almost choking to death with Allen, Banning flew the wreck across the Delaware River, not far from Yardley, Pennsylvania, and then managed to slam it down at Mercer Airport, West Trenton, New Jersey.

As the Eagle Rock bounced and swerved and lurched towards a fence at the far of the field, smoke poured from the engine, and it blew, loudly, and completely.

They completed airport formalities, asked directions, and walked a mile and a quarter to a bus stop, where they waited for a ride into town.

Now, just one hop away from the New York landing, and a flight record, the situation was truly desperate. Allen had made a careful check of the engine and though the problem was not as drastic as the aviators had anticipated, replacement parts would be needed. The airport mechanics were instructed to complete the job, stake the plane down for the night, and have her ready for a morning take-off. A quote of fifteen dollars and sixty cents had been made, and the office wanted half in advance.

Swallowing his pride, Banning had made collect calls to Hapgood, the Los Angeles promoters, and two dear friends in San Francisco, both women, and the response from all had been negative. Eventually, because the airport manager considered the Eagle Rock to be a worthless junk heap, it had been decided that the aviators could leave their watches – both precious gifts – and their leather flight jackets, as a deposit, returnable only when the Mercer Field repair bill was officially stamped paid in full.

And so, money had to be raised, before morning. They were tired, and very hungry, but food and beds were not their primary concern at the moment.

They had been waiting for almost an hour, and there was still no sign of a bus, and hardly any traffic. Finally, a car headed their way, and the driver switched on his headlights, as twilight cast dark shadows over the West Trenton suburbs. The vehicle came to a halt in front of the aviators. It was a New Jersey State police car, driven by a bull dog-faced trooper, who poked his head out of the window for a closer inspection of the Negroes. An equally unpleasant-looking uniformed officer sat beside him.

'What the hell are you characters wearing?' the gravel-voiced driver asked, while his eyes raked them up and down.

'Flying suits,' Allen replied. 'We're aviators.'

'Aviators,' the driver repeated, shooting a fast glance at his smirking colleague. 'Show us your identification.'

Allen and Banning obliged.

'Los Angeles, California,' the driver mumbled, studying the licences and other documents. 'What are you doing here?'

'We flew here,' Allen answered, forcing a nervous smile. 'And we'll be taking off for New York City in the morning,' he added, proudly. 'The end of a transcontinental flight.'

'I mean right here,' the driver said, handing the papers back to the aviators. 'What are you characters doing here on this road at night?'

'Waiting for a bus to town,' Banning answered, meeting the officer's cold stare without flinching. 'Somebody at Mercer Airport gave us instructions.'

'You've got a long wait, pal,' the officer advised, in a mocking tone of voice. 'Service was discontinued on this route about a month ago.'

'How do people come and go?' Banning asked, sceptically. 'Mercer is a fair-sized field. There must be some kind of transportation.'

'Taxis and private cars,' the officer explained, becoming impatient. 'Forget about a bus – and I would strongly advise you two men not to hitch a ride around here – for obvious reasons.'

'Well, that presents us with a mighty big problem, sir,' said Allen, scratching his chin thoughtfully. 'Is there a coloured neighbourhood in this section?'

'Not to my knowledge,' the officer replied, turning for a whispered consultation with his colleague. 'Trooper Davis thinks you should inquire at Mick Clayhorn's Bar and Grill.' He pointed down the road. 'Walk about half mile and turn right at the first intersection. You'll see and hear the place. Mick's customers know this area like a book. I'm sure they'll get you sorted out fast.'

The New Jersey State Police car sped away.

'Don't lose your temper in this joint, James Herman,' Allen warned, as they turned right at the first intersection. 'There are some bad-looking white folks prowling these parts.'

'I know.'

'Play along with anything that comes up.'

'I'll try.'

The aviators entered Mick Clayhorn's establishment – a large, smoke-filled room, scattered with crudely built tables and chairs. In the centre was an old upright piano, which someone was pounding for a groaning chorus of swaying drunks. Every table had coffee on top, bottles underneath, and five loud-mouthed boozehounds circled shoulder-to-shoulder.

Allen and Banning walked directly to a long bar at the far end, where they found two vacant stools, a small, aproned, hatchet-faced tender, and a prominently displayed sign which reminded all customers that coffee and soft drinks were the only beverages available for sale on the premises.

As the aviators took their seats, the music, singing, laughter and general hubbub tapered off, and seconds later, Mick Clayhorn's Bar and Grill was quiet.

'Is there a carnival in town?' a raspy, high-pitched voice finally asked, from one of the back tables. 'Look at what we've got at the soda fountain.'

'Don't be rude to these strangers, Gimpy,' the man behind the bar warned. 'I'm sure they'll give us a good reason for trespassing on my property – dressed for a costume ball.'

187

'Ask them, Mick.'

'I just did.'

'These are flying suits,' Allen explained, turning on his stool to face the customers. 'We're aviators – on a transcontinental flight – from Los Angeles, California.'

Ignoring the chuckles, guffaws, and racial insults, the mechanic put on his friendliest smile, walked to the nearest table, and began speaking about the Eagle Rock's mission. The coarse West Trenton drunks propped themselves up in their chairs, and pretended to listen with exaggerated interest. Unruffled and ignoring their overdone expressions of wonder, Allen continued his monologue, progressing around the room.

At the bar Mick Clayhorn, the owner of the joint, finished making a telephone call and went over to a customer who had taken a seat two stools away from Banning. Clayhorn bent low, and whispered something about fifteen cases, payment on delivery. Checking the mirror behind the bar, Banning could see that the man on the stool was of medium height, stocky, and nearly bald. His eyes were slightly crossed, and his soiled white shirt was opened to the navel, exposing a thick neck and a hairy chest.

'That last batch was putrid, Clayhorn,' the man complained, keeping his voice down. 'Full of wood alcohol – benzine – '

'You're getting real quality this time, Scott,' said the bar owner, straightening up. 'And it's got the kick of a Georgia mule.'

'I hope so – for your sake.' The man caught Banning's eye in the mirror, frowned, and then turned slightly, to glance at Allen. 'What the hell are these crazy niggers doing in here?'

'Nobody is serving them.' Clayhorn focused his attention on Banning, and the belligerent-looking customer did the same. 'We've had enough fun, black boy,' said the owner, coldly.'Get your partner and clear out,' he ordered. 'You know damn well this place is restricted.'

'Are there any coloured neighbourhoods around here?'

'Hell, no – and thank God,' Clayhorn replied, exchanging a smirk with Scott, the customer. 'We've got a crummy nigger section in town – and that's bad enough. You'd better head that way, right now.'

'Did you hear what my friend said about our flight?'

'Not interested.'

'We need some money desperately, Mr Clayhorn,' said Banning, submitting to necessity. 'Maybe you have some odd jobs we could do – sweeping – cleaning – dish washing – mechanical repairs – anything.'

188

'I have an odd job you can do for me, nigger.' Scott fingered his trouser buttons. 'Come over here and get on your knees.'

Banning clenched his teeth, and fists, and stared down at the bar counter, doing everything possible to maintain control.

At the same moment, Allen, who was standing by a table near the piano, had also inquired about odd jobs, and a chance to earn some urgently needed money.

'Tap dance for us, nigger,' a loutish drunk orderd, starting to clap his hands in what he thought was a rhythmical fashion. 'Play a real hot tune for him, Gimpy.'

A small, wizened character, with thinning grey hair and a toothless mouth, got up and staggered to the piano. The audience applauded. After taking a bow, which almost made him overbalance, Gimpy sat on the wobbly bench and immediately began thumping out a melody which bore a slight resemblance to Sophie Tucker's 'Some of These Days', a speeded-up version.

'Come on dance, nigger!' one of the guzzlers yelled. 'Shake your black ass and pick up some money!' He tossed a coin and it landed at Allen's feet. 'That's what you want, ain't it?'

Banning glanced over his shoulder and met his partner's look. Each read the humiliation, anger, and frustration in the other's eyes.

Suddenly a huge theatrical grin took over Allen's face, and he began dancing wildly to Gimpy's piano music. With his arms waving, and his ass shaking, the mechanic performed his own spirited and outlandish versions of the buck and wing, time steps, waltz clogs, turns, and even painful splits, whooping and hollering the song's lyrics whenever he had enough breath.

Allen's boisterous and inebriated audience egged him on with stomps, whistles and cheers. More important, coins were being thrown from all directions, landing at the dancer's feet.

Even Clayhorn, leaning on the end of the bar, had his eyes glued to the performance. But the customer, Scott, appeared to be interested only in James Herman Banning. And Banning, attempting to block out the degrading spectacle that Allen was making of himself, and at the same time avoid serious trouble with Scott, had his head down, and his gaze fixed on the same spot on the counter.

'I made you an offer, nigger.' Following the bar's standard drinking procedure, negotiated during a local police pay-off, Scott took a long swig of whisky, and then put the bottle down on the floor. 'Are you turning me down?'

Banning ignored him.

'Did you hear my question, nigger?' Scott slurred, moving closer to Banning. 'What a pity – if God made you black – and deaf too.'

'Why don't you just leave me alone, mister?' Banning circled a stain on the counter slowly with his finger and did not look up. 'I have problems – and a quick temper.'

'You have a lot of problems, black boy,' Scott snarled, leaning close to Banning's face. 'And I don't give a shit about your temper.'

'Then leave me alone.'

'After you learn a few lessons. You two coons swagger into a white establishment, dressed up cute – plop your asses down where they don't belong – and take over the place.'

Banning did not react in any way.

'Nigger boys bow – and nigger girls curtsy – when I'm around.' Scott reached down for the bottle, took another gulp and, disregarding the house rules, smacked it down on the bar in front of him. 'You are definitely out of line, boy,' he slobbered, wiping his mouth with the back of his hand. 'In Trenton, niggers haul garbage – they don't fly airplanes.'

'Hey, Scotty!' Clayhorn yelled from his position at the end of the bar. 'You're missing a great show!' He pointed at Allen. 'That darky is funny as hell!'

'Did you hear me?' Scott asked Banning, paying no attention to Clayton. 'Take my good advice – and you might stay alive in this town tonight.' He poked a chubby finger into Banning's arm. 'Now get that crazy black brother of yours and crawl out of here fast – or I'll have you delivered to the appropriate part of Trenton in a very special way.' He poked again, more insistently. 'It won't be the first time, you know.'

Banning finally stopped tracing the round stain on the counter. 'Talk all you want, mister,' he said sombrely, glaring at Scott in the mirror. 'But don't touch me again.'

'What's that?'

'Just keep your hands off me.'

'I think our friendly little chat is over, nigger.' Scott gripped the back of Banning's flying suit collar. 'Now get up and do as you're told.'

Like a bolt of lightning, the pilot's closed fist swung back, and the powerful, unexpected blow caught Scott flush on the chin. He toppled off the stool backwards and landed with a thud on Clayhorn's linoleum.

Unaware of the incident, the customers went on cheering the

unexpected floor show. Only Clayhorn came running up. 'What the hell is going on here?'

Scott pulled himself up to a sitting position. Suddenly he produced a switchblade knife, flicked it full open, and held it menacingly. 'Now you can watch a better show, Mick,' he said, his face contorted and beet-red. 'I'm going to slice me a nigger.'

'Better run, boy,' Clayhorn advised nervously, as Banning watched the customer get up and move towards him, with the sharp blade poised for action. 'That man intends to use his weapon.'

'Put it down, goddamn it!' Banning pleaded, keeping his opponent under close observation. 'I don't want any trouble!'

'I'll put it down, all right,' said Scott, within striking distance now. 'But first, get ready for surgery – you arrogant black bastard.'

Smoothly and unexpectedly, Banning reached for Scott's bottle, and smashed it violently against the side of the bar. Gripping the neck tightly, he held the jagged edge inches away from Scott's face. 'Go ahead – you do yours – and I'll do mine – or drop that damn thing – and I'll do the same. It's your play – you arrogant white bastard.'

At the sound of shattering glass, the music and the cheering had stopped instantly. The whole room, including Allen, was transfixed by the tense drama unfolding at the bar.

Seconds passed, and both men held their ground, with the knife and broken glass poised to rip flesh and draw blood.

'You'd better drop it, Scott.' Clayhorn was directly behind Banning. 'We can't afford a homicide investigation right now. Know what I mean?'

Scott looked over Banning's shoulder, caught Mick Clayhorn's eye, and finally nodded. Then he shifted his attention back to the pilot, and gave him a quick, sardonic smile. 'I guess you win this one, nigger.' He tossed the knife and it slid across the floor. 'But you won't be so goddamn lucky next time.'

Without a word, or any visible emotion, Banning placed the broken bottle on the table, and turned to face Scott again.

At that moment, Clayhorn grabbed him by the hair, and pulled his head back, giving Scott an opportunity to ram a massive right fist into his stomach. The punch doubled Banning over.

'GET THE NIGGER!' one of the drunks shouted, and they all lurched towards the bar, screaming like wild Indians on a rampage.

Making a fast decision, Tom Allen, left alone near the piano, dropped to his knees and began frenziedly scrabbling for the coins.

191

While Banning was busy taking and throwing punches in all directions, Allen crawled along the floor, snatching up dimes and cramming them into his flying suit pockets. When he had prised the last one from under a piano leg, he jumped to his feet, raised both fists, and screamed over the din of battle, 'KEEP PUNCHING, JAMES HERMAN – HERE I COME!!'

His pockets jingling and his arms rotating like spinning propellers, Allen flew into the thick of the brawl, catching one burly drunk on the chin immediately, putting him down and out cold even quicker than Eddie Lyons.

The furniture-busting free-for-all continued, with Allen and Banning giving almost as good as they got, until a sudden shrill female voice peaked higher and louder than any of the male shouts and groans and war cries.

'STOP – AT ONCE – MICK CLAYHORN!'

The voice, apparently well known to all the Bar and Grill patrons, brought an immediate cease-fire, and absolute silence.

All eyes were on the figure of an elderly woman standing at the bottom of some wooden stairs which, according to a printed notice posted above the open door, led to a restricted area of the establishment. Tiny and stooped, she cradled a huge double-barrelled shotgun in her arms.

'Tell your drunks to clean this place up, and then throw them out!' she commanded Clayhorn. 'And what the hell are two niggers doing here?'

'They just drifted in, Ma,' said Clayhorn, motioning feebly at Allen and Banning. 'Real trouble-makers,' he added. 'We had to defend ourselves and the property.'

'Well, call the law or boot them out – right now,' the old woman ordered. 'And don't bring me downstairs again, or I'll use this damn thing – and get rid of all of you – once and for all.'

She turned and slowly climbed the stairs, one step at a time, carrying the shotgun military-style on her emaciated shoulder.

'Close that door, Gimpy!' Mick Clayhorn barked, getting down to business, as directed. 'We'll clean this place up, and stay quiet, for Ma's sake.' He walked over the aviators. 'You niggers should be locked away for trespassing – assault – property damage – and a lot more. But I'll give you a break – and you'd better appreciate it. Get the hell out of here – and don't come back this way again – ever.'

'We'll do exactly as you say, Mr Clayhorn – for Ma's sake,' said Allen. He followed Banning out without waiting for a reaction.

*

192

Allen and Banning made an important decision before reaching the State road intersection. The planned visit to Trenton, New Jersey's coloured neighbourhood, was cancelled. Instead, with empty stomachs, battered bodies, and a desperate need for sleep, the aviators hiked the mile and a quarter back to Mercer airport. Concerned about Clayhorn's rowdy gang of customers as well as prowling cops, they hugged the shadows all the way, and lay low in bushes whenever an occasional car drove by.

'Like goddamn fugitives,' Banning grated bitterly.

After explaining their predicament to a greedy night attendant at the field, the aviators handed over a one dollar tip in return for the use of the toilets, the floor of a spare tool room, and two hot coffees in paper cups. A 6:00 am reveille was also part of the arrangement.

They reviewed their situation as soon as they had settled against the grease-smeared wall of their windowless, claustrophobic sleeping quarters. The repaired Eagle Rock had been staked down at the far end of the field. A fifteen dollar and sixty cent bill would have to be paid before take-off. Thomas 'Bojangles' Allen had solicited six dollars and ten cents by making a damn fool out of himself at Clayhorn's Bar and Grill. It was all the money they had. Their leather flight jackets and watches were being held as security by the Mercer airport management.

They would have to strike a deal. Because New York and the one thousand dollar prize money were just a short hop away, Banning suggested starting with a plea for credit, and a written promise of quick repayment. If negative, he proposed offering one flight jacket or a watch, as collateral for the loan. Or, possibly a jacket or a watch, along with a few dollars in cash. Or some other practical combination.

'Suppose they accept one watch as security?' Allen had propped himself in a corner, under a row of wrenches, hammers, and other tools hanging from metal hooks. 'Are you prepared to leave yours, James Herman?'

'We flip a coin.'

'Absolutely not,' Allen snapped back. 'I've got two hundred dollars of my own money invested in this flight. 'Have you forgotten already?' he added, closing his eyes, and preparing for sleep.

'And what about my contribution?'

'I'm speaking financially.'

'To hell with all that petty crap, Thomas.' Banning, in a dreamy state of ecstasy, was flat on his back, oblivious to a

193

nearby heap of oily rags. 'We're almost there – and I can hardly believe it.'

They were silent for a moment.

'James Herman?'

'Yeah?'

'Are we really landing in New York tomorrow?'

'You damn right.'

'It's like a dream.'

'Not to me.'

'Can I bring her down – for old times' sake?'

'Keep on dreaming – that's as close as you'll get.'

17

In the morning, after twenty minutes of frantic negotiations, it was agreed that, along with a five dollar payment, Banning's watch would be held as security for the repair bill balance of ten dollars and sixty cents. The leather flight jackets and Allen's watch were returned.

With mounting excitement, Banning phoned Lippy Hapgood collect, and briefed him, while Allen made the final Eagle Rock flight inspection.

At 9:00 am, the aviators shook hands, and wished each other good luck. Just after 9:15 am, the Eagle Rock rumbled across the field, and picked up just enough speed for take-off. But while climbing, both men heard a rattle, followed by a loud cracking sound, and the wings began to shudder even more than usual.

The fluttering became much worse as they gained more altitude and flew unsteadily north-east, towards Staten Island, New York.

At last, flapping its wings like a giant bird, the plane swung east over the Island, and Allen and Banning caught a heart-throbbing, pulse-racing, tear-jerking glimpse of what they had pictured in their minds, day and night, ever since leaving Dycer Airport – the Statue of Liberty.

Allen raised both arms high in the air and screamed until the veins in his neck nearly burst. Banning, fighting to control the wing problems, and experiencing new complications, descended a bit, and started respectfully circling the famous land-mark, determined to get a closer look regardless of the risks.

While the aviators stared down in awe at the 152 foot statue on its 300 foot pedestal, tourists walking around the base of the monument looked up at the sky, and pointed to the strange airborne creature.

Allen's emotions ran deep, and his heart was full as they went round and round the uplifted torch and crown of the lady who stands at the mouth of New York harbour. Banning recalled a few lines of the poem by Emma Lazarus which is inscribed inside the pedestal, under the statue. 'Give me your tired, your poor, your huddled masses yearning to breathe free,' he thought. 'Like we don't have enough here at the moment,' he added to himself with a momentary bitterness, soon forgotten as the dream became more and more of a reality.

Numb with anticipation, the aviators bounced and quivered, flying east over Jamaica, and then Queens, to Valley Stream, New York.

With the plane's wings now dangerously close to breaking off, Banning circled the field erratically, smacked down, harder than usual, and taxied in a zig-zag to the line.

Containing himself with difficulty, Tom Allen jumped out of the Eagle Rock and cut off the gas before removing his helmet and goggles. Banning sat in the cockpit until the engine ran down, then climbed to the ground and took off his headgear. Allen walked slowly towards him and stood close.

'Well,' he said casually. 'Here we are.'

'Yep,' Banning responded. 'Here we are.'

And then, emotionally, the aviators embraced and, for the first time either man could remember, the tears flowed, despite all their efforts to restrain them.

18

The first Negro transcontinental flight ended at 10 am on Sunday morning, 9 October 1932. The Eagle Rock had flown approximately three thousand three hundred miles, in forty-one hours and twenty-seven minutes, although the actual trip had taken twenty-one days, because of stop-overs and delays. Four hundred and ten gallons of gasoline had been used. The aviators had spent approximately one hundred and fifty dollars between Los Angeles and New York. And after taking a cross-country beating, the remodelled 0XX6 looked more suited for the Mosby brothers' junk heap than the Smithsonian Institute, Washington.

About sixty enthusiastic Negro spectators – men, women and children – were gathered on the field to welcome them, and they applauded and cheered loudly when the aviators marched past them on the way to the administration building. Beaming, and enjoying the sincere attention – a rare occurrence since leaving LA – Allen and Banning waved, blew kisses, and gave victory salutes to the crowd. The white people present, including the airport staff and ground crew members, stared curiously. There were some chuckles, and a few derogatory remarks, as usual. It was obvious that Lippy Hapgood's much vaunted publicity campaign had been aimed specifically at New York's black population.

Dazed and delighted, Allen and Banning were later driven through the streets of Harlem to the Hotel Olga, where more applauding and cheering supporters were waiting out front, and crowding the lobby. Getting their first real taste of celebrity status, and loving every minute of it, the aviators grinned and waved, shook hands, and signed their names as an assortment of papers and objects were thrust at them by their admiring fans. A large banner over the check-in desk read – 'WELCOME TO THE LINDBERGH AND CHAMBERLIN OF THE NEGRO RACE.'

Upstairs in their spacious, comfortably furnished rooms, Allen and Banning were greeted by Lippy Hapgood, together with two other smartly dressed, big-city types, and a pretty, light-skinned young girl, with ample breasts and shapely legs.

'Hail the conquering heroes,' the pudgy publicity man exclaimed, grabbing the aviators' hands and shaking them vigorously. 'I didn't have one doubt in my mind.'

Allen and Banning smiled and stood awkwardly.

'We'll disappear in a few minutes and let you boys settle in and get some rest,' said Hapgood, using his hands and arms again to emphasize each word. 'I just want to cover a few basics at the moment,' he added, flashing his large diamond pinky ring. 'This family will be living together for the next few weeks.'

Allen and Banning sat down and the others found places opposite them.

'Hope the accommodation is suitable,' said Hapgood, glancing around at the fancy surroundings. 'Everything, including food and extras, paid for by an appreciative black community.'

'This is really something,' Allen managed to blurt out, in a voice that had no resemblance to his own. 'We'll need a little time to come down to earth, Mr Hapgood.' He gave Banning a quick look. 'Right, James Herman?'

'Right.'

'And that's why I want to be as brief as possible this morning, boys,' the publicity man explained, getting down to business. 'You have a very busy schedule starting today.'

Hapgood introduced Joseph Gates and Aubrey McVey, two of his senior associates, and Miss Daisy Patton, his personal assistant. All three had been involved in the campaign preparations, he said.

'We've scheduled a quiet business lunch here at the Olga,' he went on. 'And then prepare for a big Sunday.' He motioned to Daisy Patton. 'The Eagle Rock agenda, please, dear.'

'Two o'clock – a private appointment for clothes shopping at Hall and Dillinghams,' the secretary read, without looking up from her pad. 'Three-thirty – interviews and photographs at the *Amsterdam News*. 'Four-fifteen – interviews and photographs at the *New York Defender*. Seven o'clcock – dinner and a celebrity reception at the Tivoli Ballroom.'

'And that's just today, boys,' Hapgood added, with his hands and arms in motion. 'Wait until sweet Daisy hits you with the rest of the week.'

'How about collecting the prize money at the *Defender*?' Banning asked. 'Or do they contact Mr Cunningham first?'

198

The publicity men exchanged quick, worried glances.
'You might have a little problem, boys,' Hapgood finally admitted, folding and unfolding his arms nervously. 'I phoned the *Defender* after you called me from Trenton.'
'And?' Banning's eyes had narrowed, his jaw muscles had tightened, and his voice was cold. 'What do you mean – we might have a little problem?'
'Now stay calm, Banning.'
'Get to the point, Hapgood.'
'I will – but stay calm.'
The *New York Defender* had telephoned Mr John Radcliff Cunningham, in Norfolk, Virginia, reminding him of his published intentions, and announcing that the Eagle Rock had reached Trenton, and was poised for a Valley Stream landing – the completion of the first, successful Negro transcontinental flight. Cunningham had been asked how he intended paying the promised one thousand dollar prize.
'At first,' related Hapgood, 'Cunningham played dumb about the whole thing. And then he claimed the prank started at the Cotton Club – a drunken bet with friends – and then the gentleman swore that somebody else had placed the ad without his knowledge or consent – because he would never put up one thousand dollars for a coloured flight anywhere – and then – he hung up.'
The aviators sat dumbfounded, grappling with their own thoughts and feelings. Hapgood and his entourage were also wisely silent, allowing the shock and disappointment to register.
'Cunningham sure did play a funny little white trick on all of us,' Banning finally rasped. 'Do they have the gentleman's address in Norfolk?'
'That won't help a damn bit, James Herman,' Allen advised, more sad than angry. 'Black folks get a jail term for sneezing too loud in that town.'
'Absolutely correct,' said Hapgood, ready to participate again. 'Now remember,' he went on. 'I had five per cent of that money – and it's gone – and I should be roaring mad – but I'm not, because we've got bigger and better things on our plate. Want the floor, Aubrey?'
McVey, a tall, thin, big-eared man, rose slowly from his chair, and began a nasal monologue, while Allen and Banning watched and listened grim-faced, unable to shake off the effect on them of Cunningham's default.

Little by little, however, the aviators found themselves being drawn into Aubrey McVey's speech. He was talking about a wealthy Harlem businessman, who had expressed his great interest in the historic transcontinental flight. After discussions with Lippy Hapgood, the man, Louis C. Towbury, had offered to finance the complete repair and overhaul of the Eagle Rock, together with the installation of a new engine to any specification they recommended.

'We're organizing a tour,' Hapgood continued, after Aubrey McVey had sat down. 'A series of exhibitions in cities across the land. The famous Eagle Rock – and the transcontinental flight heroes – will stimulate Negro interest in aviation – inspire black youth – and generate lots of money.'

'Lippy?' Joseph Gates, a younger, even pudgier version of the publicity man, raised his hand for permission to speak. 'Our newspaper, radio, and magazine campaigns will promote the tour. And we've set you up to address civic receptions and youth clubs, business associations, fraternal orders, church congregations – even theatres, night spots, and street parties.'

'The whole black world is going to applaud this great achievement.' Hapgood leered discreetly at his assistant's shapely legs as she crossed them. He studied the aviators' troubled expressions. 'Are you boys still upset about Cunningham?'

'Of course,' said Allen instantly. 'It's a very big disappointment. We were counting on the money – for a lot of important reasons.'

'Don't worry about nickels and dimes now,' Hapgood advised, checking his watch under the sleeve of a gaudy but expensively tailored jacket. 'Take a rest – have lunch – do some shopping – deal with the papers – and prepare for the time of your lives tonight. Ever meet Broadway Jones or Louis Armstrong? What about Cab Calloway or Pegleg Bates?'

'Are you in a position to come up with immediate cash, Mr Hapgood?' Banning asked flatly. 'Without Cunningham's prize money, we're finished – broke.'

'I'm in a position to *raise* immediate cash.'

'Well, raise ten bucks right now.'

'You've got more than anybody needs – rooms – food – transportation – clothes – entertainment.' The publicity man was irritated. 'What do you have to buy?'

'A little self-respect,' Banning replied tersely. 'How can two black American heroes walk around with empty pockets – especially in front of people like Cab Calloway and Louis Armstrong?'

200

'You'll get the money back very quickly, Mr Hapgood,' said Allen. 'Take it out of our first earnings.' He smiled. 'And there should be plenty. Right?'

'I told you before – no advances – that's my policy.'

'Screw your policy,' Banning retorted. 'We need five bucks each right now.'

'Big heads already,' the publicity man muttered, turning to Joseph Gates. 'Give them ten dollars and mark it red in the books.'

The cash was handed over and accepted without thanks.

'About this tour, Mr Hapgood,' said Allen. 'We intend to contact the Smithsonian Institute about putting the Eagle Rock on permanent display.'

'When the tour is over.'

'Can we make long distance calls from the hotel?' Banning asked, getting to his feet, after Hapgood and the others had stood.

'Go ahead,' said Hapgood. 'Your bill is being covered by the Harlem Businessmen's League. But be reasonable – and don't rack up unnecessary expenses. In fact, the League has already been criticized by the Harlem Co-operating Committee on Relief and Unemployment, even though they appreciate your important accomplishments.'

'Just one last question, Mr Hapgood,' said Allen, stopping him on the way out. 'Why do you only concentrate on getting black publicity? The white people ought to know about our achievement as well. Don't you agree?'

'Of course, I agree,' Hapgood replied. 'But things don't work that way, Allen. Right now, practically speaking, we've got an important *black* story. The whites – at the moment – won't touch it – or they'll three line it – or poke fun at it – or get nasty.'

'We heard that in Pittsburgh.'

'Pittsburgh was right,' said Hapgood. 'First, we have to announce it to the entire black population – present two new heroes – show that we've taken a major step forward in the white world of aviation – where courage, and brains, and strength, and technical skills are needed. All the things most white people think we lack.' He paused. Right now as far as the whites are concerned, you two men are just threats – intruders – annoyances. So, they'll either ignore you – or laugh you off. Sad, but that's the way it is – and that's the way it'll stay, for a long, long time to come.'

'Don't take bets on it – Lippy.'

'Be downstairs for lunch at twelve-thirty,' Hapgood instructed them. 'Get some rest. And don't worry. White people will know

201

about it. They won't wave banners, or and send out marching bands – but they'll know about it – and think about it – and, deep down, they'll respect you for it. And you can't ask for anything more than that, the way things are today.'

After a good rest, Allen and Banning were up, and their mood had changed completely. The safe landing in New York City, had finally registered as reality, and they felt both proud and happy, and full of excited anticipation.

They made high-spirited phone calls to Celene, Banning's father, and the useless promoters and fund-raisers in Los Angeles. Allen's mother and younger brother were contacted in Oklahoma City, and Banning even spoke to a delighted Lieutenant Craig Meredith, in Des Moines.

The rest of the day passed smoothly according to Hapgood's schedule: they lunched, shopped, and were interviewed and photographed by the Press. The *Amsterdam News* made an appointment to take further pictures of them with the Eagle Rock. A senior editor from the *New York Defender* arrived to offer personal and corporate apologies, and regrets, for the disgusting behaviour of Mr John Radcliff Cunningham. He assured them that a mention of the cruel deception would be included in their coverage of the story.

Later, at seven-fifteen, the aviators found themselves in a dream sequence, one they would remember for the rest of their lives.

The immense Tivoli Ballroom had been expertly and securely arranged for this very special occasion. As Allen and Banning, in proper attire, made a nervous and rather hesitant entrance with Lippy Hapgood, the crystal-chandeliered foyer was bustling with newly arrived guests. They stood in noisy groups, sipping champagne, gulping booze, calling out greetings, slapping backs, and shaking hands. Music could be heard drifting from the main room.

At first, the aviators felt as though it was all happening to two other human beings, who resembled them, while they stood on the side, watching and listening, as Hapgood introduced them from group to group. They found themselves shaking hands with famous idols like Cab Calloway and his wife, Fats Waller, Duke Ellington, Ethel Waters, Don Redman, Louis Armstrong, Bill Robinson and his wife, young Lena Horne, Pegleg Bates, Adelaide Hall, and Paul Robeson. And there were authors, like Langston Hughes, and boxers, and church leaders, and businessmen, and NAACP officials, and newspaper publishers, and a State Assemblyman, and a New York City police surgeon – and more – and they all congratulated the new black heroes – and the new black heroes were completely dazed.

After several large drinks, snatched off passing trays, Allen and Banning, with their celebrity following, walked down three short steps into the enormous Ballroom, where they found the orchestra, elegantly decorated tables, and a huge banner proclaiming: HARLEM SALUTES OUR TRANSCONTINENTAL FLIGHT HEROES.

During a sumptuous banquet, the aviators, seated at the table of honour, talked informally with their fellow guests about their historic adventure, and later both men were led to the Ballroom's raised platform by Lippy Hapgood, and once again they told the Eagle Rock story, and received a standing ovation from their audience.

Hapgood announced that the money donated so generously for seats in the star-studded Tivoli, had been pledged to the Harlem Co-operating Committee for the benefit of the community's hungry and homeless. The prominent guests applauded loudly.

As the orchestra began to play, and people moved on to the dance floor, Allen leaned close to Banning. It was the first opportunity they had had to exchange a few words. 'Are you sure we didn't get killed along the way – and I am now in heaven?' he whispered.

'No, Thomas,' Banning whispered back, sipping fine quality whisky from a delicate glass. 'If you had been killed along the way, you wouldn't be sitting at this table with Mr Louis Armstrong, drinking champagne and listening to good music. This place would be a bottomless pit – with fire and brimstone – and a guy with horns and a pitchfork.'

'Why don't you go there right now, James Herman?'

The next day, the aviators met Mr Louis C. Towbury, a squat character in his late fifties, with a bow tie, a shiny black toupée, and the manners of a man used to having money and exercising authority. Towbury owned a New York company which imported cocoa, nutmeg, cinnamon and other spices from the West Indies. Grumpy and humourless, he was, nevertheless, extremely interested in the Eagle Rock and the flight, and appreciated the need for more Negro aviation enthusiasts.

He confirmed that he would finance the repairing, overhauling, and fitting of a new engine for the old 0XX6, but the operation would take time, because Towbury had money invested in an out-of-town aircraft factory and, for economic and promotional reasons, he wanted all the parts, including the engine, shipped from Garson Aeronautics, Colorado Springs. The aviators requested a Wright Whirlwind J5 engine and Towbury agreed to supply one, and also to cover their expenses from the time they left New York City until the first exhibition had been completed.

Because the wealthy businessman had not insisted on any returns for himself, Allen and Banning would receive ninety-five per cent of the ticket admission income, with five going to Lippy Hapgood, as they had agreed. Operational costs, if any, at each stop along the way, were the responsibility of the aviators. Hapgood had to cover his own publicity and scheduling expenditures, including telephones, telegrams, business meals, drinks, personal and staff transportation, bribes, and other pertinent incidentals.

'What about our original promoters and fund raisers?' Allen asked Banning later, after their productive meeting with Towbury. 'Do they get a split of our ninety-five?'

'Let's see how things go,' Banning advised, thoughtfully. 'After all, the Eagle Rock wouldn't be the Eagle Rock if Phil Nash and Little Dandy hadn't smashed the damn thing to bits.'

'James Herman?'

'What?'

'This mission has sure turned commercial.'

'I told you it would.'

'Well – we did get skunked out of a thousand dollars.'

'Don't remind me,' Banning said grimly. 'I might still push Lippy into arranging a very special exhibition in Norfolk, Virginia.'

While waiting for the plane to be repaired and refitted, Allen and Banning, now recognized celebrities in New York, followed Daisy Patton's crowded agenda. They were adulated at a Sunset Café dinner and a YMCA banquet, where they were given a year's honorary membership of the New York City 135th Street Branch. They were guests of the Charles E. James Aero Club, and became permanent members. They spoke at churches, youth clubs, civic gatherings, businessmen's functions, fraternal organizations, and Harlem Relief assemblies. There were street parties. And house parties. Night-spot bows. And theatre introductions.

There were also opportunities to observe poverty and hunger, homelessness, helplessness, and hopelessness, and though Banning felt certain that the Eagle Rock's success would provide black people with a glimmer of light in the distance, like a permanent aviator's beacon – an encouraging example, a reason to get off their knees and try to better themselves, any way they could, Allen remembered the expressions and comments of the Negro beggars on the streets, and wondered about Banning's theory. He prayed that it would somehow prove to be sound. He missed Celene, worried about her pregnancy, and yearned to get home. Banning, needless to say, had a constant supply of beautiful and eager bed partners.

Lippy Hapgood, a man with Washington contacts, according to Lippy Hapgood, had undertaken to deal with the Smithsonian. He planned to visit the Capital and make the necessary arrangements as soon as the Eagle Rock exhibition schedule had been finalized.

On Thursday, 10 November 1932, exactly four weeks and one day since Allen and Banning landed in New York, the meticulously repaired and refitted Eagle Rock was sitting on the Valley Stream Airport runway, gassed up, and ready for take-off. The wings had been fixed and the tail section strengthened. Even so, from the outside at least, it looked like the same old pieced-together flying contraption, scrubbed clean, and freshly painted. Allen and Banning were excited and anxious to fly again.

Lippy Hapgood had set the first exhibition at Bettis Field, Pittsburgh, Pennsylvania. The record-breaking aviators were expected to display their famous plane, execute some thrilling flight manoeuvres, then give a brief talk, answer questions, sign autographs, distribute souvenir photos, and shake as many hands as possible. Hapgood assured them he had contacted Edmund Drum of the black *Pittsburgh Courier,* and every prominent Negro group and individual in town. He expected Bettis Field to be packed with cheering admirers, paying seventy-five cents for adults, and fifty for children.

Over a hundred black supporters had crowded into a partitioned viewing area of the Valley Stream Airport to watch the Eagle Rock take off. There were banners, and flags, and placards, congratulating the heroes. Mr Louis C. Towbury, Hapgood and his associates, and several celebrities, church and business leaders, and other important New York Negroes were in a special section, closer to the plane and the runway. Photographers from the *Amsterdam News* and the *New York Defender* had been shooting from every angle since the aviators arrived at the field. No white newspapers were represented, although a few had carried four or five lines, buried deep inside

205

each edition, dwelling mainly on the number of stops, and the fact that the Negro flyers had taken twenty-one days to make the trip. The last line of each mentioned that Colonel Lindbergh would be making a transcontinental flight on behalf of President Hoover's re-election.

The Negro spectators cheered and applauded, and the white onlookers stared as Allen and Banning waved and saluted from their cockpits.

Picking up speed faster than usual, and rolling more smoothly, the Eagle Rock raced down the Valley Stream runway, and lifted off.

Flying west to the Statue of Liberty, and then swinging southwest, both men looked over their right shoulders, and saw New York disappear in a fog.

The aviators flew to Harrisburg, Pennsylvania, and spent the night in a cheap room. At the airport early the following morning, they were amazed to find that, for some unknown reason – possibly faulty installation – the new Wright Whirlwind J5 engine would not start. Allen worked until three in the afternoon, before locating and solving the problem.

The Eagle Rock finally took off once again for Pittsburgh. But as they passed over Altoona, Banning noticed that an air-show was in progress. Feeling cocky in his newly overhauled aircraft, the pilot began to perform some of his most complicated and breath-taking stunt manoeuvres.

Screaming and pounding the fuselage, Allen finally succeeded in interrupting the wild barnstorming demonstration, and Banning levelled off, and continued on his normal flight path.

Moments later, the plane ran up against the strongest headwinds the aviators had ever encountered, which slowed their progress, and threatened the gas supply. To make matters even worse, darkness was falling early, and a rattling had started up front, presumably the engine again. Earlier, Allen had discovered warped brackets on the Whirlwind mounting, the responsibility of Garson Aeronautics of Colorado Springs.

As Banning approached Blairsville, Pennsylvania, he spotted a large and relatively level cow pasture, and indicated that they should take the Eagle Rock down at once, instead of gambling on a Pittsburgh landing, with so many problems stacking up. Allen waved his agreement.

On the roll out, in the dim lighting, Banning saw a high fence, too late to take evasive action. As he attempted an emergency turn, the pilot hung a wing on the sturdy barrier, crushing the leading edge, and leaving the fabric. They were grounded – and in serious trouble.

After taking a bus to Pittsburgh, a disgruntled Banning contacted the local Curtis Wright Plant and organized a rescue operation. Mechanics would travel to the cow pasture near Blairsville, dismantle the Eagle Rock, and bring it back to Pittsburgh for repairs. Meanwhile, the aviators planned to hire a different plane, go ahead with the scheduled Bettis Field exhibition anyway, and hope that the spectators would be sympathetic.

Banning phoned Louis C. Towbury in New York, briefed him on the unfortunate situation, and was shocked by the business-man's unexpected reaction.

'I am a careful investor, Banning,' said Towbury coldly. 'How could you possibly have wrecked a completely overhauled aircraft with a new engine – on a short flight to Pittsburgh?'

'We had an accident, Mr Towbury.'

'A responsible pilot would have anticipated strong headwinds and early darkness,' Towbury criticized. 'Why did you take off late from Harrisburgh?'

'I've already explained.' Banning was struggling to maintain control of his temper. 'Garson Aeronautics fouled up the Whirl-wind engine mounting – and we had to make repairs.'

'Don't shift the blame,' Towbury snapped. 'The Garson engi-neers are the most reliable in the country. You must have loosened –'

'Mr Towbury!' Banning had heard enough. 'We didn't loosen anything. There is a definite fault – Garson's responsibility. Will you pay the repair bill?'

'Under no circumstances,' Towbury replied fiercely. 'I've put out a substantial amount of money already. Nobody has unlimited funds these days.'

'You'll be reimbursed quickly.'

'My contribution has been large enough,' Towbury interrupted. 'You should fly more carefully in the future.'

'That's unfair, Mr Towbury.'

'Don't expect another dime from me.'

The New York line went dead.

'I assume his answer was negative,' said Allen, studying the pilot's face.

'Shit.'

'Well,' Allen rationalized, 'in a way, you can't blame him.'

'Shit, again.' Banning glared at the phone. 'Very few people go far enough – and nobody goes all the way – and that's why we take one step forward – and two steps back.'

'Ungrateful – like I said before.' Allen was serious. 'We just flew across the United States of America in a beat-up old airplane. And we needed a lot of help to do it. Remember the Gold Book? And what about the history books? Hell, man, we made it! When will you be satisfied?'

Banning sat pensively gazing at the mechanic for a long moment, and then smiled broadly. 'I will be satisfied – when we return to Los Angeles – and get divorced.'

'Amen!' Turning serious again, Allen began scribbling with pad and pencil. 'What do you figure the damage will cost?' he asked, finally looking up. 'I say about three-fifty or four hundred dollars.'

'Probably.'

'We'll need a few thousand paying adults.'

'Probably.'

'Hapgood might be full of crap.'

'Very possibly.'

'Then why aren't you more concerned?'

'Because,' said Banning, 'nobody can hold the Eagle Rock in Pittsburgh for a repair bill. We now have a famous plane – a part of aviation history – one that will soon be on display in the Smithsonian.'

19

The Bettis Field exhibition proved to be a humiliating experience, and a financial disaster. Only fifty-eight spectators attended; all prominent and well-off members of the black Pittsburgh community. Edmund Drum of the *Courier* claimed that Hapgood had phoned him about the proposed event, requested co-operation, but refused to buy any advertising space. Lippy had contacted a few civic, business, church, and fraternal leaders, and begged them to appear and applaud the historic Negro achievement, and that was the extent of his high-powered publicity campaign. There were no billboard rentals, no circular deliveries, no public relations handouts, mailings, or advertisements of any kind. A Mr Joseph Gates had told Drum that the New York campaign's momentum would carry over to Pittsburgh, and only a few key contacts were needed to start a word-of-mouth tide of publicity.

With Banning at the controls, and Allen in the rear cockpit, the disheartened aviators performed several unspectacular flight manoeuvres, landed, and faced a barrage of protest from the onlookers, who had come to see and photograph the original Eagle Rock, and now felt cheated.

When the aviators phoned Lippy Hapgood's Harlem office collect, Daisy Patton informed them that the publicity man was out for the day, busy with a promotion for the Mills Brothers' appearance at the Lafayette Theatre.

The repaired Eagle Rock – the famous airplane destined for the Smithsonian Institute, Washington – would, by order of the management, continue sitting in the Curtis Wright plant in Pittsburgh, until Allen and Banning, or someone else, settled a four hundred and seventy-five dollar bill. Offers of promissory notes and other proposals were rejected out of hand. Curtis Wright's local officials were adamant – payment in full or no Eagle Rock.

Allen and Banning, now desperate, telephoned Louis C. Towbury again and explained, pleaded, begged, and promised, but the New York businessman was just as angry, and even more uncompromising.

'Not another dime,' he repeated to Banning. 'Don't call this number again.'

The wealthy New York businessman clicked off.

Now that the first exhibition had been completed, Towbury's expense money was no longer forthcoming, so Allen and Banning would have to check out of the dingy Pittsburgh hotel by twelve noon the following day, or begin paying for the room, meals, phone calls and other incidentals. And, as they saw, they could make no further appearances without the Eagle Rock. However, after paying Lippy his five per cent of the Bettis Field take – which Banning thought should be withheld – they still had the publicity man's two five dollar bills, and twenty-four dollars earned, because Edmund Drum had arranged a very special price for the plane rental. But they still needed four hundred and forty-one dollars for Curtis Wright, or the Eagle Rock would be locked away in Pittsburgh forever.

Banning was too angry to deal with Lippy Hapgood, so Allen made the collect call from their hotel room and, miraculously, the publicity man was available.

In his even-tempered way, Allen explained their predicament and Hapgood listened, and sympathized.

'Will you be able to pay the repair bill, Mr Hapgood?' Allen asked, taking the plunge. 'It's the only way we can continue the tour.'

The publicity man started laughing.

'Is something funny, Mr Hapgood?'

'You want me to shell out four hundred and seventy-five dollars for a wrecked airplane?' Hapgood asked, abruptly becoming serious. 'Only a man like Towbury has that kind of money these days. And if I did have it, you wouldn't get it anyway. You were told at the start – I am not a bank – remember?'

'But you're a partner,' said Allen. 'With five per cent.'

'Don't make me laugh again,' Hapgood retorted. 'The phone call to Drum in Pittsburgh cost me more that I'll pull from the Bettis Field fiasco.'

'That's your fault,' Allen reminded him, beginning to lose his composure. 'Where was the hot-shot, big-city, advertising and promotion campaign you promised us?'

Furiously, Banning grabbed the phone away from Allen, and unleashed all of his pent-up emotions. 'Will you lay out the Eagle Rock repair money, Hapgood?'

'Not a chance.'

'Then our deal is over right now,' Banning announced. 'We'll arrange the exhibitions – do our own publicity – and handle the Smithsonian. You take care of the Mills Brothers and forget our five per cent.'

'We have a fifteen-page legal and binding contract.'

'Stick it up your ass – or between Daisy Patton's legs – and every scrap will disappear – and be lost forever, in either place – I can assure you.'

The aviators sat in the dismal Pittsburgh hotel room, without speaking, or even glancing at each other, as bitterness, disillusion and frustration, drove out the last vestige of any exhilaration they had felt about the flight and their achievement.

The phone rang, startling them out of their despondency. Allen lifted the receiver, praying that Louis C. Towbury or Lippy Hapgood had changed his mind about settling the Curtis Wright repair bill.

'What did you say?' his hand was trembling on the receiver. '*What did you say*?!' he repeated in a strident voice. And then he listened, and nodded his head repeatedly, before speaking again, quietly this time, and with an unfamiliar stutter. 'I will find a way – indeed – and thank you – for phoning.'

'That has to be more bad news,' Banning commented, studying his utterly shaken partner, who was nervously tapping his finger on the base of the telephone. 'Was it Curtis Wright?'

Allen stared, and blinked, and finally took a deep, uneven breath, before speaking in a tight-voiced monotone.

'After succeeding – even Little Dandy, Phil Nash and the Mosby brothers – should be able to help us collect enough money on the Avenue – and around town – to bail the Eagle Rock out of Curtis Wright.'

'Have you finally gone mad?'

'At least we'll be around friendly and familiar folks.'

'What the hell are you babbling about?'

'If we need a few bucks – Drum will help – in a case like this.'

'A case like what?'

'Humanitarian.'

'Who was on the phone?'

'Tina Blandford.'

'*Who*?'

'My neighbour.'

'Get to the damn point, Thomas!'

211

'Celene is in the hospital – about to give me a son.'

Dressed in his smartest outfit, and armed with a large bouquet of flowers, James Herman Banning arrived at the Los Angeles Pickford Clinic, walked to the reception desk on the second floor, and asked for Mrs Thomas C. Allen.

At the end of Ward B, in a corner bed, Banning found Celene sitting up, looking brighter, prettier, and more cheerful than ever. Her proud and gloating parents were in chairs nearby. And Tom Allen was standing holding a small blanket-wrapped bundle.

Banning smiled, handed Celene the flowers, and kissed her on the forehead. The greetings and congratulations over, he focused his attention on Allen.

'All right, Thomas,' he said, pretending to be irritated. 'I've played the game long enough.' His eyes were on the bundle. 'Even the hospital refused to leak any information this morning. Do you have a boy or a girl, dammit?'

'Come over and look.'

Banning stood beside his partner and stared as Allen drew the blanket away revealing a small, dark face.

'I still can't tell, Thomas.'

Holding the bundle carefully with one hand, and cupping his mouth with the other, Allen imitated a trumpet fanfare. 'You are gazing at – Orrin Allen – my son,' he announced.

'A boy!'

'That's a brilliant deduction.'

'You lucky devil!'

Instead of reacting with smiles and thanks, jokes and horseplay, Banning was silent. He looked down at the infant's face, obviously moved, and in deep thought. The others watched, without speaking, until Celene finally said, in a gentle voice, 'Why don't you pick him up, James Herman?'

The suggestion seemed to break into his thoughts, and he looked away from the child, and glanced at Celene. 'I'm clumsy with babies – a hopeless type.'

'Ridiculous,' said Celene pointing at her husband. 'Look at that baboon.' She smiled at the way Allen was cradle-rocking the bundle. 'Thomas holds our child like a new engine part.'

'And that is exactly how it should be done, my darling wife,' Allen responded. 'With care – respect – love – and great appreciation. And with the knowledge that you can't get a replacement from the manufacturer.'

212

'Well spoken, Thomas,' said Banning, himself again. 'I always knew you'd make a great daddy.'

'And what about you, James Herman?' Celene asked, taking the bundle from Allen, and placing it next to her on the bed. 'Messing around with airplanes all the time won't produce anything like we've got.' She fixed the blanket neatly around the infant's head. 'All of your priorities are wrong – and life is short.'

'Well, maybe I'll get lucky – someday,' Banning responded, taking another quick peek at the bundle. 'Orrin,' he murmured. 'I like that – very much.'

'Go find your own, partner,' said Allen, sitting on the bed beside his son. 'And don't forget to stick a Thomas in the name – give the kid some class.'

'You seem to forget,' said Banning, 'I already have a baby of my own. Some people are holding it – against my will – in Pittsburgh.' Once again, his mood changed as deep-seated emotions surfaced. 'But I intend to get that baby back – some way – and as quickly as possible.'

'Amen, James Herman,' said Allen. 'I'm with you.'

'Curtis Wright should release the plane at once.' Mr Pendleton, Celene's rather stern-looking father, asserted. 'The Eagle Rock has made history for the Negro race.'

'Curtis Wright *will* release the plane at once, Daddy Pendleton,' Allen explained, leaning close to his wife and son for maximum effect. 'All you have to do is give them four hundred and seventy-five dollars.

'Your family savings have already been gambled away on the flight, Thomas,' Mr Pendleton scolded. 'The few dollars we have – hard earned and dwindling reserves – must be kept to provide for our grandson. Because you, Thomas, are an unreliable provider – a hero, and we're all proud – but an unreliable provider, nevertheless.'

'Oh, thank you, Daddy Pendleton,' said Allen, grinning broadly, and taking his wife's hand. 'That is truly the nicest thing you've said to me since I married your daughter – I mean the hero part – of course.'

Allen and Banning embarked on an exhausting and, at times, humiliating campaign to raise the funds needed to ransom the Eagle Rock. Armed with an album of their photographs, taken with celebrities and influential black leaders in New York, newspaper clippings, and other documents, verifying the first successful Negro transcontinental flight, they approached every conceivable target, on the Avenue and off, and the results were shocking and depressing.

Conditions had worsened, especially in the coloured neighbourhoods, where the inhabitants struggled for the necessities of life. Hungry beggars crowded the streets. Sickly children had stopped playing. Morale had been shattered completely. Churches, business leagues, civic, fraternal, and political groups were doing all they could to help the needy. Bailing out an airplane in Pennsylvania, even a famous one, was certainly not a top priority for the potential donors, regardless of the aviators' inspiring messages about Negro progress, goals, and incentives.

In any case, nearly everyone had already been ineptly and unsuccessfully solicited, on numerous occasions, by Little Dandy and Phil Nash. Some of the more astute among those approached wanted to know why this record-breaking achievement had not been more widely publicized, on a national basis, and in white newspapers, too.

After tapping all possible sources, including friends and relations, the aviators had a not-so-grand total of thirty-four dollars and sixty cents.

'I'm afraid our panhandling days are over, James Herman,' said Allen, as they sat dejectedly at the counter of a Central Avenue coffee shop. 'There is only one thing we can do now to pick up some money, without crawling on our hands and knees.'

'What?'

'Go to work.'

'Doing what?'

'Well, considering that I have a wife – and a new baby – to support, I should be arranging for some steady – you know – full-time – mechanical job, if possible.'

'Nobody is stopping you, Thomas.

'I said that I *should* be arranging for some steady mechanical work – but I won't right now, because we have to stay together – until that Eagle Rock settles down in the Smithsonian.'

'We don't *have* to do a damn thing together.'

'Oh, yes, we do, James Herman,' said Allen. 'That airplane is just as much my baby as yours – more – because I put up and lost a lot of money.'

'Who flew the damn thing?'

'And who kept it running for you? Listen to me.' Allen was

214

unusually sombre. 'Little Dandy called with a proposition a few days ago. I didn't mention it because – well – the damn thing was so – depressing. A black man – name of Colonel Bud Oliver – has a small, low geared, travelling – air circus.'

'God almighty,' moaned Banning, shaking his head in disgust. 'I know that fat hog – and his two-bit operation.' He glared at the mechanic. 'Are you asking me to wallow in Bud Oliver's shit?'

'We've got to rescue the Eagle Rock,' Allen responded, determinedly. 'Little Dandy says the man will pay us good money for special guest appearances. He wants to meet at Mosbys' garage and discuss the details.'

'And what do you think – flight hero of the black race?'

'Maybe we should go – and listen – and then make a decision,' the mechanic answered, watching Banning shove his unfinished cup of coffee aside. 'Unless you have some better ideas.'

'I should have ordered tea,' said Banning, making a face, and holding his stomach. 'That damn mud got me sick enough to puke.'

'I feel exactly the same, James Herman,' Allen remarked, quietly. 'And it has absolutely nothing to do with the coffee.'

The original members of the Eagle Rock team assembled at Mosbys' garage, where Little Dandy explained that Colonel Bud Oliver, an old business acquaintance, had expressed great interest in the flight, the aviators, and the possibilities of capitalizing financially on their magnificent achievement. His travelling air circus troupe, The Daring Blackbirds, would like very much to employ Allen and Banning as special guest stars.

Because of the way they had funded their flight, the Colonel wanted them to be introduced, advertised, and known as 'The Flying Hobos'. Along with greeting the crowds, and handing out photos and autographs, Banning was to perform his well-known stunt manoeuvres, with the spectacular help of a young, black, female parachutist. Allen, of course, would be employed as a mechanic.

'You'll get fifty bucks apiece for each performance – free transportation – and a night's lodging,' Little Dandy urged, searching the aviators for a spark of interest. 'A cool one hundred per show – in hard cash – and the Colonel has one a week lined up for twelve weeks.'

'Can we quit before that?' Allen asked.

'You have to do a minimum of six.'

215

Allen turned to his sullen, grim-faced partner. 'Could we put up with it, James Herman?' he finally asked, quietly. 'Six hundred dollars would get us the Eagle Rock.'

'Just a minute, Thomas.' Little Dandy jumped the pilot's response. He crossed to the work bench, where Phil Nash, Floyd, and Booker T. were seated, watching and listening attentively. 'We had a meeting before you two guys arrived. Part of the Colonel's payment will have to split with us, gentlemen. And I know you'll agree, that's only fair.'

'We all did count on that white man's prize,' Phil Nash finally interjected. 'And not one penny came to us – from anywhere – and we had a firm deal – with spelled out percentages.'

'It is a true fact,' Floyd Mosby monotoned, from his nearly hidden position behind a pile of tools. 'The wreck belonged to Little Dandy and Phil Nash. And me and Booker T. loaned our garage – and food – and drinks – and a right good amount of time – and sweat – and muscle.'

'And the hay wagon too,' Booker T. added, 'My farmer friend tells me that one of his old horses still has a bad stomach problem due to strain.'

'We've agreed to the following Daring Blackbirds pay allocation, gentlemen,' Little Dandy announced officially. 'Fifty dollars each for me and Phil Nash – owners of the Eagle Rock wreckage.' He waited for his associate to nod and then continued. 'Twenty-five dollars each for Floyd and Booker T. Mosby – and you were just reminded of their valuable services. A four hundred and fifty dollar balance plus your pocket money – or a small loan from family or friends – other than us – will get the famous plane out of hock in Pittsburgh, Pennsylvania. How does all this sound to you – James Herman?'

Banning stood abruptly, marched to the window, and stared out for a moment. He spoke as though no one else was in the cluttered workshop.

'We're the first Negro aviators to fly a plane across the United States,' the pilot reminded himself bitterly. 'And soon this information will be printed in history books all over the world. But the whites ignore it – or make a joke of it. And the blacks, instead of being proud – inspired – supportive, chop it down – turn it into nigger shit – The Flying Hobos – and – and hell, man, we deserve a lot more recognition – and a lot more respect.'

'You might be right, James Herman.' Little Dandy had softened. 'But the Eagle Rock is still sitting in Pittsburgh – not Washington. And Bud Oliver has the money ready. Where else will you find six hundred dollars so fast? Unless you rob a bank.'

'Not a bad idea.'

'You'd be strung up or shot dead.'

'A sure way to make the white newspapers.'

'What do I tell the Colonel, Thomas?' Little Dandy asked, shifting his attention to the mechanic. 'Bud has to know in a couple of days.'

'Tell him we're giving his proposition some deep thought,' Allen replied, as Banning turned and faced him, glowering. 'And add that we appear to be – very interested.'

On the following day, Banning called Allen's home, bubbling with excitement. Lieutenant Craig Meredith was in town, on an unexpected business trip, and he wanted to meet for a chat. Because Celene was still hospitalized, and Banning's bedridden father was now sharing the pilot's apartment, Allen suggested that they get together at his place. Banning agreed, gratefully, and Allen noted how high his partner's morale had soared, with the prospect of seeing the white man from Des Moines.

After congratulating the aviators on their remarkable achievement, Meredith displayed genuine disappointment and anger over the indifference to the historic flight shown by both the white and black populations of Los Angeles. He promised to contact the proper officials at the Smithsonian Institute immediately upon his return home. Mainly, he was appalled that Curtis Wright had refused to release the Eagle Rock, because of the repair bill. And, sickened by Colonel Bud Oliver's proposal to exhibit them in an air circus, Fisher advised the flyers to decline the invitation at once, and they agreed.

'Unfortunately,' he apologized, 'like most other people these days, I'm in debt, and unable to make a worthwhile financial contribution. But this is a solemn promise: we'll get the Eagle Rock away from Pittsburgh, in an honourable and dignified fashion. I have a few ideas already. Give me some time to organize them properly. And once again, congratulations. I can honestly say that I'm very, very proud to know both of you.'

During the first week of January 1932, Allen began searching locally for a full-time aircraft mechanic's job, and found unemployment lines instead of vacancies. Freelance assignments were just as impossible to secure. He realized that, temporarily at least, he would have to abandon the field of aviation, and explore less technical sources of income.

Banning's father was now very ill. He needed constant attention at home and expensive medication. Like Allen, the pilot had attempted to pick up full or part-time aviation assignments, in and around Los Angeles, without much success. And, in a short time, he too lowered his sights considerably, and was willing to take any employment, in order to support himself and his father. Even more so than Allen, the aftermath of the Eagle Rock flight had left him full of resentment, despair, and tightly clamped rage.

On 20 January 1933, when the aviators had started to lose all hope of retrieving the Eagle Rock from Pittsburgh, Banning received the long-awaited phone call from Des Moines, Iowa.

'First I'll hurt you with the bad news,' Fisher said bluntly. 'But don't get too mad until you hear the rest of my story.'

'I'm prepared.'

'Good. I spoke to Mr Theodore Kunstadt of the Smithsonian Institute. He was quite interested in the flight and agreed that it would be recorded as a great advancement for the Negro people – a major achievement.'

'But?'

'But – they don't want the plane.'

'Why not?'

'Mainly, considering the number of stops, the length of travelling time involved, and – other factors – Kunstadt doesn't believe that the event is important enough to put the Eagle Rock on permanent display in the Smithsonian.'

Banning was struck silent by anger and disappointment.

'You promised not to get mad,' Meredith reminded him, rather sternly. 'This is Kunstadt's opinion – I don't agree – but he works for the Institution and we have to accept his judgement.'

'Thomas Allen and myself are the first black men to fly a plane transcontinental,' Banning pointed out scathingly. 'And that's aviation history. The Eagle Rock rates being on permanent display.'

'Fine,' said the Lieutenant, eager to keep the long-distance conversation moving. 'But it won't be at the Institution. We'll find a proper setting at one of the National Air Museums.'

'The Smithsonian in Washington is the only place I'm interested in,' the pilot stated passionately. 'That was our goal, and I won't rest until the Eagle Rock sits there.'

'We'd better get it out of Pittsburgh first.'

'Sorry, Lieutenant.'

'Can I switch to the good part now?'

'Yeah.'

The Lieutenant explained that, with the help of an Army Major Warren Dodge, a friend of his, he was in the process of organizing a large, high quality air show, at an abandoned airfield, Camp Kerney Mesa, south of San Diego, near the Mexican border. Invitations had already been sent out to well-known airmen, flight enthusiasts, aircraft builders and designers, journalists, and a number of public officials.

Although the United States Army was not officially involved, a sharp team of military pilots, friends of Major Dodge, had been granted special permission to perform a series of precision manoeuvres, and a mock combat display in the Army's new, recently delivered fighter aircraft.

However, the main purpose of the gathering at Camp Kerney Mesa, was to introduce and commemorate the first successful Negro transcontinental pilots, James Herman Banning and Thomas C. Allen. A trophy and a framed certificate would be presented to the aviators by the senior representative of the nation's Flying Clubs. And Banning, the first black to be licensed by the Department of Commerce, and certainly one of the best race flyers in the world, would be invited to demonstrate his extraordinary ability before this prestigious and influential audience.

'One thing is absolutely certain,' Meredith concluded. 'I will personally guarantee that the donations will more than cover the operation to recover the Eagle Rock.'

Banning was speechless.

'Most importantly,' Meredith continued, 'you and Allen will finally get the recognition you both deserve – from the white people in this country – as well as the coloured – because we're also setting up a special section for invited Negro guests – and you can add to our list.'

'I –' Momentarily thrown off his brash, confident, sometimes arrogant course, Banning groped for words. 'Can I ask a question?'

'Go ahead.'

'What do *you* get out of all this?'

'Great satisfaction,' Craig Meredith replied, without a hesitation. 'I taught you how to fly – remember?' He paused for a moment before speaking again. 'And I don't like to see capable human beings shoved around because of prejudice and ignorance.'

'Your wife hates black people.'

'I can't quarrel much with that,' Fisher responded openly. 'I'd be a hypocrite if I did. 'You see – for many reasons – I can't accept Negroes all the way, either. I don't live with them, or sleep with them, or want my kids to marry them. Maybe I wouldn't mind if other white people did these things – but they don't, so I conform – and stop short at a certain point. That's a character weakness of mine. Do you understand?'

'Most of it.'

'Just realize that we're not organizing an air show for the sake of the Negro race,' Meredith went on. 'I'm only concerned about you and Allen – two damn good and determined aviators – who deserve the proper amount of credit for a great achievement – against tremendous odds.'

Banning was silent.

'The Camp Kerney Mesa date is fifth February,' Fisher continued, 'I'll be in touch with all the details. Are you there?'

'I'm here,' said Banning, having a difficult time controlling his feelings of excitement and deep appreciation. 'I'll never forget anything you've taught me,' he added, haltingly. 'And – you've taught me more than anyone will ever realize – and I'm very, very thankful.'

20

On the evening of 4 February 1933, the Allen household was full of hustle and bustle and laughter as Thomas and Celene, aglow with excitement, packed for their ten o'clock commercial flight to San Diego.

'It's just a shame that my mother and brother can't make the trip from Oklahoma City,' Allen remarked, pensively. 'Both of them would be mighty proud.'

'They'll hear about it, and read about it, and see all kinds of pictures of it,' said Celene, taking his arm, and squeezing it lovingly. 'And so will that boy upstairs, when he gets a little older.'

Allen beamed with delight.

'You should be able to find steady employment after this San Diego tribute, Thomas,' Celene's mother said, fixing him with a dissatisfied stare. 'You won't have any excuses from now on.'

'Get off his back, Mama,' said Celene, stroking Allen's cheek, while he purred like a contented kitten. 'Tomorrow is my man's big day, and we should all be very proud of him.'

'We are,' said Mr Pendleton sincerely. 'And so should any white employer be – even without a vacancy for an experienced mechanic, some clever boss is going to make room for a national hero, and capitalize on the publicity. Don't you agree, Thomas?'

'Thank you very much for the trophy and certificate, Mister Sullivan,' Allen recited, staring through his father-in-law, as though in another world. 'We will – *cherish* these possessions and remember this glorious day – for the rest of our lives.'

Celene applauded softly.

On the same evening, in an apartment across town, James Herman Banning had completed his packing alone. After pouring a very large tot of bootlegged whisky, he went quietly into a small, stuffy bedroom and stared at the frail form of his father, under covers, beside a stack of medicine bottles.

Moments later, an elderly black woman in a tattered nightgown poked her head inside an inquired softly, 'Is he all right?'

'He's fine, Mrs Ogden.'

The pilot turned abruptly, and walked back into the living-room, with the old woman behind him.

'Your Papa sure would have been proud to be in San Diego tomorrow, James Herman,' Mrs Ogden said, blinking away tears. 'And your Mama too, God rest her soul.'

'I know that, Mrs Ogden.'

'Enjoy this great honour and don't worry about your Papa,' the old woman advised. 'I'll take real good care of him. That's what old friends are for.'

'We both appreciate it, Mrs Ogden.'

'He appreciates *you*, James Herman,' the old woman remarked. 'Riley told me last night that him and Cora were blessed with a boy like you. What a reward, he said, to have a son go so far in a mean world like this.'

'They worked very hard to give me the chances,' said Banning, taking a seat on the couch, still holding his drink. 'I'll always be grateful.'

'Well, I'll be off to bed now.'

'Goodnight, Mrs Ogden. Sleep well.'

Banning sat for a while in a gloomy mood, and then his eyes fell on the packed suitcase on the floor, and his handsome features softened, and a broad smile appeared. He drained his glass, and removed a neat address book from his back pocket. With his feet propped on a table, he flipped through a page at a time, muttering, 'No, no, no, no, no.' Eventually his finger stopped, his eyes sparkled, and his smile became a lustful grin. 'Yes, yes, yes, indeed,' he murmured, reaching for the telephone.

'Sylvia? This is James Herman Banning. Forgive the short notice, but – how would you like a – ceremonial drink with me tonight? *Who*? Ridiculous! Cancel him, dear. OK? Good, that's my girl. I'll be at your place in fifteen minutes. With refreshments. And don't get dressed. Sylvia – I *mean* don't get dressed – because I have to jump a commercial flight at ten o'clock.'

On the afternoon of 5 February 1933, over two thousand spectators had filled the improvised stands at Camp Kerney Mesa. In perfect weather, a slight breeze fluttered American flags, and several banners welcoming the first successful Negro transcontinental flyers. Balloons in assorted colours were tied to poles and rafters, and held in the hands of children. A costumed marching band was, at the moment, providing a medley of stirring patriotic pieces for the enthusiastic and very receptive crowd.

The military pilots had just thrilled the spectators by performing a series of precision manoeuvres in the Army's latest fighter aircraft.

The next event, according to a crackling loud speaker, would be James Herman Banning's spectacular exhibition of stunt aviation. A voice informed the crowd that Banning, one of the world's best and most experienced race flyers, was the first Negro to be licensed by the United States Department of Commerce, and reminded them that with Thomas C. Allen, he had very recently completed a history-making transcontinental flight, from Los Angeles to New York City.

Following Banning's performance, the cross-country heroes were scheduled to be formally introduced and honoured in a brief ceremony, presided over by Mr William E. Sullivan, Vice-President of the National Association of Flying Clubs. A large raised platform had been specially built and positioned on the field, in front of the stands, close to the airfield's one newly renovated runway. Red, white, and blue silk draped the sides. At one end of the stage sat Mr William E. Sullivan, a tall, grey, distinguished-looking gentleman, with his shorter, younger, and obviously ill-at-ease assistant beside him. Two impressively designed trophies and glass-framed certificates rested conspicuously on the table before them.

At the other end of the platform, facing Sullivan and his assistant, were two rows of metal folding chairs, three in front, and four behind. Thomas C. Allen and Celene had the front places of honour, next to a vacant chair, which had presumably been reserved for Banning. The mechanic, smartly dressed in a dark suit, sat awe-struck, gripping his wife's hand tightly and gazing at the predominantly white audience. His usual easy smile did not accurately reflect the heart-thumping, nerve-twitching, stomach-churning sensations he was trying so desperately to control. In contrast, Celene both looked and felt radiant and composed, as she enjoyed every thrilling moment of this remarkable tribute to her hero husband – an experience which would be recounted in detail, over and over again, as Orrin Allen grew older.

Behind them, staring straight ahead and avoiding the inscrutable gaze of Mr William E. Sullivan and his assistant, sat Little Dandy, Phil Nash, and the Mosby brothers. Little Dandy was outfitted in his gaudy best. The shirt, tie, suit and shoes had been especially selected to dazzle the white guests, and make a memorable impression on the assembled blacks.

Phil Nash had decided on a casual sweater, slacks, and moccasin-type footwear. The overall effect was pure sloppiness. Floyd and Booker T. Mosby were dressed as though there had just been a death in the family and, in addition, everything was much too short, and too tight for them.

While the guests on the platform and the excited spectators waited for the next event, the music blared, the band marched, and Lieutenant Craig Meredith conferred anxiously with Major Warren Dodge about the delay in James Herman Banning's appearance.

Fisher had rented a plane for Banning's exhibition, but it needed a few minor engine repairs, and these were being done at nearby Lindbergh Field, the San Diego Naval Air Station. The Lieutenant figured that the work should have been completed about fifteen minutes earlier. Both men were concerned about the dignitaries and the crowd, hoping that they would not become too impatient and bored with the band's second playing of the 'The Star-Spangled Banner.'

At Lindbergh Field, becoming anxious himself now at the delay, Banning went to the hangar where the repairs were being carried out and discussed the situation with a supervising mechanic. He was told that, because of unexpected complications, the job would take approximately another hour.

Banning was not satisfied. Dressed sharply in a new and perfectly fitted flying suit, supplied by the air show's organizers, he reported to the Naval Air Station's duty office, where he filed a complaint with Lieutenant Commander Frank Penner.

'We can't rush them, Mr Banning.' The tall, smooth-faced officer had a thick Southern drawl, and a condescending manner. 'Release orders are only signed for aircraft in perfect flying condition,' he went on, eyeing the Negro with obvious distaste. 'This field is run by the United States Navy.'

'I know that, Commander,' Banning said, as respectfully as he could. 'But we've got about two thousand people waiting at Kerney, and I'm sure they're getting impatient by now. Can't you move things along?'

'No.'

'I'll speak to Lieutenant Fisher.'

'Use the phone on the table.'

*

224

After a brief discussion, Meredith and Dodge decided that Banning should make the short flight to Camp Kerney in any available aircraft, and proceed with the formal introductions, platform ceremonies, and presentations by Mr William E. Sullivan. Afterwards, while explanations and rescheduling announcements were being made to the crowd, Banning would fly back to Lindbergh, pick up his repaired airplane, and then perform his stunts.

At exactly 4.00 pm, James Herman Banning, walking beside Lieutenant Commander Penner, crossed Lindbergh Field, and approached a two-seater Travelair, his transportation to Camp Kerney Mesa.

Ready with his helmet and goggles, Banning stopped abruptly just before reaching the plane. He stared curiously at a young, white, pock-marked enlisted sailor, who was sitting in the rear cockpit, at the controls, ready for take-off. The boy had an ugly smirk on his face.

'I don't understand,' Banning said courteously.

'You don't understand what?' Panner asked.

'My chauffeur.'

'That's Aviation Machinist's Mate Second Class Albert Burghardt,' Penner announced. 'He's one of our very promising young student pilots.'

'Very good,' said Banning, evenly. 'But I'm quite capable of flying this airplane to Camp Kerney on my own.'

'So is Albert Burghardt.'

'A ceremony has been planned for us at Kerney, Commander,' Banning reminded him, tight-voiced, aware that his temper was being tested. 'I would like to arrive as a solo pilot.'

The young sailor snickered.

'Get one thing straight, Banning,' said Penner, tiring of the conversation. 'You can do anything you want with that hired airplane back in the hangar. That's not my responsibility – once the repairs have been completed and approved. But no aircraft under my supervision will leave this Station in the hands of a civilian – a stranger – especially a stranger who happens to be a circus stunt flyer.'

'Are you trying to say something, Commander?'

'You heard every word clearly.'

'Do you doubt my ability as a pilot?'

'We all have our own standards for judging qualified aviators.' Penner was standing next to the grinning sailor's cockpit. 'And my standards are very high.'

'Want to check my flying hours and experience?'

'I'm talking about *inbred* and *consistent* reliability.'

'You know something, Commander? Banning faced the officer, his shoulders back, head held high, eyes blazing. 'I know exactly what you're talking about,' he said, in a firm, steady voice. 'And for the first time in my life, I feel sorry for ignorant bastards like you.'

The two glared at each other while Burghardt sat in the cockpit with the same mocking grin on his face.

'Get off the field right now with my pilot, Banning,' Penner finally ordered, looking away. 'Or I'll haul this plane back into the hangar.'

Banning stood for another moment, and then, realizing that there was no alternative, he moved slowly to the Travelair, without glancing at the officer or the grinning sailor, who had been given command of the ship.

On the Lindbergh Field runway, just before taxiing for the take-off, Albert Burghardt yelled at the back of Banning's helmeted head, 'HEY, STUNT FLYER!'

Banning, sitting in the front passenger's cockpit, without any controls, refused to turn his head.

'YOU'RE GOING FOR A NICE RIDE!'

There was still no response from Banning.

'MAYBE I'LL SHOW THAT CROWD A FEW OF MY OWN TRICKS!'

The Travelair moved down the runway, picked up speed, and lifted off easily, heading for Camp Kerney Mesa.

Watching the sky from his seat next to Celene, Tom Allen heard the engine noise, and was the first to spot the plane. He nudged his wife, pointed, and then turned around to Little Dandy, Phil Nash and the Mosby brothers. Lieutenant Craig Meredith, using Banning's front row chair temporarily, already had his eyes on the approaching aircraft.

'That big ham-bone is coming in mighty low and fast,' Allen remarked, a little surprised. 'I thought the stunts were scheduled for later.'

'He's making a low pass over the platform,' Meredith commented, showing irritation, as he watched, shading his eyes with his hand. 'Why show off now and waste more time? It's not like Banning.'

The Travelair, flying at high speed, swooped very low over the platform and the guests, and then made a sharp climbing turn, gaining altitude, as it circled the airfield, obviously preparing for more flight manoeuvres.

'It's not him!' Allen yelled, as Lieutenant Meredith got up, jumped from the platform, and ran towards a nearby administration shack. 'What the hell is going on up there?'

'Explain, Thomas,' Celene demanded nervously.

'Somebody else is in the rear cockpit with the controls,' Allen told her, unable to hide his concern. 'James Herman is up front – a passenger.'

The Travelair descended a little, and executed a few sloppy loops, fish tails, and side slips. The band stopped marching and playing in mid-tune, as the restless members of the audience focused their attention on the aerial display.

'Thomas!' Lieutenant Meredith had returned and was calling from the side of the platform. 'A young Navy enlisted man is at the controls of that plane,' he explained, uneasily. 'The boy has no authority to play around. His superior, Lieutenant Commander Penner, is furious.'

'Can he fly?'

'He's a good student – and that's all.'

'White?'

'So what?'

'Just curious, Lieutenant.'

'I'll be in the administration shack,' Fisher said. 'Get set for the introductions and presentations. Don't worry, Banning will be down safely in a few minutes.'

'Sure.'

At that precise moment, as though he knew exactly what to expect, Allen took Celene's hand, and squeezed it, staring up at the sky just as the student flyer pulled the nose of the plane up into a climb, a steep climb, a very, very steep climb.'

'TURN AWAY!' Allen screamed at Celene, as he released her hand, and jumped to his feet. 'DON'T WATCH!'

'I don't understand –'

'TURN AWAY, GODDAMMIT, CELENE!' Allen yelled again, unable to take his eyes off the Travelair, as the ship reached the peak of the climb, and stalled. 'DON'T WATCH!'

'Oh, my God,' Celene muttered, as she obeyed.

Little Dandy, Phil Nash and the Mosby brothers were on their feet with Tom Allen gazing in stunned disbelief. The plane rolled on its back for a moment, and then plunged into an uncontrollable spin.

A gasp of horror went up from the crowd as the aircraft spun towards the ground in a terrifying slow-motion sequence, until it finally hit the runway, and exploded with tremendous force, scattering mangled pieces in all directions.

Seconds later, as the dense smoke rose, and hazy figures ran to the scene, Celene Allen, with her face buried in her hands, screamed hysterically – a long, piercing, continuous wail.

'Little Dandy!' Tom Allen shouted. 'Take Celene to the administration shack! And the rest of you get over there too!'

'Come with us, Thomas,' the badly shaken Central Avenue operator advised, as Phil Nash and the Mosby brothers moved zombie-like to the platform steps. 'You can't do a damn thing for James Herman standing here.'

'Get moving!' Allen blurted. 'I want to be alone right now. Just make sure my wife is all right.'

Tom Allen stood by himself on the platform, and squinted at the frantic activity going on around the remains of the Travelair. William E. Sullivan and his assistant had rushed to the scene immediately after the crash. The police had moved in quickly to control inquisitive spectators. And a medical team, organized in advance by Meredith and Dodge, was in action with a group of firemen, attempting to extricate two bodies from the tangled wreckage.

Allen had witnessed these emergency procedures several times before, after other air disasters. At the moment, he was observing in a detached way, delaying the physical and emotional collapse he knew would be inevitable, once the reality of the situation registered.

Now the police were forcing an opening in the crowd which had gathered around the crash site, and Allen had a clear view of two ambulance attendants coming through, carrying a broken body on a stretcher. He caught a quick glimpse of Naval blue before someone threw a sheet over it, and the medics moved, without any sense of urgency, to their waiting vehicle.

A strange tingling sensation began at the back of his head and neck, as the ambulance men brought out another corpse, covered with a sheet. Feeling weak, nauseous, and light-headed, Allen forced himself to watch, as the body was being hoisted into the hospital van. As the stretcher tilted, an arm fell from under the sheet, and dangled limply over the side. The mechanic could plainly see the sleeve of James Herman's new flying outfit.

He could no longer postpone reality. His partner was under that sheet. Not just some dead pilot, but James Herman Banning. He felt like jumping off the platform, rushing to the ambulance, and ripping the damn sheet away. He would grab the big ham-bone, and hug his busted body, and shake him awake. And he'd get up. Oh, hell, yes, he'd get up. James Herman always got up. How could he be dead? *DEAD? James Herman was dead.* Oh, my God, no. 'NO! NO! NO!' he screamed.

The ambulance doors slammed shut, and the vehicle drove slowly away. With the entire field spinning, and his legs giving way, Allen staggered to the presentation table, flopped in a chair, and put his head on his arms. He closed his eyes tightly. The darkness helped, momentarily.

Five days later, on 10 February, Lieutenant Craig Meredith went to the Curtis Wright plant in Pittsburgh to settle the long overdue bill of four hundred and seventy-five dollars.

'Sorry about the delay,' he told Gerald Ambrose, the assistant manager, removing a cheque book from his inside jacket pocket. 'The owners have had a few financial problems – like everybody else these days.'

'Thomas Allen and James Herman Banning,' the assistant manager murmured, studying the Eagle Rock file. 'Our people went to a cow pasture near Blairsville, dismantled the aircraft, and did a major repair job here.'

'Correct.'

'11 November, 1932.'

'That was the date.'

'We wrote and demanded settlement on 28 November, 15 December, 22 December and sent a final notice on 8 January this year,' the assistant manager recapped, reading from a file copy. 'Our letters were ignored.'

'Ignored?' Were they sent to Allen or Banning?'

'Both,' Ambrose replied, looking up. 'In care of a Mr Eugene Hapgood at a New York City address.'

'Oh, I see.' Fisher smiled. 'Hapgood was acting as their agent at the time. They must have given Hapgood's address and forgotten to contact you with a change after they dismissed him.'

'Someone should have answered.'

'Quite so, Mr Ambrose,' said Meredith pleasantly, getting his pen ready for the cheque. 'But surely that's of little importance now,' he went on, poised to write. 'How do I make this out?'

'I'm afraid you don't.'

229

'What's that?'

'After formal legal notice, the plane was sold on 13 January,' Ambrose declared, in a rather apologetic manner. 'Only the new engine was of value,' he added, checking the file again. 'We failed to recoup the entire debt, and consequently wrote off the balance.'

Craig Meredith's thin, pale face was flushed. 'Do you have the name of the buyer?' he asked huskily. 'And his address and phone number, please?'

'Of course.' Once again, the assistant manager referred to his documents. 'The plane was purchased by Mr Howard Roebuck, of 1174 Lakehurst Boulevard, Pittsburgh. Telephone 483 – 762.'

'Does he have a company?'

'Spare parts – and scrap.'

'I don't believe it.'

'Apart from the engine, it wasn't much of a plane, according to our mechanic's report. Was there some kind of sentimental value attached to it?'

'I would say so, Mr Ambrose. 'Do you mind if I use a phone somewhere in the plant?' Fisher asked. 'I want to call Howard Roebuck.'

'Use mine,' Ambrose said obligingly. 'If it's so important to you, I sure hope you get the plane back from Roebuck.'

'So do I,' said Fisher, grimly reaching for the phone.

Mr Howard Roebuck confirmed that he had indeed purchased an old and remodelled 0XX6 Eagle Rock from Curtis Wright, on 13 January.

Matter-of-factly, he explained that his company had made a small profit on the new Wright Whirlwind J5 engine, the steel propeller, and the repaired wings, although these had had to be repainted, because of some names scribbled on the lower left tip. The rest of the plane had been dismantled, and sold in pieces, to various buyers, as aircraft scrap.

Numbed, Lieutenant Craig Meredith slowly replaced the receiver.

21

Somehow, with the help of Celene and his son, Tom Allen battled his way through the agonizing weeks following Banning's death, and the news that the Eagle Rock had been destroyed. On the recommendation of Meredith and Major Dodge, he had been hired as a full-time mechanic at Lockheed Aircraft. The rigid schedule and challenging work kept his mind off the recent disappointments and tragedies, at least partially, but only during the daylight hours. His nights were restless; when he slept the images of the spinning Travelair and James Herman's dangling arm would jolt him awake in a cold sweat of horror.

The trophy and the framed certificate had been consigned to a shelf in the closet, and Allen intended to keep them there indefinitely. Riley Banning, James Herman's father, now twice as sick and in constant mourning, had the treasured mementoes on public display, just behind his medicine bottles. He seldom took his eyes from them.

During these unhappy times, Tom Allen had very little contact with Little Dandy, Phil Nash, the Mosby brothers, and Central Avenue. He had become withdrawn, more serious, more responsible and mature, and much more family-conscious.

Celene welcomed most of these changes in her husband, but she missed his smile, his laugh, his jokes, and the extrovert way he had enjoyed life. And she worried about his refusal to talk about James Herman Banning, the Eagle Rock, or the flight. Every night, while Allen stared silently up at the ceiling, she prayed that something would happen to bring him out of the shell he had formed around himself.

One day at the beginning of April Celene found a short, official-looking letter in the bedroom drawer, under a stack of her husband's clean underwear. It was addressed to him and dated three weeks earlier.

A Mr Claude Douglas, of the National Association for the Advancement of Colored People, in Washington, DC, invited Thomas C. Allen and his wife to visit the nation's capital on

25 April. A very special ceremony, honouring the first successful Negro transcontinental flyers, was planned for 26 April, at 3:00 pm. All expenses would be paid by the NAACP. Mr Douglas asked Allen to contact him as soon as possible, so that arrangements could be made for travel and hotel accommodation. All the members of the organization's Washington branch were looking forward to meeting them.

That night Celene cautiously mentioned finding the letter, and Allen tried to treat the subject lightly, at first. But Celene persisted.

'Did you answer Mr Douglas?'

'Of course not.'

'How can you possibly ignore –'

'I don't want to talk about it.'

'Listen to me, Thomas,' Celene pleaded quietly, intensely. 'You've got to face this Eagle Rock business sooner or later.' She watched him shove his coffee cup aside, stand up, and begin pacing the room. 'It won't go away,' she continued. 'And it should never go away. Why the hell did you and James Herman do it?'

'That's a good question.'

'You have to go to Washington, for Banning's sake,' Celene whispered, treading gently, on very dangerous ground. 'How can you deprive him of this honour – after he did so much – and gave up his life?'

Instead of exploding, or leaving the room, Allen stared at the wooden propeller, hanging from the ceiling on its short chain. 'James Herman would never have gone to yet another black gathering, full of bullshit and no action,' he said quietly. 'We've had enough of them.'

'How about a white gathering?'

'We went once – and James Herman died there – remember?'

Celene watched his back, as Allen continued to stare at the ceiling propeller. She was pleased that he was talking so calmly about Banning, and seemed prepared to talk some more.

'I thought about this Washington visit a lot,' Allen confided sombrely. 'And it scares hell out of me. Because I'd never be able to follow through. Stand up and preach about what? Cunningham's prize money? James Herman's crash? The loss of the Eagle Rock?'

'The main thing is – you and Banning flew across the United States – and no other Negroes have ever done it before, and that's history.'

'And who cares?'

'I do,' said Celene proudly. 'And your son will. And there are plenty of others out there, too. And more to come in the future.'

'Not without a permanent Eagle Rock display,' Allen said ruefully. 'And that's what James Herman wanted more than anything else.'

'Take me to Washington, Thomas.'

'It might be a disaster.'

'You'll do fine.' Celene waited, as Allen continued to study the propeller.

'I'll take a shot, Celene,' Allen finally replied, turning to his wife. 'But – don't be surprised if I – crack a little – or even fall apart completely.'

'You'll do fine.

Mr and Mrs Thomas C. Allen were picked up by an NAACP car at the Capital Arms Hotel, in Washington, DC, on the morning of 26 April 1933.

Allen had been quiet and edgy during the long train journey from Los Angeles. Celene had put up with his distant and, at times, ill-humoured behaviour. Expecting a large, noisy, and organized welcoming committee, the mechanic was relieved to find only Mr Claude Douglas, and two other senior NAACP representatives, waiting at the station. Their greetings had been cordial, respectful and subdued, and mindful of their guests' weariness after the long trip, they had driven the Allens straight to their hotel.

'This afternoon's ceremony has been arranged entirely by Mr Jason Riker and his staff,' Claude Douglas explained, in a rather evasive manner. 'Our organization is holding a celebratory dinner tonight and you'll meet our members there – but this afternoon's event has nothing to do with us.'

Douglas and his two associates were sitting with Tom and Celene Allen, in the NAACP's spacious Washington office.

'What am I supposed to do at this ceremony today?' Allen asked, slightly confused. 'Do I have to speak or answer questions?'

'Only Mr Riker knows that,' Douglas replied patiently. 'His car will collect you and Mrs Allen in about twenty minutes. I assume he will tell you all about it then.'

'Is Mr Riker with the NAACP?' Celene asked.

'No, Mrs Allen,' one of the associates answered. 'But he knows two of our very prominent members: the Reverend Fletcher

233

Brown of the Abyssinian Baptist Church, and Dr Alain Fauset of Howard University. He contacted them about the proposed ceremony, and they notified us. We thought it would be a fine idea to invite you for Mr Riker's event, and have our own honorary dinner on the same night. And here we are.'

'A church or a school presentation,' Tom Allen mumbled, fidgeting in his chair. 'That means a speech and some kind of interview session.' He glanced at Claude Douglas and frowned. 'I'm really not prepared for anything formal.'

'My husband has been under a terrible strain lately, Mr Douglas,' Celene explained, concerned about Allen's uneasiness. 'As you must realize, this visit is a difficult one for him – because of recent events.'

'We are all very much aware of the sad circumstances, Mrs Allen,' Douglas responded. 'There will be no need for speeches or interviews at tonight's dinner. Just good food, some drink, and a jolly crowd of members, all anxious to meet you and your illustrious husband.'

'That's extremely kind of you,' said Celene, smiling. 'We're very appreciative.' She looked at her husband. 'Isn't that right, Thomas?'

Allen, who had been staring gloomily at a spot on the floor, suddenly lifted his head and spoke with unusual forcefulness. 'My illustrious partner would have appreciated all this, too,' he declared, staring straight at the NAACP official. 'I'm sorry he couldn't make the trip with us.'

'And so are we, Mr Allen,' Douglas asserted sincerely. 'But he will certainly be on our minds tonight,' he added. 'And in our hearts, too.'

Fifteen minutes later, Allen and Celene were ushered to a waiting car, parked outside the NAACP offices. They climbed into the back seat, and found themselves beside a white man with a wide, friendly smile on his face.

'My name is Jason Riker,' he announced, extending his hand first to Celene, and then to Allen. 'I'm very pleased to meet both of you.'

Riker, a confident, amiable-looking man in his late thirties, was obviously at pains to make the couple feel comfortable and at ease.

After some small talk about their journey from Los Angeles, and the dreary Washington weather, Allen loosened up enough to ask a few questions.

234

'Is this ceremony being held in a Negro church or school?'

Jason Riker, furrowing his brow, looked past Celene to Tom Allen. 'No,' he replied flatly. 'Neither. Why do you ask?'

'Your NAACP friends.'

'Oh.' Riker smiled again and settled back in the seat. 'Douglas must have mentioned Reverend Brown and Alain Fauset.' Changing the subject, he asked, glancing at Celene, 'Is this your first visit to Washington?'

'Yes, it is.'

'You'll have plenty to see,' Riker remarked. 'I'll arrange for a complete tour,' he added, as the car slowed down, and moved to the right-hand lane. 'Will tomorrow morning be convenient?'

Celene looked at her slightly bemused husband and waited for his nod of approval. 'That would be marvellous, Mr Riker,' she said finally. 'We're very much obliged to you.'

'Mr Riker,' Allen leaned forward. 'About today's ceremony. Can I ask –?'

'Excuse me,' Riker interrupted, pointing out of the window at a large, impressive-looking building. 'We'll start your Washington tour here. You can see all the other sights tomorrow.'

'Where are we, Mr Riker?' Celene inquired, peering out through the rain.

'Put the car in my place, Travis,' Riker said to the driver, as they rolled into a private parking area. 'We'll walk from there under cover.'

'Yes, sir.'

'Sorry, Mrs Allen,' said Riker, turning to her. 'This is the Smithsonian Institution. I am one of the directors.'

In his modest office on the second floor of the building, Jason Riker explained to the astounded Allens that a special exhibition room was being opened to the public on the following morning. It contained a display of aviation photographs which would be maintained on a permanent basis, and updated and augmented as flight improvements were made and accomplishments recorded, until an actual Air Museum could be established as part of the Smithsonian.

'I've been told by some enthusiasts that you would be extremely interested in our collection, Mr Allen,' said Riker, smiling broadly. 'Would you care for a private view?'

Tom Allen sat and stared at the man, unable to speak, hardly able to breathe. Finally, Celene accepted the invitation, with pleasure, for both of them.

*

As Jason Riker and the Allens entered the huge, high-ceilinged room, the echo of their footsteps on the marble floor added to the mechanic's overpowering sense of reverence, as though he was alone with history, and his own ghosts of the past. The walls were hung with elegantly framed and annotated photographs. Allen was soon absorbed in their study. He moved from one section to another in rapt fascination.

'I have to leave now for an appointment in my office,' Jason Riker eventually whispered, breaking into his reverie. 'Keep looking, and come downstairs when you're finished.' He checked his watch. 'A group of students and their teacher from the Washington School of Manual Arts will be arriving in ten or fifteen minutes. A preview showing, because of their interest in aviation. Enjoy yourselves. We'll talk later.'

He left the room.

With Celene beside him, Allen moved on to the next partitioned section, and froze. Minutes passed before he could properly take in what his eyes were seeing.

In every photograph before him, in sharp focus, enlarged and framed, was the Eagle Rock: on airport runways at Lordsburgh, New Mexico, Oklahoma City, Pittsburgh, Pennsylvania, and Valley Stream, New York. And there were himself and Banning, in poses both formal and casual, in the cockpits, or standing beside the plane, wearing flying suits, and sometimes helmets, with goggles up, and occasionally down.

Allen's official photograph, courtesy of the *Pittsburgh Courier*, had been hung on the left of the Eagle Rock exhibit, together with his printed biographical details. Banning's picture and biography were on the right.

Above the well-organized layout, which had been lit, like the others, with dramatic effect, a large sign announced that on 9 October 1932, Thomas C. Allen and James Herman Banning, flying from Los Angeles, California, in an 0XX6 Eagle Rock, had landed at Valley Stream, New York, completing the first successful transcontinental flight by members of the Negro race.

The Allens stood motionless, as though they were paying their humble respects at a shrine, or praying before an altar.

Quite suddenly, Celene swayed slightly, reached for a handkerchief, and dabbed at her tear-filled eyes.

Like a man spellbound, Allen stepped forward and studied the photograph of their old, battered, makeshift aircraft, as it sat on the Long Island runway, after the flight had been accomplished

Standing beside the damaged wings, the aviators were grinning proudly, with their arms held high in a victory salute.

Allen gazed at the handsome pilot for a long moment, and then whispered, as though the picture could actually hear, 'You can rest now, James Herman – we're in the Smithsonian – with the Eagle Rock.'

He turned abruptly, gripped his wife's hand, and started for the doors, just as the young students and their teacher from the Washington School of Manual Arts entered. They were black, and bright-eyed, and obviously eager to see the exhibition.

Before leaving the display room, Allen glanced back over his shoulder, and saw the children gathered in front of the Wright Brothers, and Charles Lindbergh, and the two Negroes who had successfully flown transcontinental.

He smiled his old, familiar smile, held Celene's hand tighter, and walked down the Institute's corridor, erect, assured, and with as much spring in his step as ever.